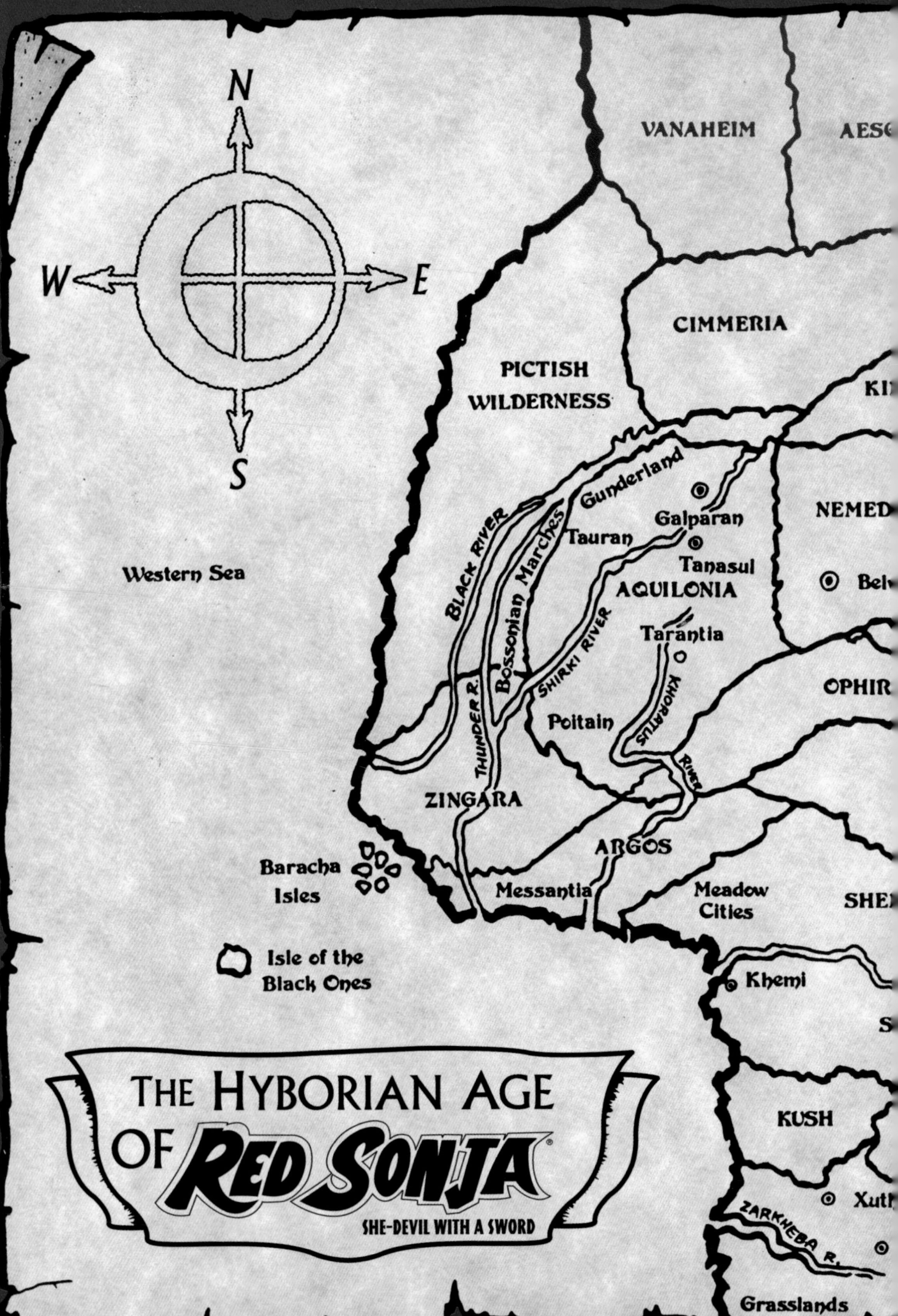

N
W
E
S
VANAHEIM
AESG
CIMMERIA
PICTISH
WILDERNESS
KI
Gunderland
Galparan
NEMED
BLACK RIVER
Bossonian Marches
Tauran
Tanasul
Western Sea
AQUILONIA
Bel
Tarantia
SHIRKI RIVER
OPHIR
THUNDER R.
Poitain
KHORATUS
RIVER
ZINGARA
ARGOS
Baracha
Isles
Messantia
Meadow
Cities
SHE
Isle of the
Black Ones
Khemi
THE HYBORIAN AGE
OF RED SONJA
SHE-DEVIL WITH A SWORD
KUSH
Xuth
ZARKHEBA R.
Grasslands

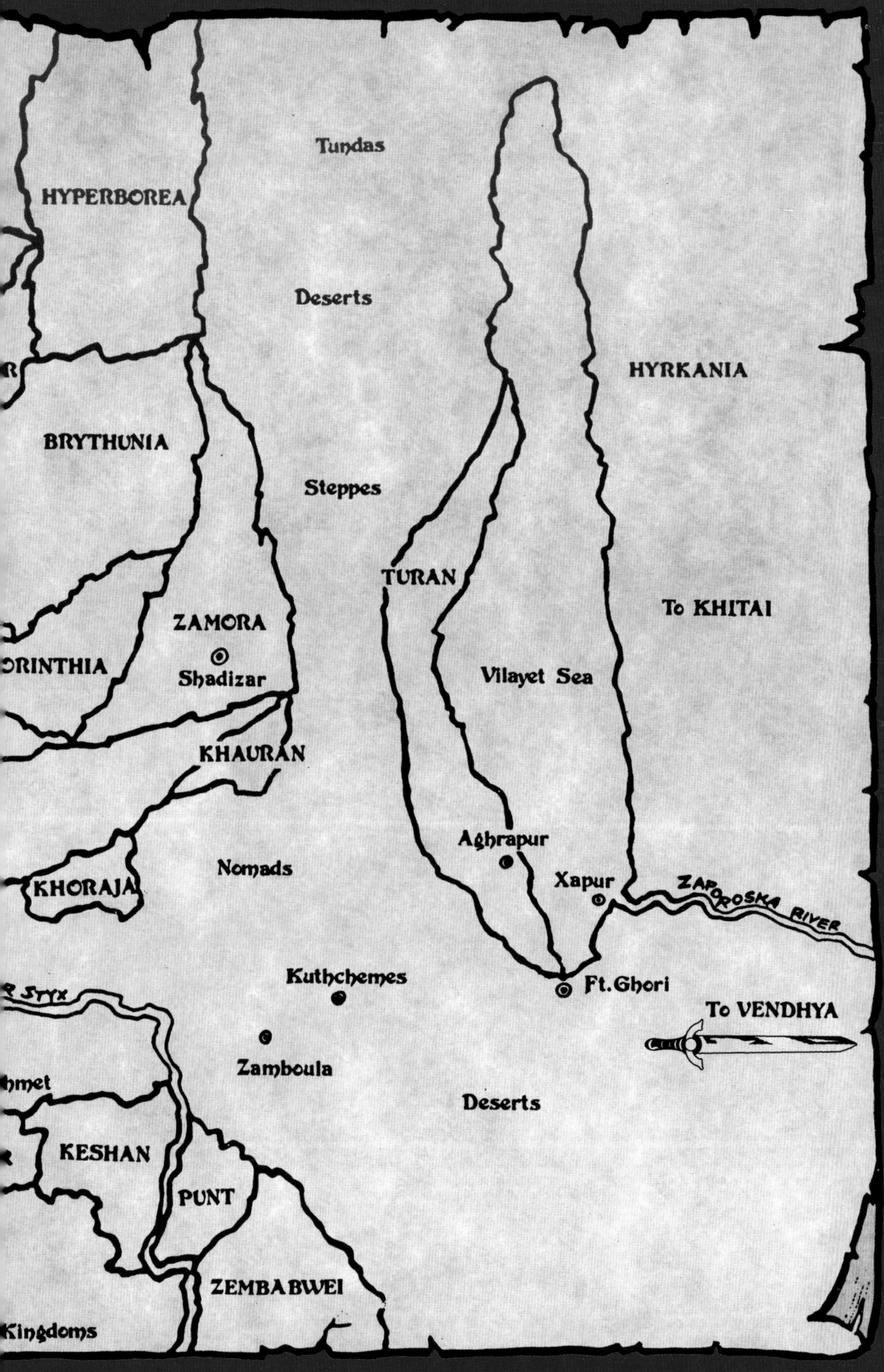

Tundas
HYPERBOREA
Deserts
HYRKANIA
BRYTHUNIA
Steppes
TURAN
To KHITAI
ZAMORA
Shadizar
ORINTHIA
Vilayet Sea
KHAURAN
Aghrapur
Nomads
Xapur
KHORAJA
ZAPOROSKA RIVER
Kuthchemes
Ft. Ghori
To VENDHYA
Zamboula
hmet
Deserts
KESHAN
PUNT
ZEMBABWEI
Kingdoms

Dynamite Entertainment Presents

RED SONJA®

SHE-DEVIL WITH A SWORD

Volume V: World On Fire

Dedicated to **Robert E. Howard**

■ WRITTEN BY
MICHAEL AVON OEMING
BRIAN REED

■ ART BY
HOMS

■ COLORS BY
VINICIUS ANDRADE

■ LETTERING BY
RICHARD STARKINGS
AND COMICRAFT

■ COVER BY
HOMS

THIS VOLUME COLLECTS RED SONJA: SHE-DEVIL WITH A SWORD ISSUES TWENTY FIVE THROUGH TWENTY NINE BY DYNAMITE ENTERTAINMENT.

BASED ON THE HEROINE CREATED BY
ROBERT E. HOWARD

EXECUTIVE EDITOR - RED SONJA
LUKE LIEBERMAN

SPECIAL THANKS TO ARTHUR LIEBERMAN
AT RED SONJA LLC.

DYNAMITE ENTERTAINMENT
NICK BARRUCCI — PRESIDENT
JUAN COLLADO — CHIEF OPERATING OFFICER
JOSEPH RYBANDT — DIRECTOR OF MARKETING
JOSH JOHNSON — CREATIVE DIRECTOR
JASON ULLMEYER — GRAPHIC DESIGNER

DYNAMITE
ENTERTAINMENT®
WWW.DYNAMITEENTERTAINMENT.COM

To find a comic shop in your area, call
the comic shop locator service toll-free
1-888-266-4226

First Edition
SOFTCOVER ISBN-10: 1-933305-83-5   ISBN-13: 9781933305837
HARDCOVER ISBN-10: 1-933305-82-7   ISBN-13: 9-781933305820
10 9 8 7 6 5 4 3 2 1

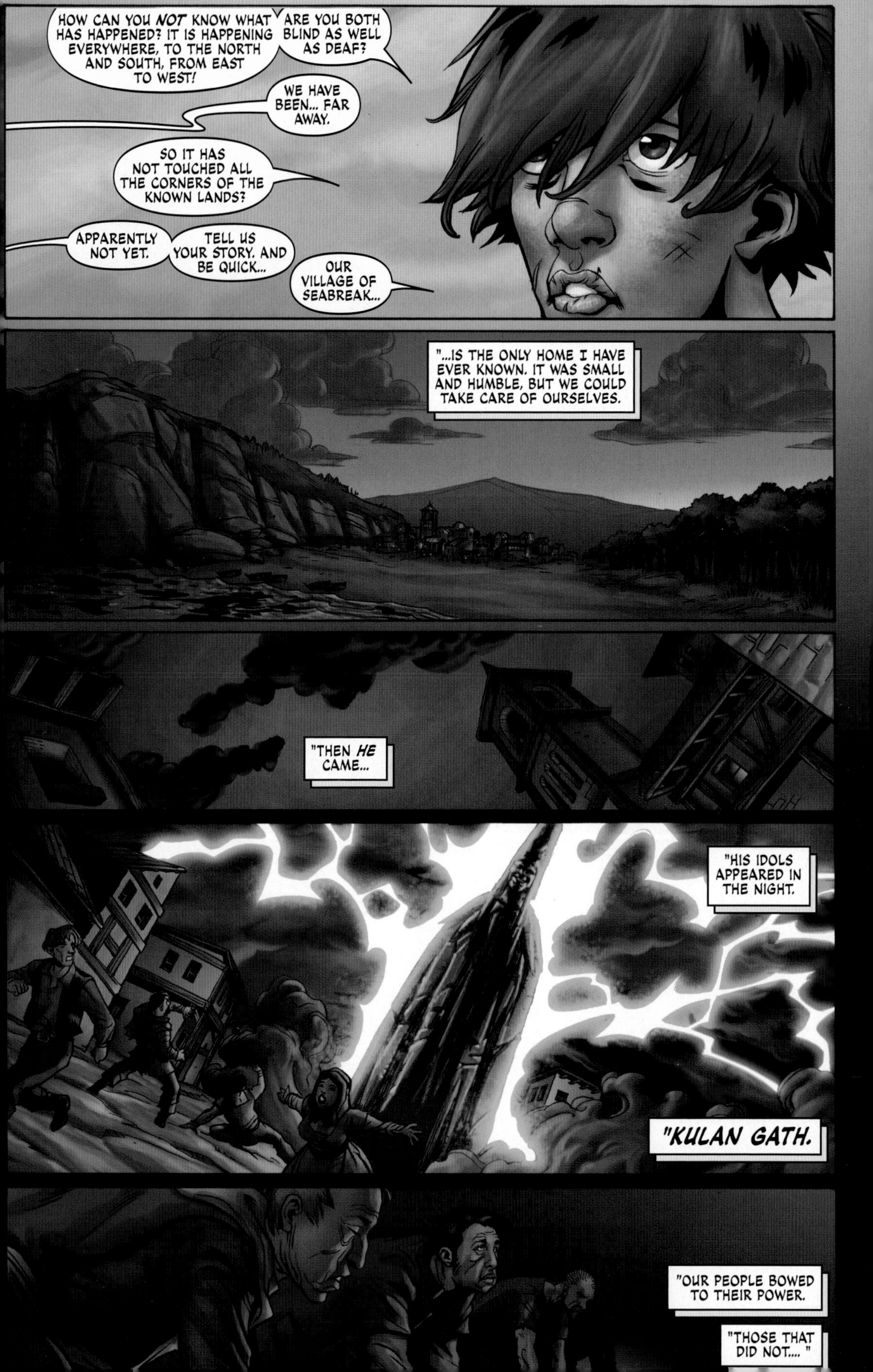
HOW CAN YOU *NOT* KNOW WHAT HAS HAPPENED? IT IS HAPPENING EVERYWHERE, TO THE NORTH AND SOUTH, FROM EAST TO WEST!
ARE YOU BOTH BLIND AS WELL AS DEAF?
WE HAVE BEEN... FAR AWAY.
SO IT HAS NOT TOUCHED ALL THE CORNERS OF THE KNOWN LANDS?
APPARENTLY NOT YET.
TELL US YOUR STORY. AND BE QUICK...
OUR VILLAGE OF SEABREAK...
"...IS THE ONLY HOME I HAVE EVER KNOWN. IT WAS SMALL AND HUMBLE, BUT WE COULD TAKE CARE OF OURSELVES.
"THEN *HE* CAME...
"HIS IDOLS APPEARED IN THE NIGHT.
"KULAN GATH.
"OUR PEOPLE BOWED TO THEIR POWER.
"THOSE THAT DID NOT...."

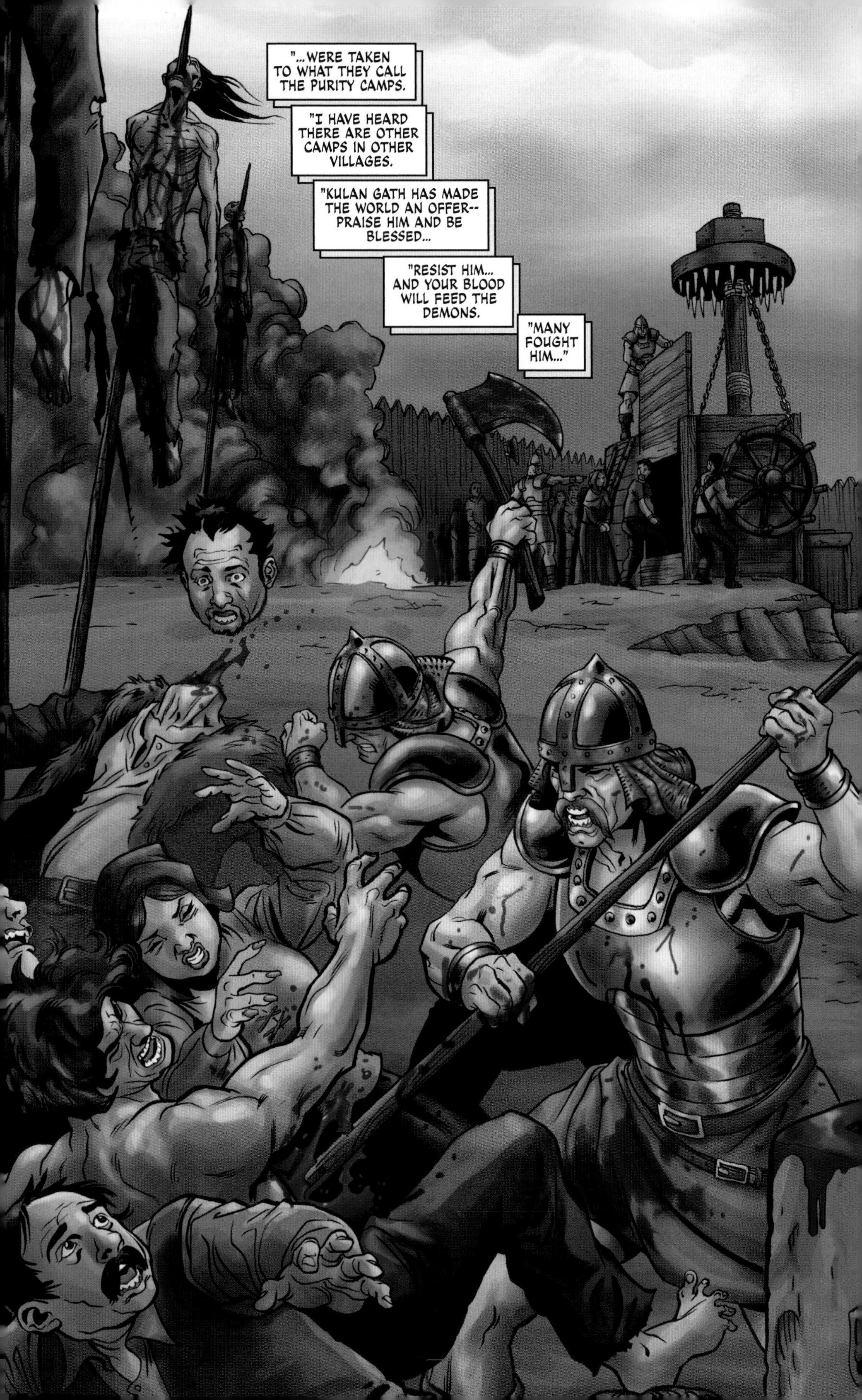
"...WERE TAKEN TO WHAT THEY CALL THE PURITY CAMPS.
"I HAVE HEARD THERE ARE OTHER CAMPS IN OTHER VILLAGES.
"KULAN GATH HAS MADE THE WORLD AN OFFER-- PRAISE HIM AND BE BLESSED...
"RESIST HIM... AND YOUR BLOOD WILL FEED THE DEMONS.
"MANY FOUGHT HIM..."

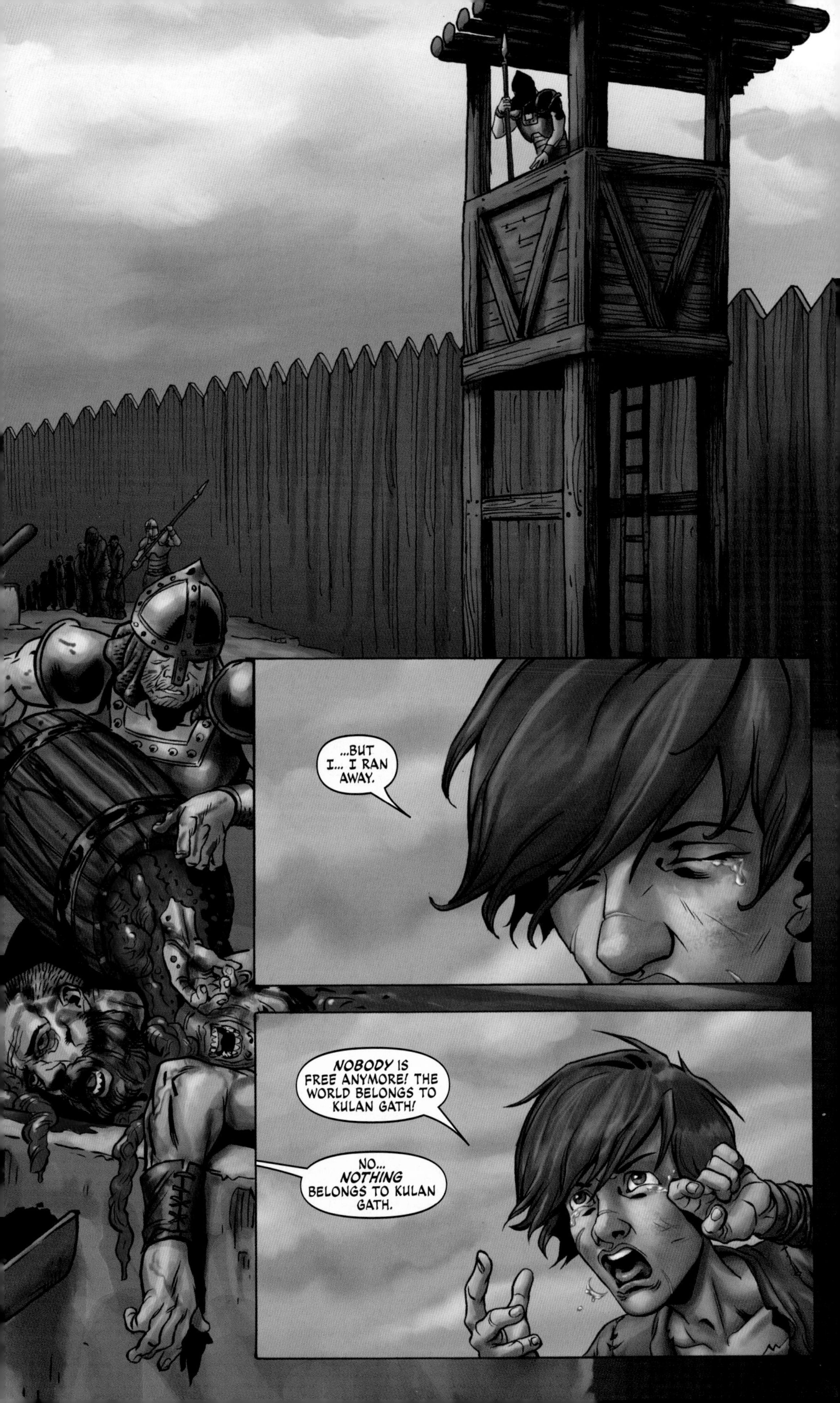
...BUT I... I RAN AWAY.
NOBODY IS FREE ANYMORE! THE WORLD BELONGS TO KULAN GATH!
NO... NOTHING BELONGS TO KULAN GATH.

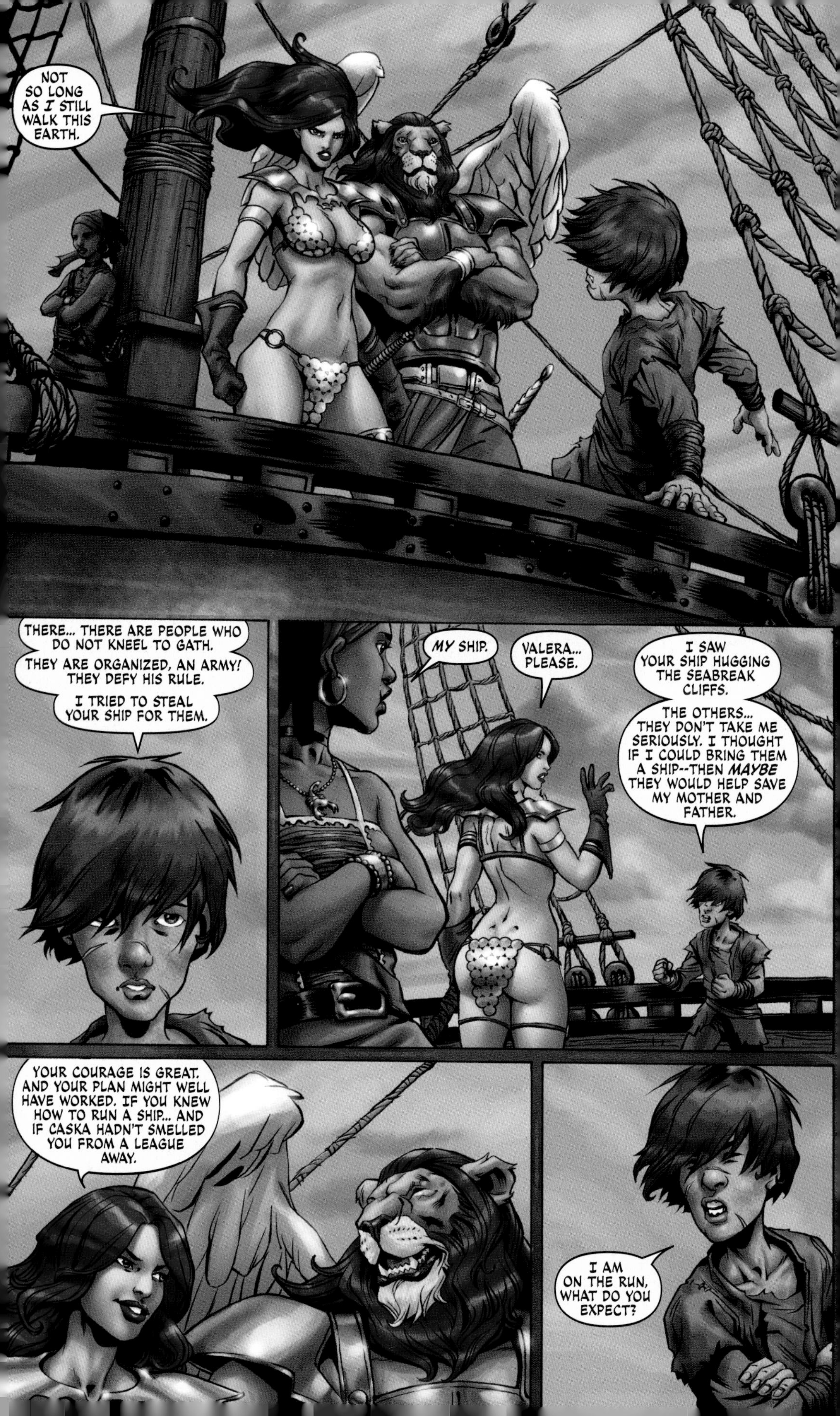

NOT SO LONG AS *I* STILL WALK THIS EARTH.
THERE... THERE ARE PEOPLE WHO DO NOT KNEEL TO GATH.
THEY ARE ORGANIZED, AN ARMY! THEY DEFY HIS RULE.
I TRIED TO STEAL YOUR SHIP FOR THEM.
MY SHIP.
VALERA... PLEASE.
I SAW YOUR SHIP HUGGING THE SEABREAK CLIFFS.
THE OTHERS... THEY DON'T TAKE ME SERIOUSLY. I THOUGHT IF I COULD BRING THEM A SHIP--THEN *MAYBE* THEY WOULD HELP SAVE MY MOTHER AND FATHER.
YOUR COURAGE IS GREAT. AND YOUR PLAN MIGHT WELL HAVE WORKED. IF YOU KNEW HOW TO RUN A SHIP... AND IF CASKA HADN'T SMELLED YOU FROM A LEAGUE AWAY.
I AM ON THE RUN, WHAT DO YOU EXPECT?

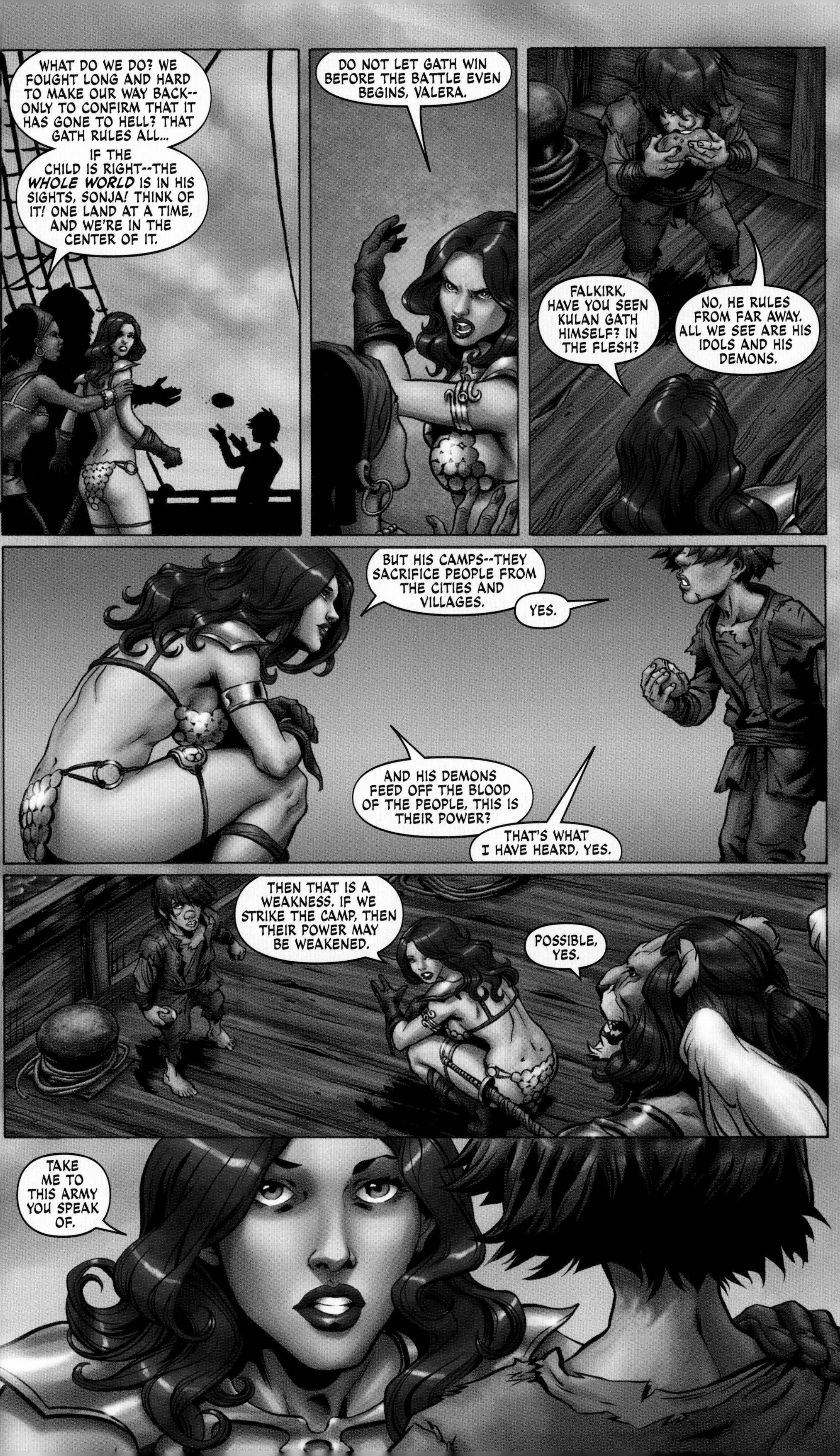
WHAT DO WE DO? WE FOUGHT LONG AND HARD TO MAKE OUR WAY BACK-- ONLY TO CONFIRM THAT IT HAS GONE TO HELL? THAT GATH RULES ALL...
IF THE CHILD IS RIGHT--THE *WHOLE WORLD* IS IN HIS SIGHTS, SONJA! THINK OF IT! ONE LAND AT A TIME, AND WE'RE IN THE CENTER OF IT.
DO NOT LET GATH WIN BEFORE THE BATTLE EVEN BEGINS, VALERA.
FALKIRK, HAVE YOU SEEN KULAN GATH HIMSELF? IN THE FLESH?
NO, HE RULES FROM FAR AWAY. ALL WE SEE ARE HIS IDOLS AND HIS DEMONS.
BUT HIS CAMPS--THEY SACRIFICE PEOPLE FROM THE CITIES AND VILLAGES.
YES.
AND HIS DEMONS FEED OFF THE BLOOD OF THE PEOPLE, THIS IS THEIR POWER?
THAT'S WHAT I HAVE HEARD, YES.
THEN THAT IS A WEAKNESS. IF WE STRIKE THE CAMP, THEN THEIR POWER MAY BE WEAKENED.
POSSIBLE, YES.
TAKE ME TO THIS ARMY YOU SPEAK OF.

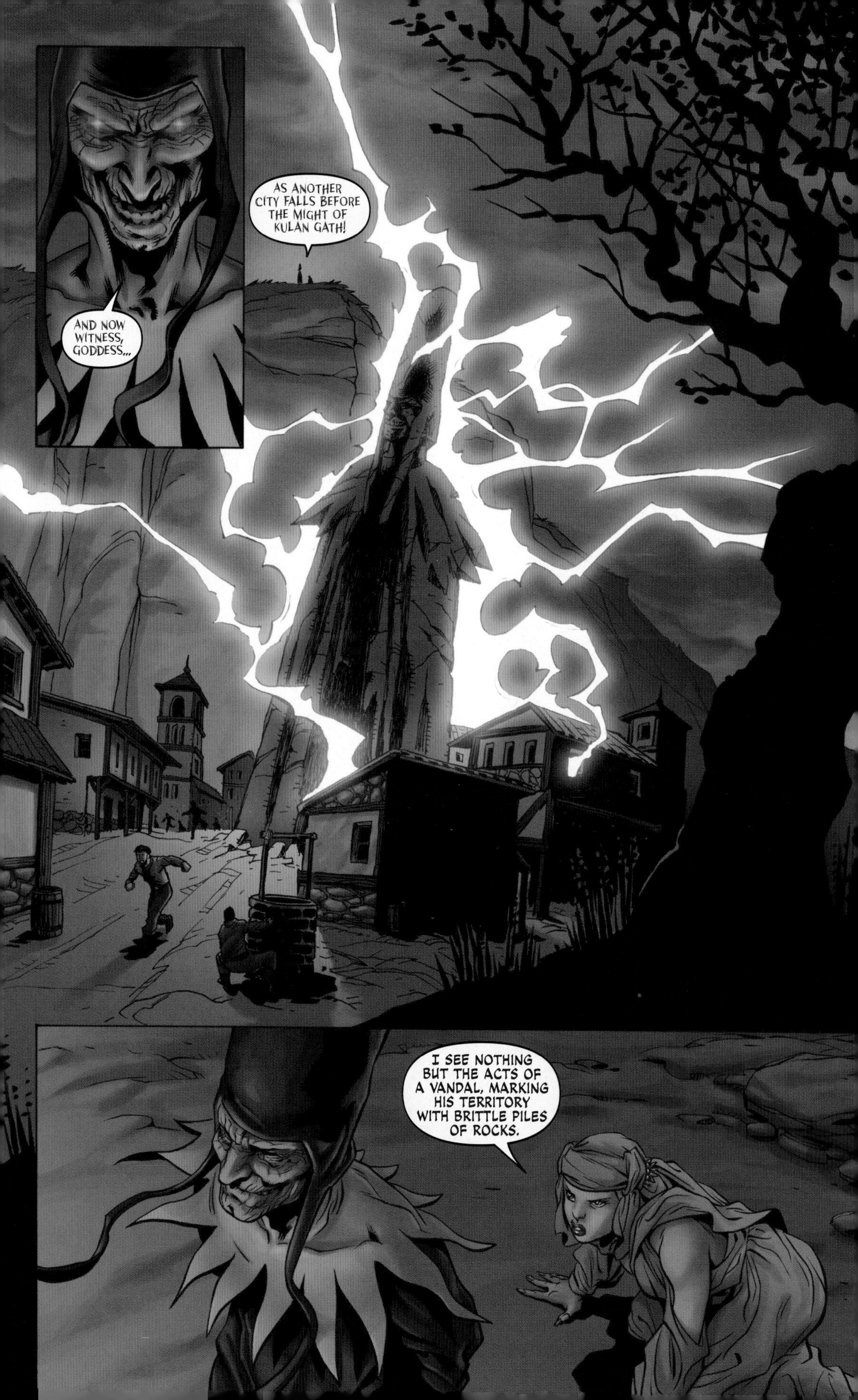
AND NOW WITNESS, GODDESS...
AS ANOTHER CITY FALLS BEFORE THE MIGHT OF KULAN GATH!
I SEE NOTHING BUT THE ACTS OF A VANDAL, MARKING HIS TERRITORY WITH BRITTLE PILES OF ROCKS.

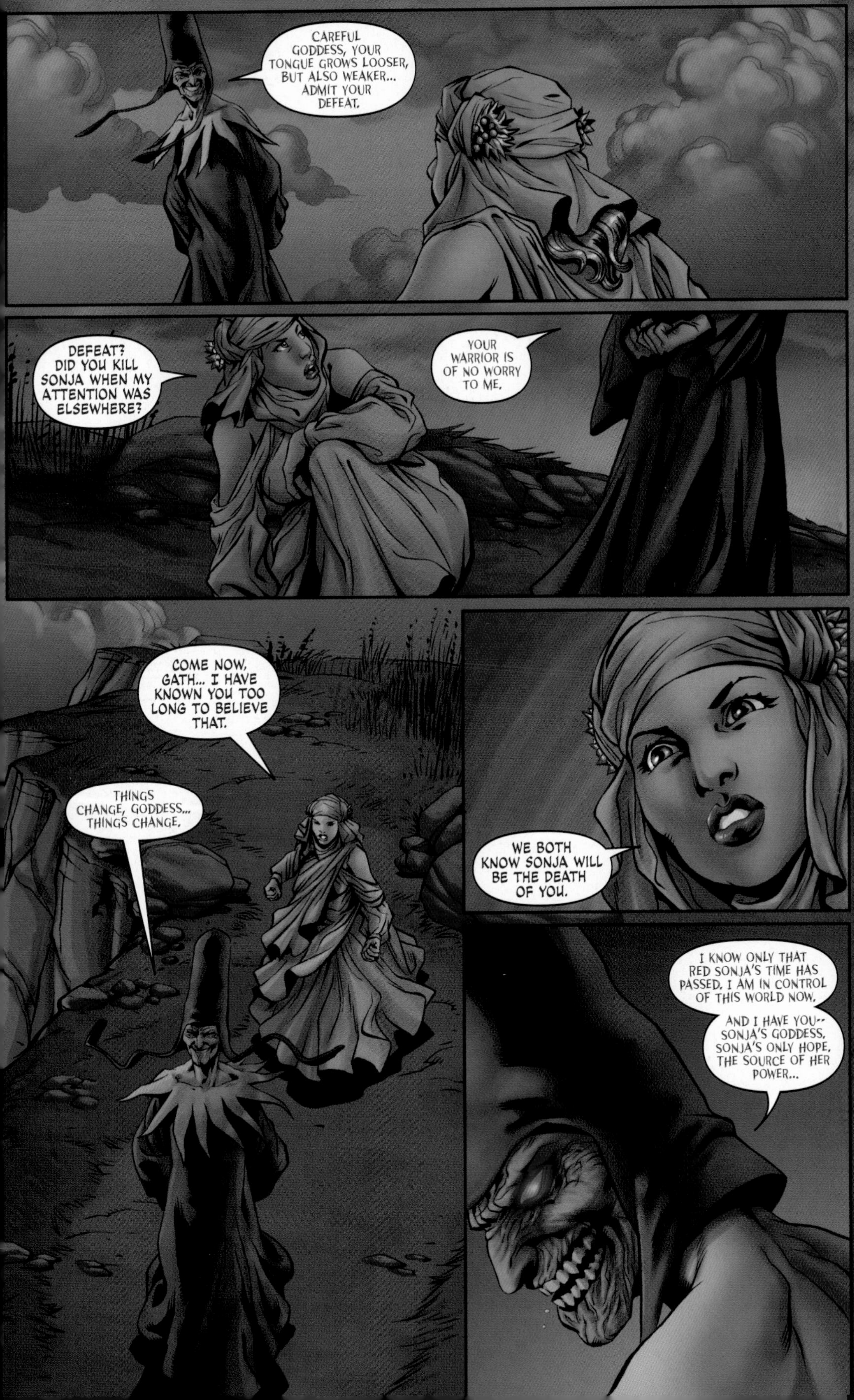
CAREFUL GODDESS, YOUR TONGUE GROWS LOOSER, BUT ALSO WEAKER... ADMIT YOUR DEFEAT.
DEFEAT? DID YOU KILL SONJA WHEN MY ATTENTION WAS ELSEWHERE?
YOUR WARRIOR IS OF NO WORRY TO ME.
COME NOW, GATH... I HAVE KNOWN YOU TOO LONG TO BELIEVE THAT.
THINGS CHANGE, GODDESS... THINGS CHANGE.
WE BOTH KNOW SONJA WILL BE THE DEATH OF YOU.
I KNOW ONLY THAT RED SONJA'S TIME HAS PASSED. I AM IN CONTROL OF THIS WORLD NOW.
AND I HAVE YOU-- SONJA'S GODDESS, SONJA'S ONLY HOPE, THE SOURCE OF HER POWER...

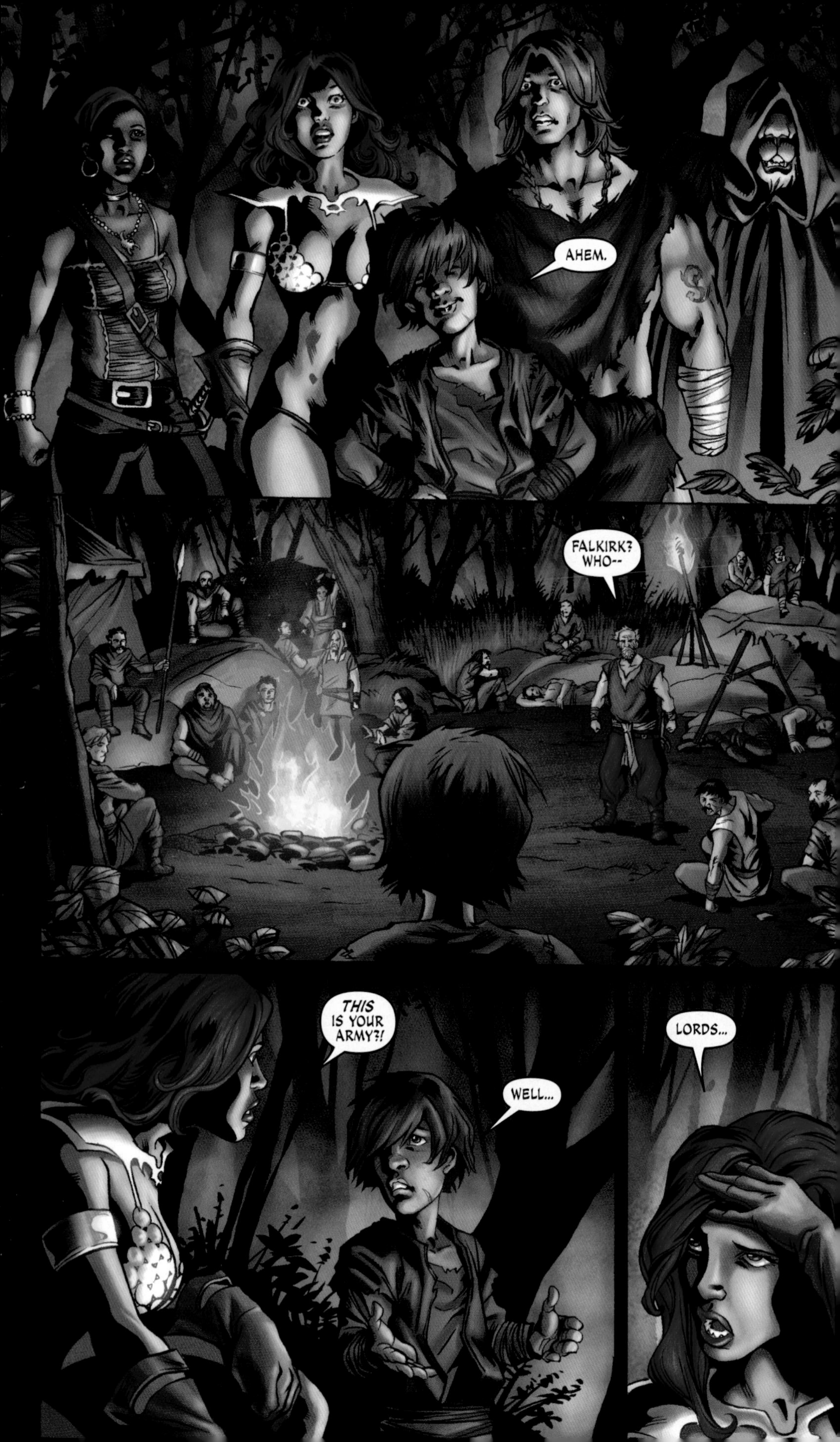
AHEM.
FALKIRK? WHO--
THIS IS YOUR ARMY?!
WELL...
LORDS...

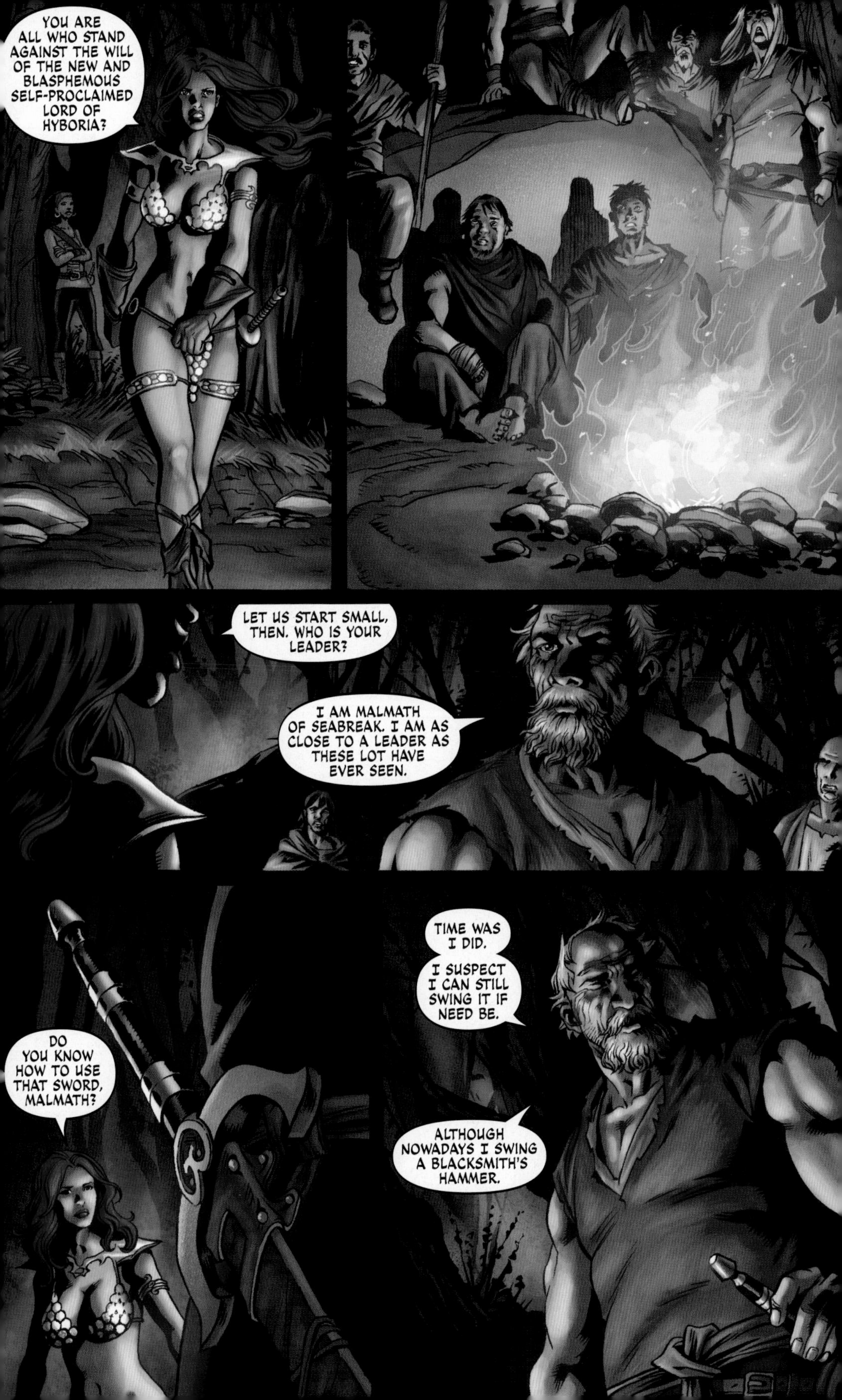
YOU ARE ALL WHO STAND AGAINST THE WILL OF THE NEW AND BLASPHEMOUS SELF-PROCLAIMED LORD OF HYBORIA?
LET US START SMALL, THEN. WHO IS YOUR LEADER?
I AM MALMATH OF SEABREAK. I AM AS CLOSE TO A LEADER AS THESE LOT HAVE EVER SEEN.
DO YOU KNOW HOW TO USE THAT SWORD, MALMATH?
TIME WAS I DID.
I SUSPECT I CAN STILL SWING IT IF NEED BE.
ALTHOUGH NOWADAYS I SWING A BLACKSMITH'S HAMMER.

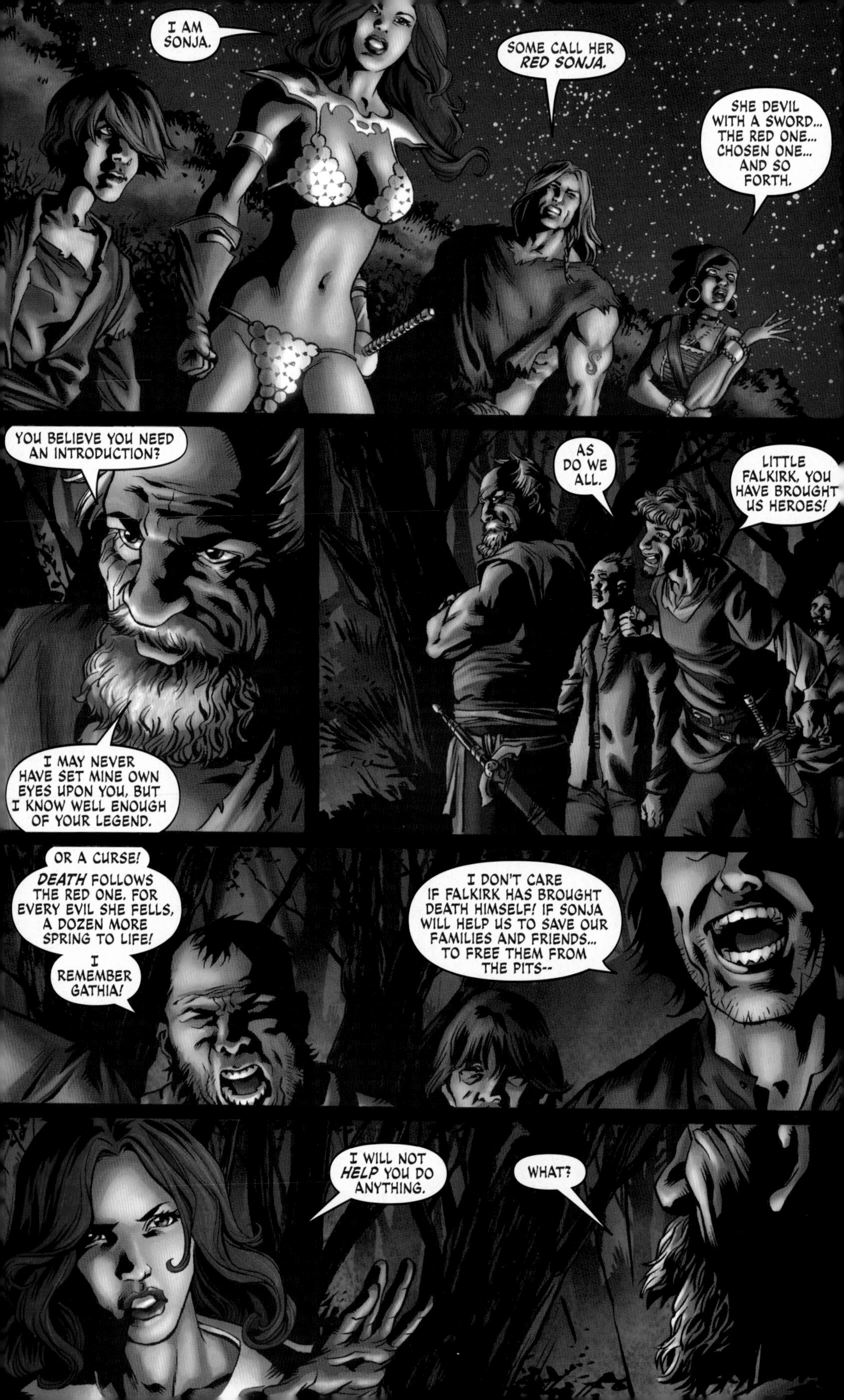
I AM SONJA.
SOME CALL HER *RED SONJA.*
SHE DEVIL WITH A SWORD... THE RED ONE... CHOSEN ONE... AND SO FORTH.
YOU BELIEVE YOU NEED AN INTRODUCTION?
I MAY NEVER HAVE SET MINE OWN EYES UPON YOU, BUT I KNOW WELL ENOUGH OF YOUR LEGEND.
AS DO WE ALL.
LITTLE FALKIRK, YOU HAVE BROUGHT US HEROES!
OR A CURSE!
DEATH FOLLOWS THE RED ONE. FOR EVERY EVIL SHE FELLS, A DOZEN MORE SPRING TO LIFE!
I REMEMBER GATHIA!
I DON'T CARE IF FALKIRK HAS BROUGHT DEATH HIMSELF! IF SONJA WILL HELP US TO SAVE OUR FAMILIES AND FRIENDS... TO FREE THEM FROM THE PITS--
I WILL NOT *HELP* YOU DO ANYTHING.
WHAT?

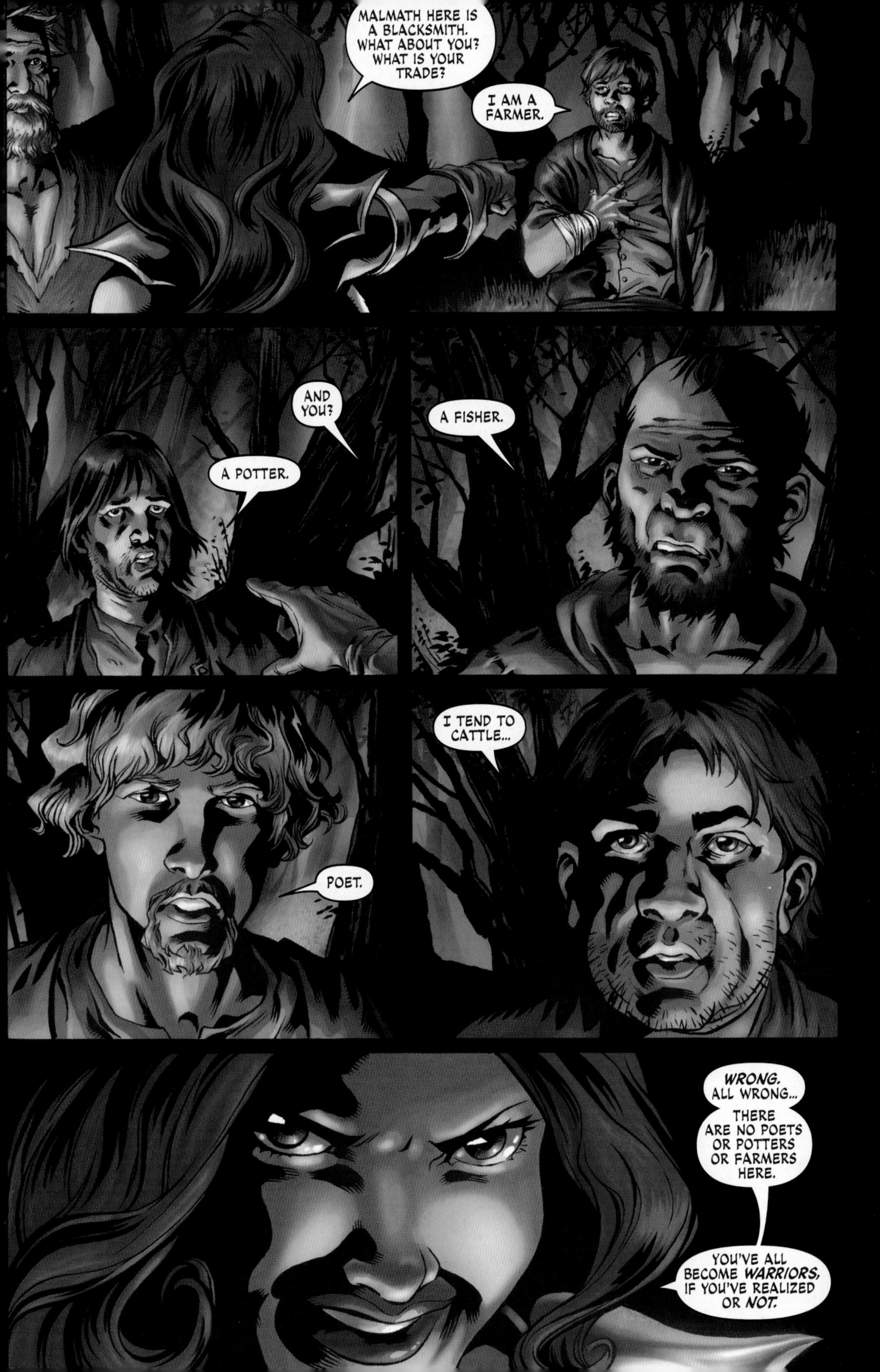
MALMATH HERE IS A BLACKSMITH. WHAT ABOUT YOU? WHAT IS YOUR TRADE?
I AM A FARMER.
AND YOU?
A POTTER.
A FISHER.
I TEND TO CATTLE...
POET.
WRONG. ALL WRONG...
THERE ARE NO POETS OR POTTERS OR FARMERS HERE.
YOU'VE ALL BECOME *WARRIORS,* IF YOU'VE REALIZED OR *NOT.*

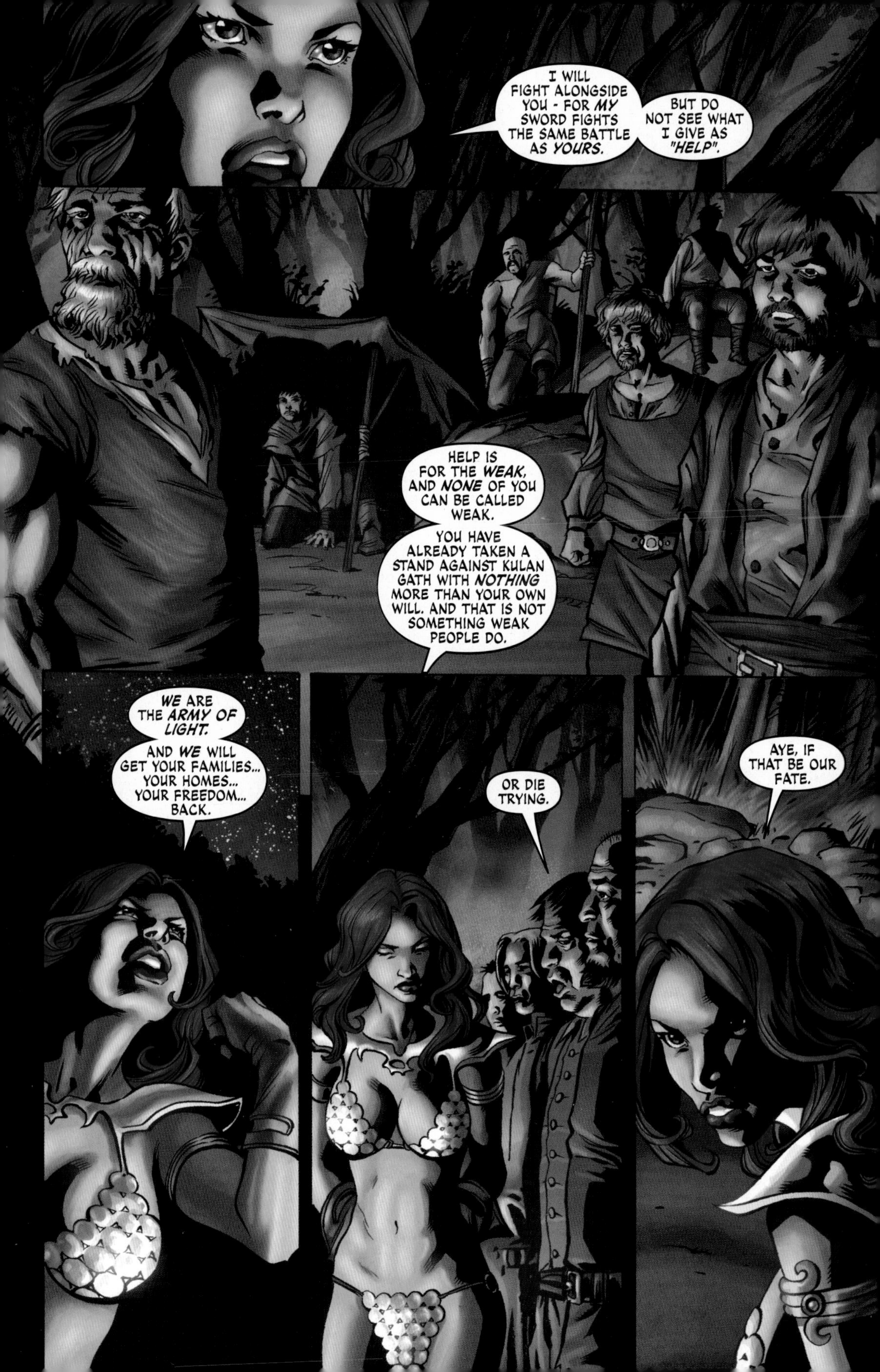
I WILL FIGHT ALONGSIDE YOU - FOR MY SWORD FIGHTS THE SAME BATTLE AS YOURS.
BUT DO NOT SEE WHAT I GIVE AS "HELP".
HELP IS FOR THE WEAK, AND NONE OF YOU CAN BE CALLED WEAK.
YOU HAVE ALREADY TAKEN A STAND AGAINST KULAN GATH WITH NOTHING MORE THAN YOUR OWN WILL. AND THAT IS NOT SOMETHING WEAK PEOPLE DO.
WE ARE THE ARMY OF LIGHT.
AND WE WILL GET YOUR FAMILIES... YOUR HOMES... YOUR FREEDOM... BACK.
OR DIE TRYING.
AYE, IF THAT BE OUR FATE.

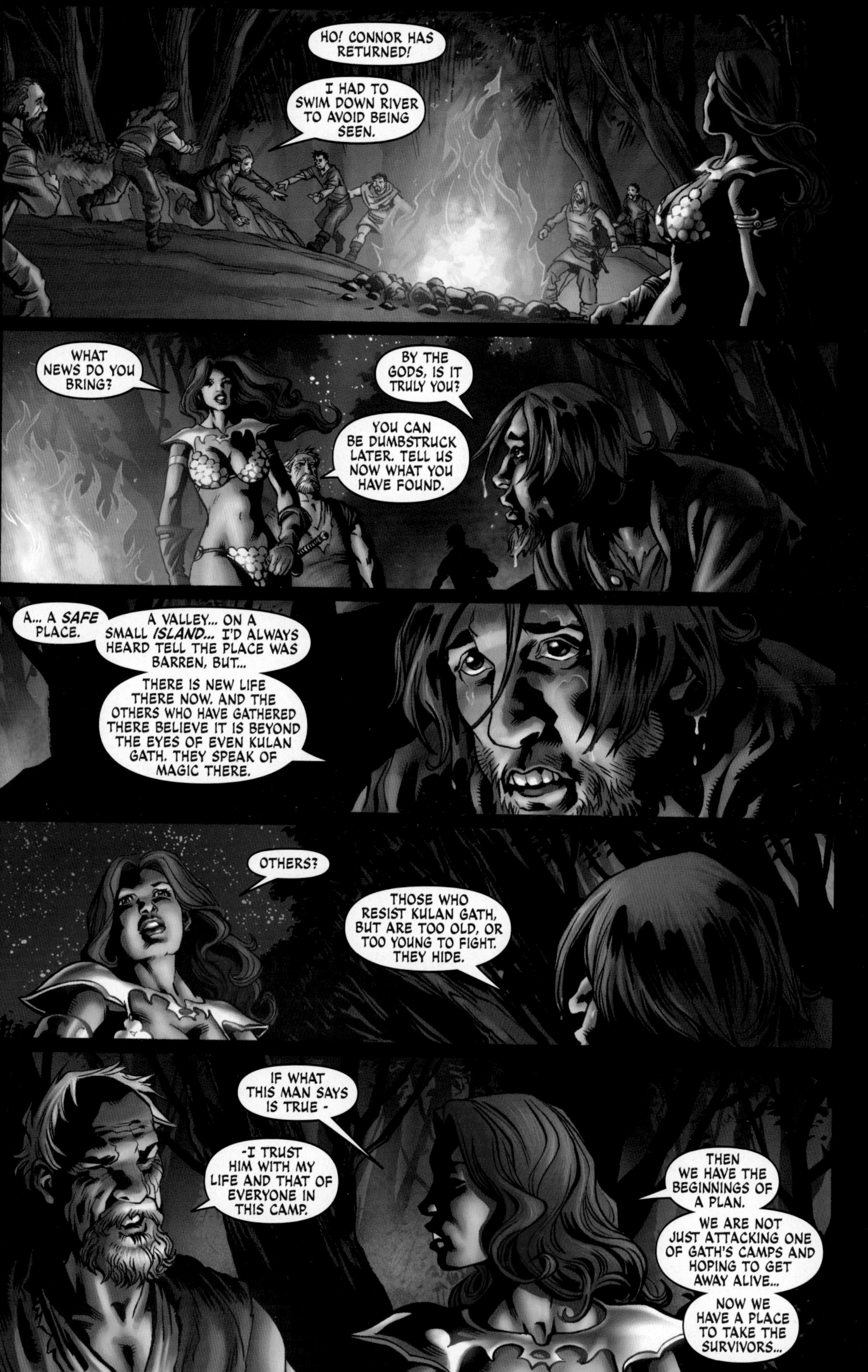
HO! CONNOR HAS RETURNED!
I HAD TO SWIM DOWN RIVER TO AVOID BEING SEEN.
WHAT NEWS DO YOU BRING?
BY THE GODS, IS IT TRULY YOU?
YOU CAN BE DUMBSTRUCK LATER. TELL US NOW WHAT YOU HAVE FOUND.
A... A *SAFE* PLACE.
A VALLEY... ON A SMALL *ISLAND*... I'D ALWAYS HEARD TELL THE PLACE WAS BARREN, BUT...
THERE IS NEW LIFE THERE NOW. AND THE OTHERS WHO HAVE GATHERED THERE BELIEVE IT IS BEYOND THE EYES OF EVEN KULAN GATH. THEY SPEAK OF MAGIC THERE.
OTHERS?
THOSE WHO RESIST KULAN GATH, BUT ARE TOO OLD, OR TOO YOUNG TO FIGHT. THEY HIDE.
IF WHAT THIS MAN SAYS IS TRUE -
-I TRUST HIM WITH MY LIFE AND THAT OF EVERYONE IN THIS CAMP.
THEN WE HAVE THE BEGINNINGS OF A PLAN.
WE ARE NOT JUST ATTACKING ONE OF GATH'S CAMPS AND HOPING TO GET AWAY ALIVE...
NOW WE HAVE A PLACE TO TAKE THE SURVIVORS...

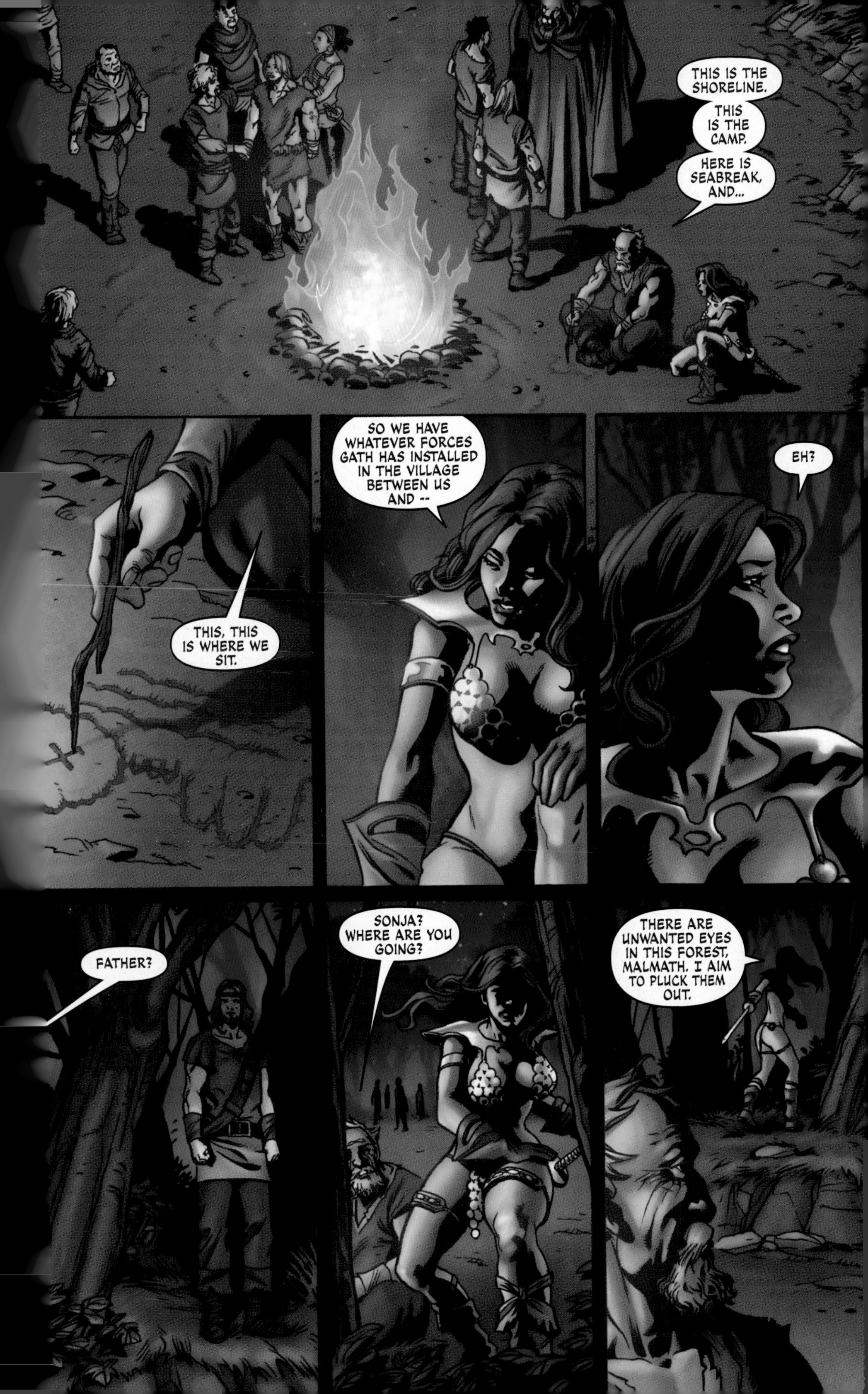
THIS IS THE SHORELINE.
THIS IS THE CAMP.
HERE IS SEABREAK, AND...
THIS, THIS IS WHERE WE SIT.
SO WE HAVE WHATEVER FORCES GATH HAS INSTALLED IN THE VILLAGE BETWEEN US AND --
EH?
FATHER?
SONJA? WHERE ARE YOU GOING?
THERE ARE UNWANTED EYES IN THIS FOREST, MALMATH. I AIM TO PLUCK THEM OUT.

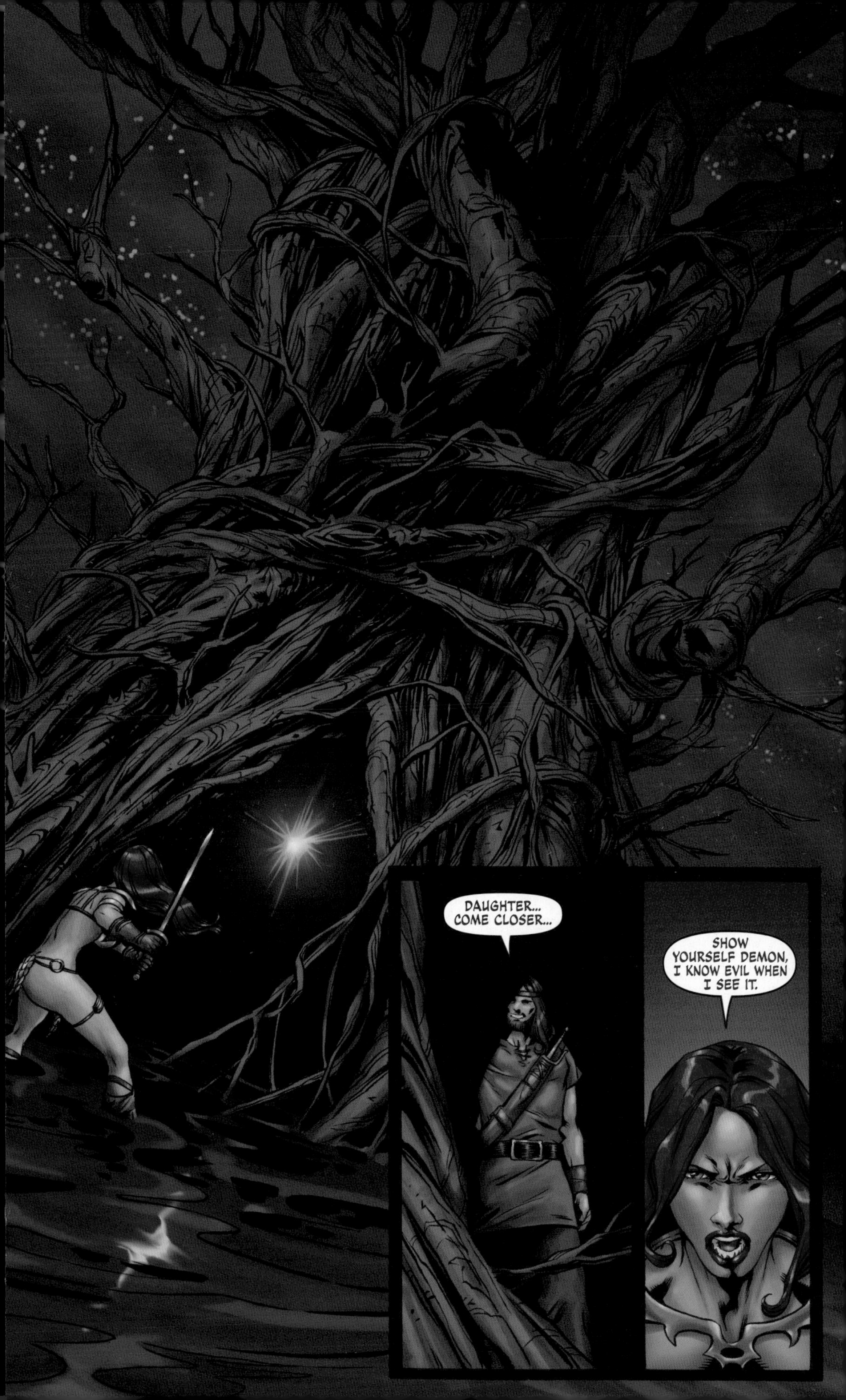
DAUGHTER... COME CLOSER...
SHOW YOURSELF DEMON, I KNOW EVIL WHEN I SEE IT.

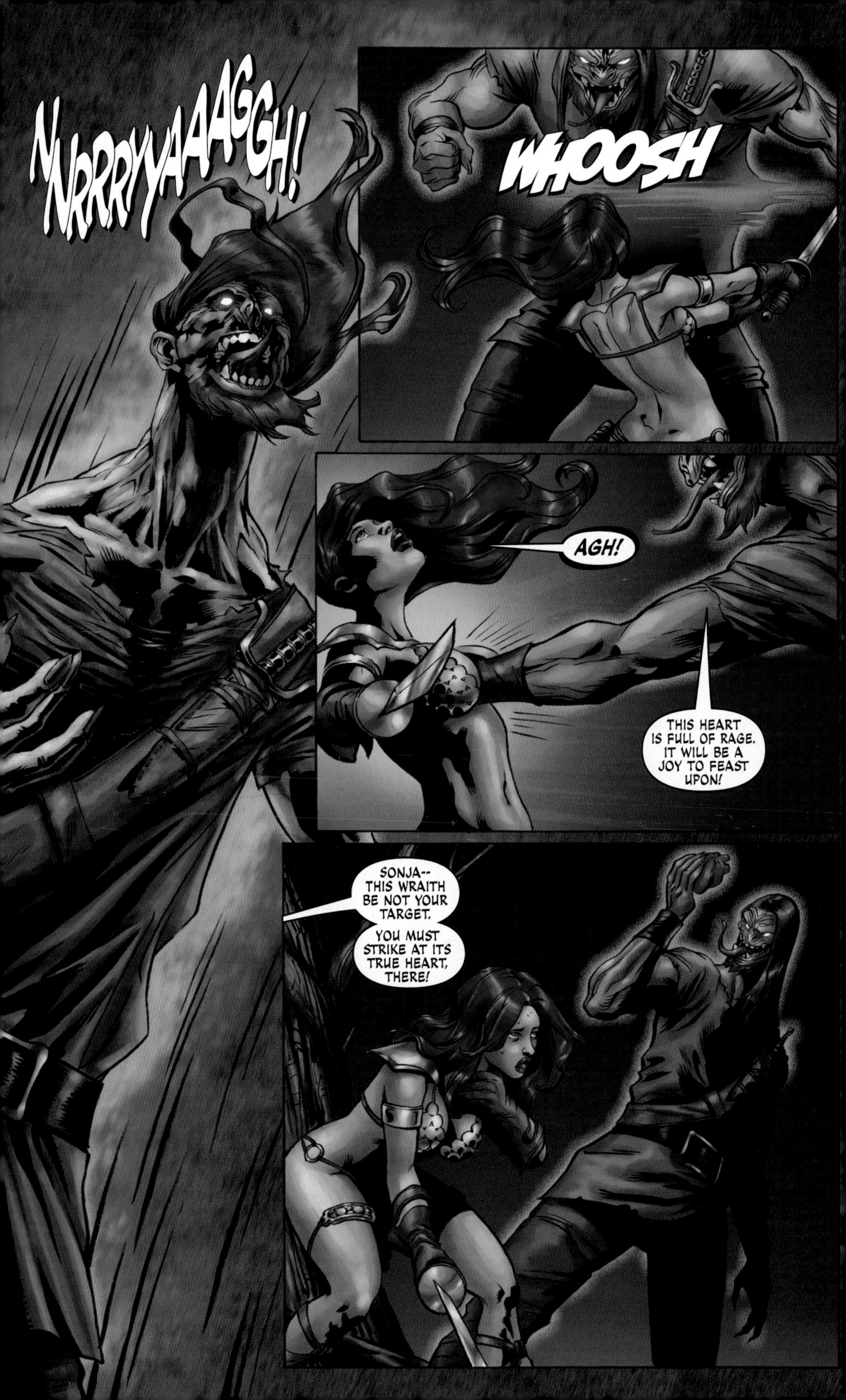
NNRRRYYAAAGGH!
WHOOSH
AGH!
THIS HEART IS FULL OF RAGE. IT WILL BE A JOY TO FEAST UPON!
SONJA-- THIS WRAITH BE NOT YOUR TARGET.
YOU MUST STRIKE AT ITS TRUE HEART, THERE!

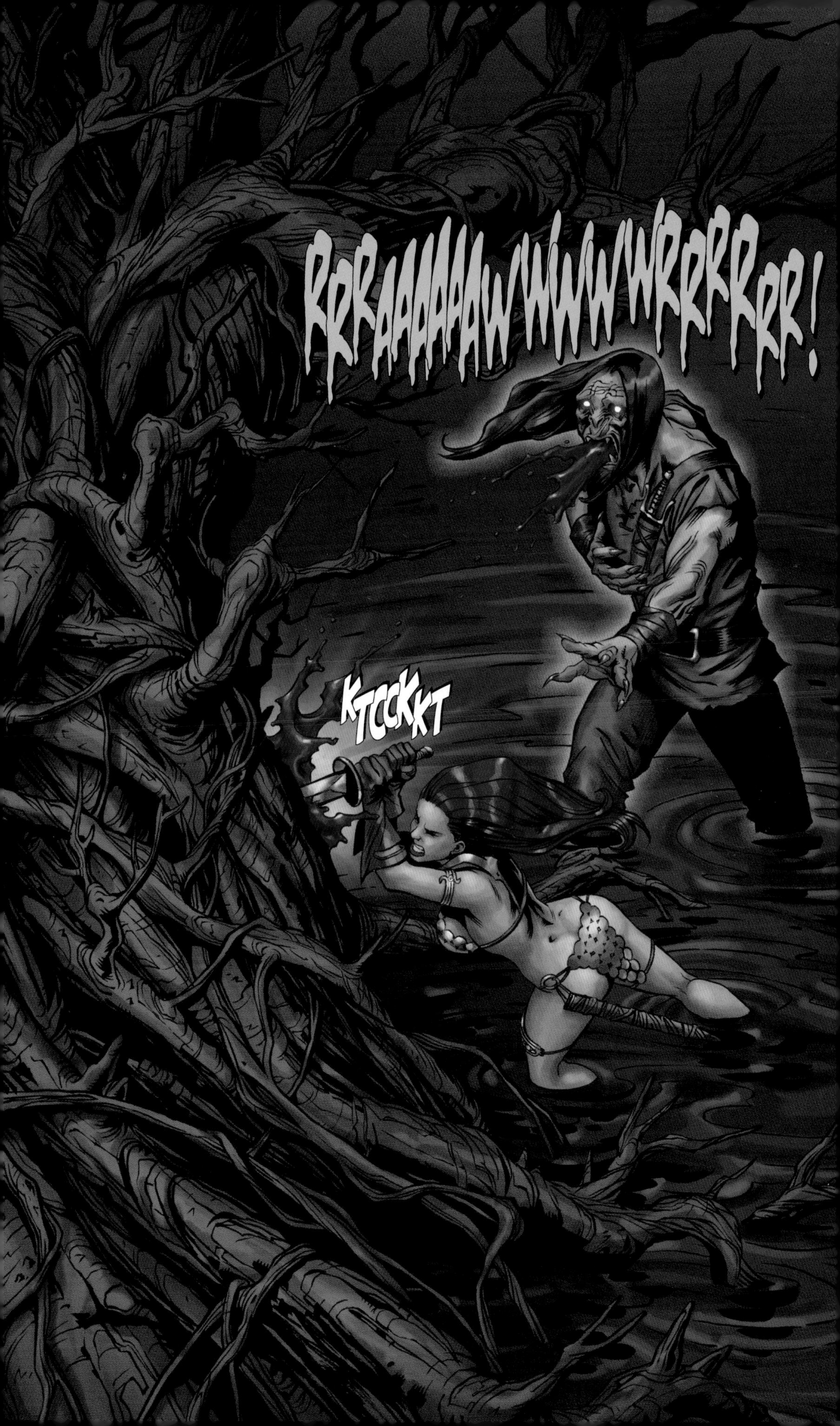
RRRAAAAAAWWWWWRRRRRR!
KTCCKKT

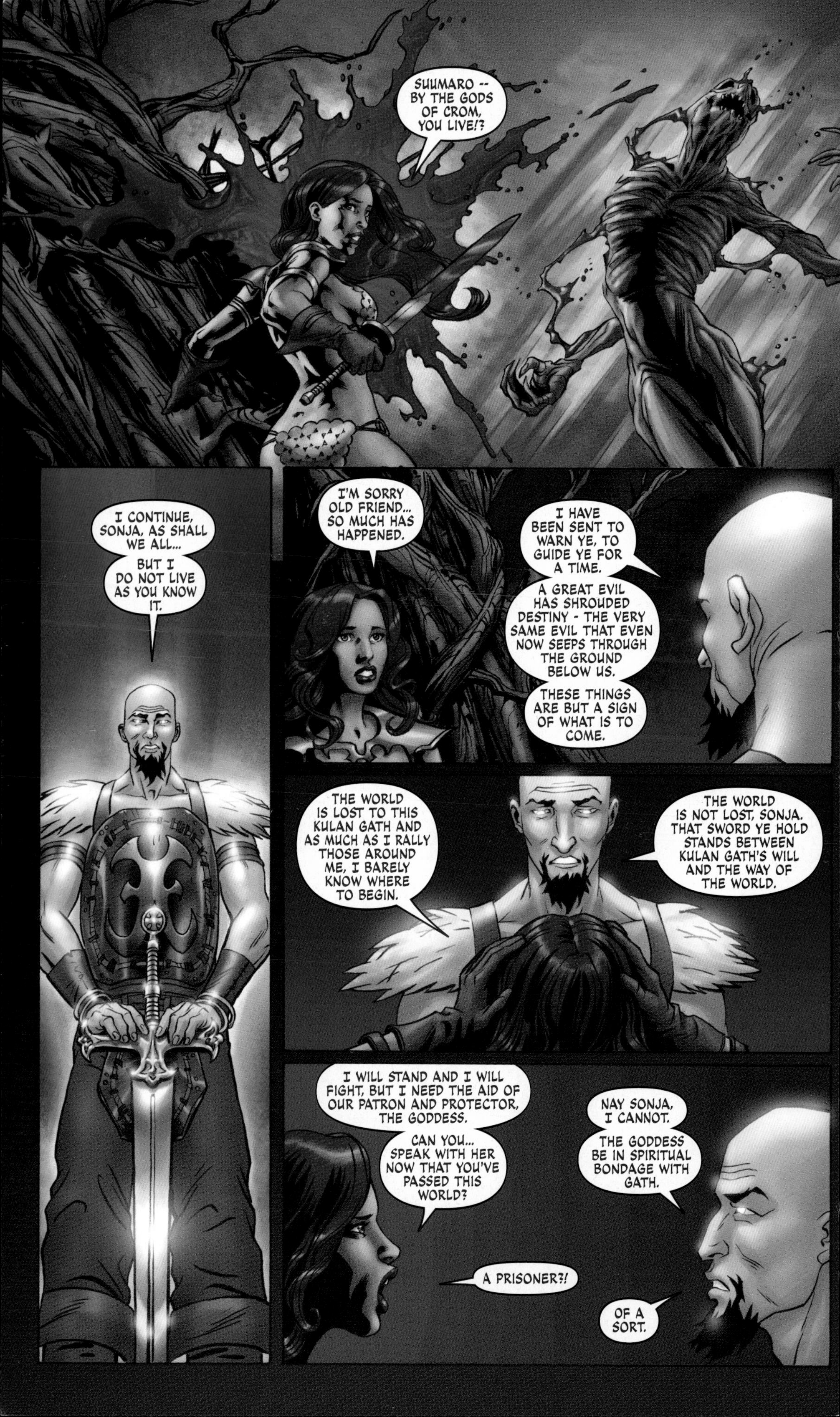
SUUMARO -- BY THE GODS OF CROM, YOU LIVE!?
I CONTINUE, SONJA, AS SHALL WE ALL...
BUT I DO NOT LIVE AS YOU KNOW IT.
I'M SORRY OLD FRIEND... SO MUCH HAS HAPPENED.
I HAVE BEEN SENT TO WARN YE, TO GUIDE YE FOR A TIME.
A GREAT EVIL HAS SHROUDED DESTINY - THE VERY SAME EVIL THAT EVEN NOW SEEPS THROUGH THE GROUND BELOW US.
THESE THINGS ARE BUT A SIGN OF WHAT IS TO COME.
THE WORLD IS LOST TO THIS KULAN GATH AND AS MUCH AS I RALLY THOSE AROUND ME, I BARELY KNOW WHERE TO BEGIN.
THE WORLD IS NOT LOST, SONJA. THAT SWORD YE HOLD STANDS BETWEEN KULAN GATH'S WILL AND THE WAY OF THE WORLD.
I WILL STAND AND I WILL FIGHT, BUT I NEED THE AID OF OUR PATRON AND PROTECTOR, THE GODDESS.
CAN YOU... SPEAK WITH HER NOW THAT YOU'VE PASSED THIS WORLD?
NAY SONJA, I CANNOT.
THE GODDESS BE IN SPIRITUAL BONDAGE WITH GATH.
A PRISONER?!
OF A SORT.

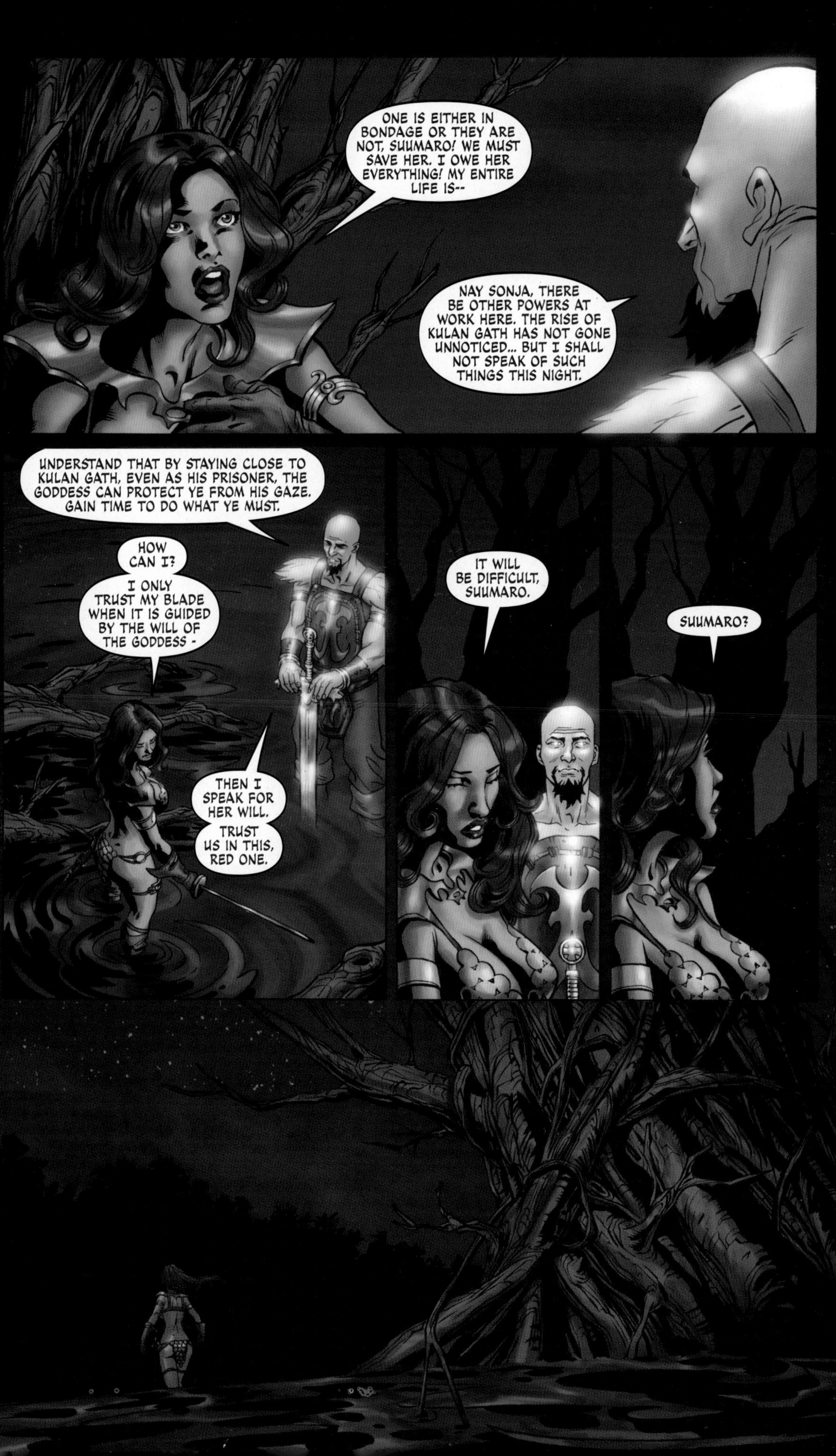
ONE IS EITHER IN BONDAGE OR THEY ARE NOT, SUUMARO! WE MUST SAVE HER. I OWE HER EVERYTHING! MY ENTIRE LIFE IS--
NAY SONJA, THERE BE OTHER POWERS AT WORK HERE. THE RISE OF KULAN GATH HAS NOT GONE UNNOTICED... BUT I SHALL NOT SPEAK OF SUCH THINGS THIS NIGHT.
UNDERSTAND THAT BY STAYING CLOSE TO KULAN GATH, EVEN AS HIS PRISONER, THE GODDESS CAN PROTECT YE FROM HIS GAZE. GAIN TIME TO DO WHAT YE MUST.
HOW CAN I?
I ONLY TRUST MY BLADE WHEN IT IS GUIDED BY THE WILL OF THE GODDESS -
THEN I SPEAK FOR HER WILL.
TRUST US IN THIS, RED ONE.
IT WILL BE DIFFICULT, SUUMARO.
SUUMARO?

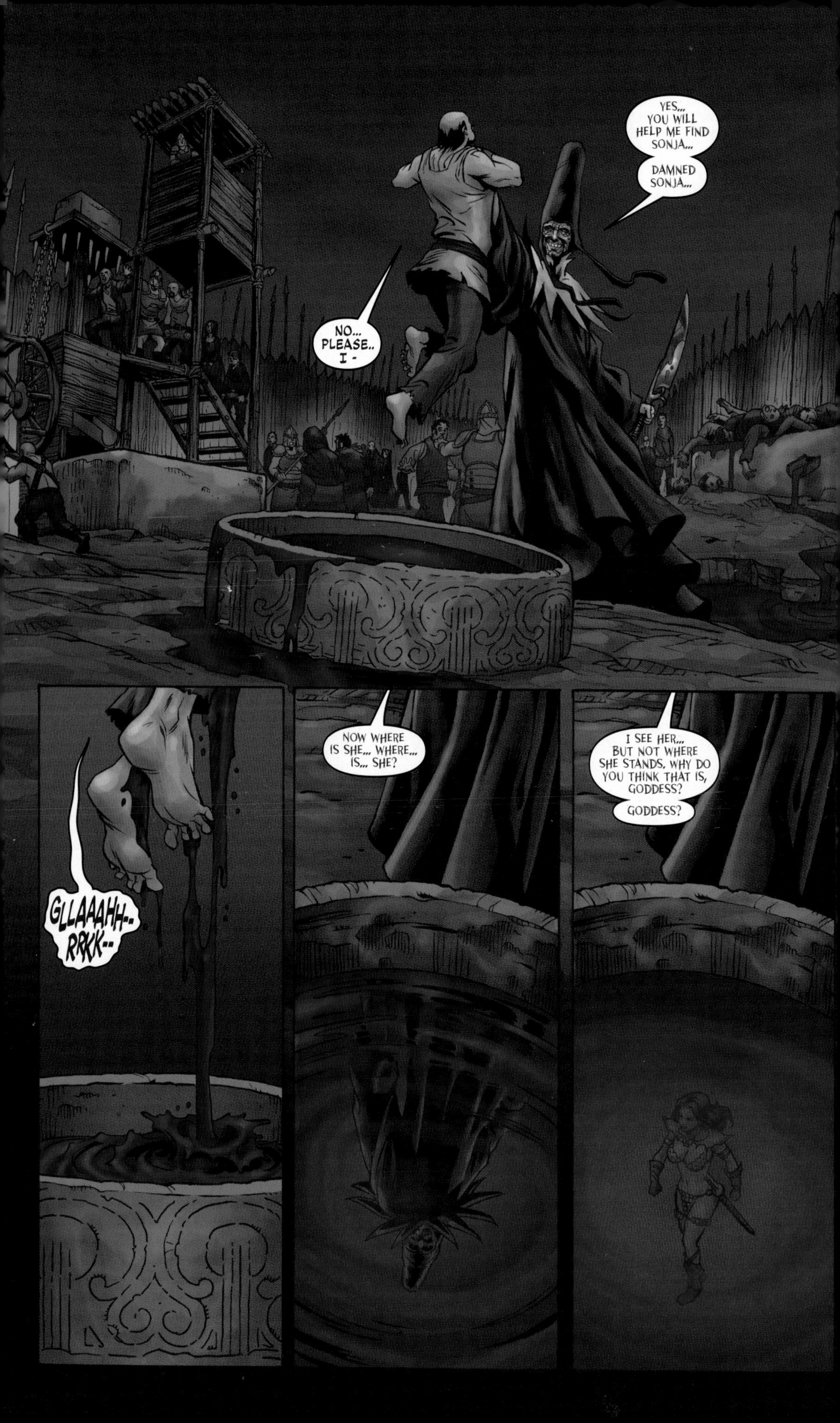
YES... YOU WILL HELP ME FIND SONJA...
DAMNED SONJA...
NO... PLEASE.. I -
GLLAAAHH-- RRKK--
NOW WHERE IS SHE... WHERE... IS... SHE?
I SEE HER... BUT NOT WHERE SHE STANDS. WHY DO YOU THINK THAT IS, GODDESS?
GODDESS?

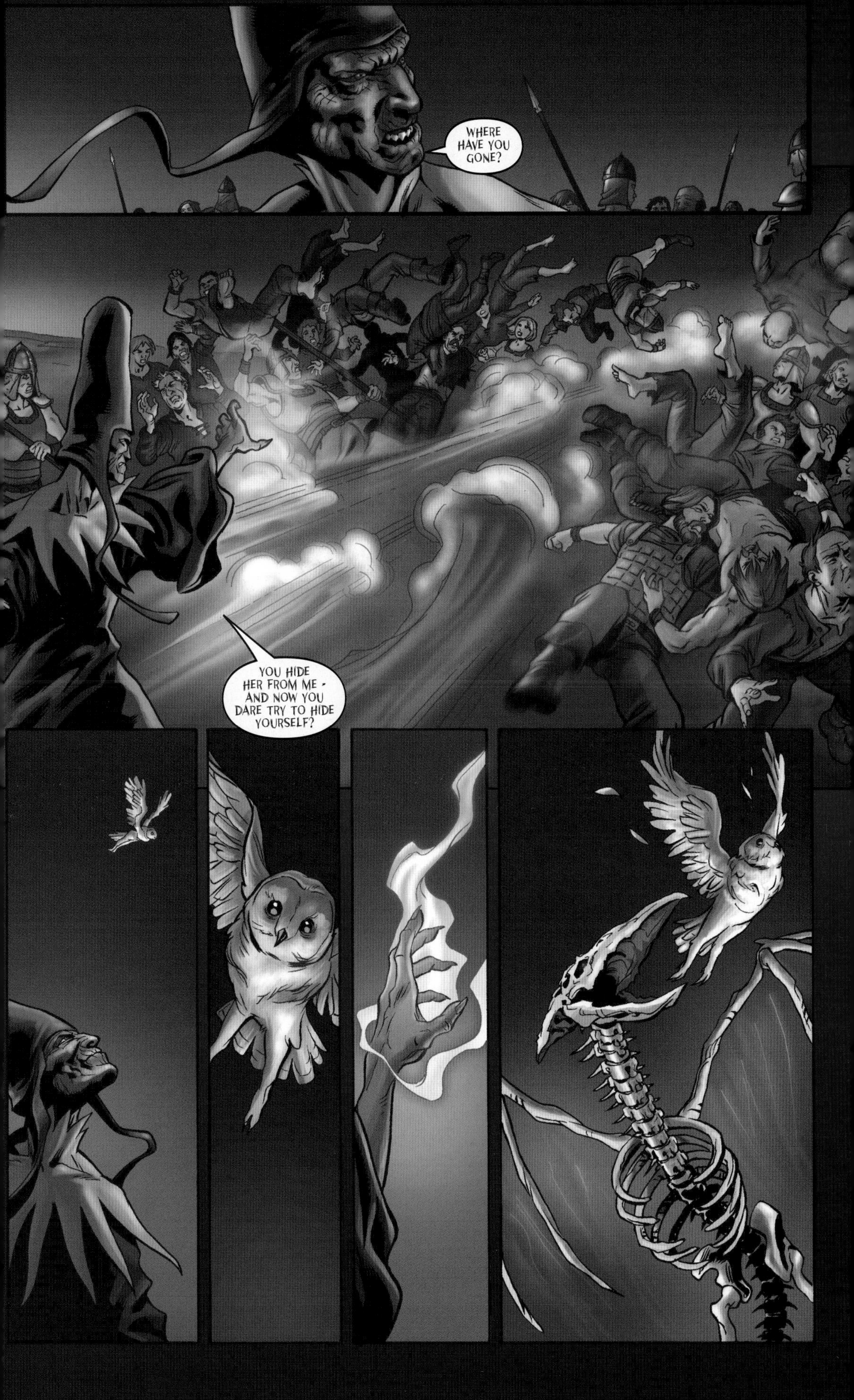
WHERE HAVE YOU GONE?
YOU HIDE HER FROM ME - AND NOW YOU DARE TRY TO HIDE YOURSELF?

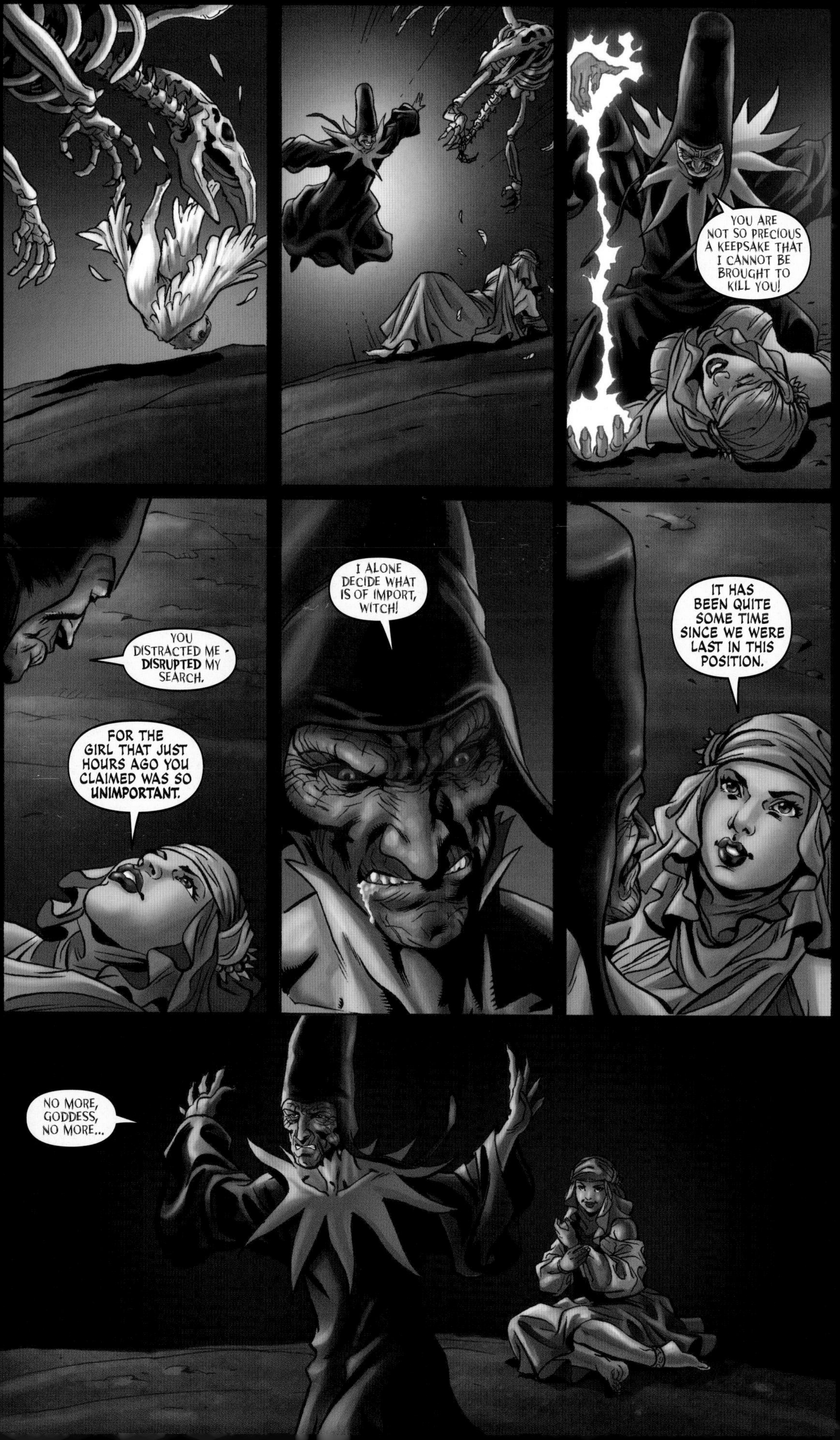
YOU ARE NOT SO PRECIOUS A KEEPSAKE THAT I CANNOT BE BROUGHT TO KILL YOU!
YOU DISTRACTED ME - DISRUPTED MY SEARCH.
FOR THE GIRL THAT JUST HOURS AGO YOU CLAIMED WAS SO UNIMPORTANT.
I ALONE DECIDE WHAT IS OF IMPORT, WITCH!
IT HAS BEEN QUITE SOME TIME SINCE WE WERE LAST IN THIS POSITION.
NO MORE, GODDESS, NO MORE...

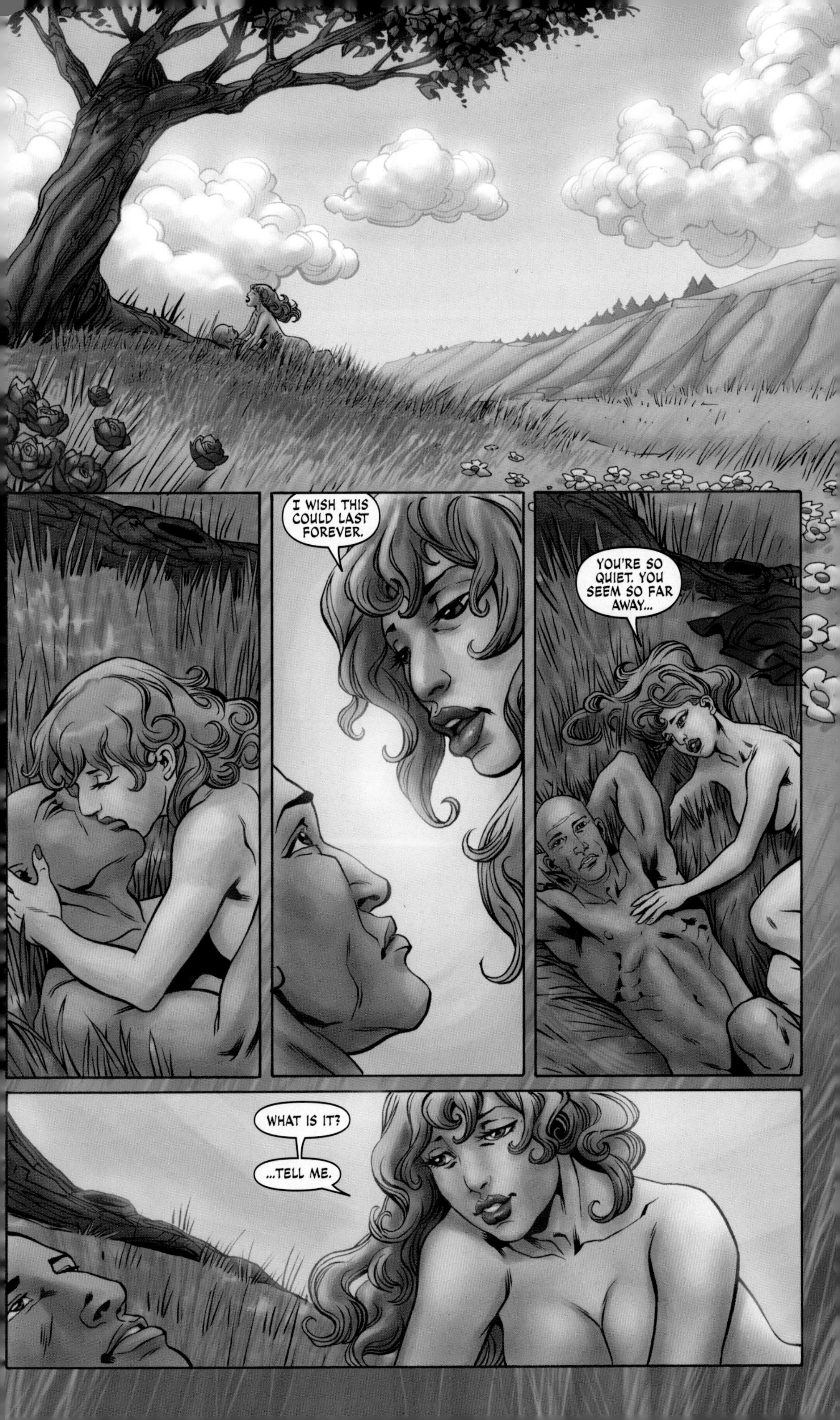
I WISH THIS COULD LAST FOREVER.
YOU'RE SO QUIET. YOU SEEM SO FAR AWAY...
WHAT IS IT?
...TELL ME.

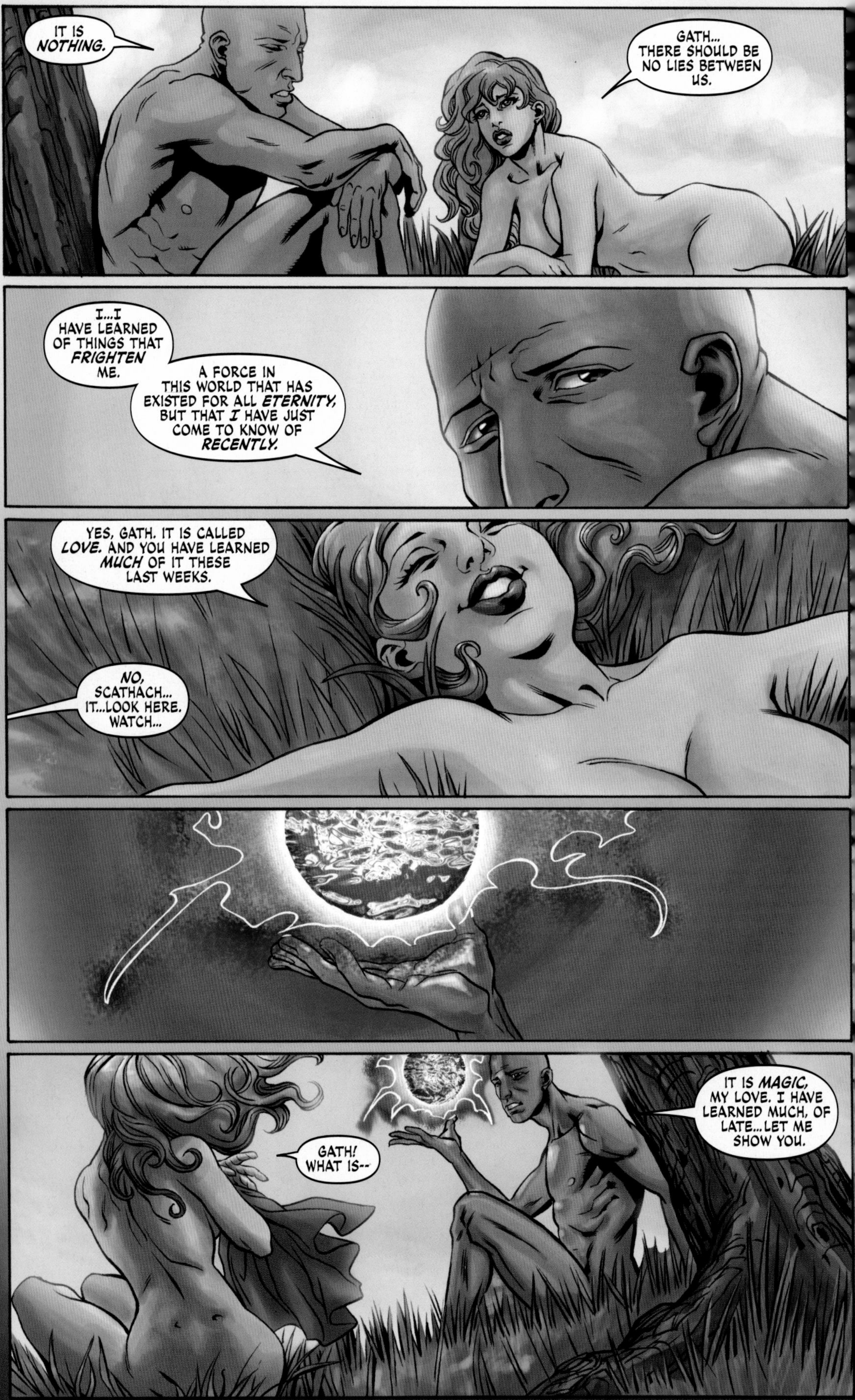
IT IS NOTHING.
GATH... THERE SHOULD BE NO LIES BETWEEN US.
I...I HAVE LEARNED OF THINGS THAT FRIGHTEN ME.
A FORCE IN THIS WORLD THAT HAS EXISTED FOR ALL ETERNITY, BUT THAT I HAVE JUST COME TO KNOW OF RECENTLY.
YES, GATH. IT IS CALLED LOVE. AND YOU HAVE LEARNED MUCH OF IT THESE LAST WEEKS.
NO, SCATHACH... IT...LOOK HERE. WATCH...
GATH! WHAT IS--
IT IS MAGIC, MY LOVE. I HAVE LEARNED MUCH, OF LATE...LET ME SHOW YOU.

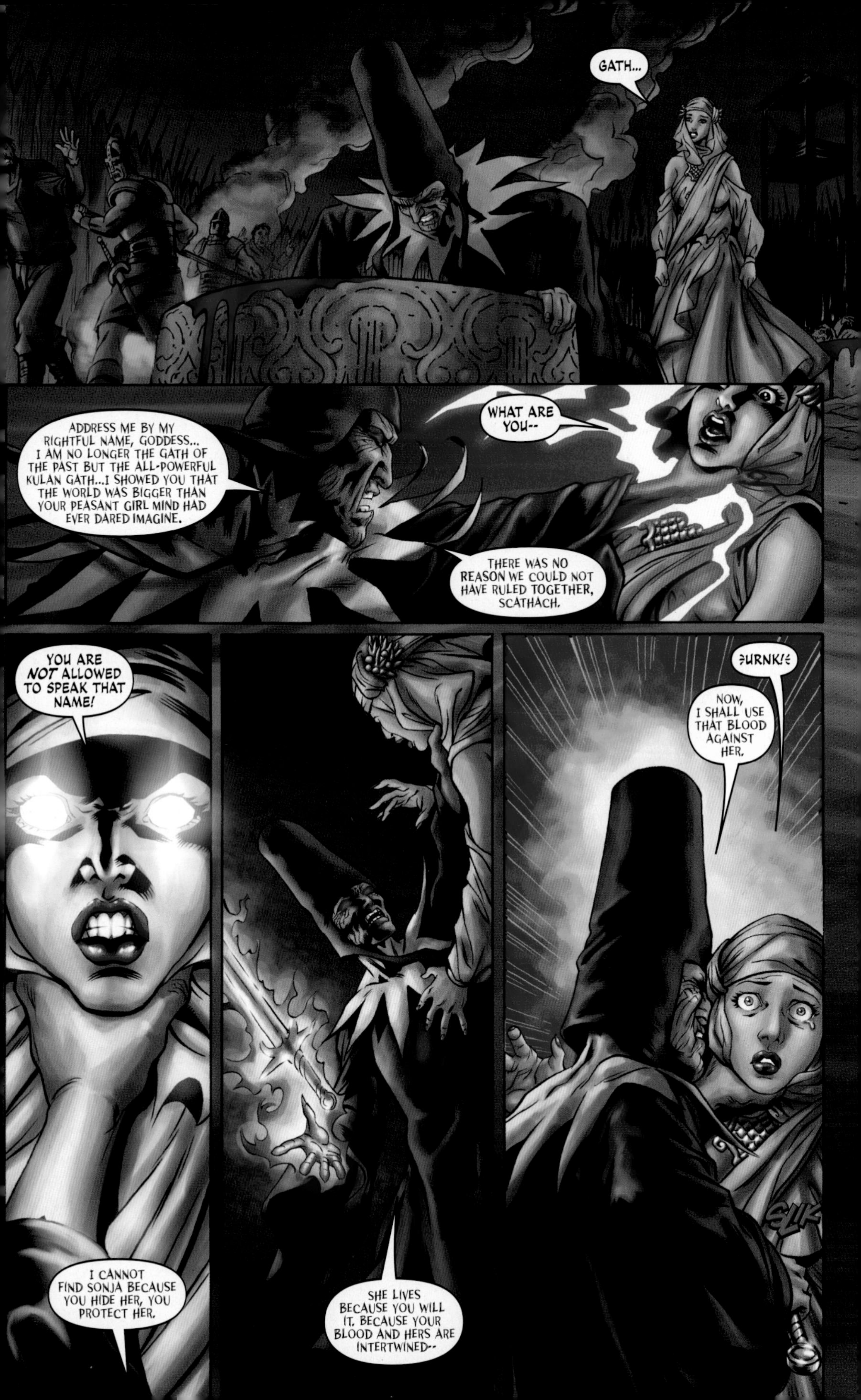
GATH...
ADDRESS ME BY MY RIGHTFUL NAME, GODDESS... I AM NO LONGER THE GATH OF THE PAST BUT THE ALL-POWERFUL KULAN GATH...I SHOWED YOU THAT THE WORLD WAS BIGGER THAN YOUR PEASANT GIRL MIND HAD EVER DARED IMAGINE.
WHAT ARE YOU--
THERE WAS NO REASON WE COULD NOT HAVE RULED TOGETHER, SCATHACH.
YOU ARE *NOT* ALLOWED TO SPEAK THAT NAME!
I CANNOT FIND SONJA BECAUSE YOU HIDE HER, YOU PROTECT HER.
SHE LIVES BECAUSE YOU WILL IT. BECAUSE YOUR BLOOD AND HERS ARE INTERTWINED--
URNK!
NOW, I SHALL USE THAT BLOOD AGAINST HER.
SLIK

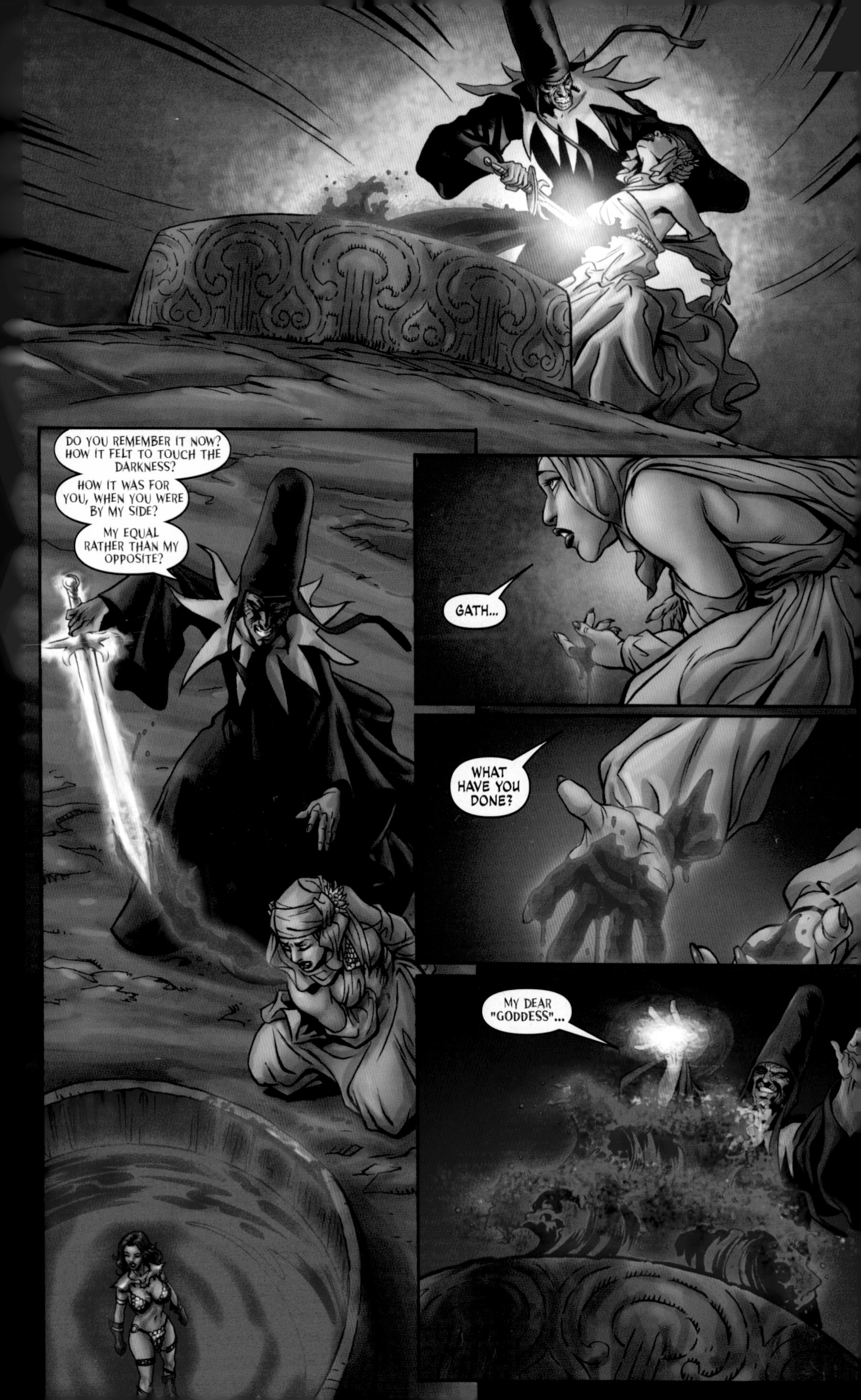
DO YOU REMEMBER IT NOW? HOW IT FELT TO TOUCH THE DARKNESS?
HOW IT WAS FOR YOU, WHEN YOU WERE BY MY SIDE?
MY EQUAL RATHER THAN MY OPPOSITE?
GATH...
WHAT HAVE YOU DONE?
MY DEAR "GODDESS"...

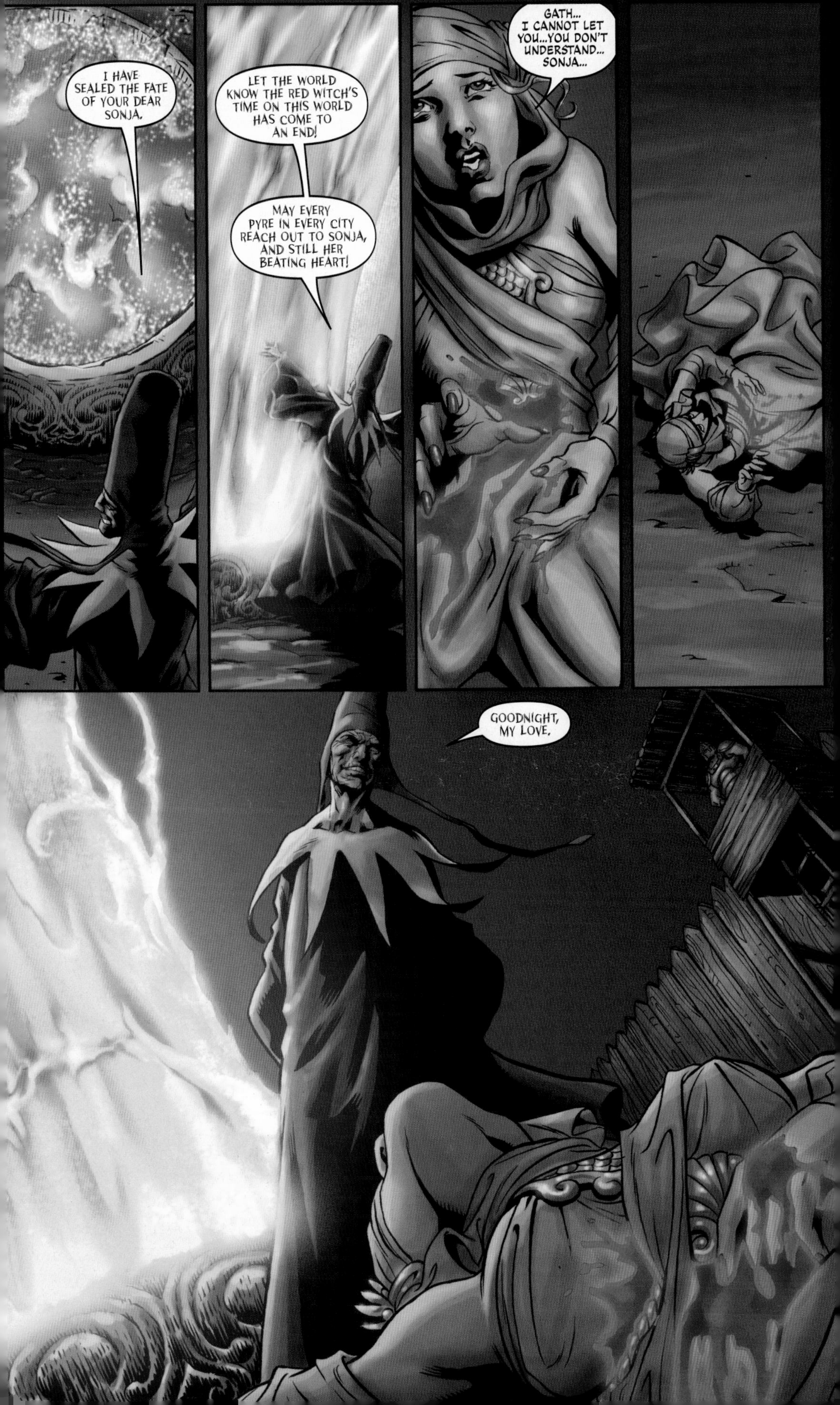
I HAVE SEALED THE FATE OF YOUR DEAR SONJA.
LET THE WORLD KNOW THE RED WITCH'S TIME ON THIS WORLD HAS COME TO AN END!
MAY EVERY PYRE IN EVERY CITY REACH OUT TO SONJA, AND STILL HER BEATING HEART!
GATH... I CANNOT LET YOU...YOU DON'T UNDERSTAND... SONJA...
GOODNIGHT, MY LOVE.

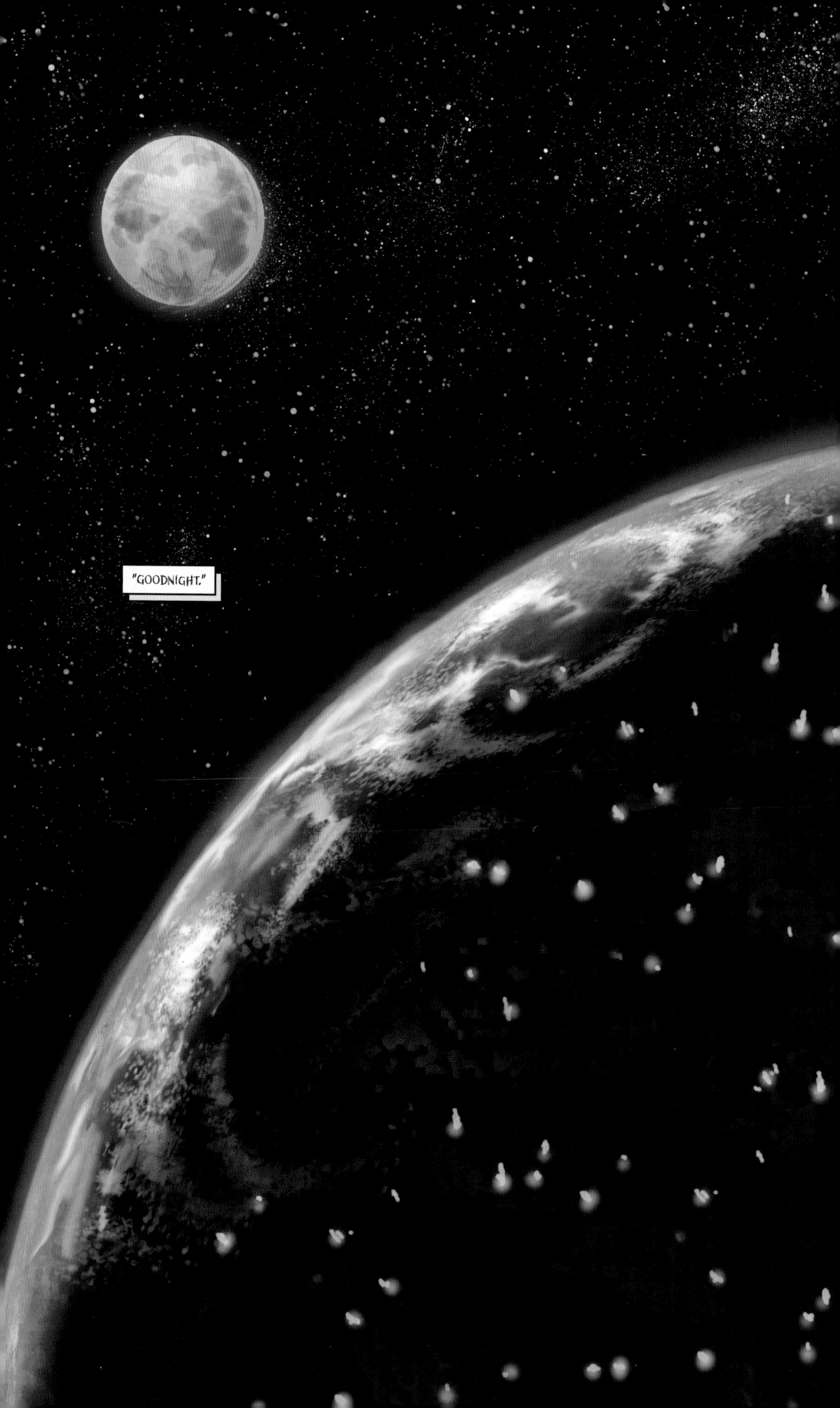
"GOODNIGHT."

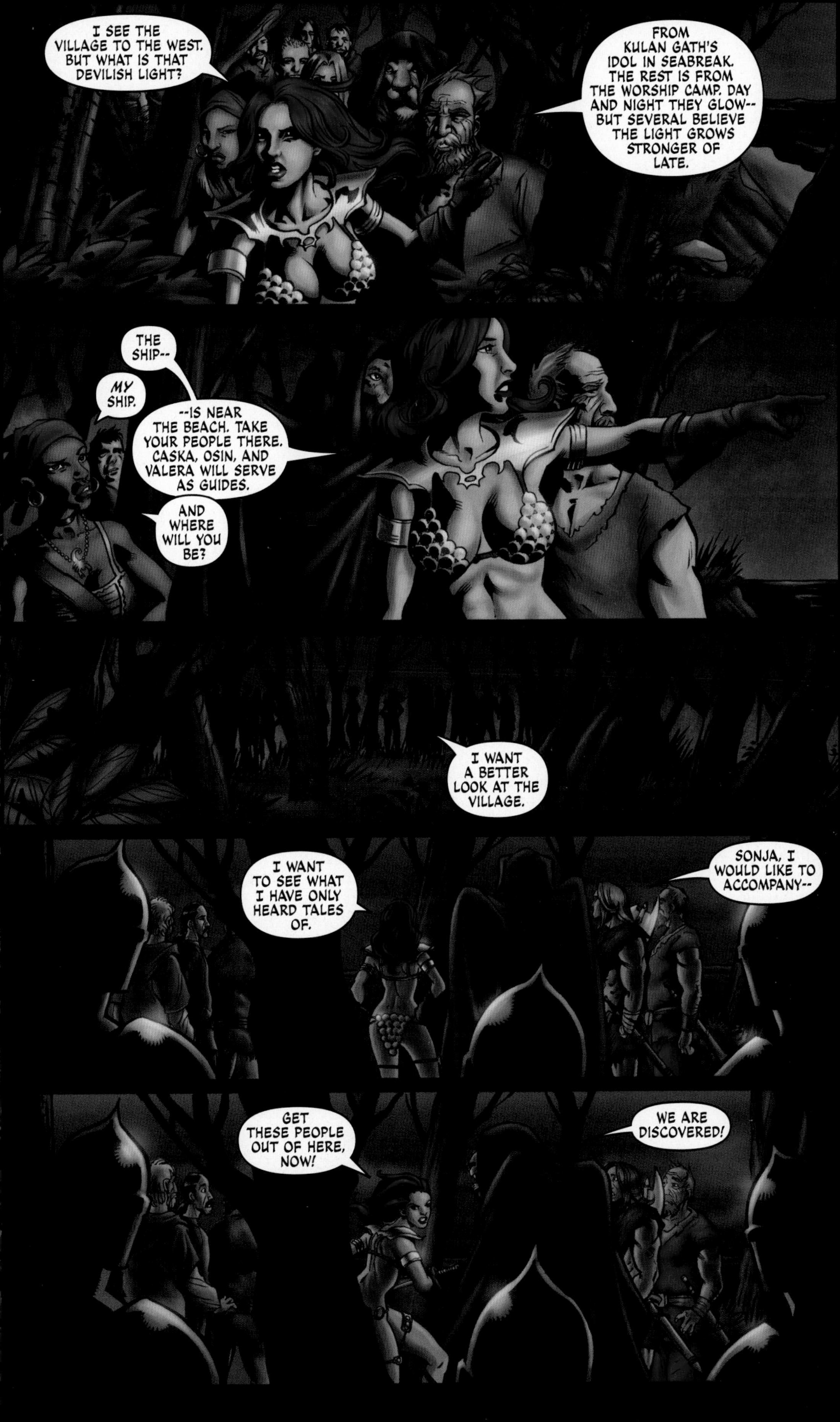
I SEE THE VILLAGE TO THE WEST. BUT WHAT IS THAT DEVILISH LIGHT?
FROM KULAN GATH'S IDOL IN SEABREAK. THE REST IS FROM THE WORSHIP CAMP. DAY AND NIGHT THEY GLOW-- BUT SEVERAL BELIEVE THE LIGHT GROWS STRONGER OF LATE.
THE SHIP--
MY SHIP.
--IS NEAR THE BEACH. TAKE YOUR PEOPLE THERE. CASKA, OSIN, AND VALERA WILL SERVE AS GUIDES.
AND WHERE WILL YOU BE?
I WANT A BETTER LOOK AT THE VILLAGE.
I WANT TO SEE WHAT I HAVE ONLY HEARD TALES OF.
SONJA, I WOULD LIKE TO ACCOMPANY--
GET THESE PEOPLE OUT OF HERE, NOW!
WE ARE DISCOVERED!

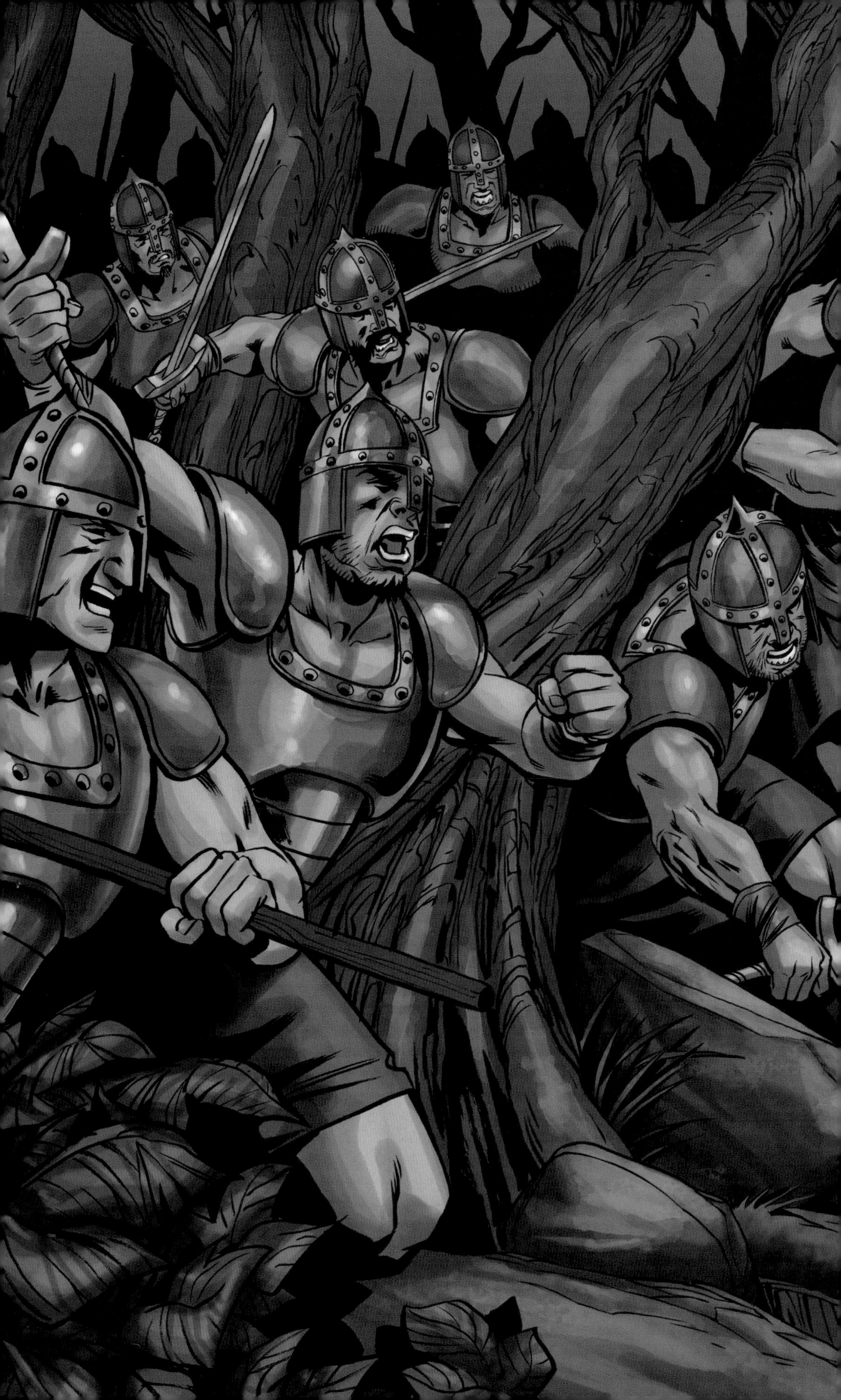

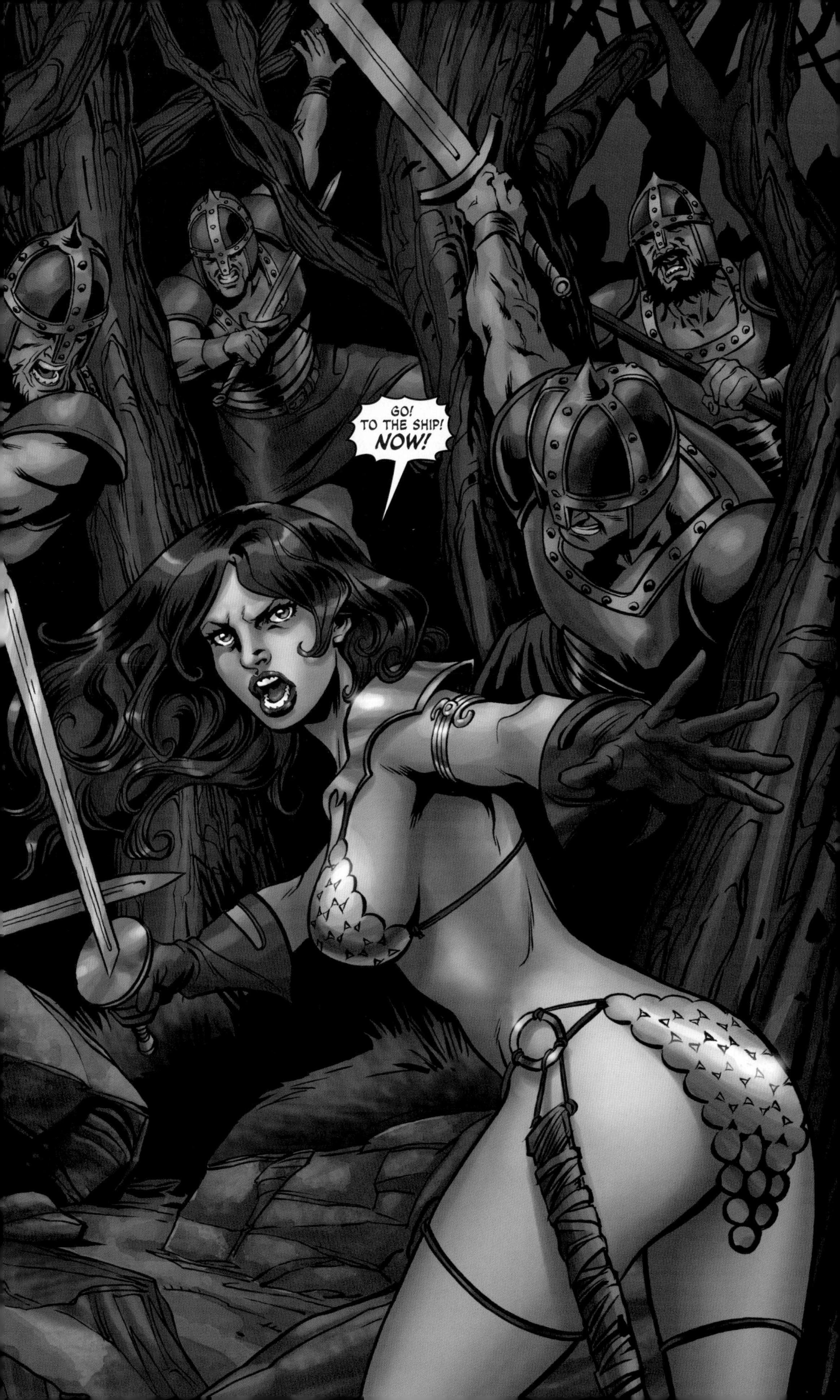
GO! TO THE SHIP! NOW!

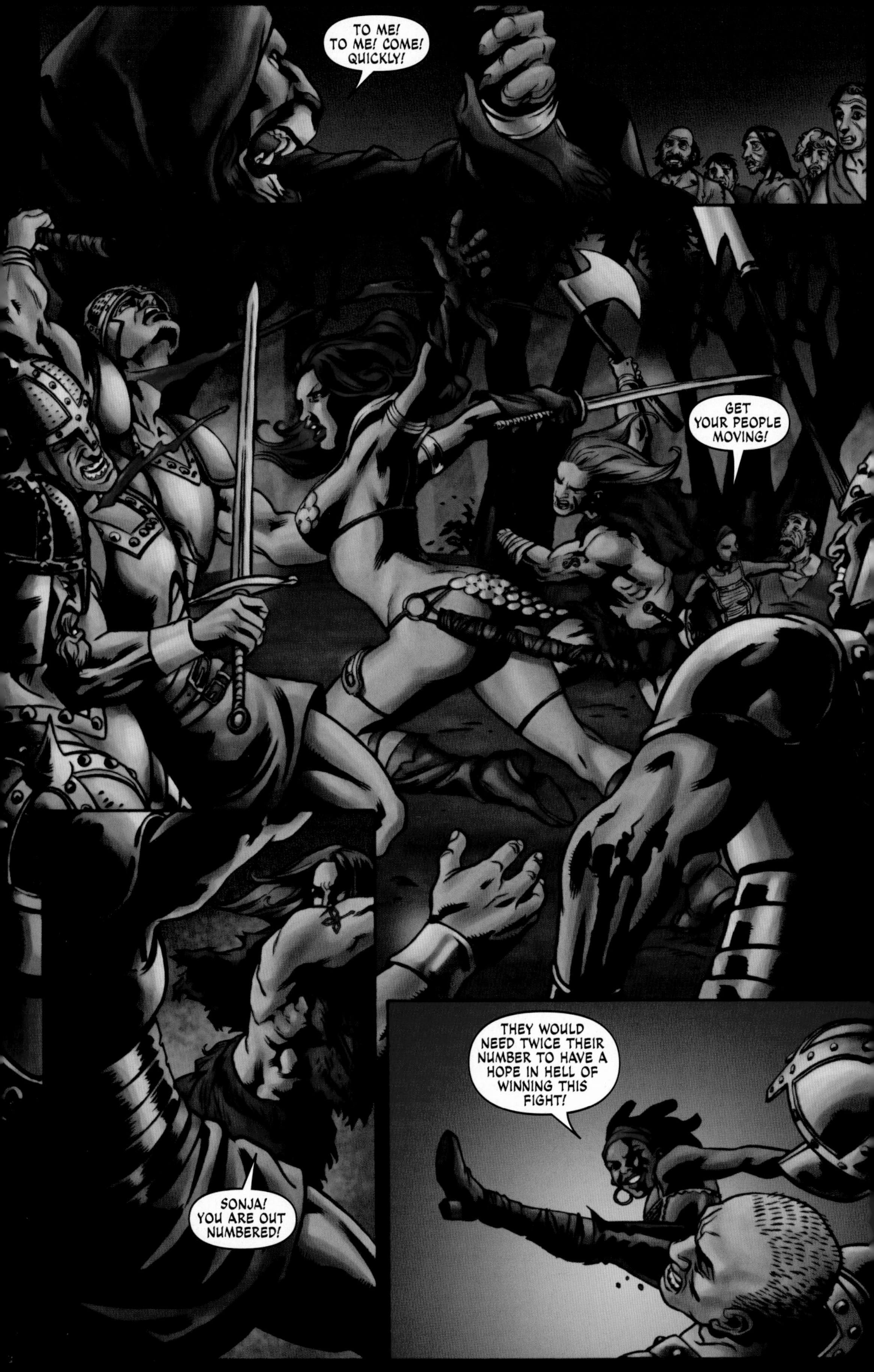
TO ME! TO ME! COME! QUICKLY!
GET YOUR PEOPLE MOVING!
SONJA! YOU ARE OUT NUMBERED!
THEY WOULD NEED TWICE THEIR NUMBER TO HAVE A HOPE IN HELL OF WINNING THIS FIGHT!

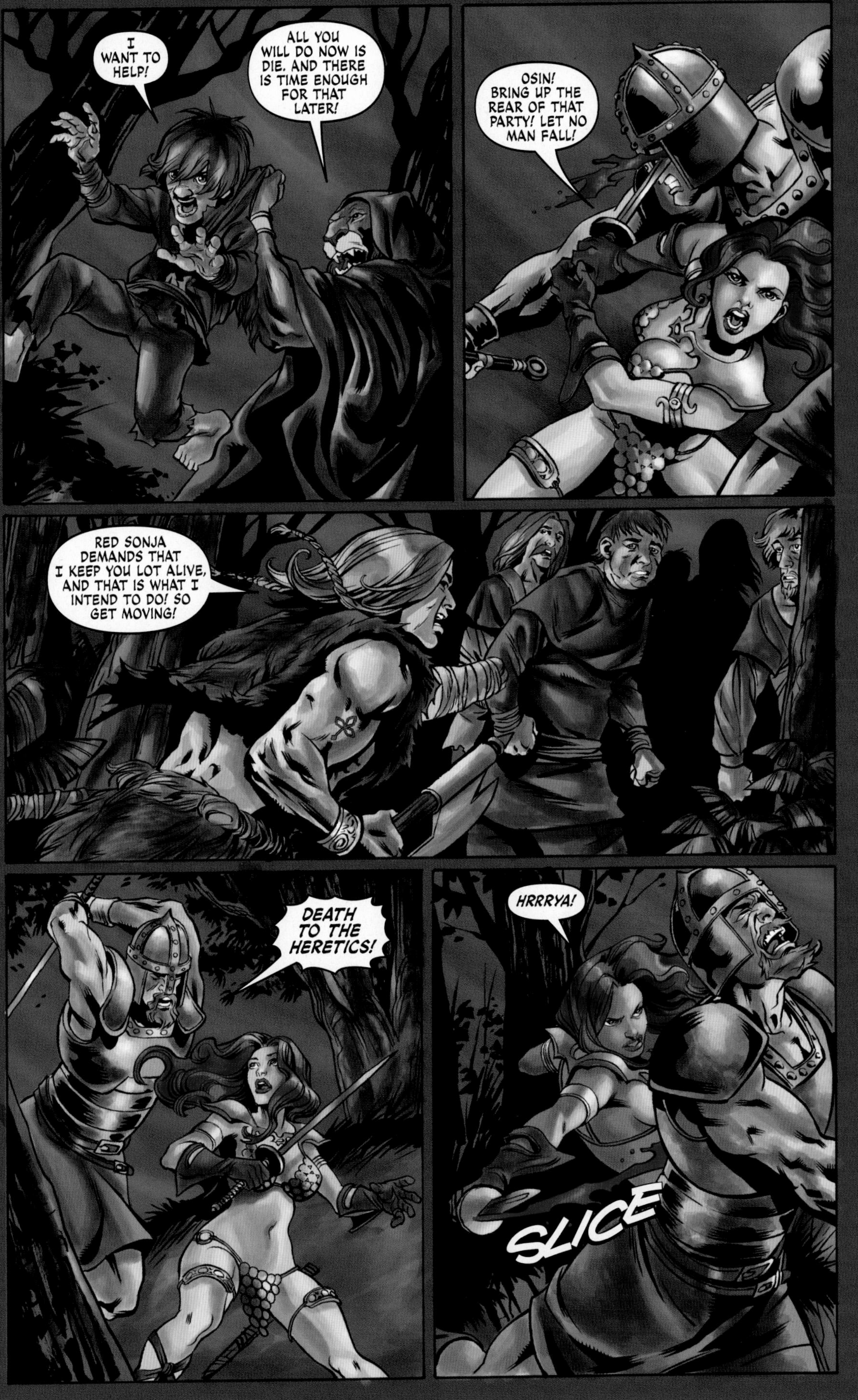
I WANT TO HELP!
ALL YOU WILL DO NOW IS DIE. AND THERE IS TIME ENOUGH FOR THAT LATER!
OSIN! BRING UP THE REAR OF THAT PARTY! LET NO MAN FALL!
RED SONJA DEMANDS THAT I KEEP YOU LOT ALIVE, AND THAT IS WHAT I INTEND TO DO! SO GET MOVING!
DEATH TO THE HERETICS!
HRRRYA!
SLICE

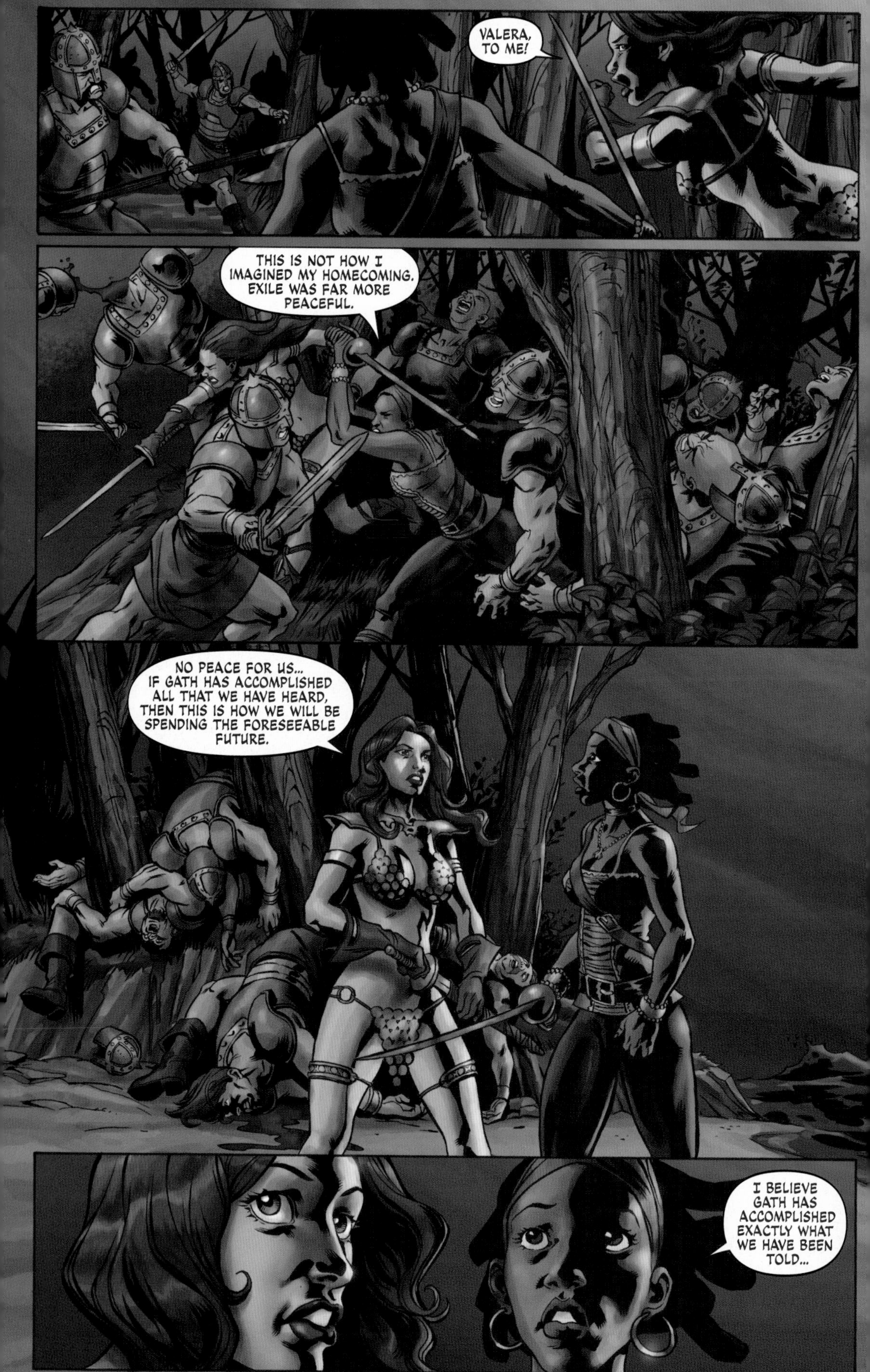
VALERA, TO ME!
THIS IS NOT HOW I IMAGINED MY HOMECOMING. EXILE WAS FAR MORE PEACEFUL.
NO PEACE FOR US... IF GATH HAS ACCOMPLISHED ALL THAT WE HAVE HEARD, THEN THIS IS HOW WE WILL BE SPENDING THE FORESEEABLE FUTURE.
I BELIEVE GATH HAS ACCOMPLISHED EXACTLY WHAT WE HAVE BEEN TOLD...

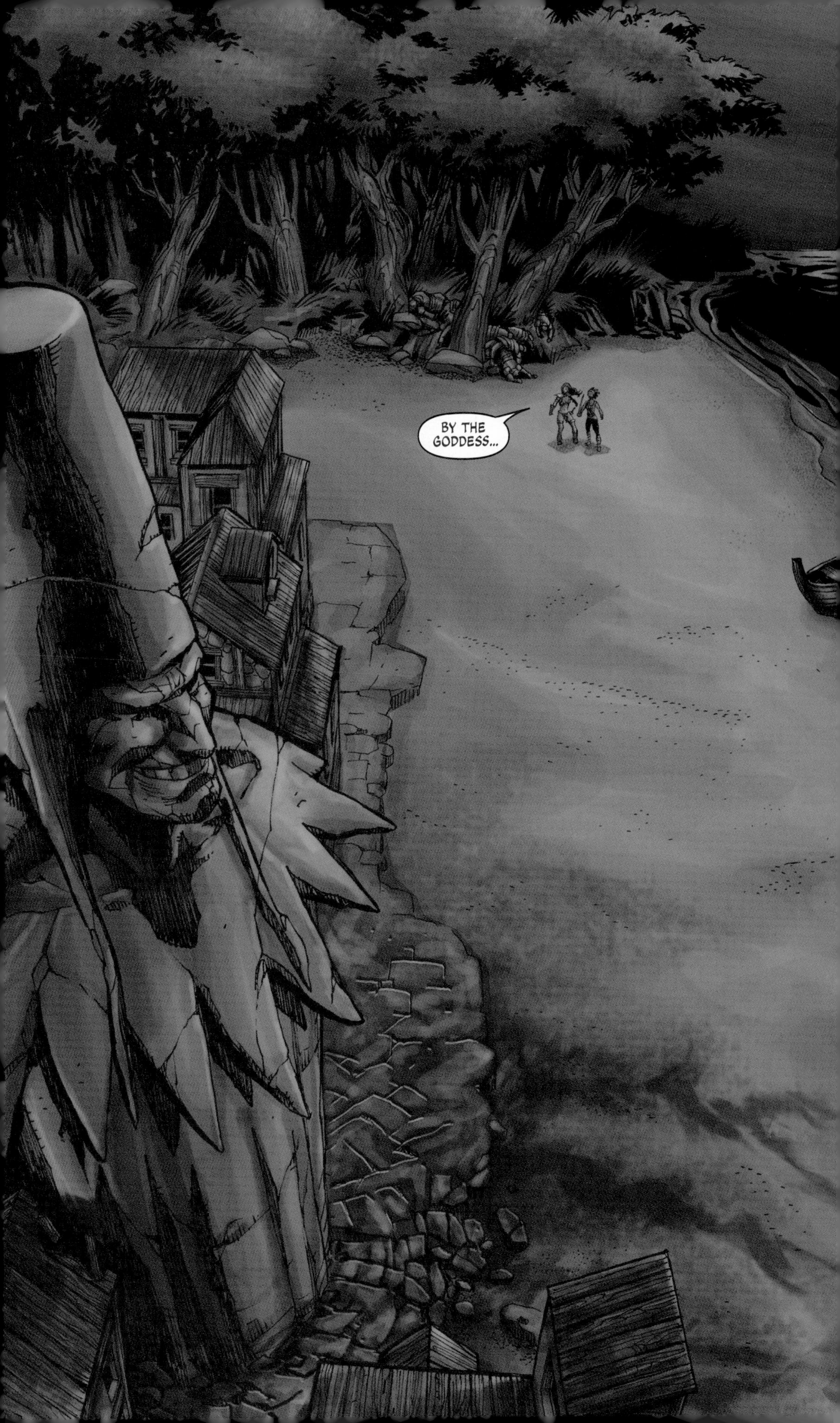
BY THE GODDESS...

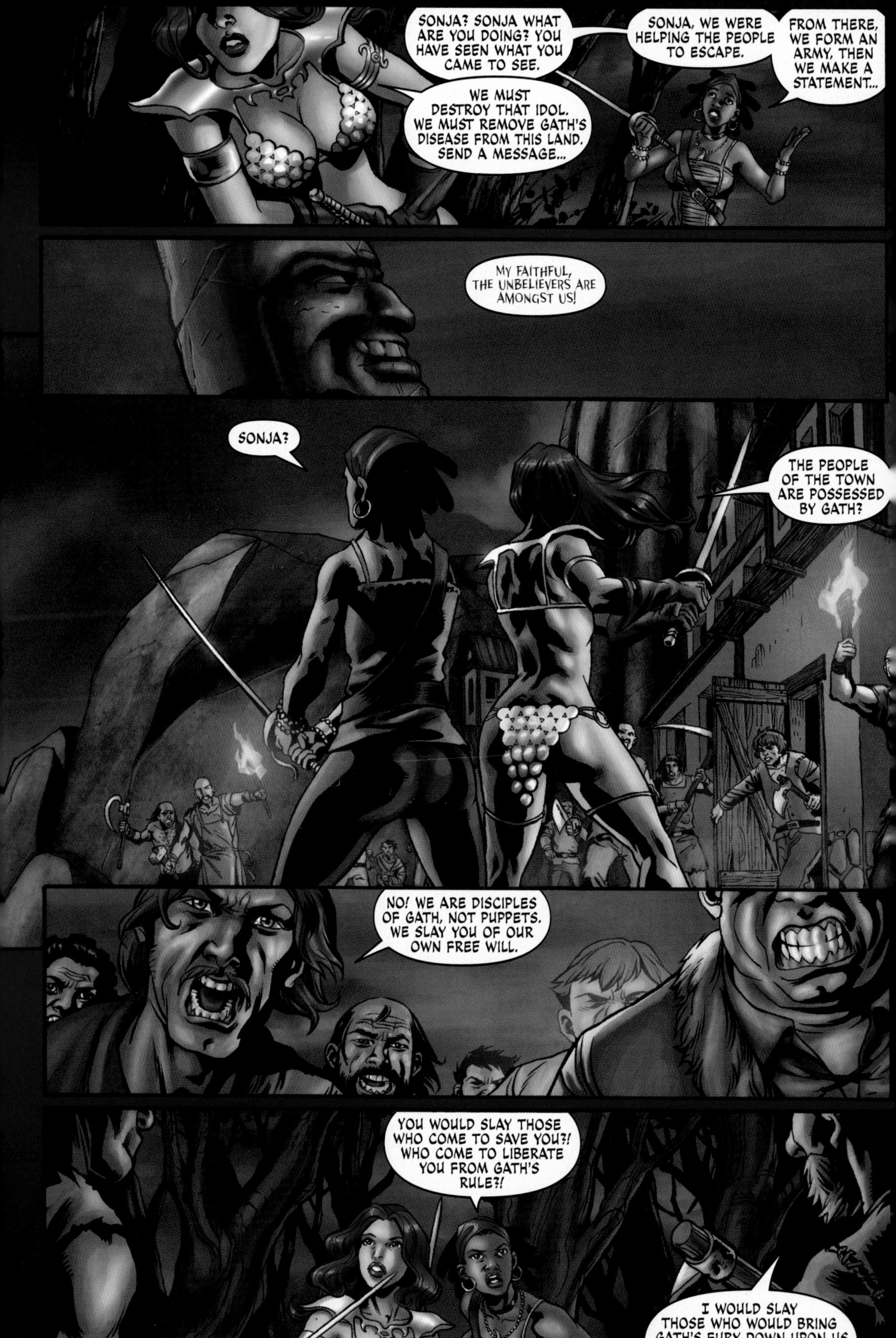

SONJA? SONJA WHAT ARE YOU DOING? YOU HAVE SEEN WHAT YOU CAME TO SEE.
WE MUST DESTROY THAT IDOL. WE MUST REMOVE GATH'S DISEASE FROM THIS LAND. SEND A MESSAGE...
SONJA, WE WERE HELPING THE PEOPLE TO ESCAPE.
FROM THERE, WE FORM AN ARMY, THEN WE MAKE A STATEMENT...
MY FAITHFUL, THE UNBELIEVERS ARE AMONGST US!
SONJA?
THE PEOPLE OF THE TOWN ARE POSSESSED BY GATH?
NO! WE ARE DISCIPLES OF GATH, NOT PUPPETS. WE SLAY YOU OF OUR OWN FREE WILL.
YOU WOULD SLAY THOSE WHO COME TO SAVE YOU?! WHO COME TO LIBERATE YOU FROM GATH'S RULE?!
I WOULD SLAY THOSE WHO WOULD BRING GATH'S FURY DOWN UPON US SHOULD WE NOT! BY COMING TO US YOU HAVE SEALED YOUR OWN FATE.

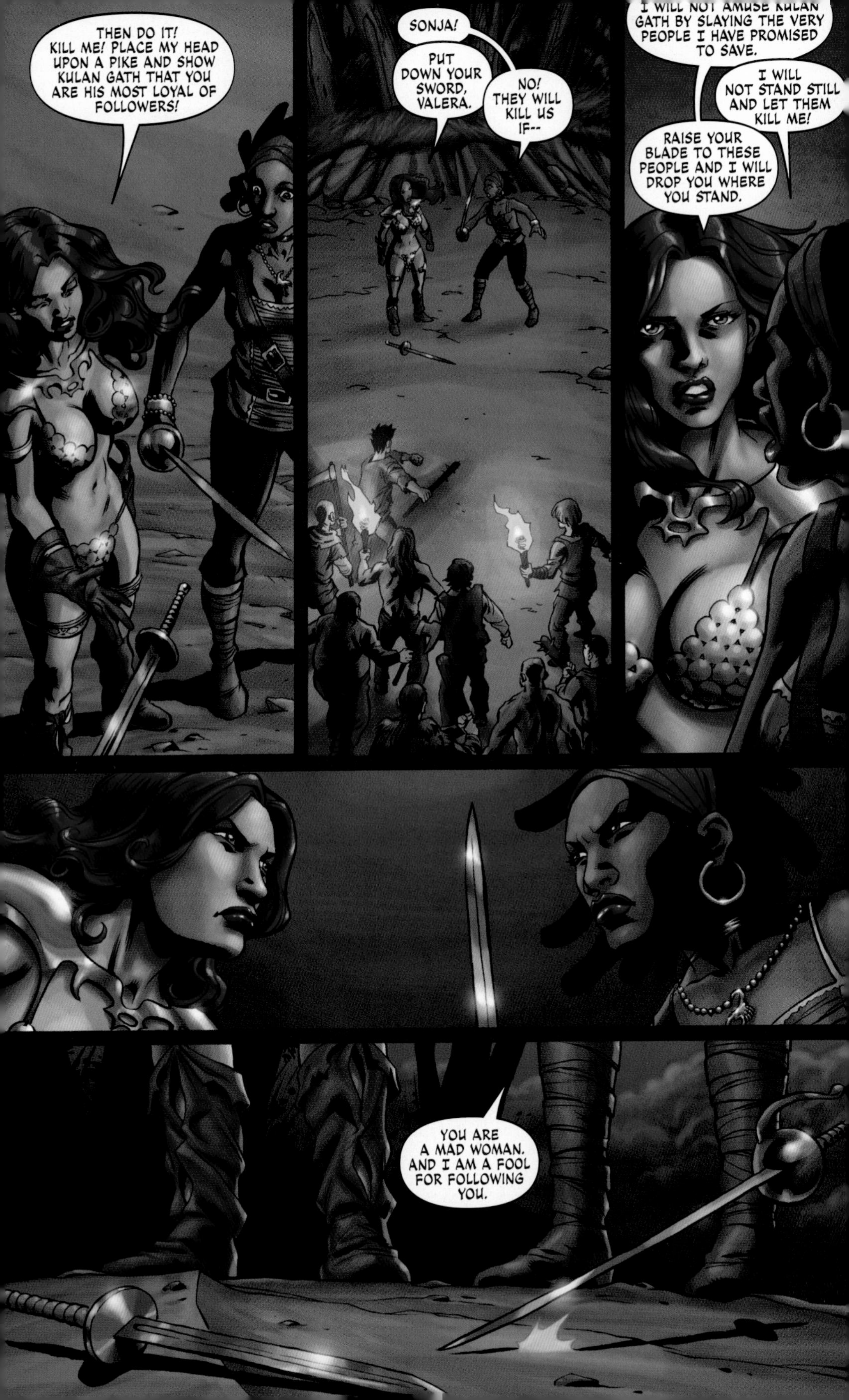
THEN DO IT! KILL ME! PLACE MY HEAD UPON A PIKE AND SHOW KULAN GATH THAT YOU ARE HIS MOST LOYAL OF FOLLOWERS!
SONJA!
PUT DOWN YOUR SWORD, VALERA.
NO! THEY WILL KILL US IF--
I WILL NOT AMUSE KULAN GATH BY SLAYING THE VERY PEOPLE I HAVE PROMISED TO SAVE.
I WILL NOT STAND STILL AND LET THEM KILL ME!
RAISE YOUR BLADE TO THESE PEOPLE AND I WILL DROP YOU WHERE YOU STAND.
YOU ARE A MAD WOMAN. AND I AM A FOOL FOR FOLLOWING YOU.

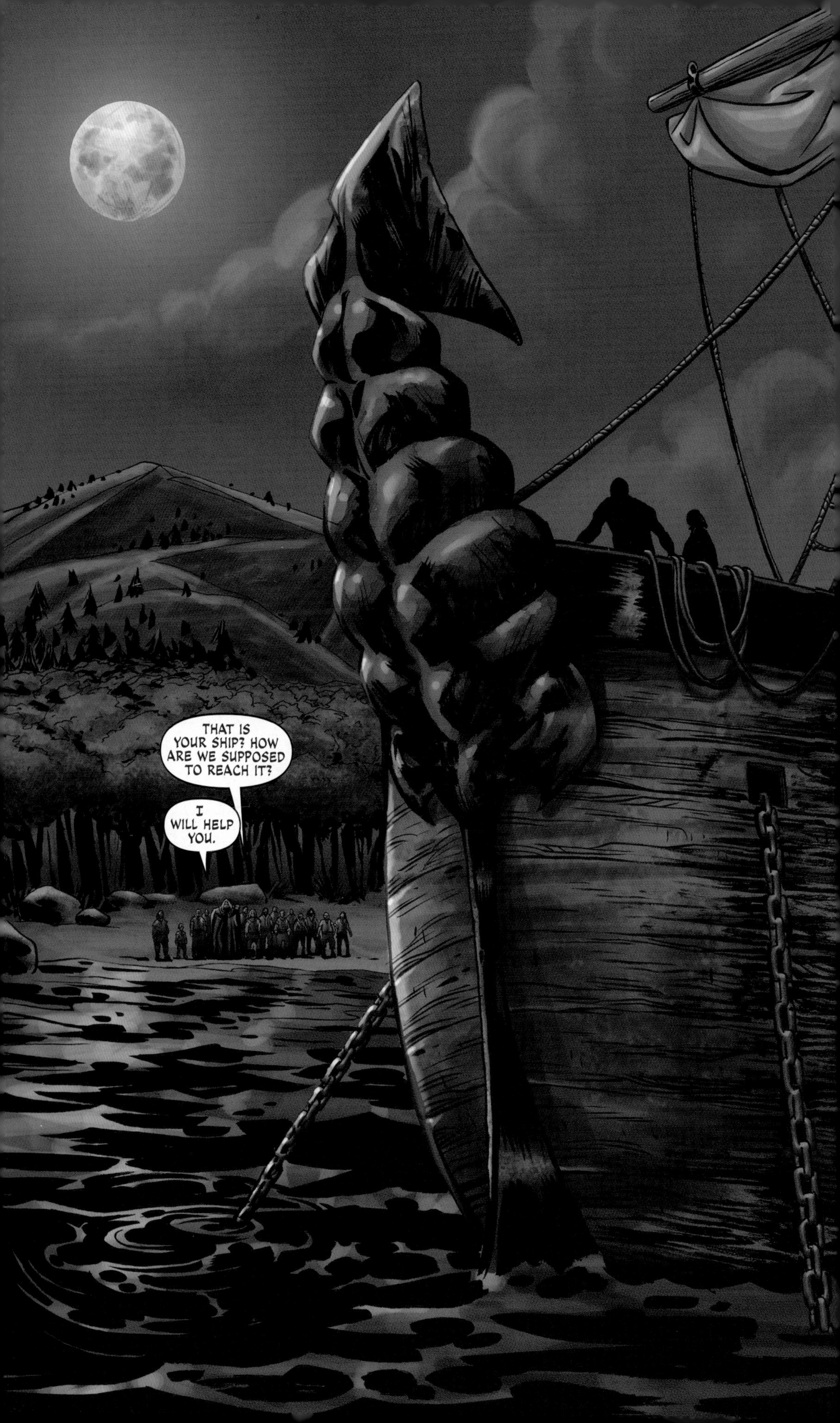
THAT IS YOUR SHIP? HOW ARE WE SUPPOSED TO REACH IT?
I WILL HELP YOU.

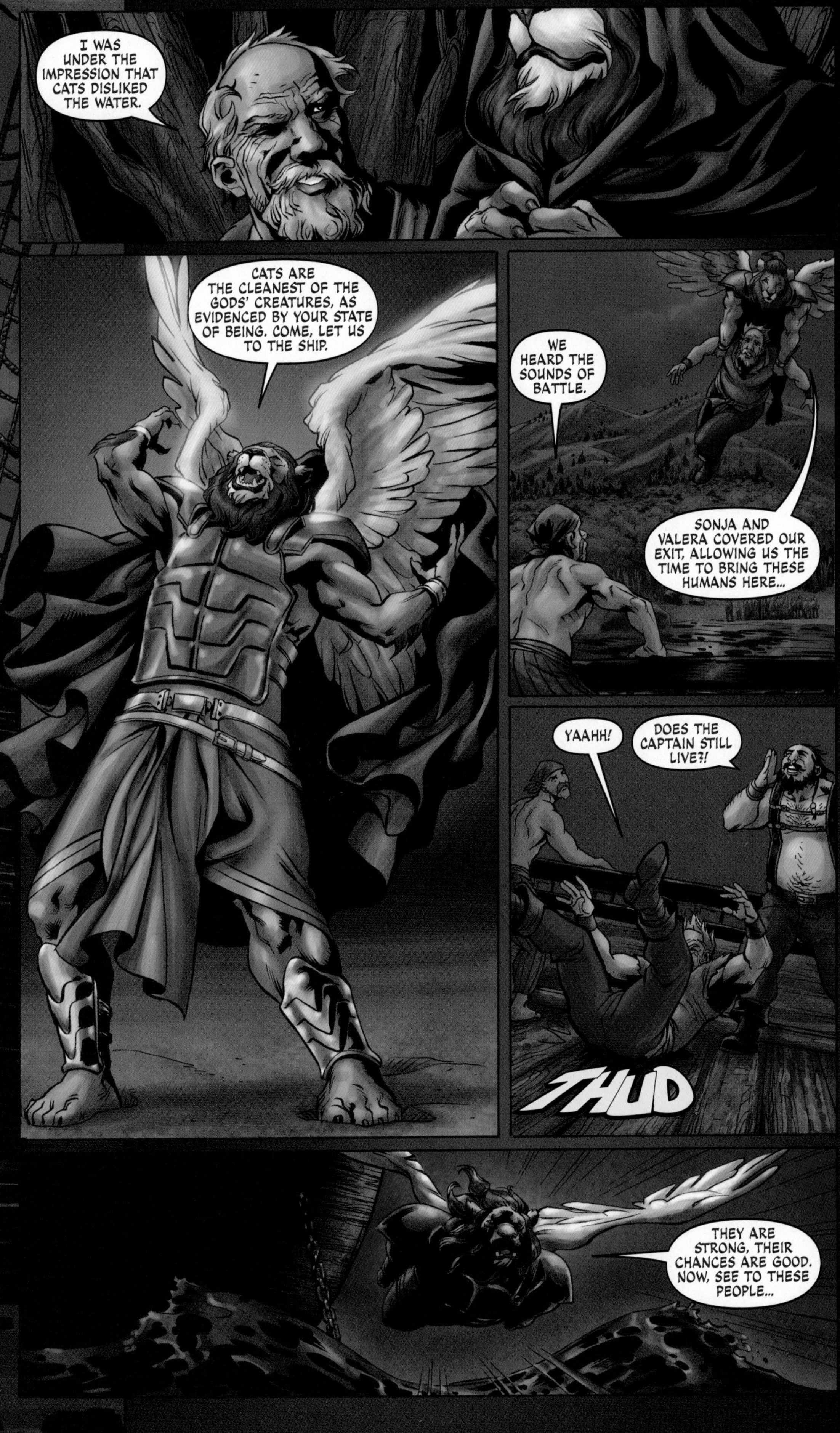
I WAS UNDER THE IMPRESSION THAT CATS DISLIKED THE WATER.
CATS ARE THE CLEANEST OF THE GODS' CREATURES, AS EVIDENCED BY YOUR STATE OF BEING. COME, LET US TO THE SHIP.
WE HEARD THE SOUNDS OF BATTLE.
SONJA AND VALERA COVERED OUR EXIT, ALLOWING US THE TIME TO BRING THESE HUMANS HERE...
YAAHH!
DOES THE CAPTAIN STILL LIVE?!
THUD
THEY ARE STRONG, THEIR CHANCES ARE GOOD. NOW, SEE TO THESE PEOPLE...

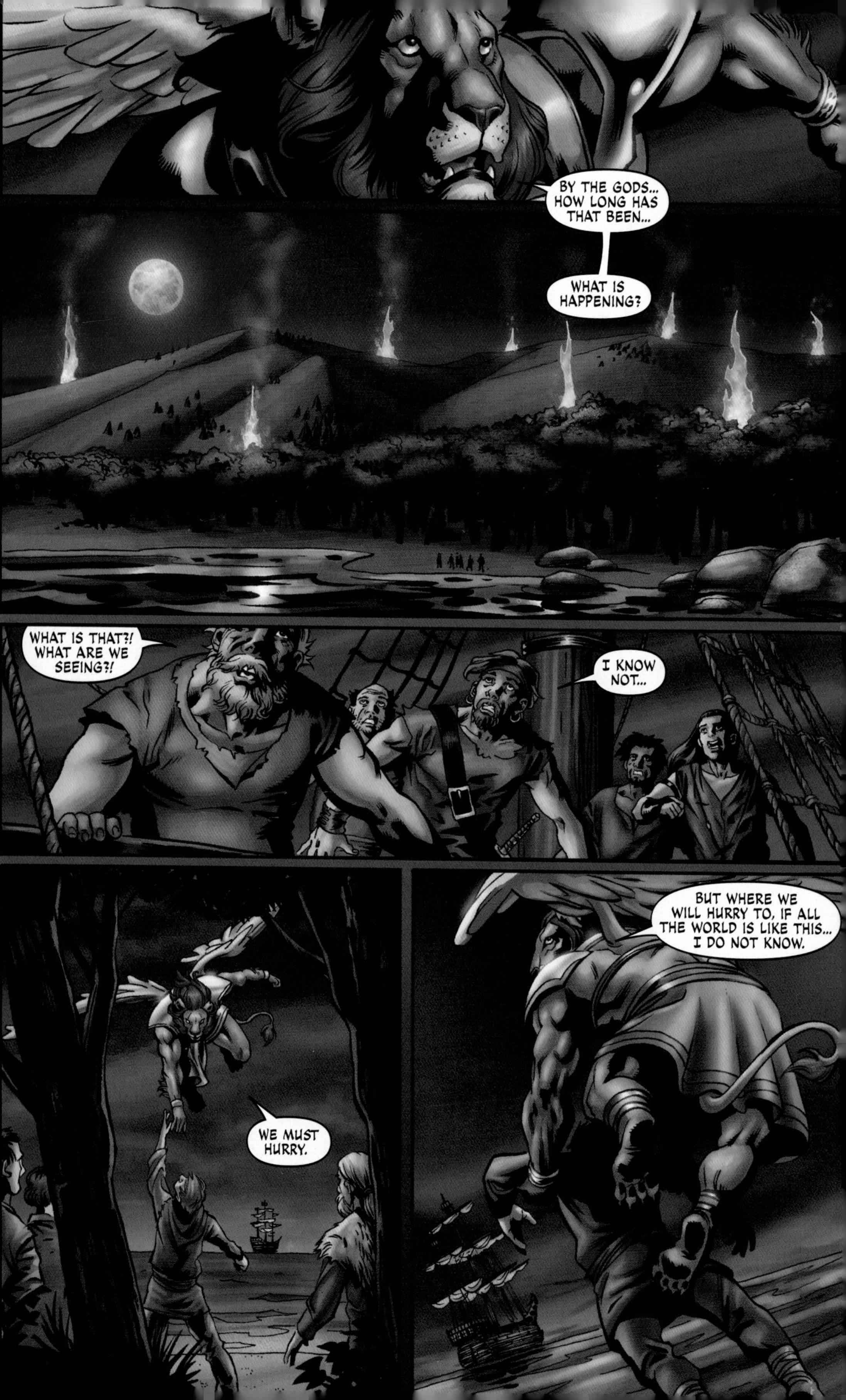
BY THE GODS... HOW LONG HAS THAT BEEN...
WHAT IS HAPPENING?
WHAT IS THAT?! WHAT ARE WE SEEING?!
I KNOW NOT...
WE MUST HURRY.
BUT WHERE WE WILL HURRY TO, IF ALL THE WORLD IS LIKE THIS... I DO NOT KNOW.

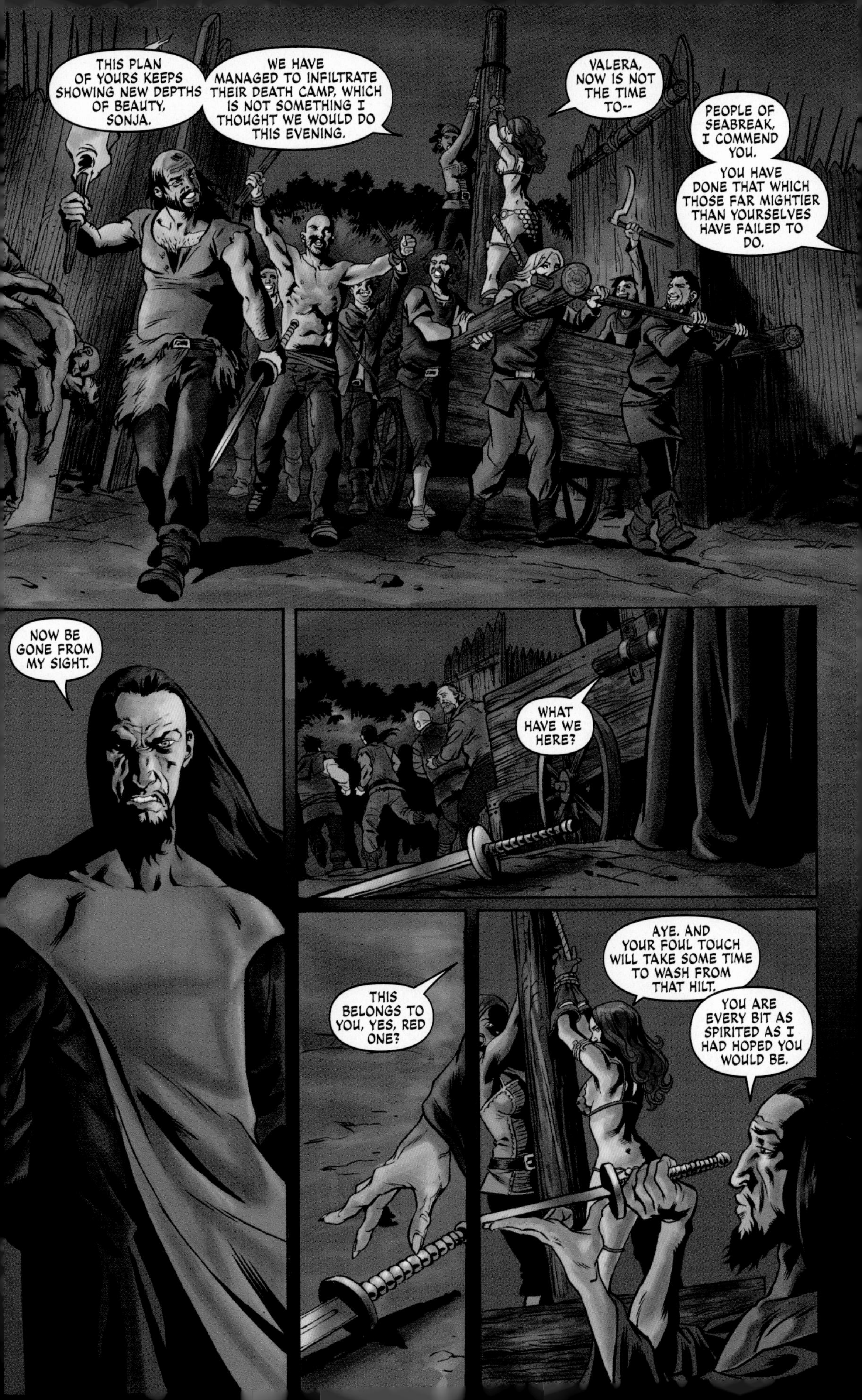
THIS PLAN OF YOURS KEEPS SHOWING NEW DEPTHS OF BEAUTY, SONJA.
WE HAVE MANAGED TO INFILTRATE THEIR DEATH CAMP, WHICH IS NOT SOMETHING I THOUGHT WE WOULD DO THIS EVENING.
VALERA, NOW IS NOT THE TIME TO--
PEOPLE OF SEABREAK, I COMMEND YOU.
YOU HAVE DONE THAT WHICH THOSE FAR MIGHTIER THAN YOURSELVES HAVE FAILED TO DO.
NOW BE GONE FROM MY SIGHT.
WHAT HAVE WE HERE?
THIS BELONGS TO YOU, YES, RED ONE?
AYE. AND YOUR FOUL TOUCH WILL TAKE SOME TIME TO WASH FROM THAT HILT.
YOU ARE EVERY BIT AS SPIRITED AS I HAD HOPED YOU WOULD BE.

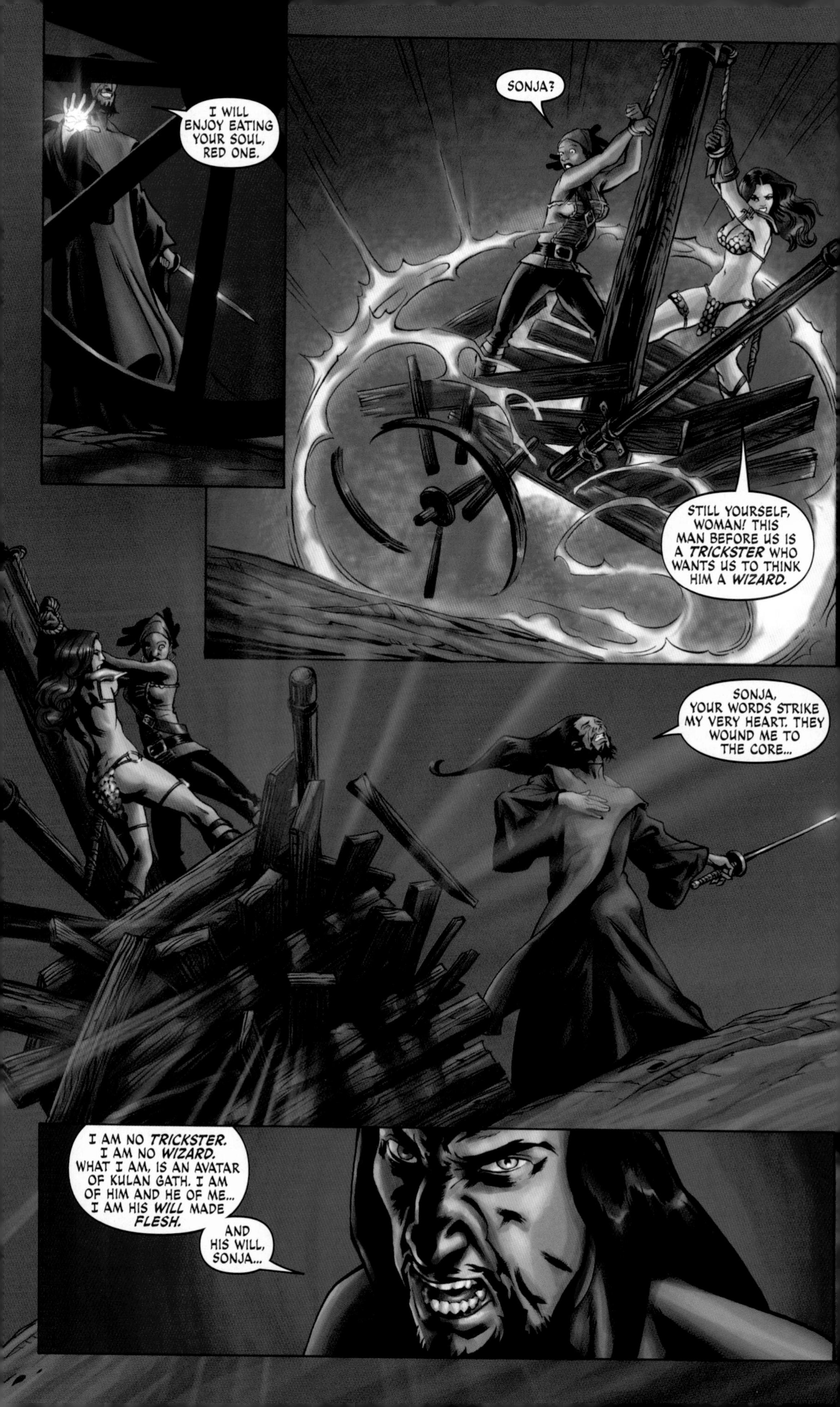
I WILL ENJOY EATING YOUR SOUL, RED ONE.
SONJA?
STILL YOURSELF, WOMAN! THIS MAN BEFORE US IS A *TRICKSTER* WHO WANTS US TO THINK HIM A *WIZARD.*
SONJA, YOUR WORDS STRIKE MY VERY HEART. THEY WOUND ME TO THE CORE...
I AM NO *TRICKSTER.* I AM NO *WIZARD.* WHAT I AM, IS AN AVATAR OF KULAN GATH. I AM OF HIM AND HE OF ME... I AM HIS *WILL* MADE *FLESH.*
AND HIS WILL, SONJA...

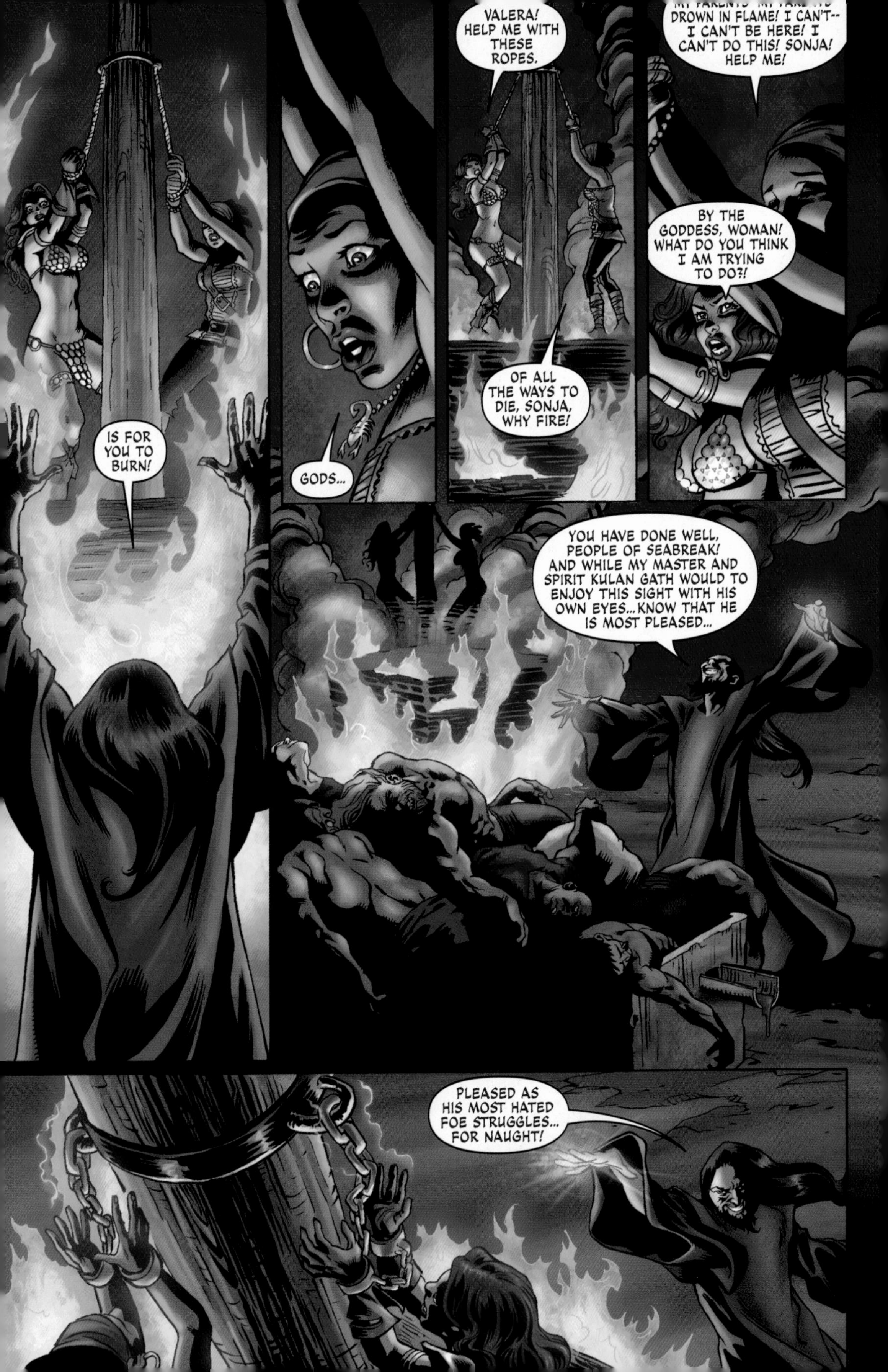
IS FOR YOU TO BURN!
GODS...
VALERA! HELP ME WITH THESE ROPES.
OF ALL THE WAYS TO DIE, SONJA, WHY FIRE!
DROWN IN FLAME! I CAN'T-- I CAN'T BE HERE! I CAN'T DO THIS! SONJA! HELP ME!
BY THE GODDESS, WOMAN! WHAT DO YOU THINK I AM TRYING TO DO?!
YOU HAVE DONE WELL, PEOPLE OF SEABREAK! AND WHILE MY MASTER AND SPIRIT KULAN GATH WOULD TO ENJOY THIS SIGHT WITH HIS OWN EYES...KNOW THAT HE IS MOST PLEASED...
PLEASED AS HIS MOST HATED FOE STRUGGLES... FOR NAUGHT!

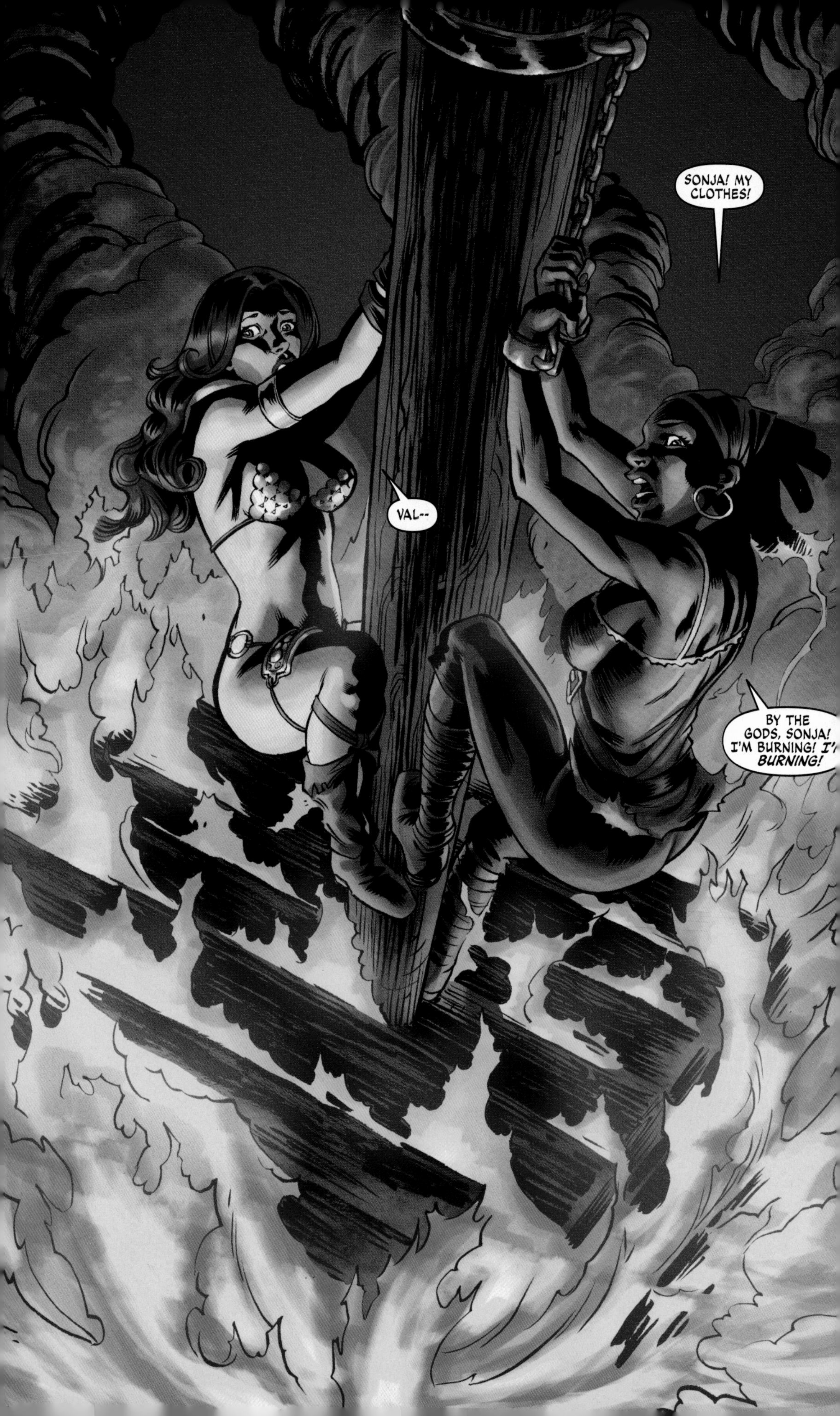

SONJA! MY CLOTHES!
VAL--
BY THE GODS, SONJA! I'M BURNING! I' BURNING!

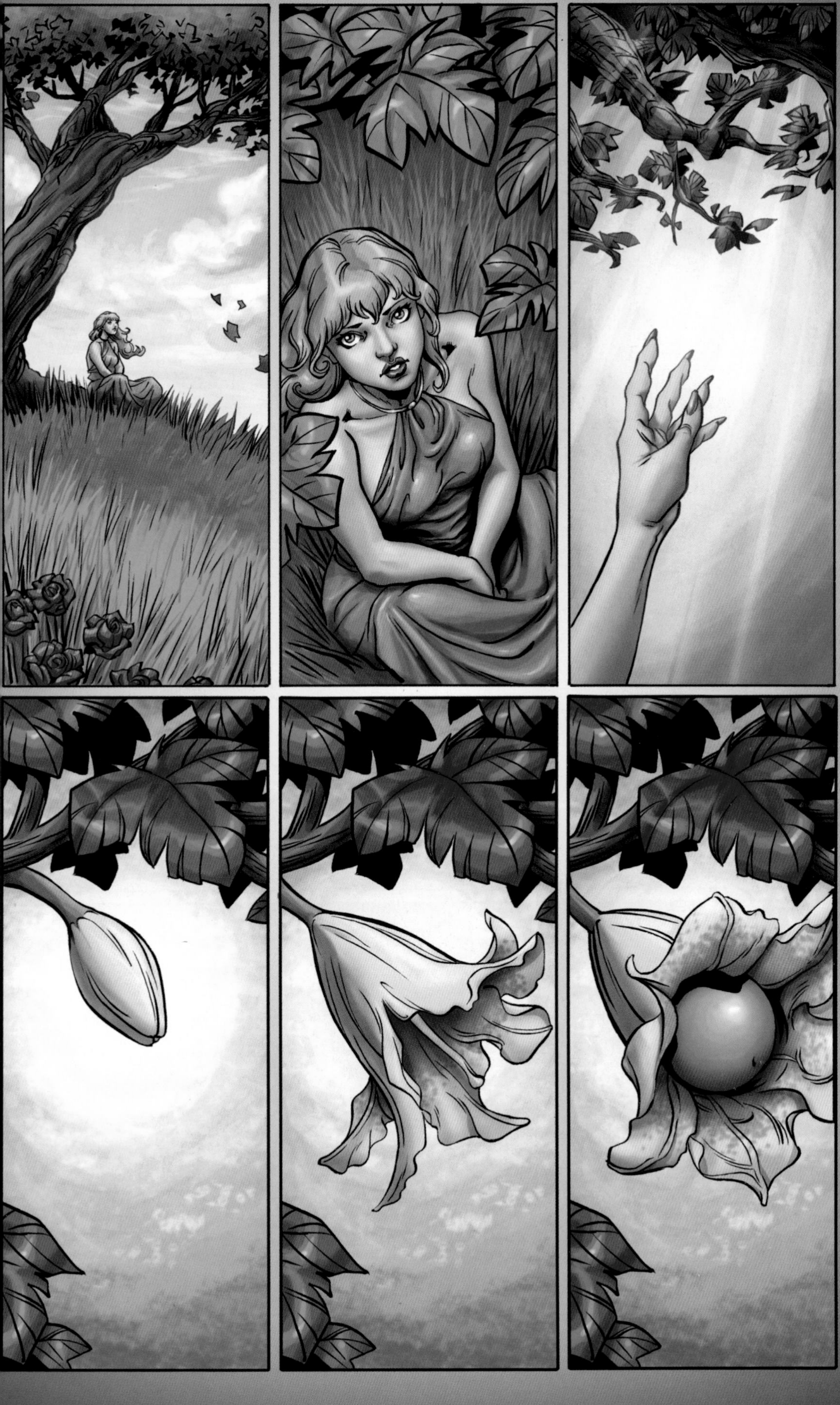

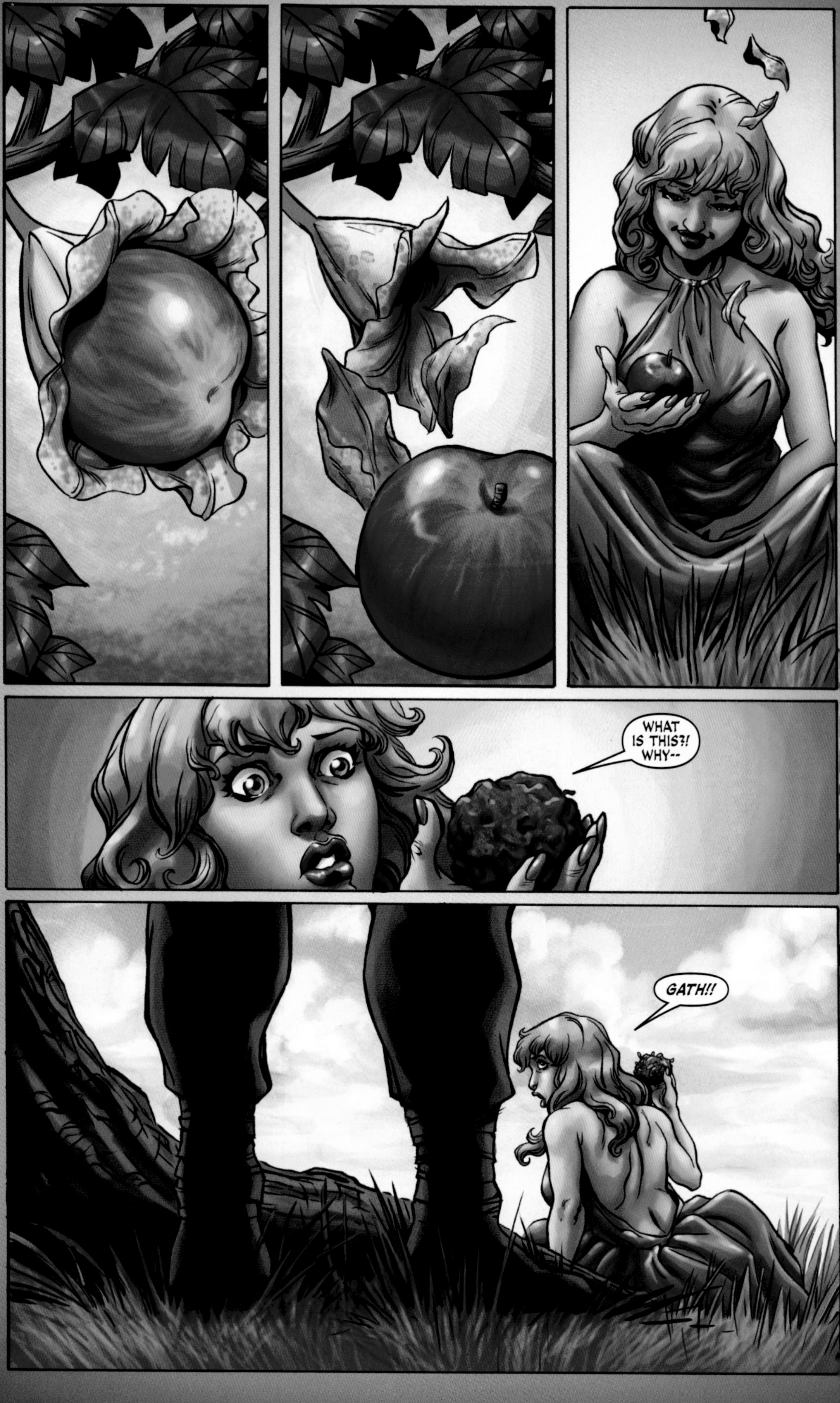
WHAT IS THIS?! WHY--
GATH!!

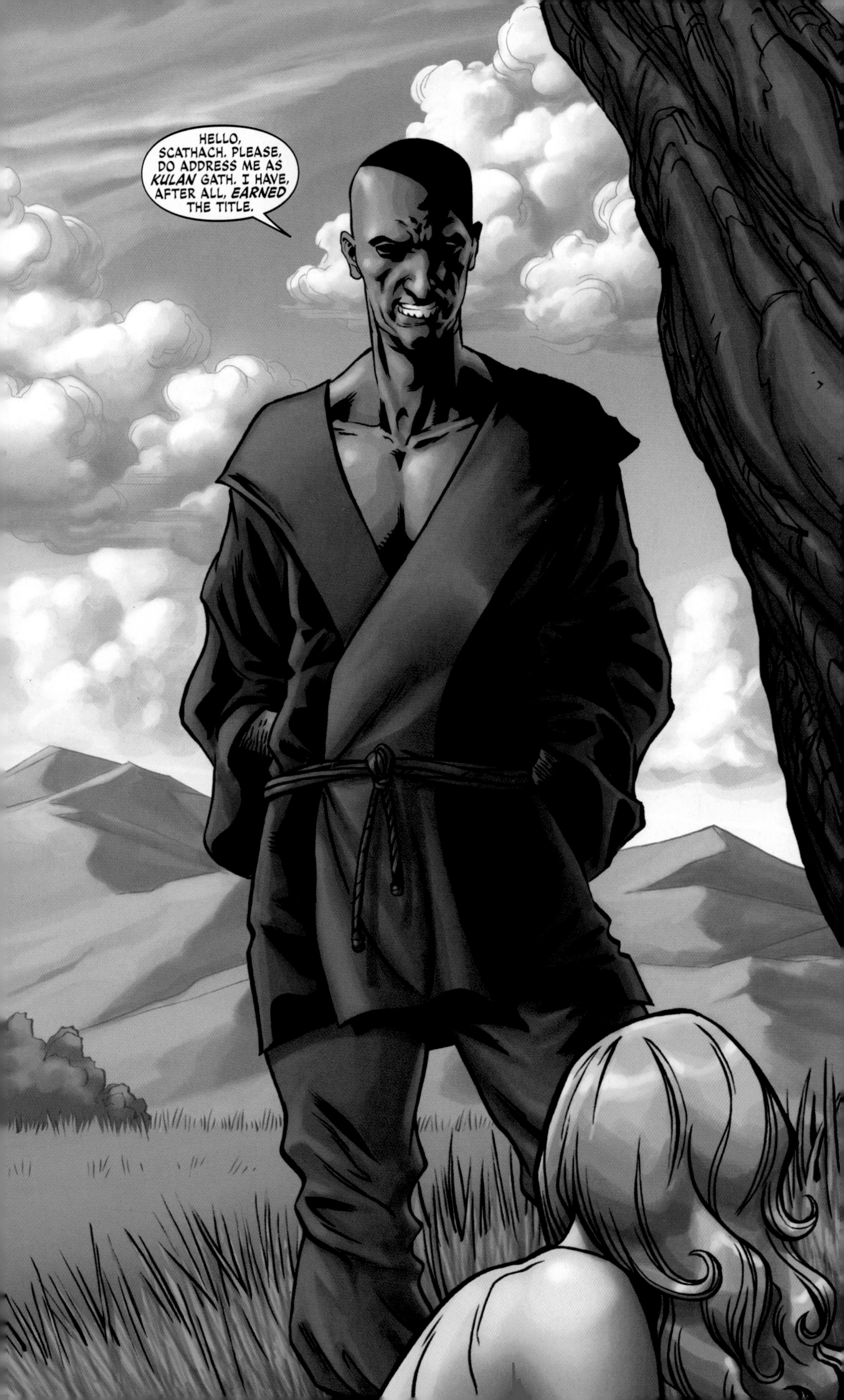
HELLO, SCATHACH. PLEASE, DO ADDRESS ME AS KULAN GATH. I HAVE, AFTER ALL, EARNED THE TITLE.

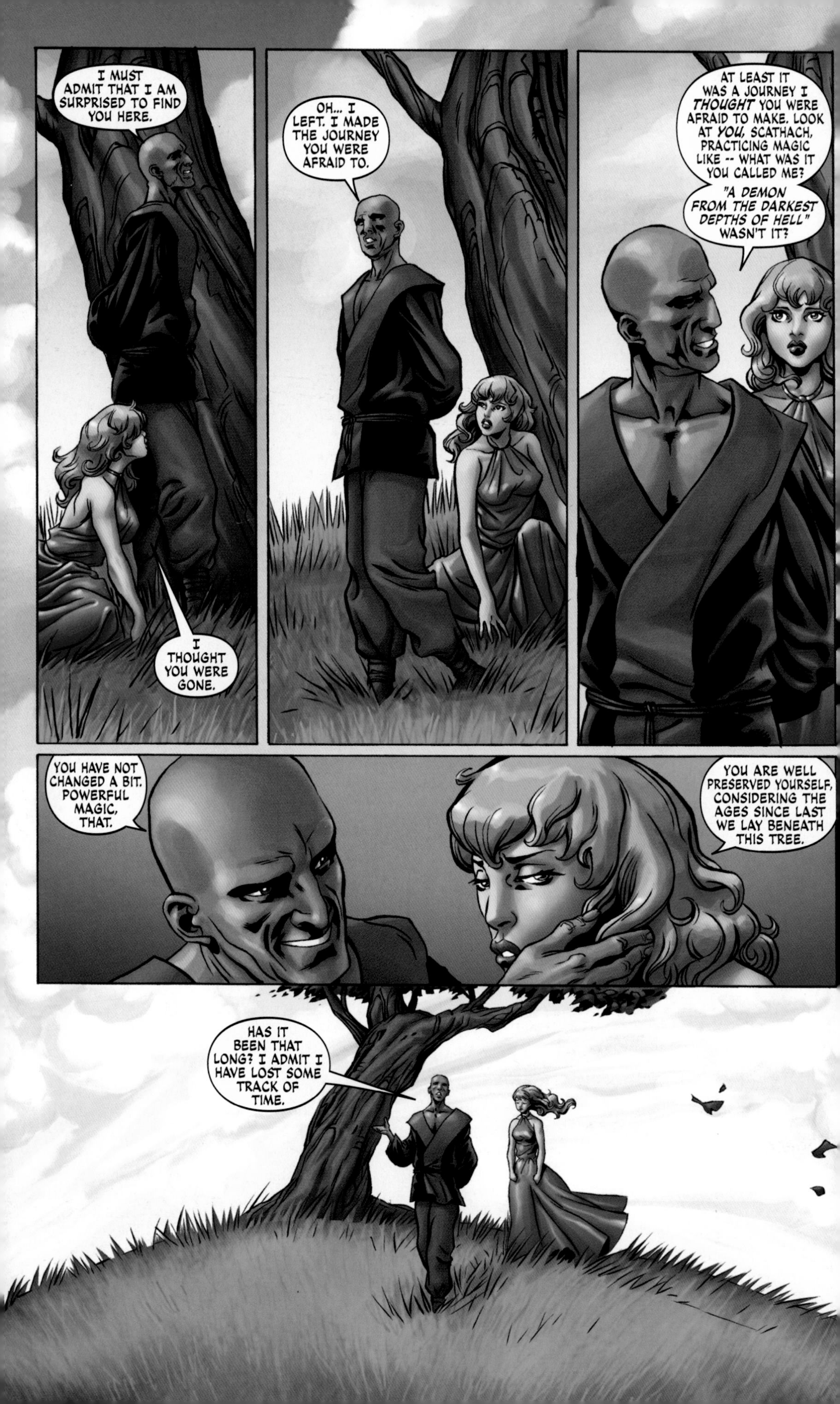

I MUST ADMIT THAT I AM SURPRISED TO FIND YOU HERE.
I THOUGHT YOU WERE GONE.
OH... I LEFT. I MADE THE JOURNEY YOU WERE AFRAID TO.
AT LEAST IT WAS A JOURNEY I *THOUGHT* YOU WERE AFRAID TO MAKE. LOOK AT *YOU,* SCATHACH, PRACTICING MAGIC LIKE -- WHAT WAS IT YOU CALLED ME?
"A DEMON FROM THE DARKEST DEPTHS OF HELL" WASN'T IT?
YOU HAVE NOT CHANGED A BIT. POWERFUL MAGIC, THAT.
YOU ARE WELL PRESERVED YOURSELF, CONSIDERING THE AGES SINCE LAST WE LAY BENEATH THIS TREE.
HAS IT BEEN THAT LONG? I ADMIT I HAVE LOST SOME TRACK OF TIME.

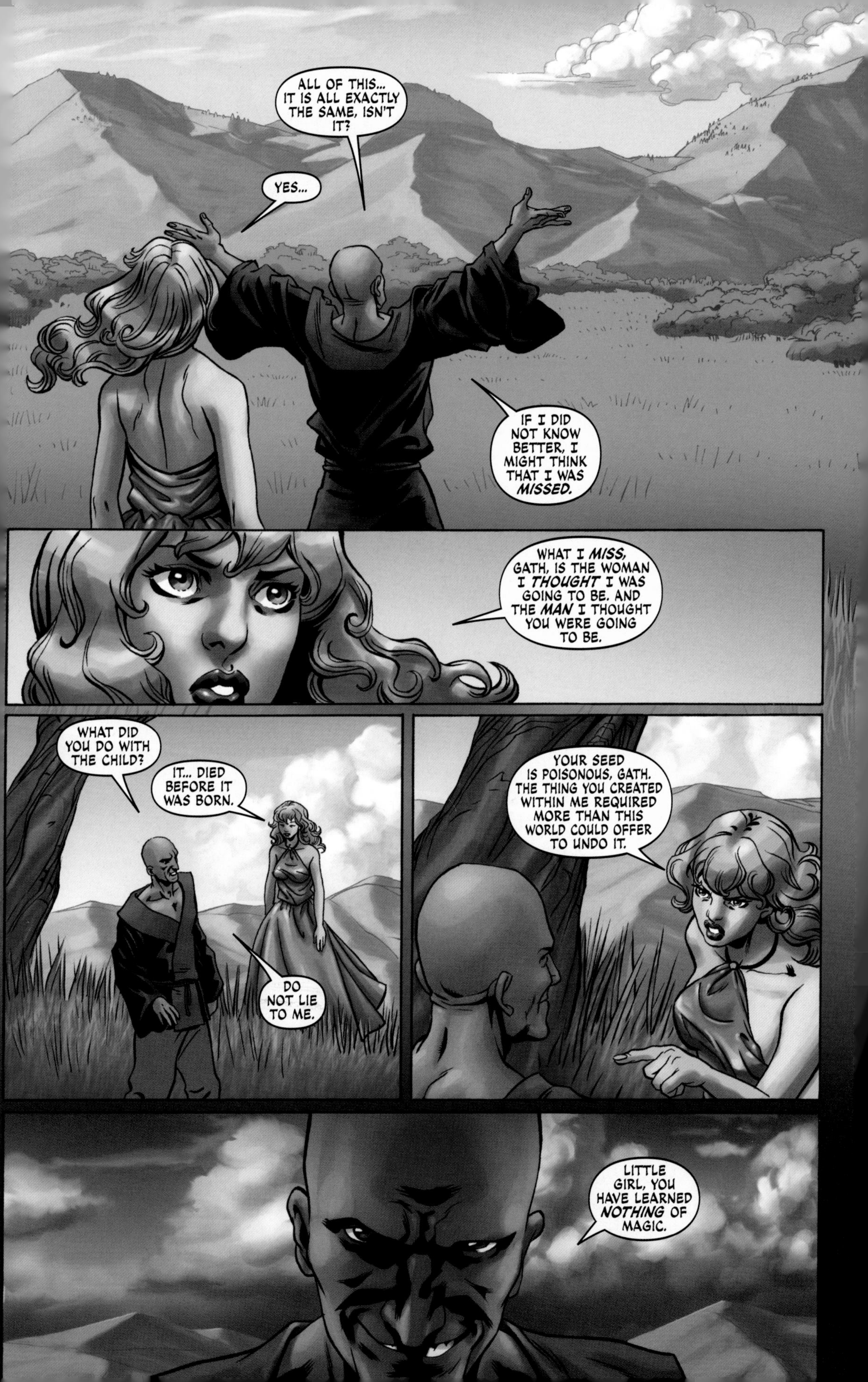
ALL OF THIS... IT IS ALL EXACTLY THE SAME, ISN'T IT?
YES...
IF I DID NOT KNOW BETTER, I MIGHT THINK THAT I WAS MISSED.
WHAT I MISS, GATH, IS THE WOMAN I THOUGHT I WAS GOING TO BE. AND THE MAN I THOUGHT YOU WERE GOING TO BE.
WHAT DID YOU DO WITH THE CHILD?
IT... DIED BEFORE IT WAS BORN.
DO NOT LIE TO ME.
YOUR SEED IS POISONOUS, GATH. THE THING YOU CREATED WITHIN ME REQUIRED MORE THAN THIS WORLD COULD OFFER TO UNDO IT.
LITTLE GIRL, YOU HAVE LEARNED NOTHING OF MAGIC.

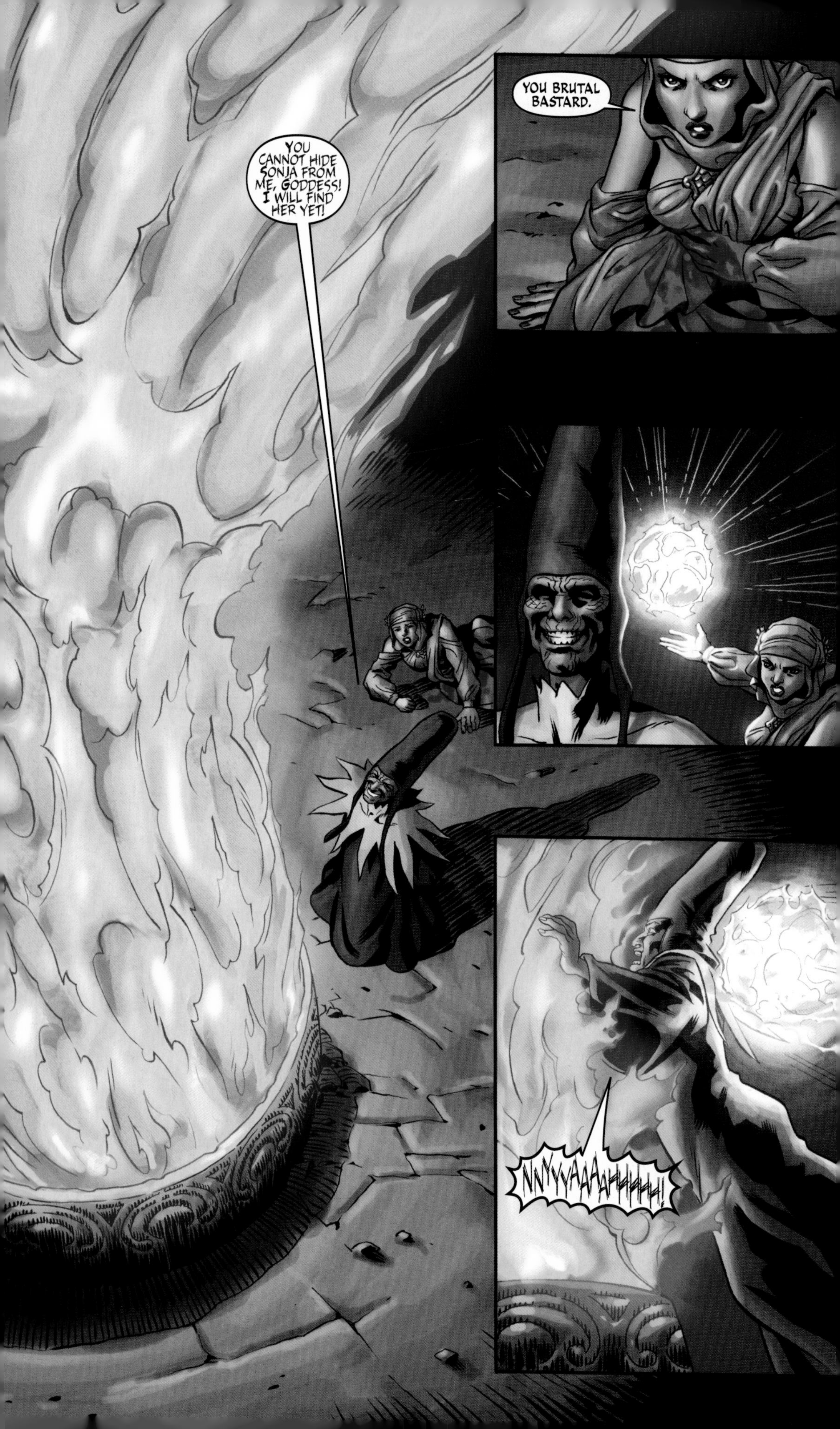

YOU BRUTAL BASTARD.
YOU CANNOT HIDE SONJA FROM ME, GODDESS! I WILL FIND HER YET!
NNYYYAAAAHHHHHH!

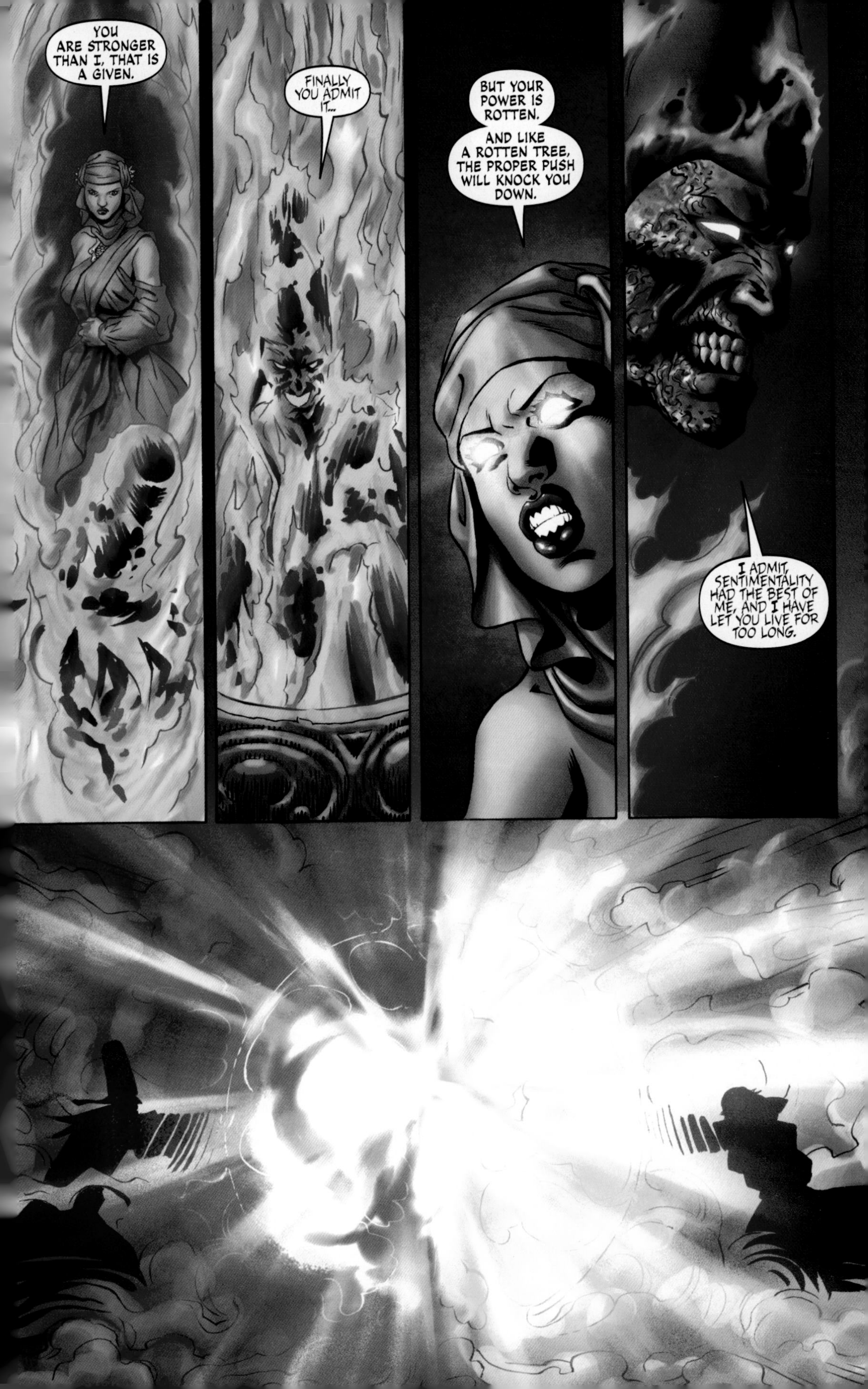
YOU ARE STRONGER THAN I, THAT IS A GIVEN.
FINALLY YOU ADMIT IT...
BUT YOUR POWER IS ROTTEN.
AND LIKE A ROTTEN TREE, THE PROPER PUSH WILL KNOCK YOU DOWN.
I ADMIT, SENTIMENTALITY HAD THE BEST OF ME, AND I HAVE LET YOU LIVE FOR TOO LONG.

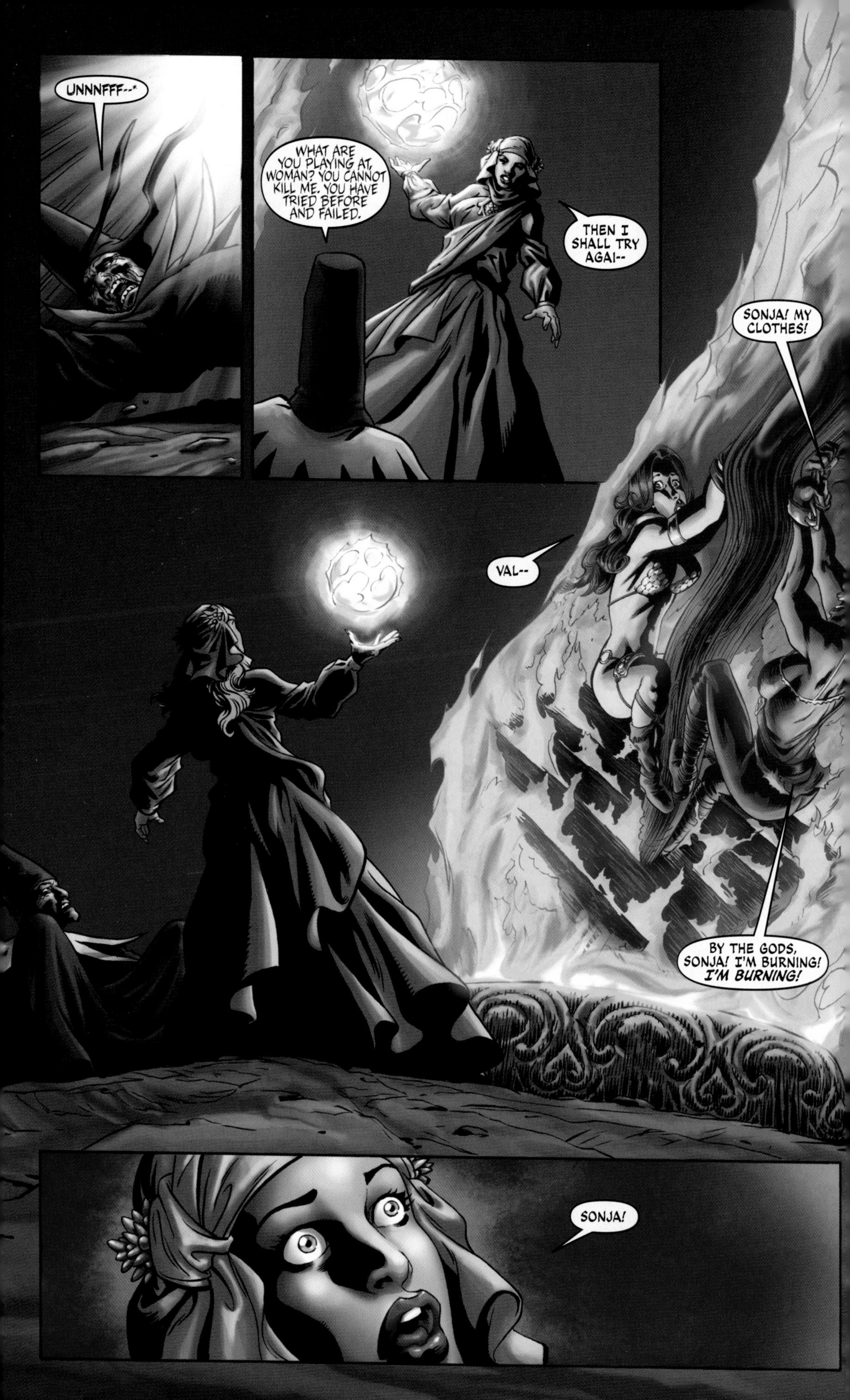
UNNNFFF--*
WHAT ARE YOU PLAYING AT, WOMAN? YOU CANNOT KILL ME. YOU HAVE TRIED BEFORE AND FAILED.
THEN I SHALL TRY AGAI--
SONJA! MY CLOTHES!
VAL--
BY THE GODS, SONJA! I'M BURNING! I'M BURNING!
SONJA!

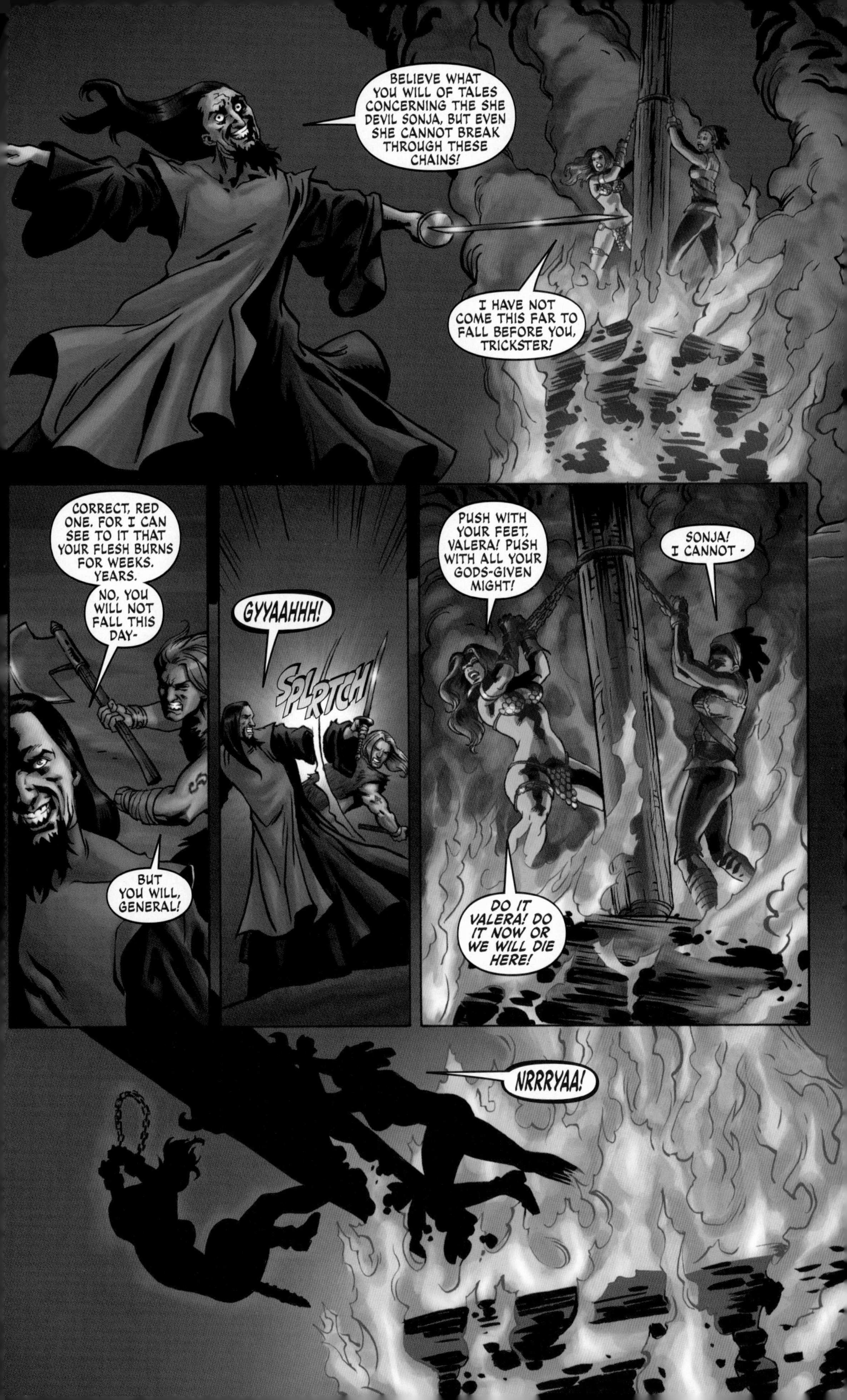
BELIEVE WHAT YOU WILL OF TALES CONCERNING THE SHE DEVIL SONJA, BUT EVEN SHE CANNOT BREAK THROUGH THESE CHAINS!
I HAVE NOT COME THIS FAR TO FALL BEFORE YOU, TRICKSTER!
CORRECT, RED ONE. FOR I CAN SEE TO IT THAT YOUR FLESH BURNS FOR WEEKS. YEARS.
NO, YOU WILL NOT FALL THIS DAY-
BUT YOU WILL, GENERAL!
GYYAAHHH!
SPLRTCH
PUSH WITH YOUR FEET, VALERA! PUSH WITH ALL YOUR GODS-GIVEN MIGHT!
SONJA! I CANNOT -
DO IT VALERA! DO IT NOW OR WE WILL DIE HERE!
NRRRYAA!

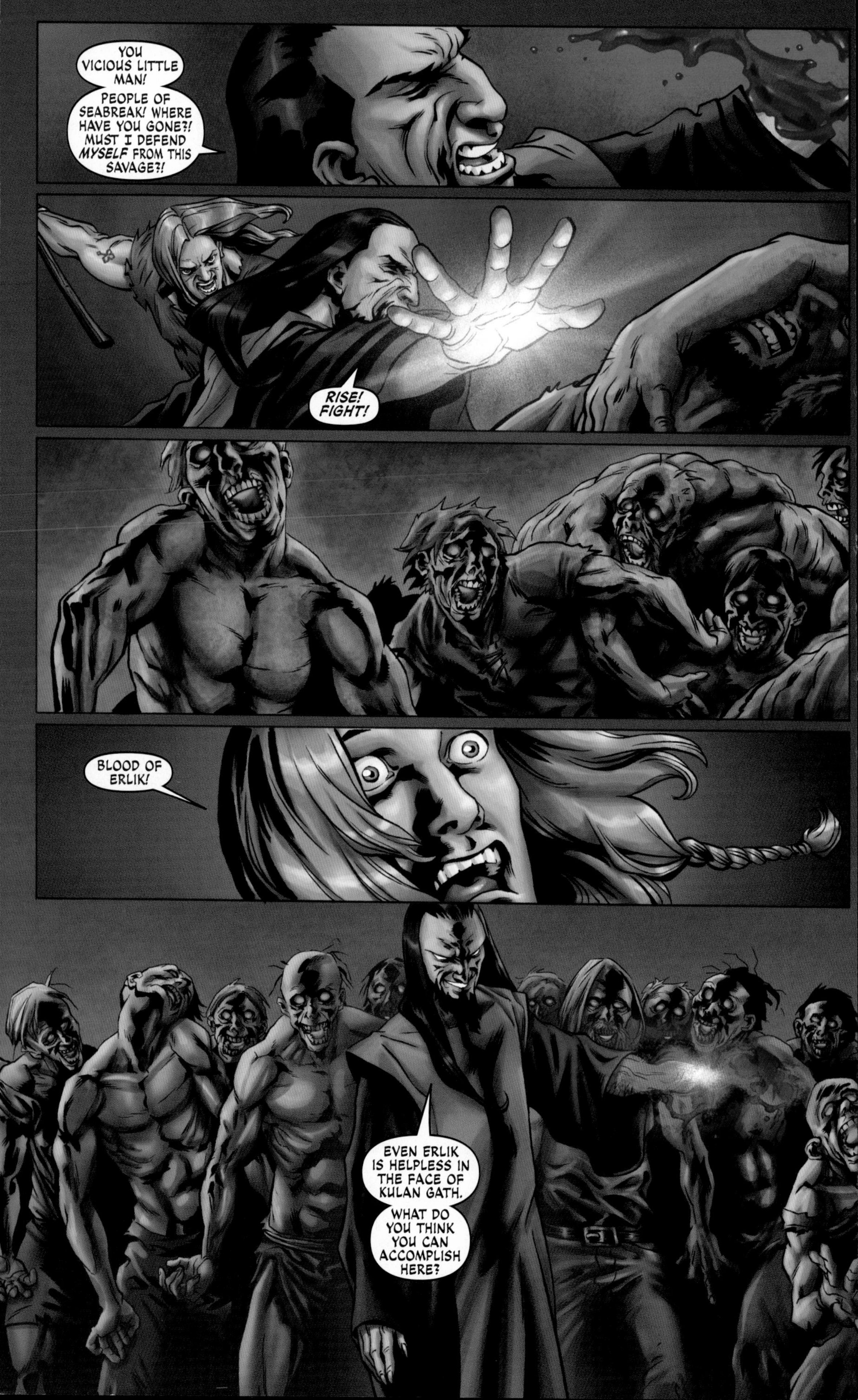
YOU VICIOUS LITTLE MAN!
PEOPLE OF SEABREAK! WHERE HAVE YOU GONE?! MUST I DEFEND *MYSELF* FROM THIS SAVAGE?!
RISE! FIGHT!
BLOOD OF ERLIK!
EVEN ERLIK IS HELPLESS IN THE FACE OF KULAN GATH.
WHAT DO YOU THINK YOU CAN ACCOMPLISH HERE?

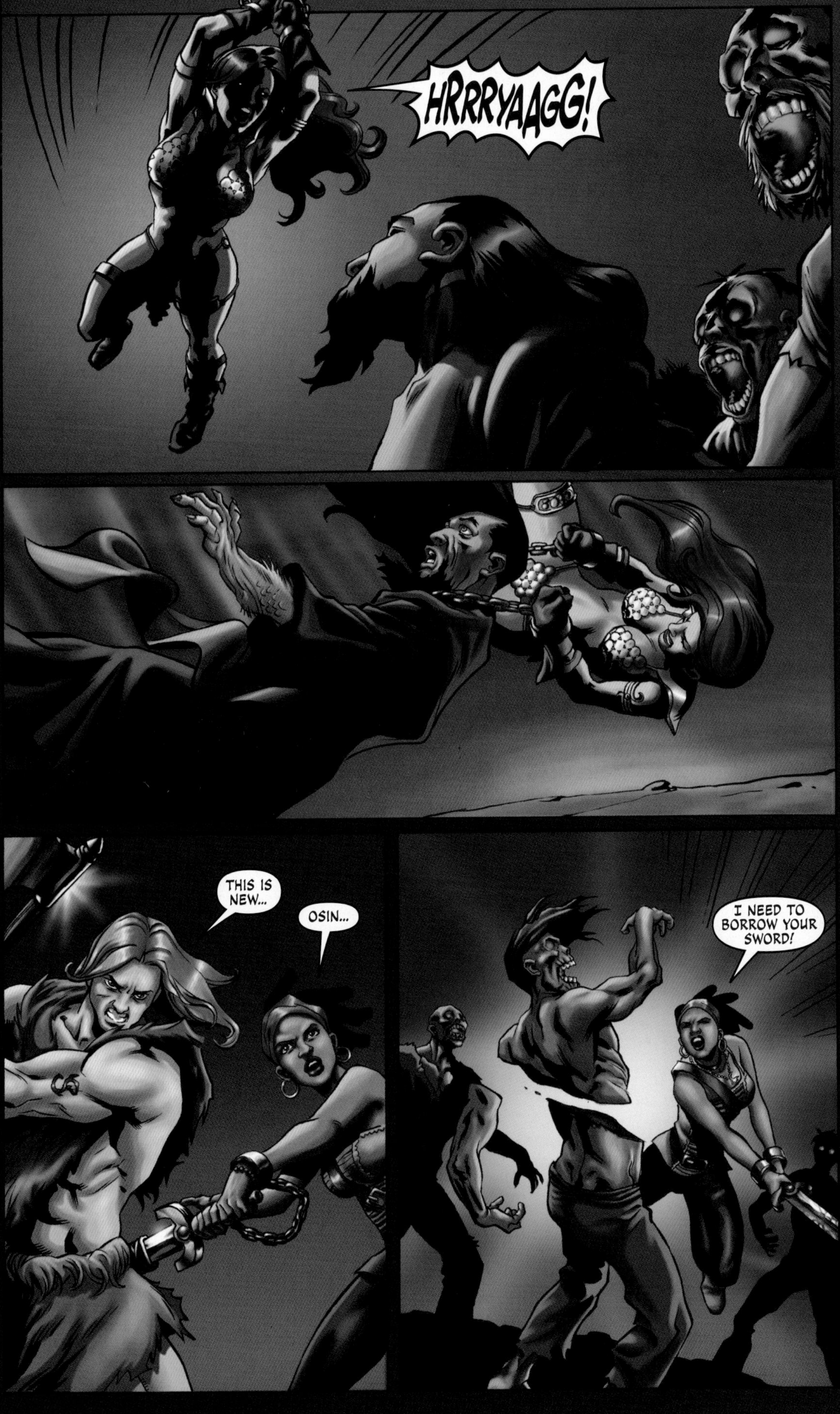
HRRRYAAGG!
THIS IS NEW...
OSIN...
I NEED TO BORROW YOUR SWORD!

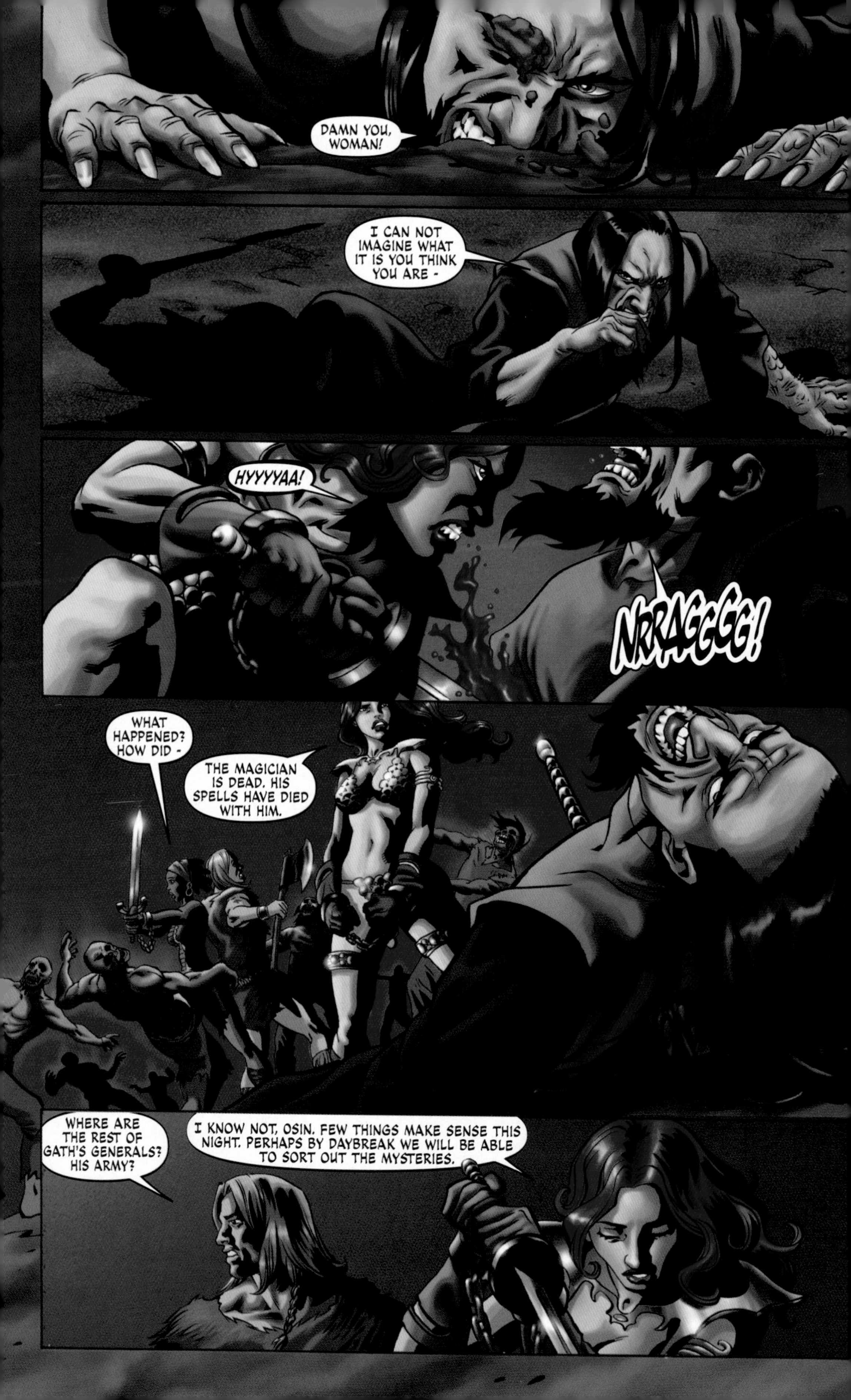

DAMN YOU, WOMAN!
I CAN NOT IMAGINE WHAT IT IS YOU THINK YOU ARE -
HYYYYAA!
NRRAGGGG!
WHAT HAPPENED? HOW DID -
THE MAGICIAN IS DEAD. HIS SPELLS HAVE DIED WITH HIM.
WHERE ARE THE REST OF GATH'S GENERALS? HIS ARMY?
I KNOW NOT, OSIN. FEW THINGS MAKE SENSE THIS NIGHT. PERHAPS BY DAYBREAK WE WILL BE ABLE TO SORT OUT THE MYSTERIES.

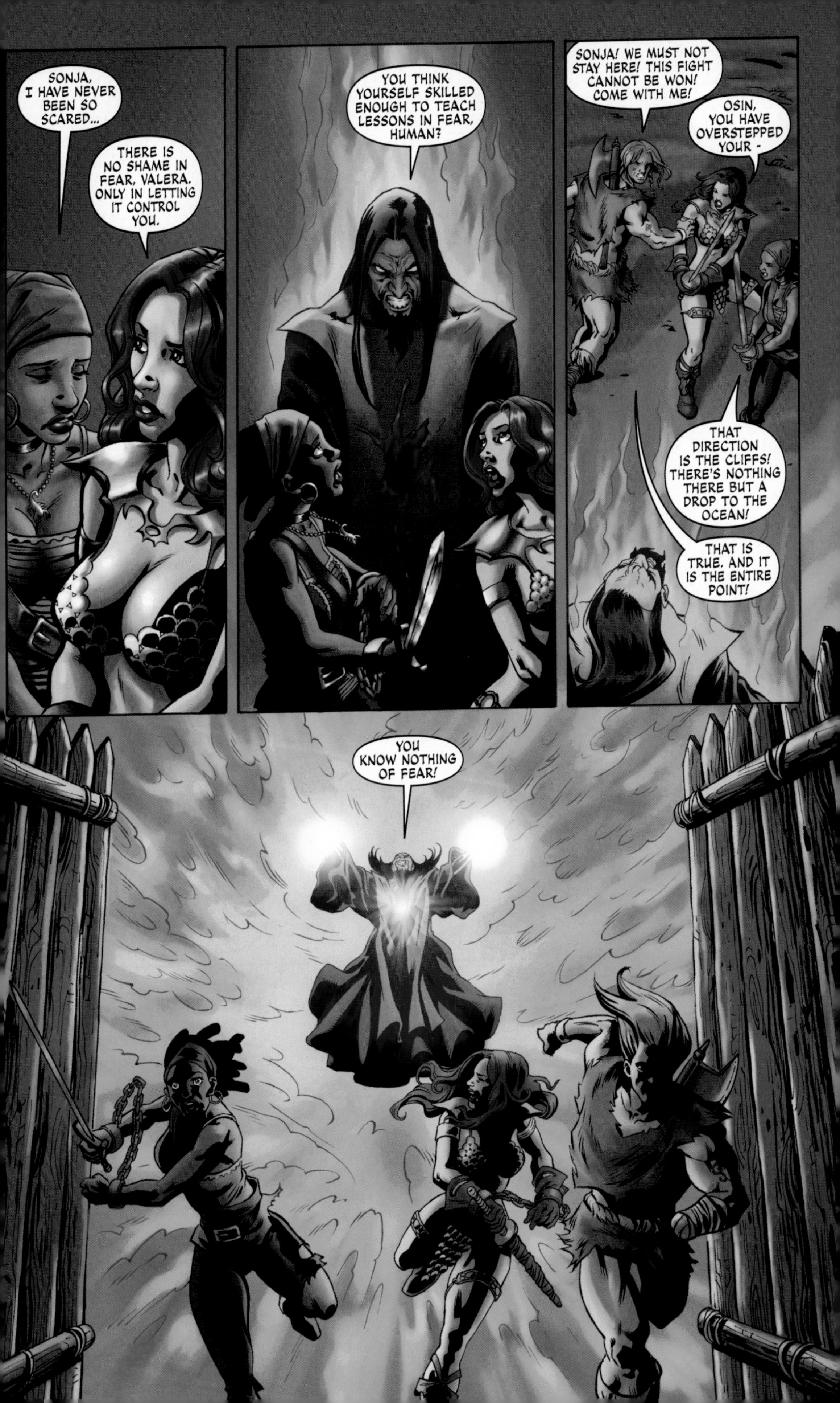
SONJA, I HAVE NEVER BEEN SO SCARED...
THERE IS NO SHAME IN FEAR, VALERA. ONLY IN LETTING IT CONTROL YOU.
YOU THINK YOURSELF SKILLED ENOUGH TO TEACH LESSONS IN FEAR, HUMAN?
SONJA! WE MUST NOT STAY HERE! THIS FIGHT CANNOT BE WON! COME WITH ME!
OSIN, YOU HAVE OVERSTEPPED YOUR -
THAT DIRECTION IS THE CLIFFS! THERE'S NOTHING THERE BUT A DROP TO THE OCEAN!
THAT IS TRUE. AND IT IS THE ENTIRE POINT!
YOU KNOW NOTHING OF FEAR!

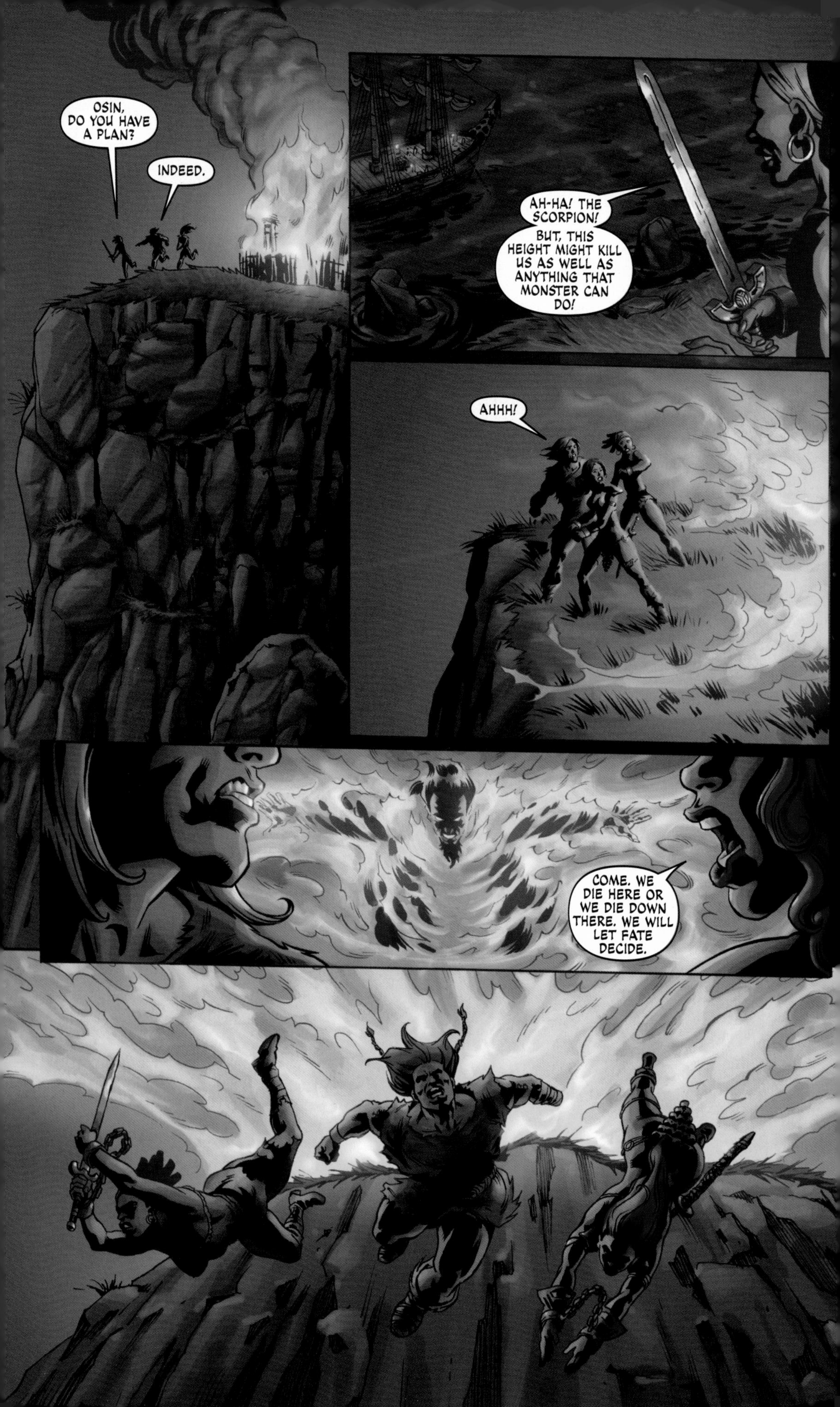
OSIN, DO YOU HAVE A PLAN?
INDEED.
AH-HA! THE SCORPION!
BUT, THIS HEIGHT MIGHT KILL US AS WELL AS ANYTHING THAT MONSTER CAN DO!
AHHH!
COME. WE DIE HERE OR WE DIE DOWN THERE. WE WILL LET FATE DECIDE.

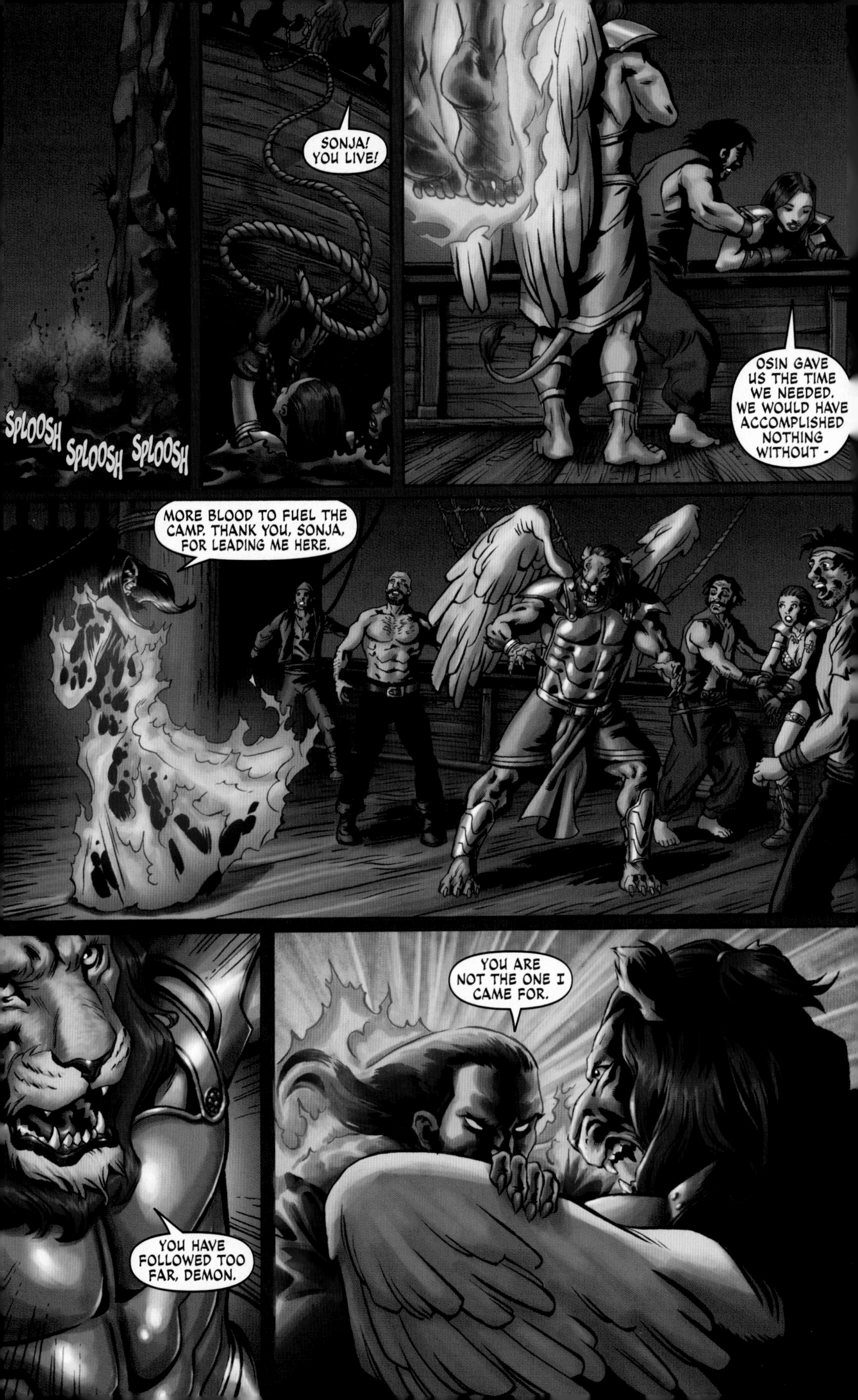
SPLOOSH SPLOOSH SPLOOSH
SONJA! YOU LIVE!
OSIN GAVE US THE TIME WE NEEDED. WE WOULD HAVE ACCOMPLISHED NOTHING WITHOUT -
MORE BLOOD TO FUEL THE CAMP. THANK YOU, SONJA, FOR LEADING ME HERE.
YOU HAVE FOLLOWED TOO FAR, DEMON.
YOU ARE NOT THE ONE I CAME FOR.

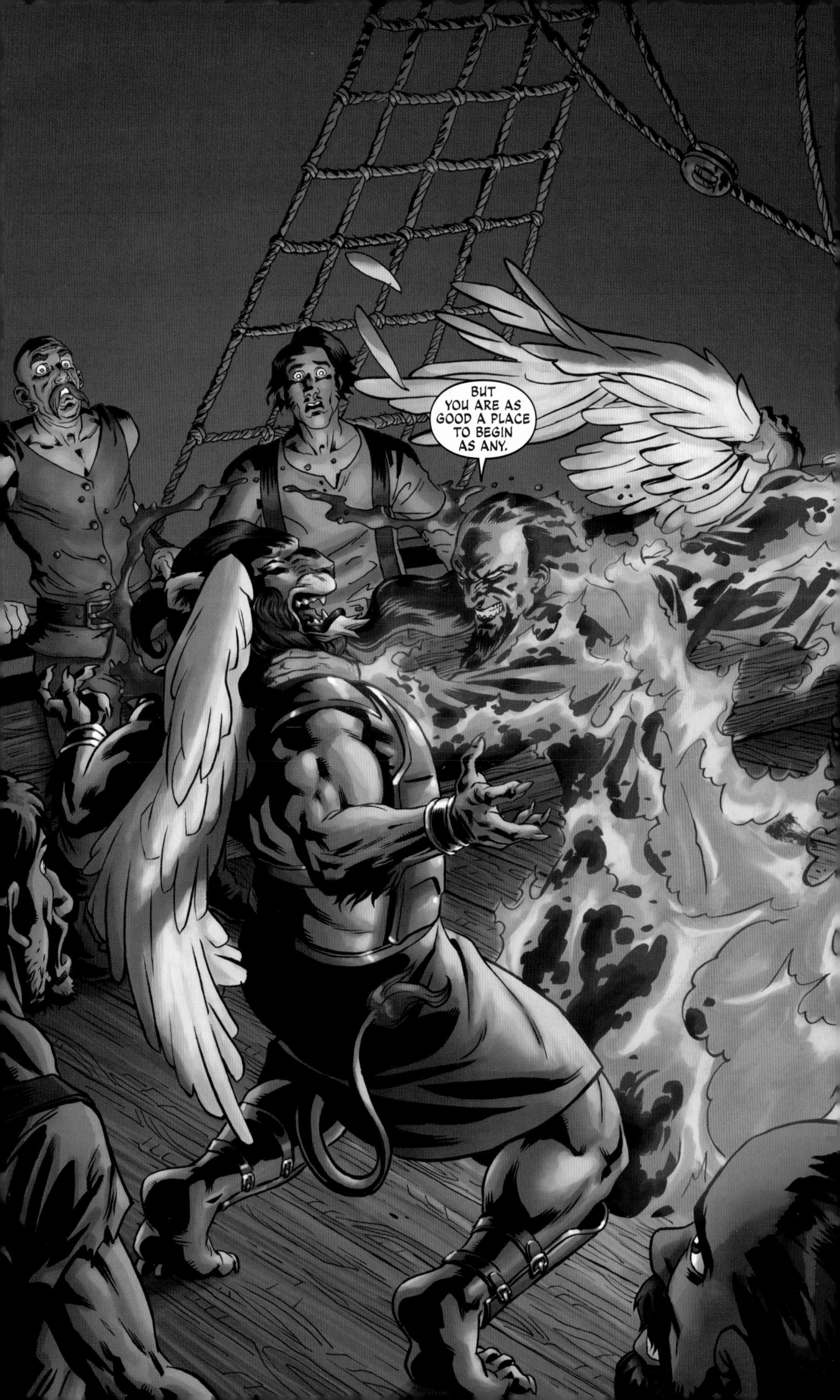
BUT YOU ARE AS GOOD A PLACE TO BEGIN AS ANY.

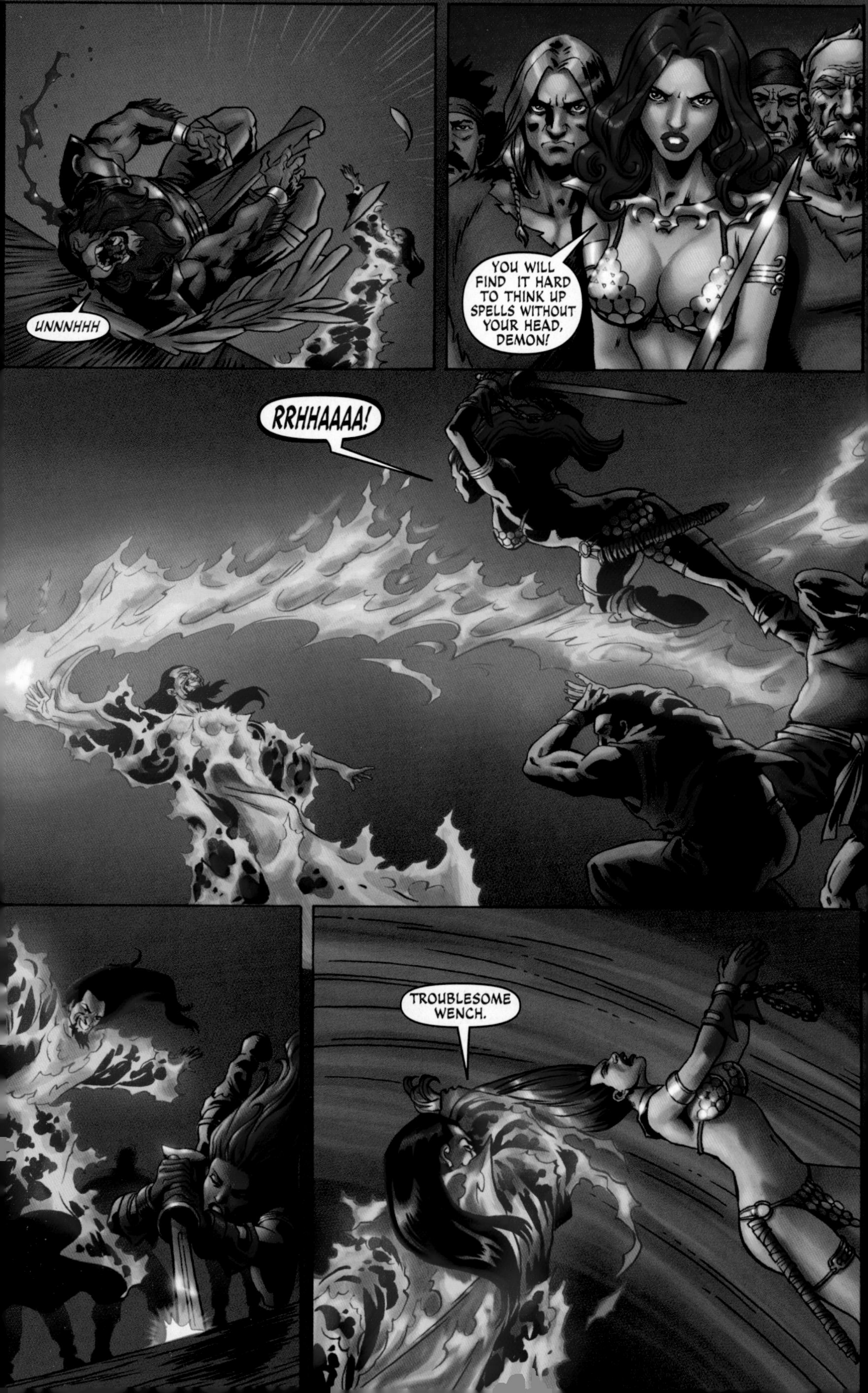
UNNNHHH
YOU WILL FIND IT HARD TO THINK UP SPELLS WITHOUT YOUR HEAD, DEMON!
RRHHAAAA!
TROUBLESOME WENCH.

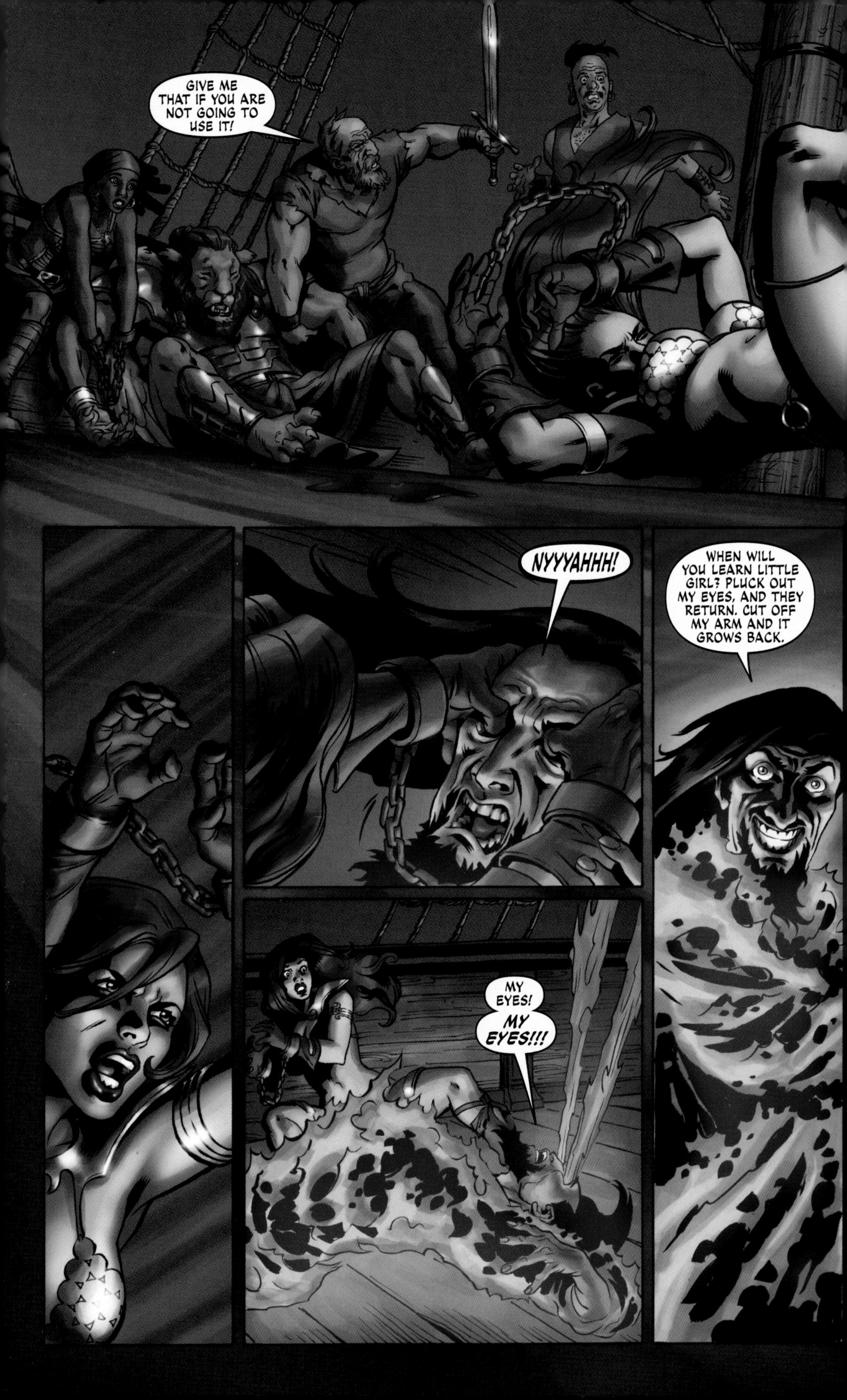
GIVE ME THAT IF YOU ARE NOT GOING TO USE IT!
NYYYAHHH!
MY EYES! MY EYES!!!
WHEN WILL YOU LEARN LITTLE GIRL? PLUCK OUT MY EYES, AND THEY RETURN. CUT OFF MY ARM AND IT GROWS BACK.

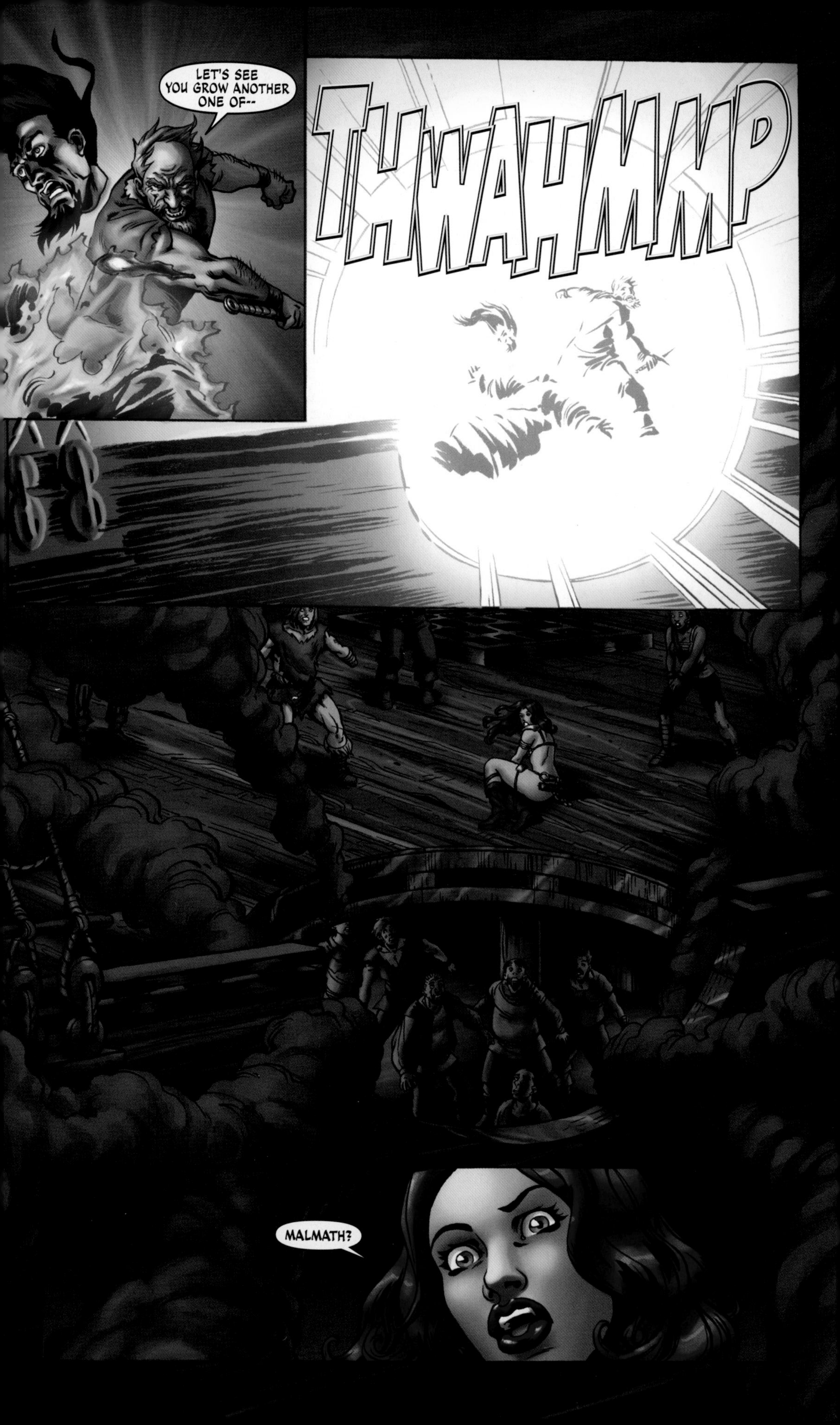
LET'S SEE YOU GROW ANOTHER ONE OF--
THWAHMMMP
MALMATH?

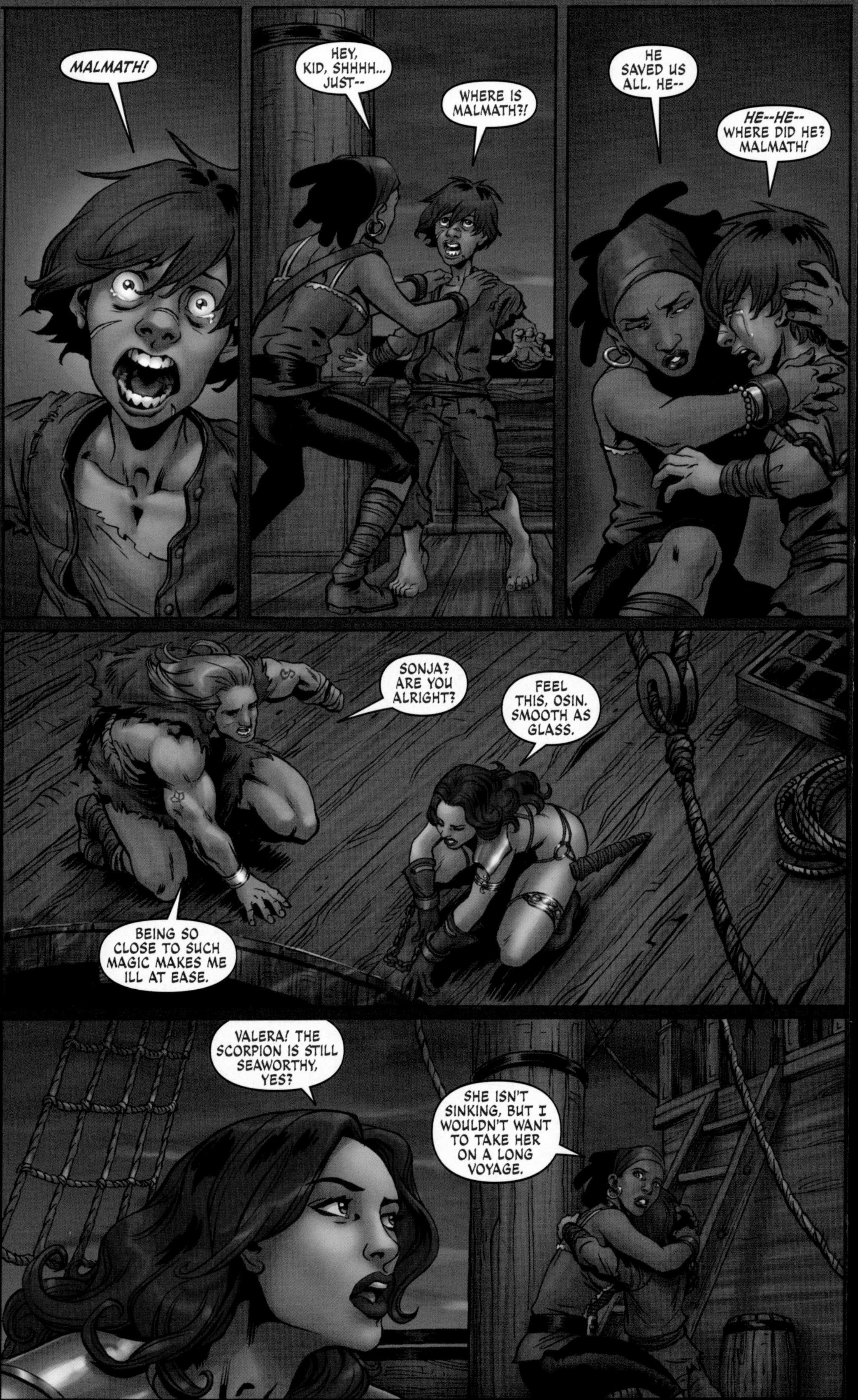
MALMATH!
HEY, KID, SHHHH... JUST--
WHERE IS MALMATH?!
HE SAVED US ALL. HE--
HE--HE-- WHERE DID HE? MALMATH!
SONJA? ARE YOU ALRIGHT?
FEEL THIS, OSIN. SMOOTH AS GLASS.
BEING SO CLOSE TO SUCH MAGIC MAKES ME ILL AT EASE.
VALERA! THE SCORPION IS STILL SEAWORTHY, YES?
SHE ISN'T SINKING, BUT I WOULDN'T WANT TO TAKE HER ON A LONG VOYAGE.

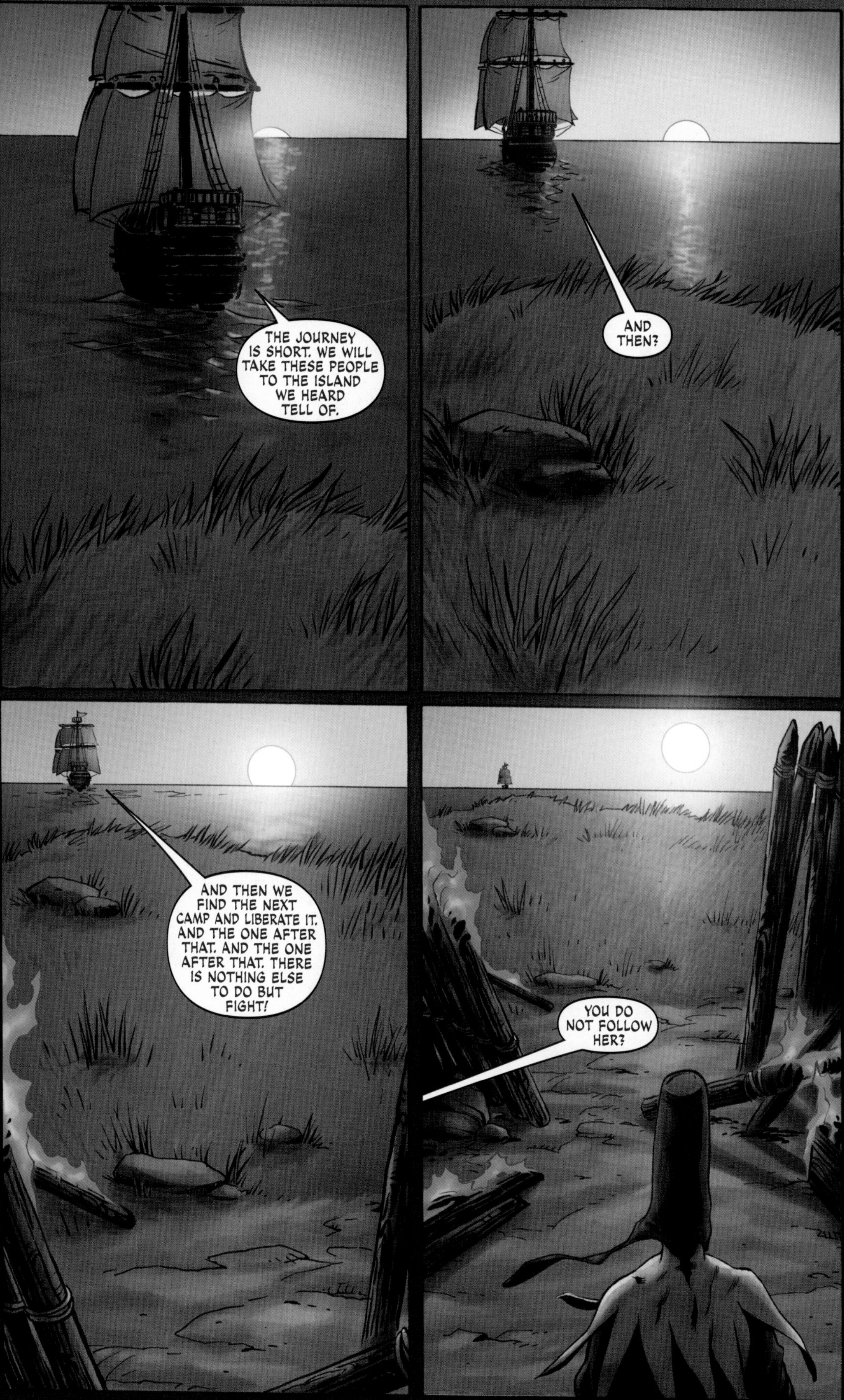
THE JOURNEY IS SHORT. WE WILL TAKE THESE PEOPLE TO THE ISLAND WE HEARD TELL OF.
AND THEN?
AND THEN WE FIND THE NEXT CAMP AND LIBERATE IT. AND THE ONE AFTER THAT. AND THE ONE AFTER THAT. THERE IS NOTHING ELSE TO DO BUT FIGHT!
YOU DO NOT FOLLOW HER?

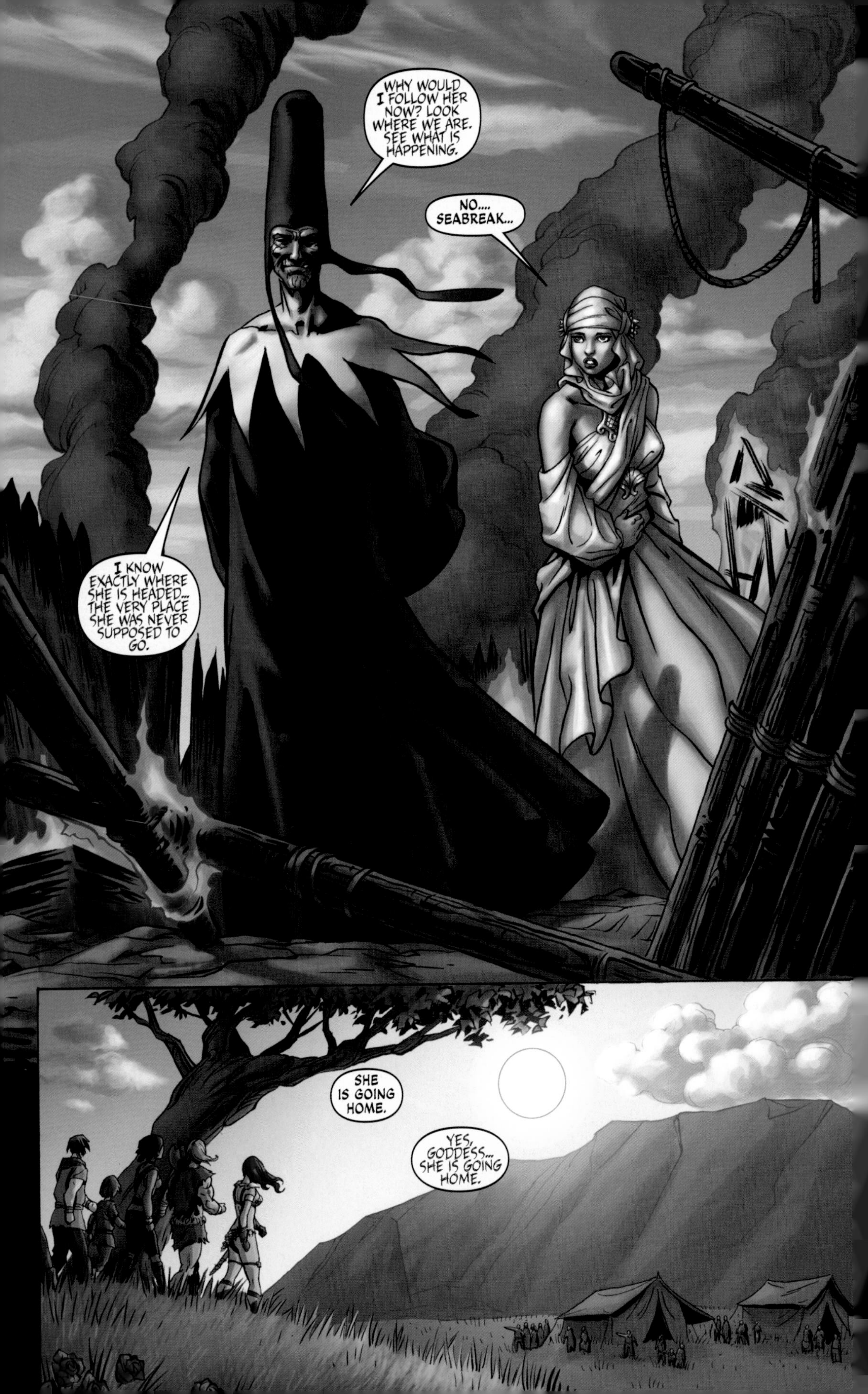
WHY WOULD I FOLLOW HER NOW? LOOK WHERE WE ARE. SEE WHAT IS HAPPENING.
NO.... SEABREAK...
I KNOW EXACTLY WHERE SHE IS HEADED... THE VERY PLACE SHE WAS NEVER SUPPOSED TO GO.
SHE IS GOING HOME.
YES, GODDESS... SHE IS GOING HOME.

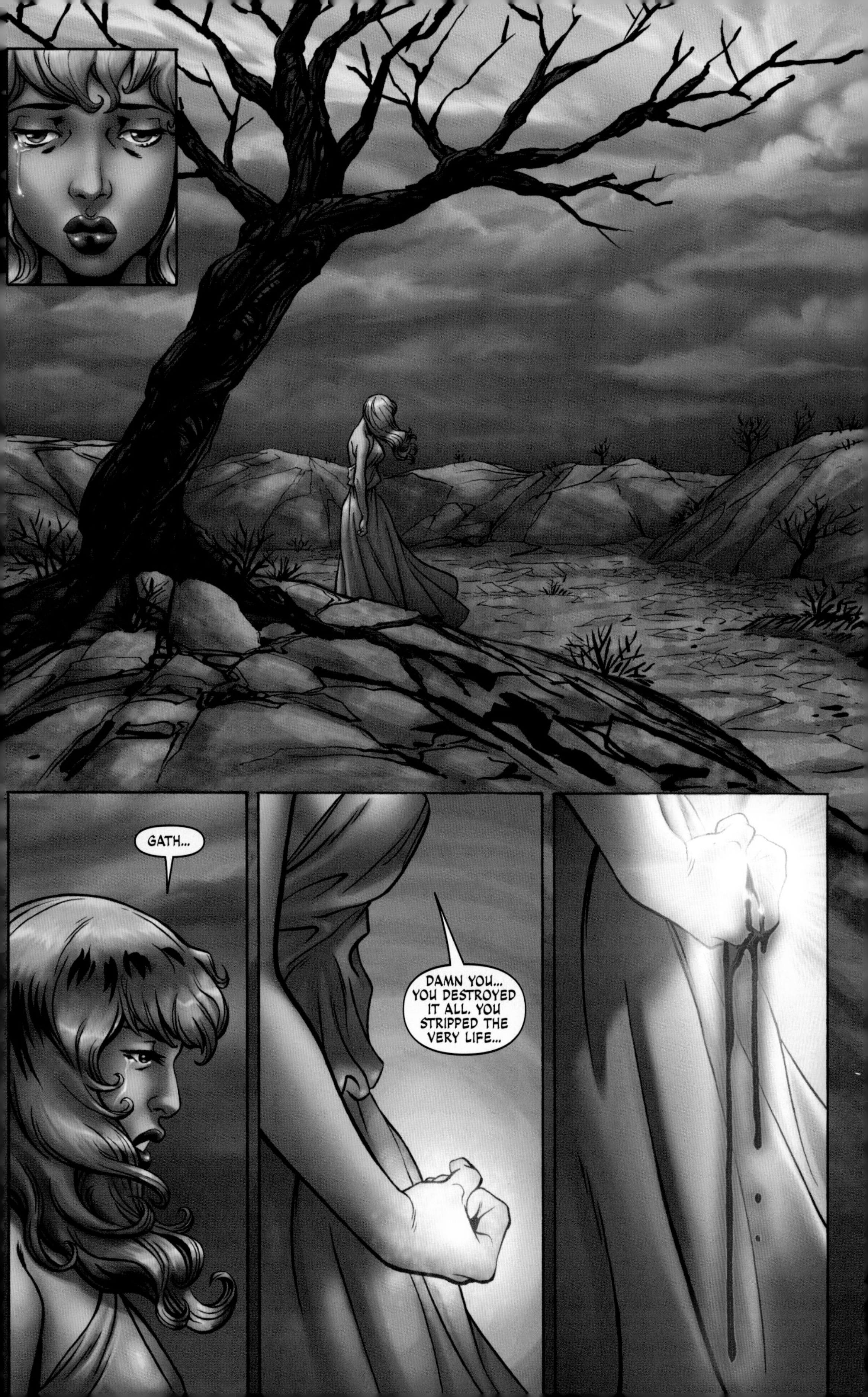
GATH...
DAMN YOU... YOU DESTROYED IT ALL. YOU STRIPPED THE VERY LIFE...

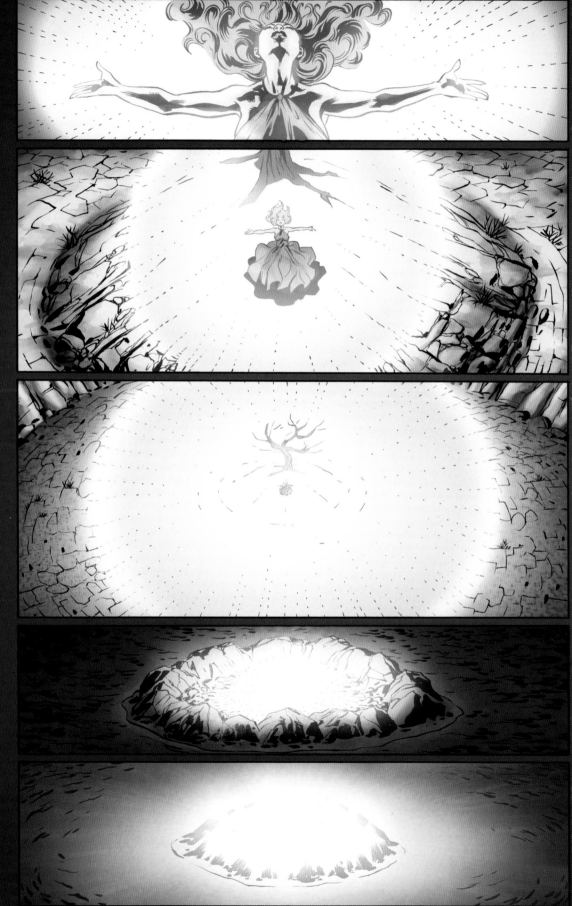

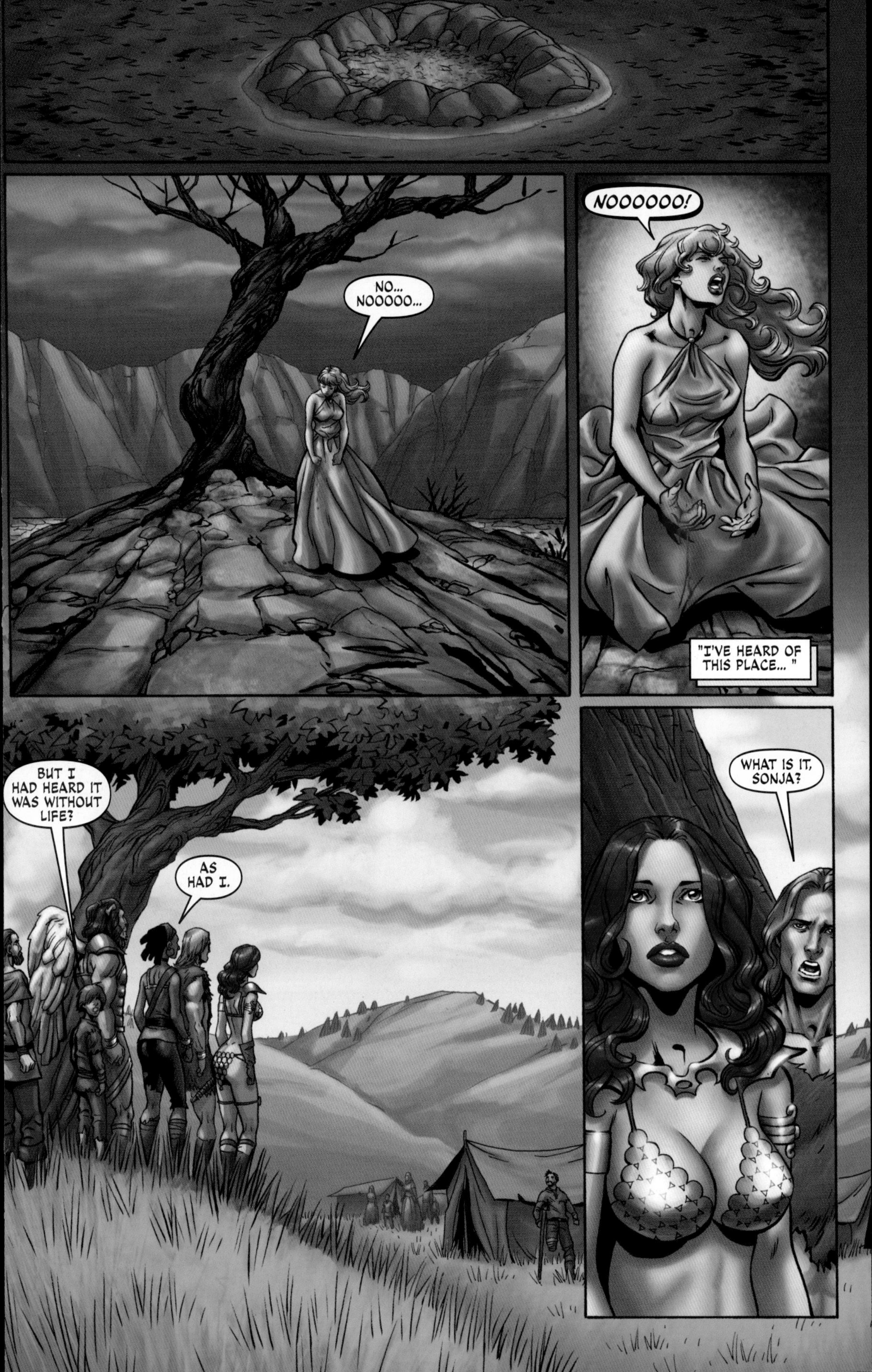
NO...
NOOOOO...
NOOOOOO!
"I'VE HEARD OF THIS PLACE... "
BUT I HAD HEARD IT WAS WITHOUT LIFE?
AS HAD I.
WHAT IS IT, SONJA?

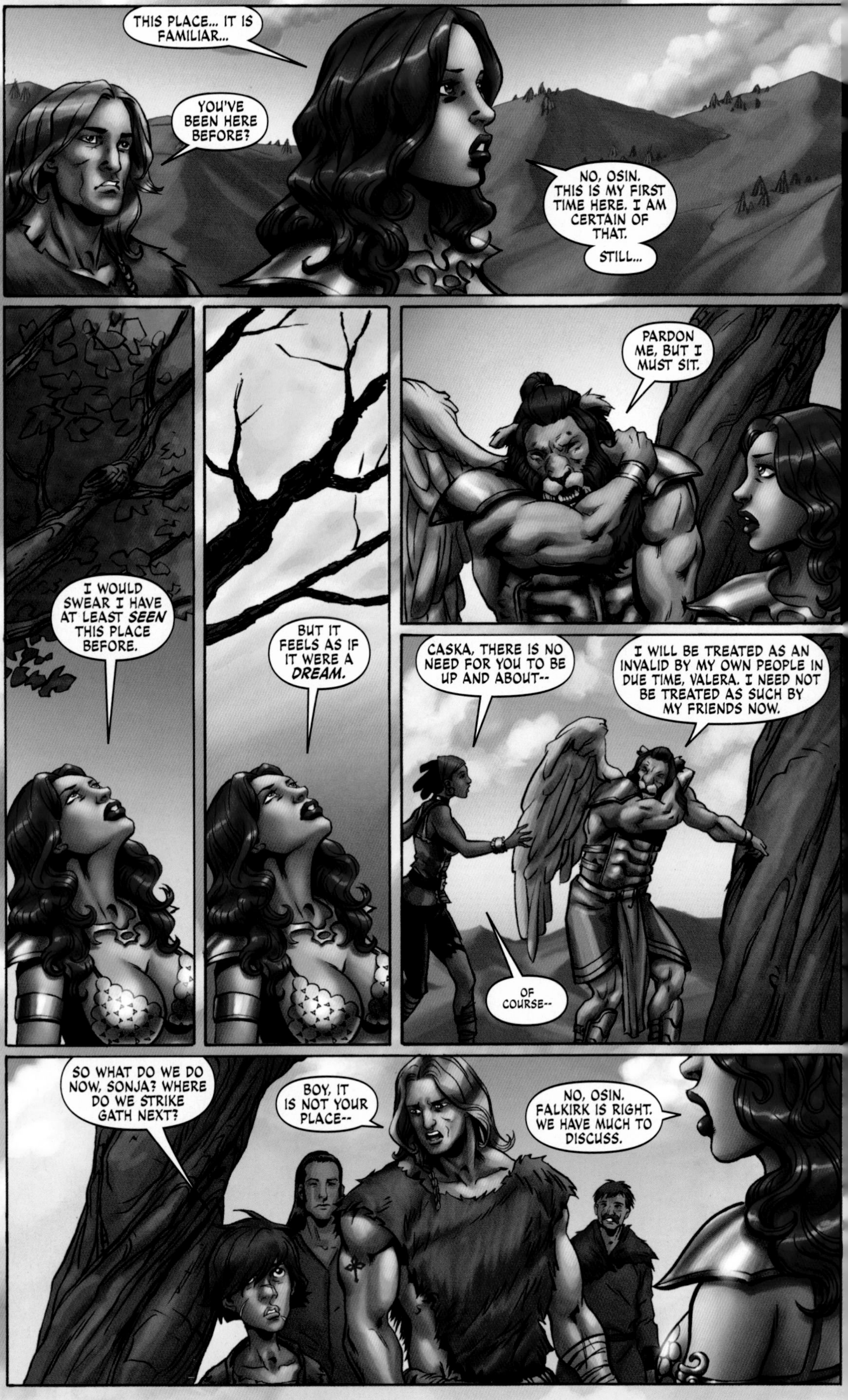
THIS PLACE... IT IS FAMILIAR...
YOU'VE BEEN HERE BEFORE?
NO, OSIN. THIS IS MY FIRST TIME HERE. I AM CERTAIN OF THAT.
STILL...
I WOULD SWEAR I HAVE AT LEAST *SEEN* THIS PLACE BEFORE.
BUT IT FEELS AS IF IT WERE A *DREAM.*
PARDON ME, BUT I MUST SIT.
CASKA, THERE IS NO NEED FOR YOU TO BE UP AND ABOUT--
I WILL BE TREATED AS AN INVALID BY MY OWN PEOPLE IN DUE TIME, VALERA. I NEED NOT BE TREATED AS SUCH BY MY FRIENDS NOW.
OF COURSE--
SO WHAT DO WE DO NOW, SONJA? WHERE DO WE STRIKE GATH NEXT?
BOY, IT IS NOT YOUR PLACE--
NO, OSIN. FALKIRK IS RIGHT. WE HAVE MUCH TO DISCUSS.

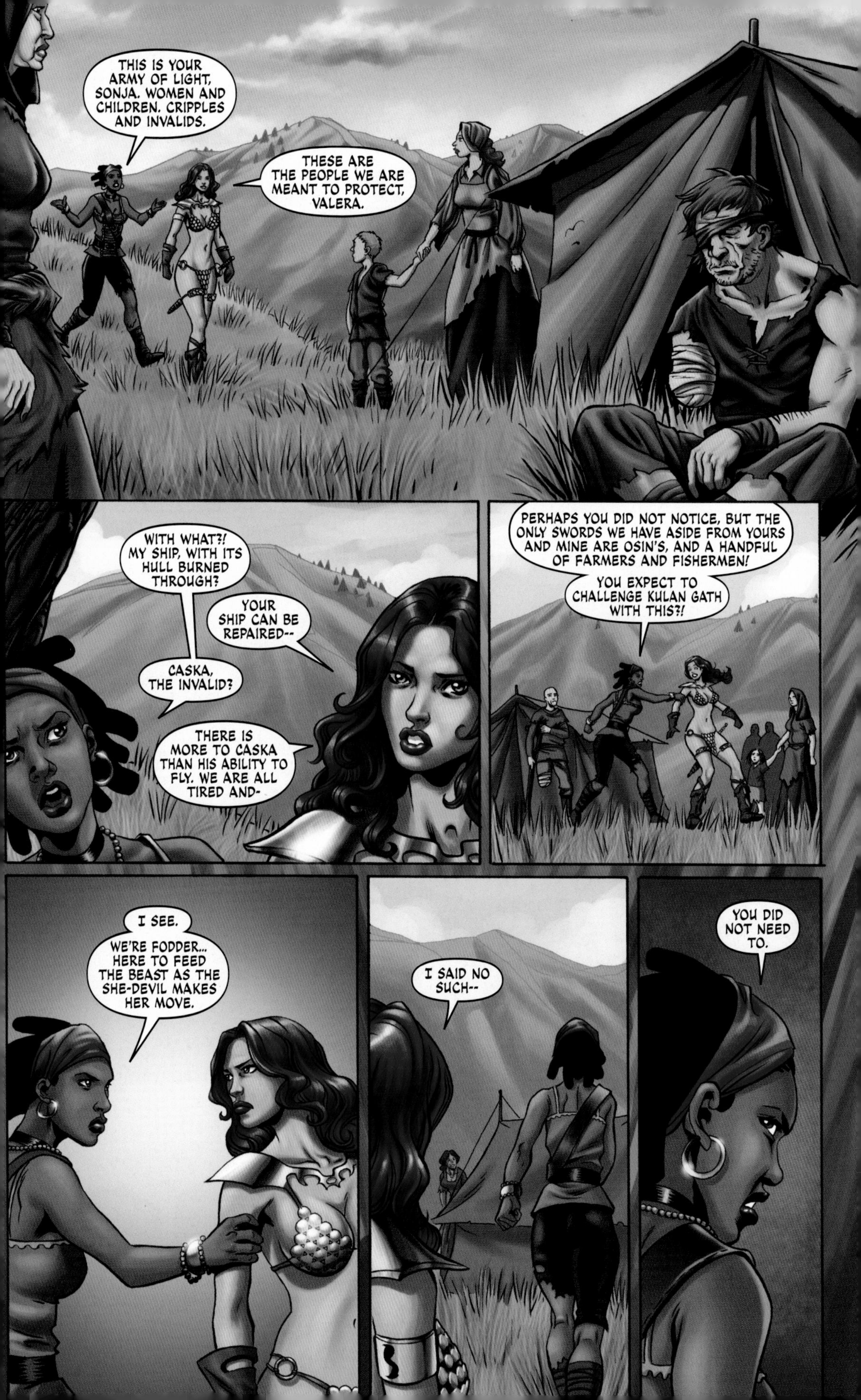
THIS IS YOUR ARMY OF LIGHT, SONJA. WOMEN AND CHILDREN. CRIPPLES AND INVALIDS.
THESE ARE THE PEOPLE WE ARE MEANT TO PROTECT, VALERA.
WITH WHAT?! MY SHIP, WITH ITS HULL BURNED THROUGH?
YOUR SHIP CAN BE REPAIRED--
CASKA, THE INVALID?
THERE IS MORE TO CASKA THAN HIS ABILITY TO FLY. WE ARE ALL TIRED AND-
PERHAPS YOU DID NOT NOTICE, BUT THE ONLY SWORDS WE HAVE ASIDE FROM YOURS AND MINE ARE OSIN'S, AND A HANDFUL OF FARMERS AND FISHERMEN!
YOU EXPECT TO CHALLENGE KULAN GATH WITH THIS?!
I SEE.
WE'RE FODDER... HERE TO FEED THE BEAST AS THE SHE-DEVIL MAKES HER MOVE.
I SAID NO SUCH--
YOU DID NOT NEED TO.

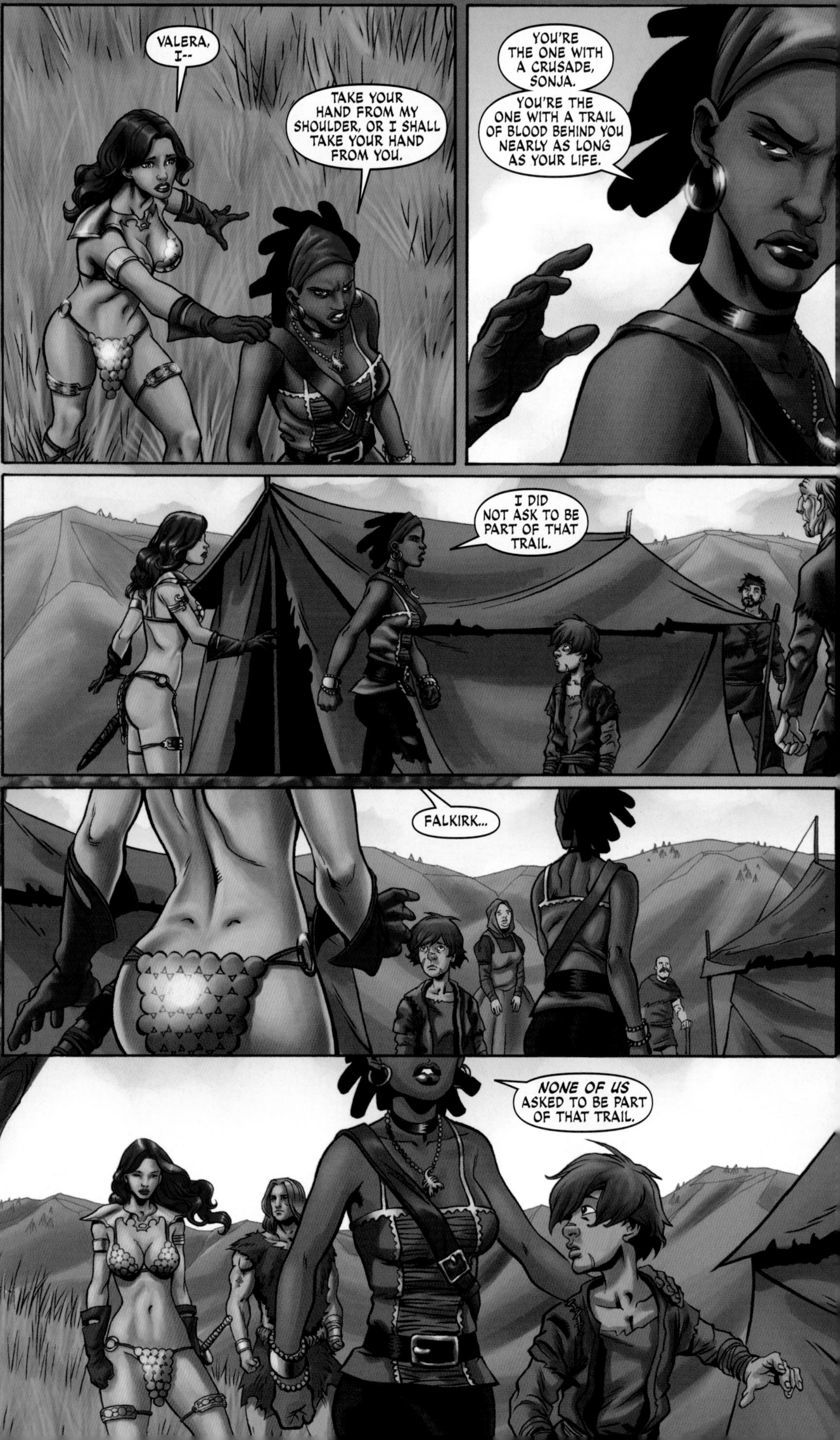
VALERA, I--
TAKE YOUR HAND FROM MY SHOULDER, OR I SHALL TAKE YOUR HAND FROM YOU.
YOU'RE THE ONE WITH A CRUSADE, SONJA.
YOU'RE THE ONE WITH A TRAIL OF BLOOD BEHIND YOU NEARLY AS LONG AS YOUR LIFE.
I DID NOT ASK TO BE PART OF THAT TRAIL.
FALKIRK...
NONE OF US ASKED TO BE PART OF THAT TRAIL.

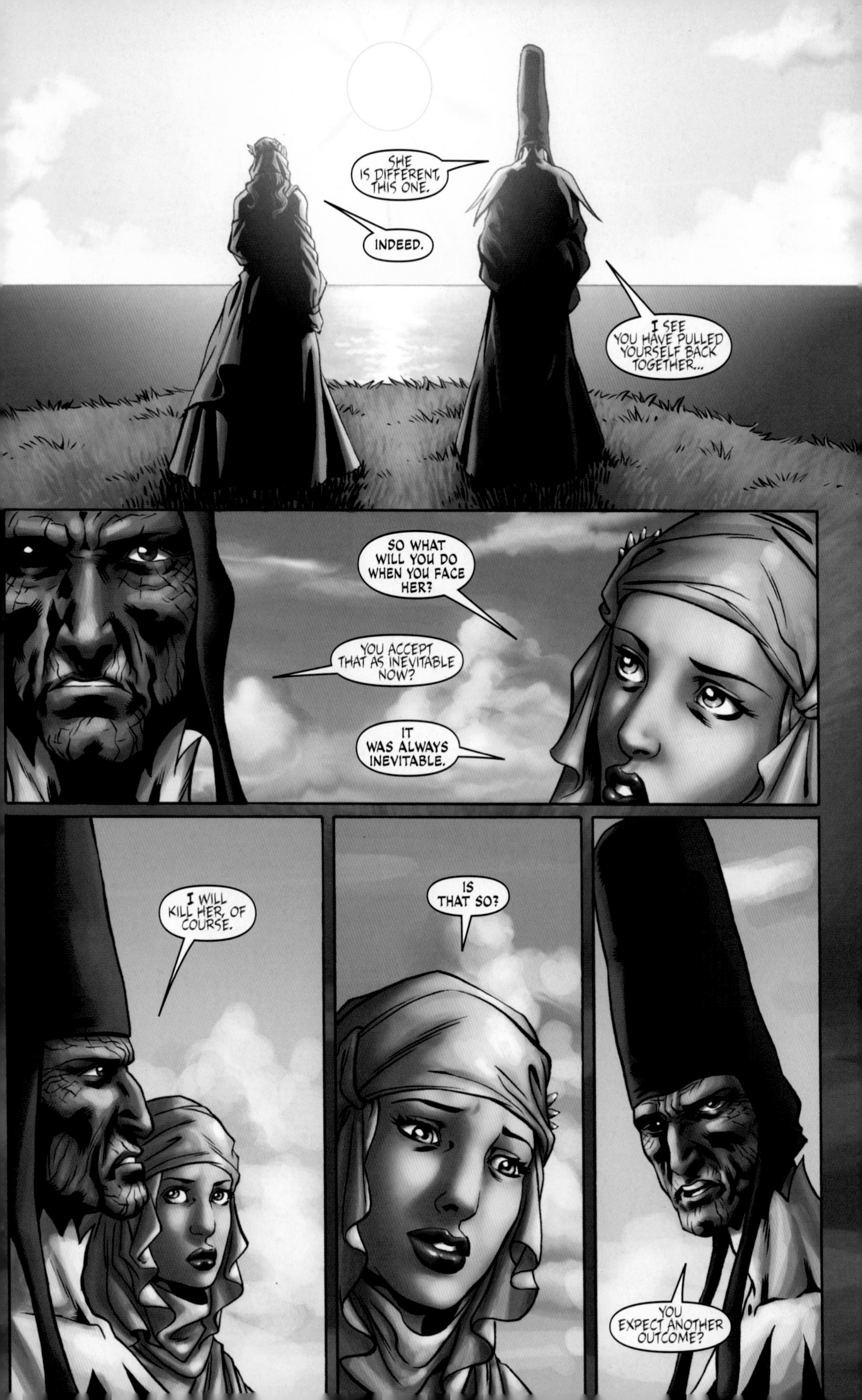
SHE IS DIFFERENT, THIS ONE.
INDEED.
I SEE YOU HAVE PULLED YOURSELF BACK TOGETHER...
SO WHAT WILL YOU DO WHEN YOU FACE HER?
YOU ACCEPT THAT AS INEVITABLE NOW?
IT WAS ALWAYS INEVITABLE.
I WILL KILL HER, OF COURSE.
IS THAT SO?
YOU EXPECT ANOTHER OUTCOME?

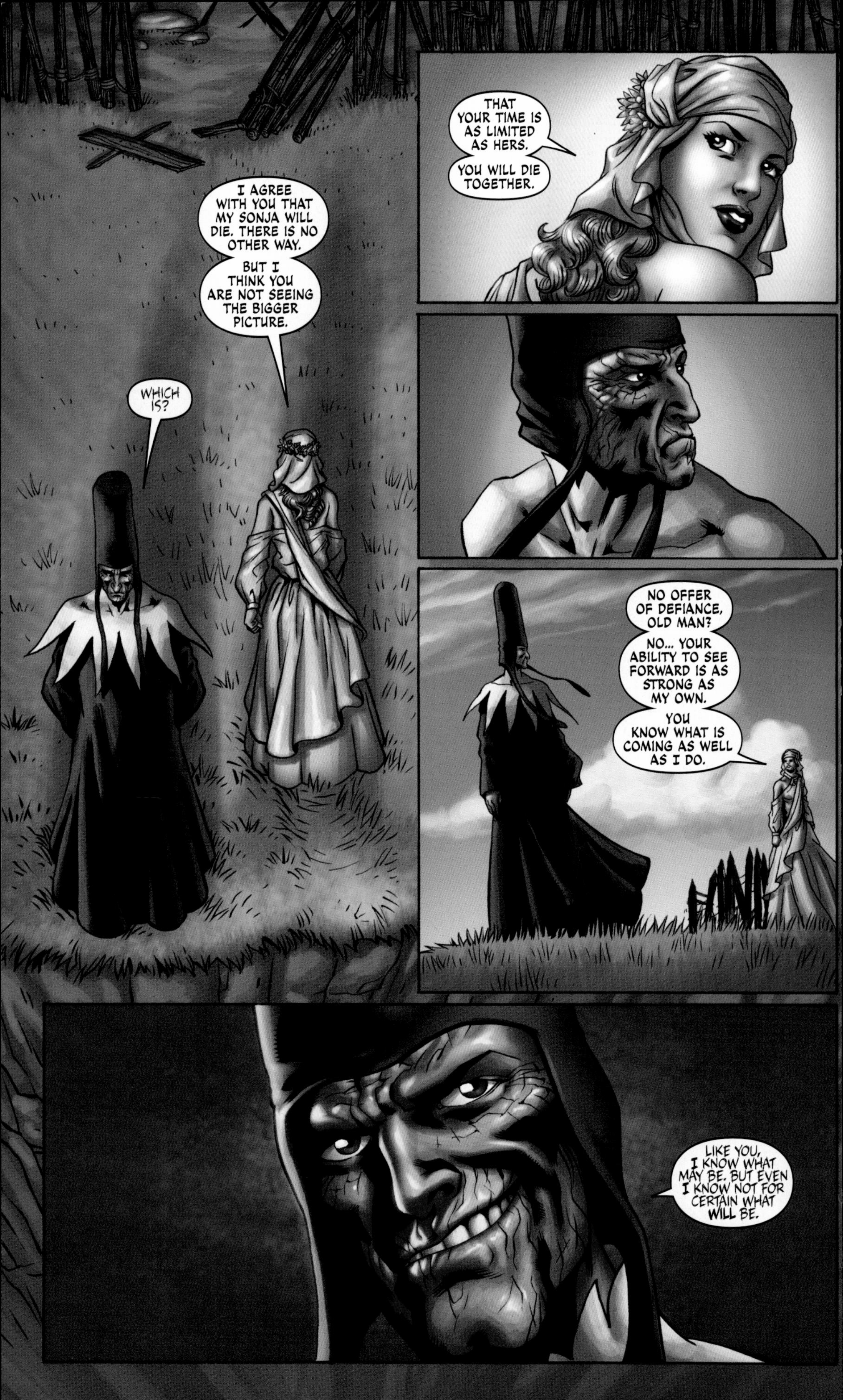
I AGREE WITH YOU THAT MY SONJA WILL DIE. THERE IS NO OTHER WAY.
BUT I THINK YOU ARE NOT SEEING THE BIGGER PICTURE.
WHICH IS?
THAT YOUR TIME IS AS LIMITED AS HERS.
YOU WILL DIE TOGETHER.
NO OFFER OF DEFIANCE, OLD MAN?
NO... YOUR ABILITY TO SEE FORWARD IS AS STRONG AS MY OWN.
YOU KNOW WHAT IS COMING AS WELL AS I DO.
LIKE YOU, I KNOW WHAT MAY BE. BUT EVEN I KNOW NOT FOR CERTAIN WHAT WILL BE.

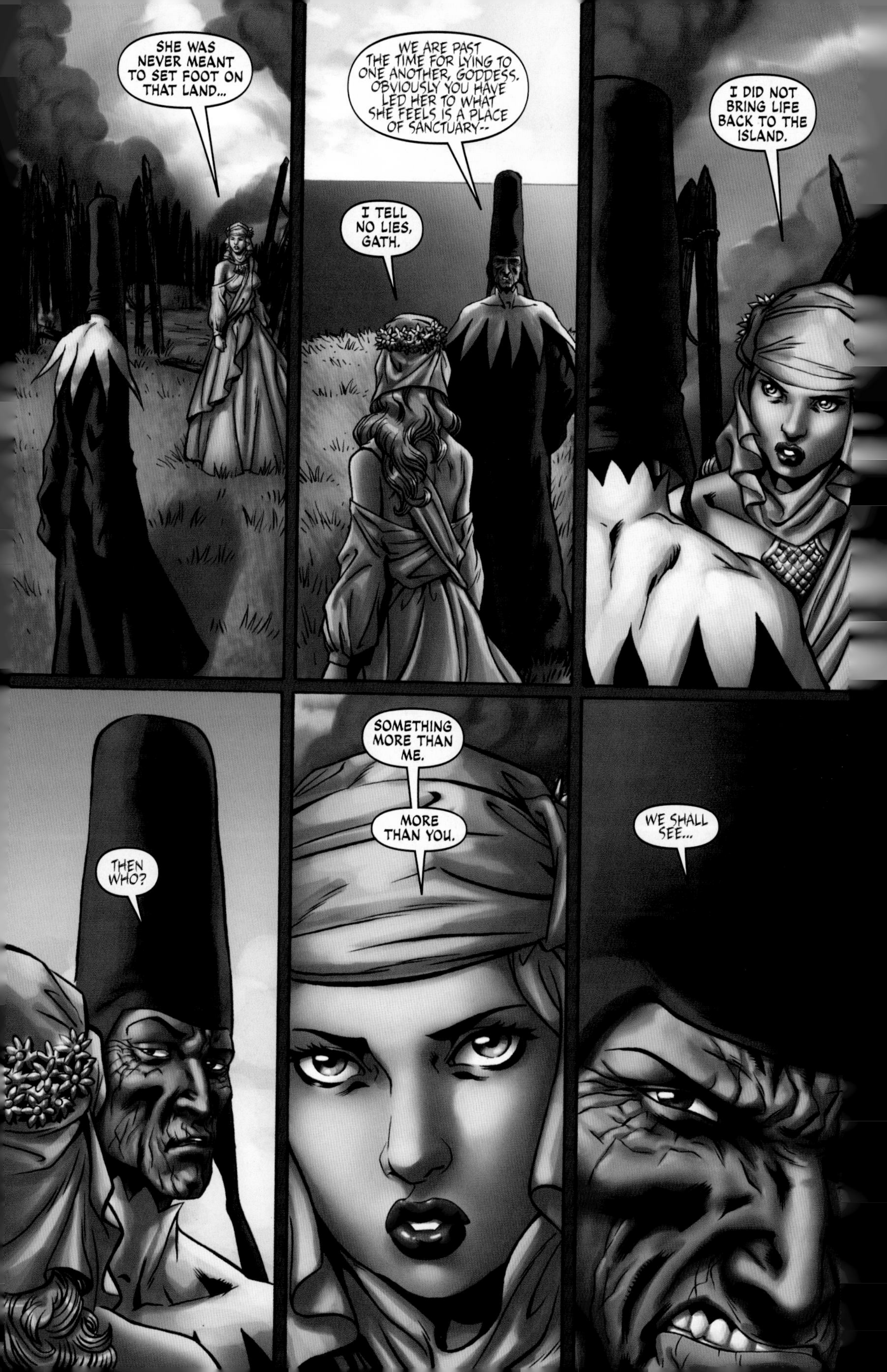
SHE WAS NEVER MEANT TO SET FOOT ON THAT LAND...
WE ARE PAST THE TIME FOR LYING TO ONE ANOTHER, GODDESS. OBVIOUSLY YOU HAVE LED HER TO WHAT SHE FEELS IS A PLACE OF SANCTUARY--
I TELL NO LIES, GATH.
I DID NOT BRING LIFE BACK TO THE ISLAND.
THEN WHO?
SOMETHING MORE THAN ME.
MORE THAN YOU.
WE SHALL SEE...

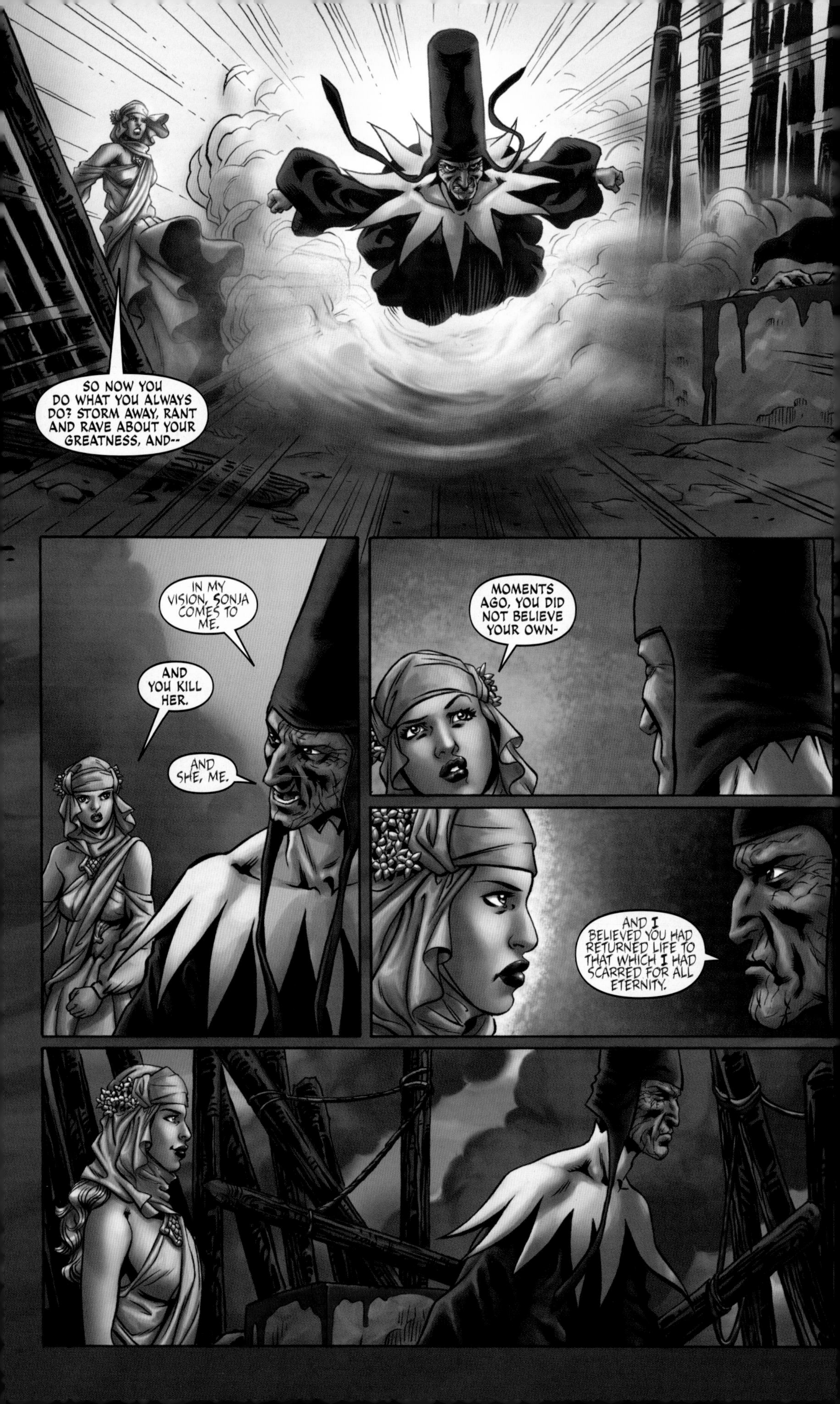

SO NOW YOU DO WHAT YOU ALWAYS DO? STORM AWAY, RANT AND RAVE ABOUT YOUR GREATNESS, AND--
IN MY VISION, SONJA COMES TO ME.
AND YOU KILL HER.
AND SHE, ME.
MOMENTS AGO, YOU DID NOT BELIEVE YOUR OWN-
AND I BELIEVED YOU HAD RETURNED LIFE TO THAT WHICH I HAD SCARRED FOR ALL ETERNITY.

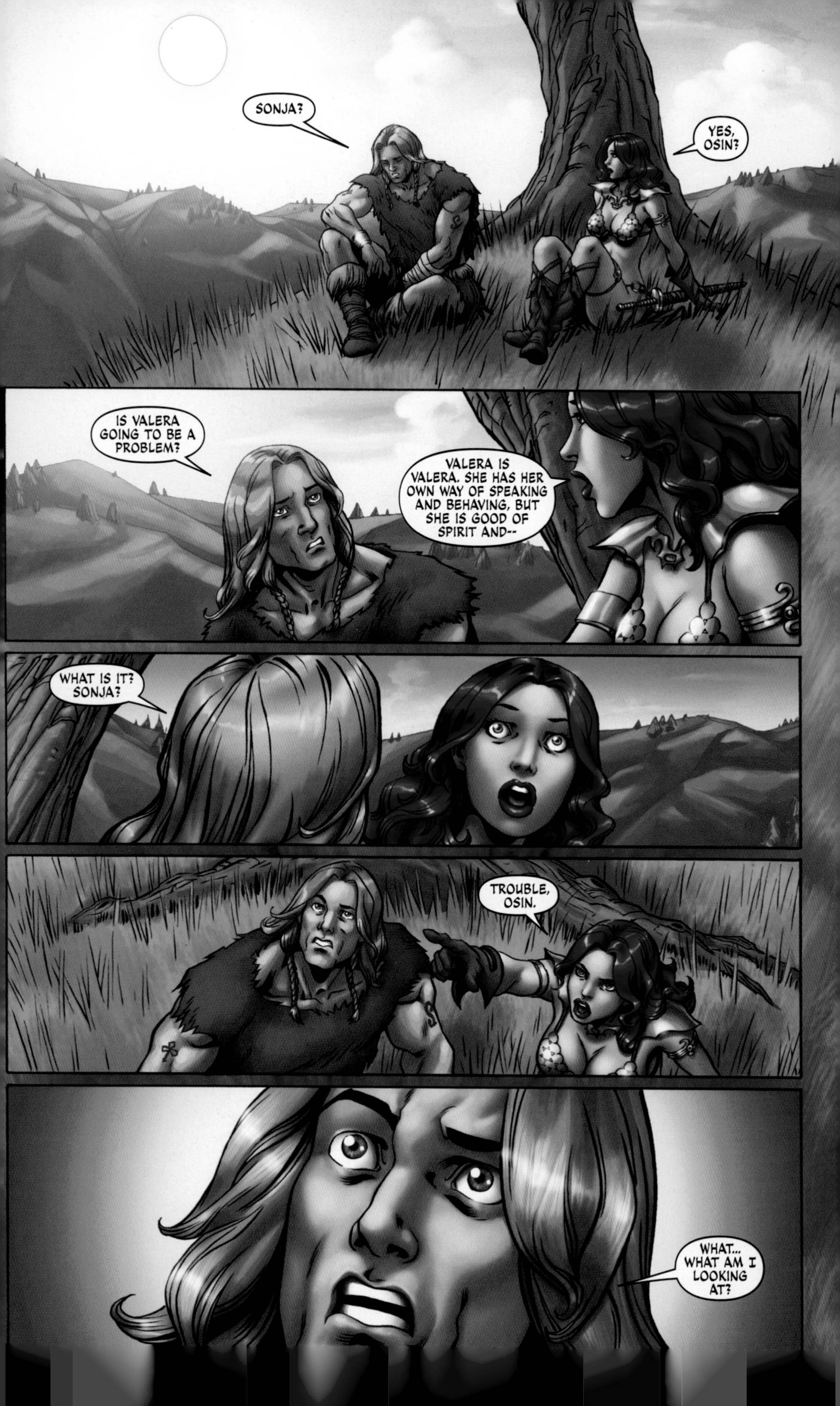
SONJA?
YES, OSIN?
IS VALERA GOING TO BE A PROBLEM?
VALERA IS VALERA. SHE HAS HER OWN WAY OF SPEAKING AND BEHAVING, BUT SHE IS GOOD OF SPIRIT AND--
WHAT IS IT? SONJA?
TROUBLE, OSIN.
WHAT... WHAT AM I LOOKING AT?

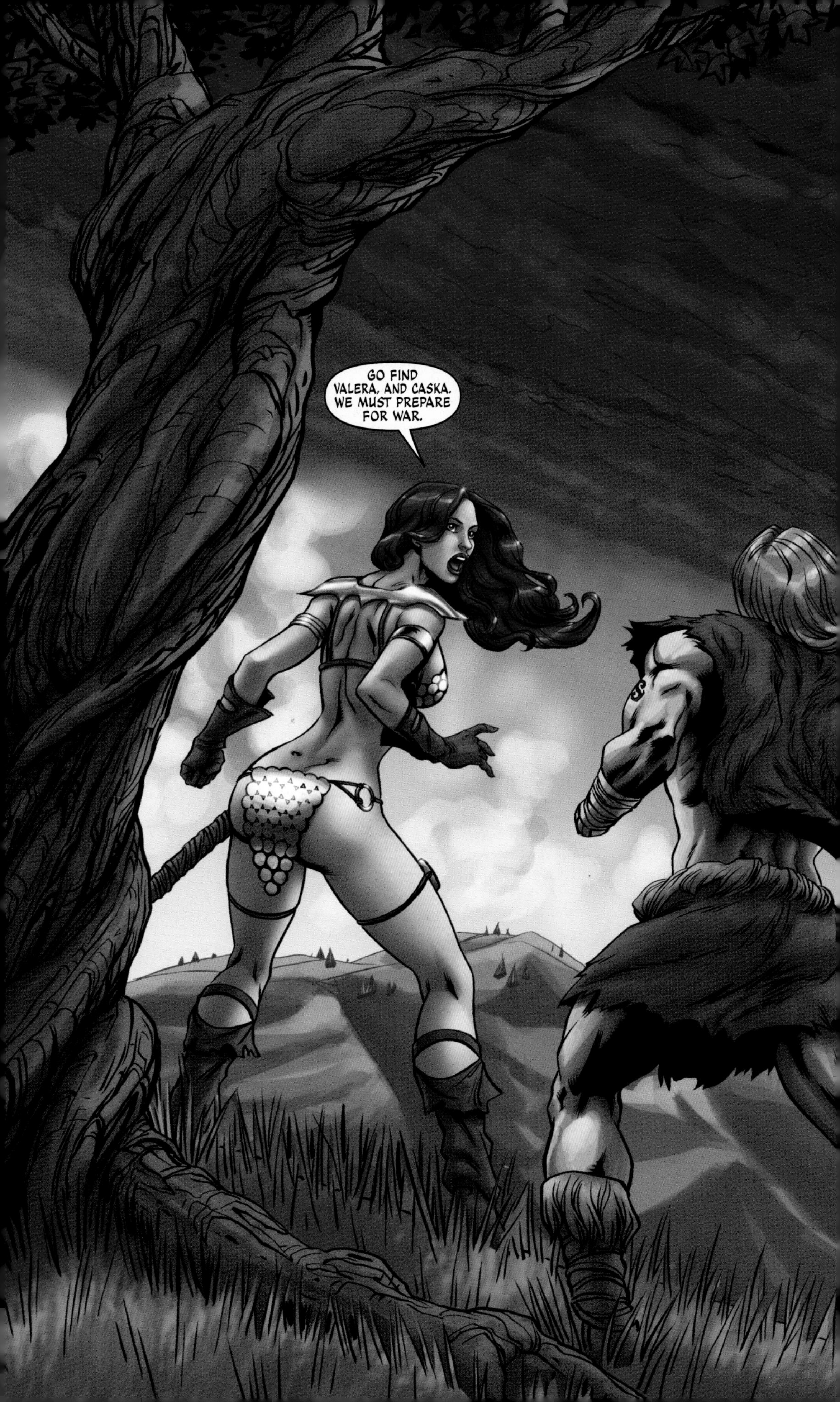
GO FIND VALERA, AND CASKA. WE MUST PREPARE FOR WAR.

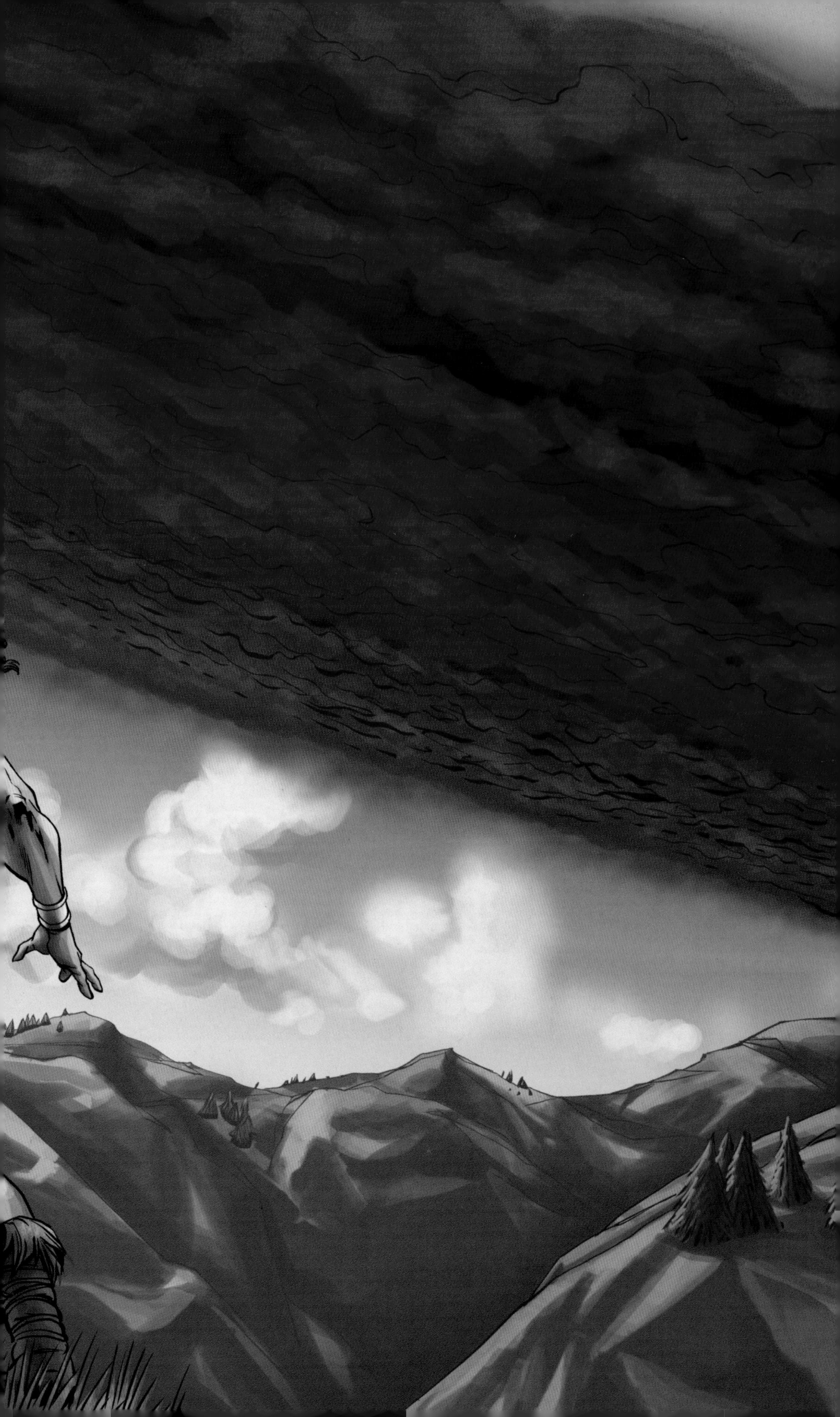

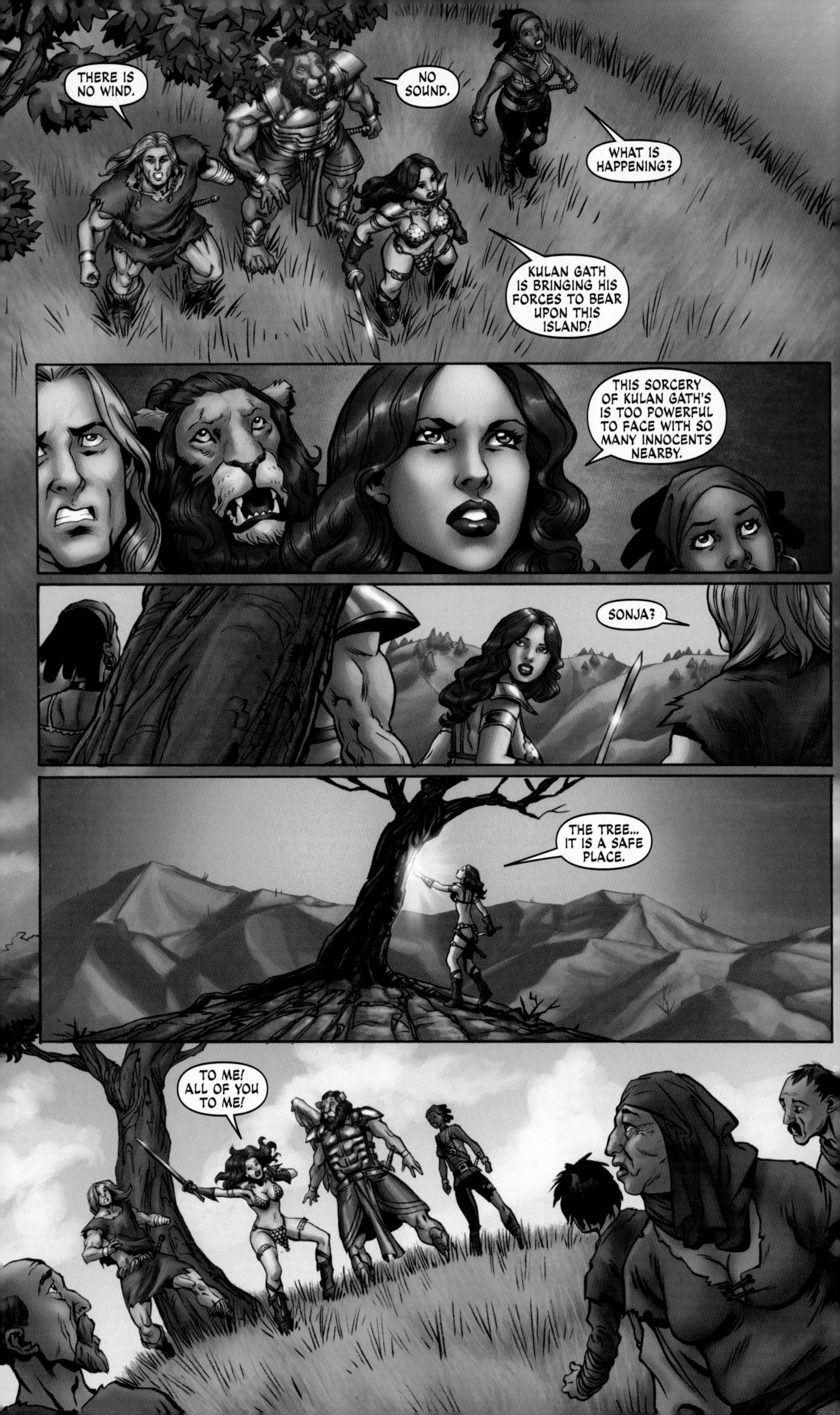
THERE IS NO WIND.
NO SOUND.
WHAT IS HAPPENING?
KULAN GATH IS BRINGING HIS FORCES TO BEAR UPON THIS ISLAND!
THIS SORCERY OF KULAN GATH'S IS TOO POWERFUL TO FACE WITH SO MANY INNOCENTS NEARBY.
SONJA?
THE TREE... IT IS A SAFE PLACE.
TO ME! ALL OF YOU TO ME!

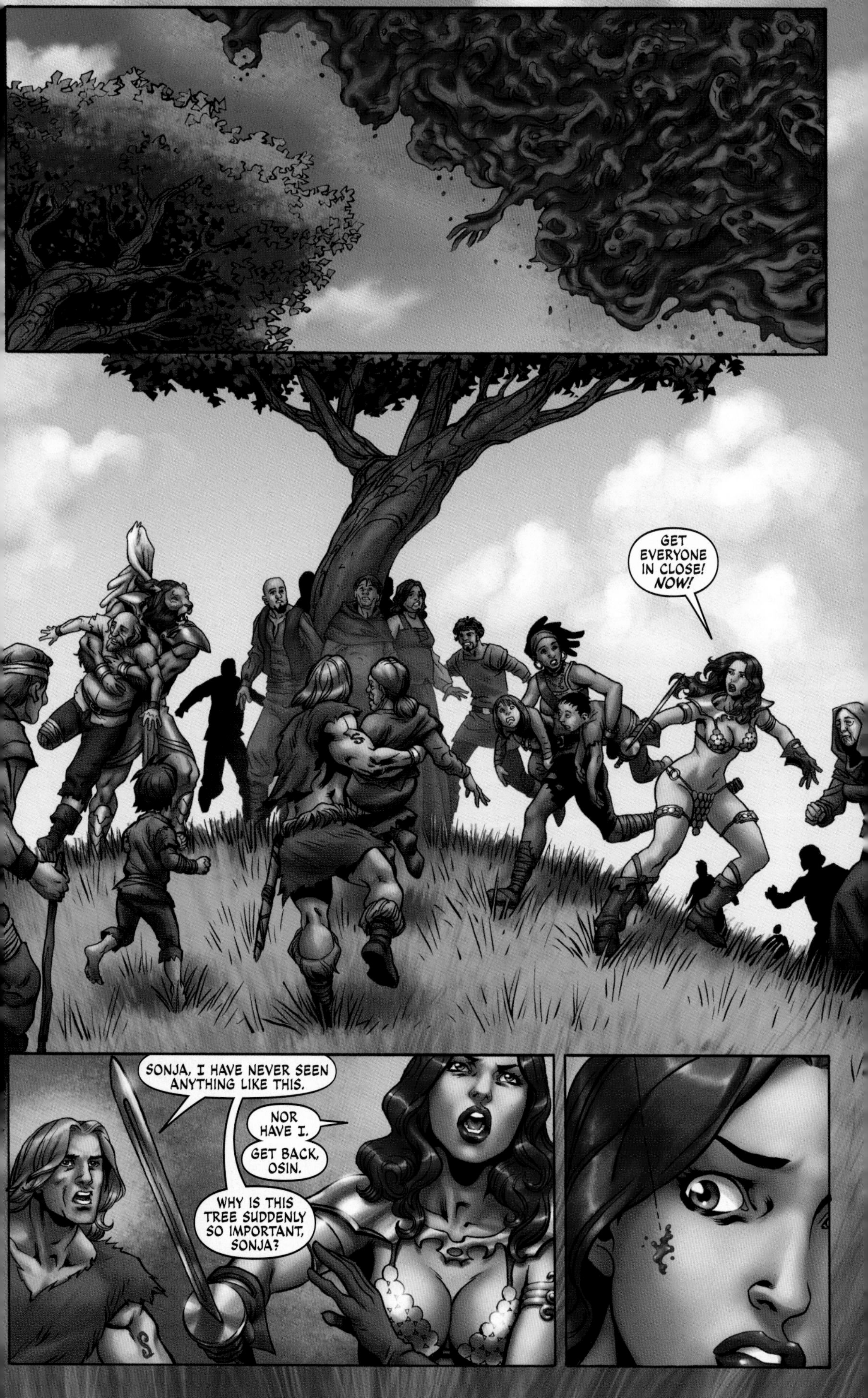
GET EVERYONE IN CLOSE! NOW!
SONJA, I HAVE NEVER SEEN ANYTHING LIKE THIS.
NOR HAVE I.
GET BACK, OSIN.
WHY IS THIS TREE SUDDENLY SO IMPORTANT, SONJA?

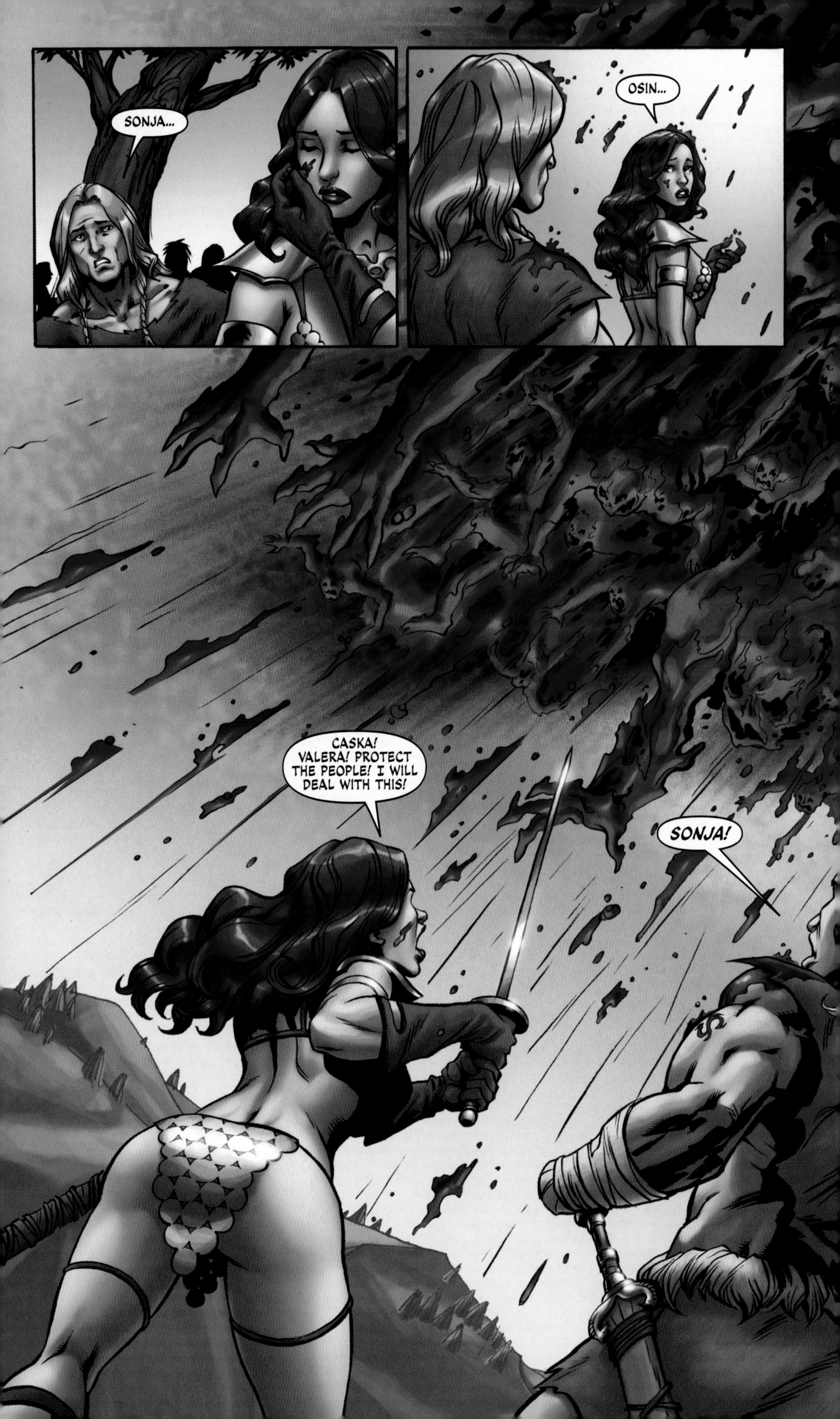
SONJA...
OSIN...
CASKA! VALERA! PROTECT THE PEOPLE! I WILL DEAL WITH THIS!
SONJA!

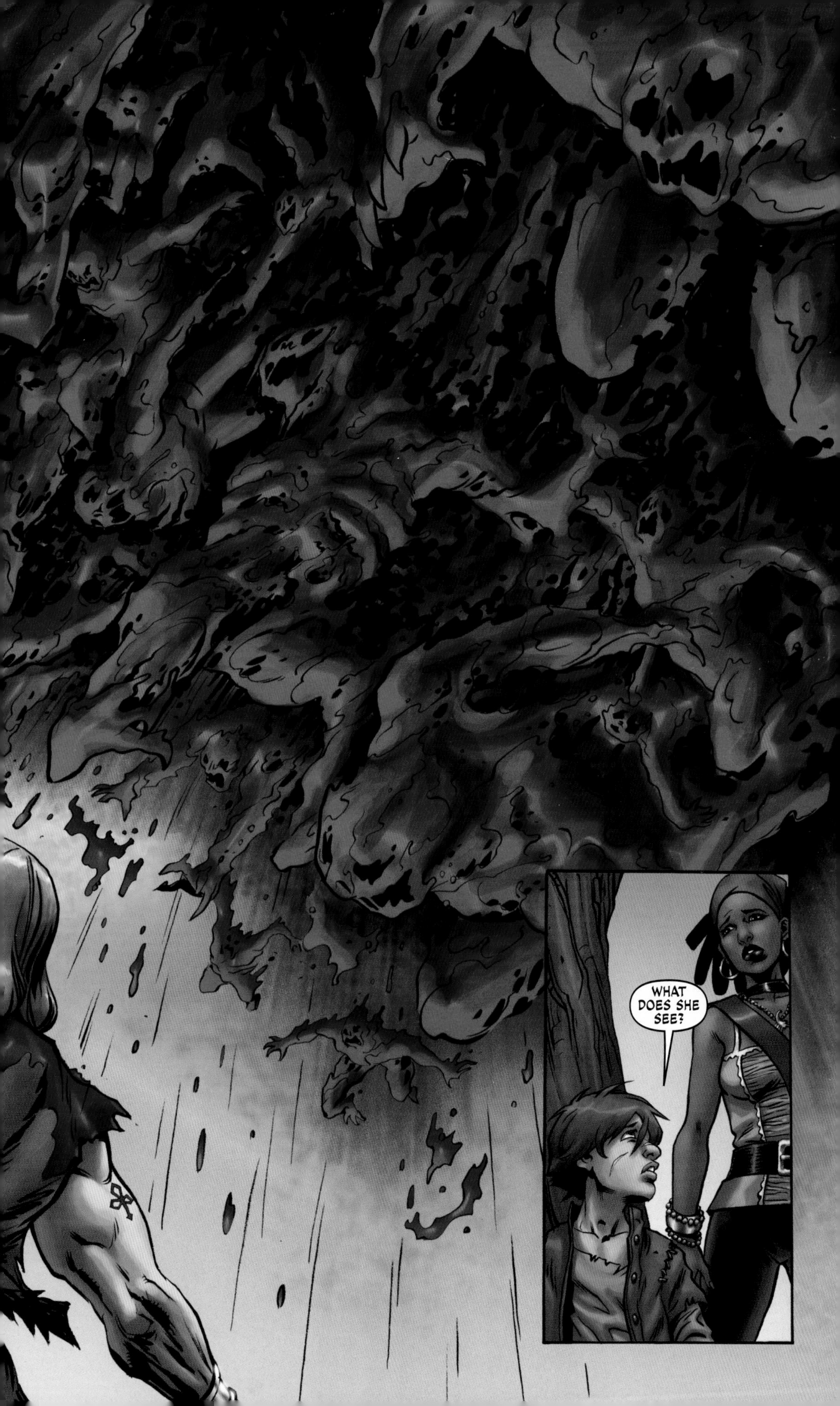
WHAT DOES SHE SEE?

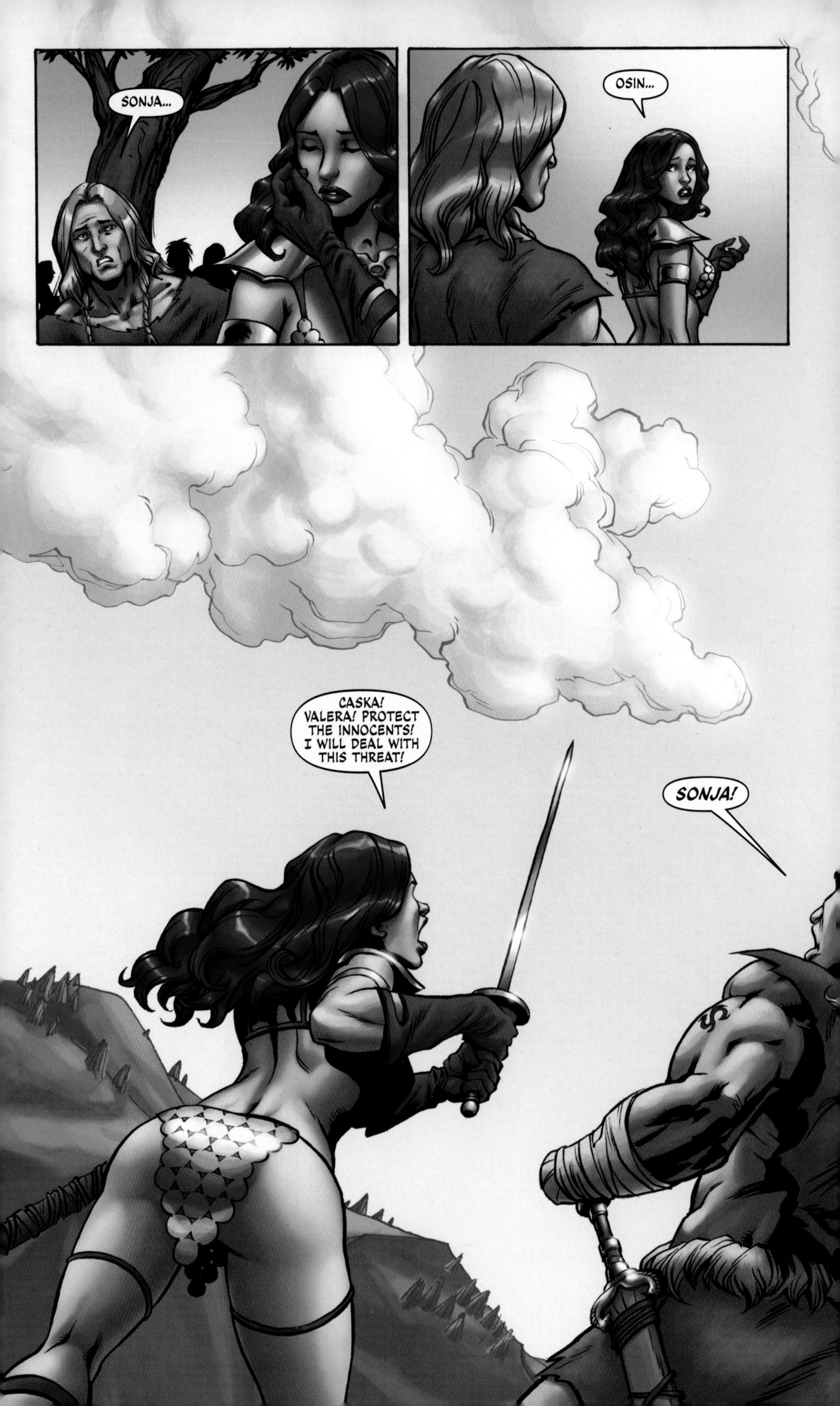
SONJA...
OSIN...
CASKA! VALERA! PROTECT THE INNOCENTS! I WILL DEAL WITH THIS THREAT!
SONJA!

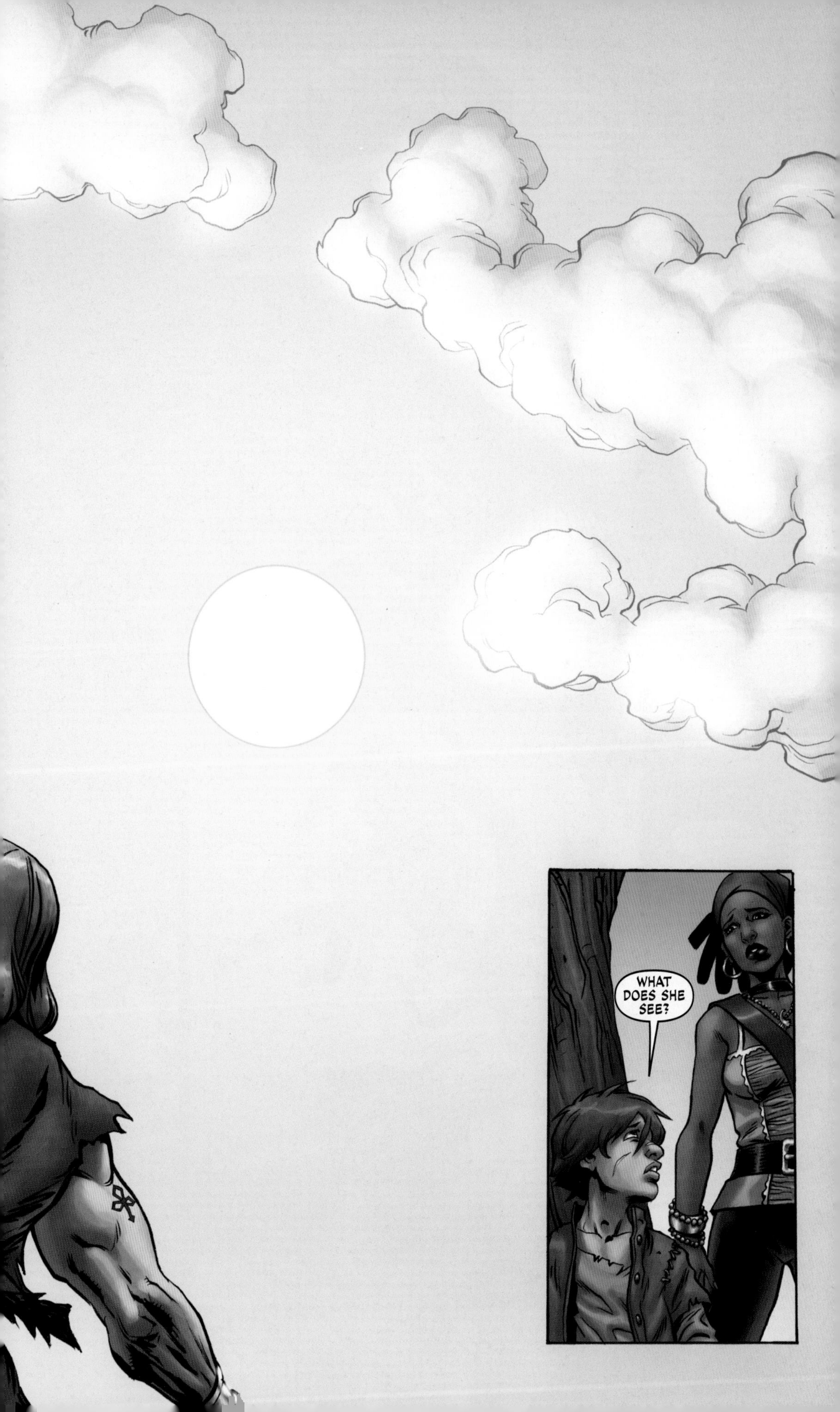
WHAT DOES SHE SEE?

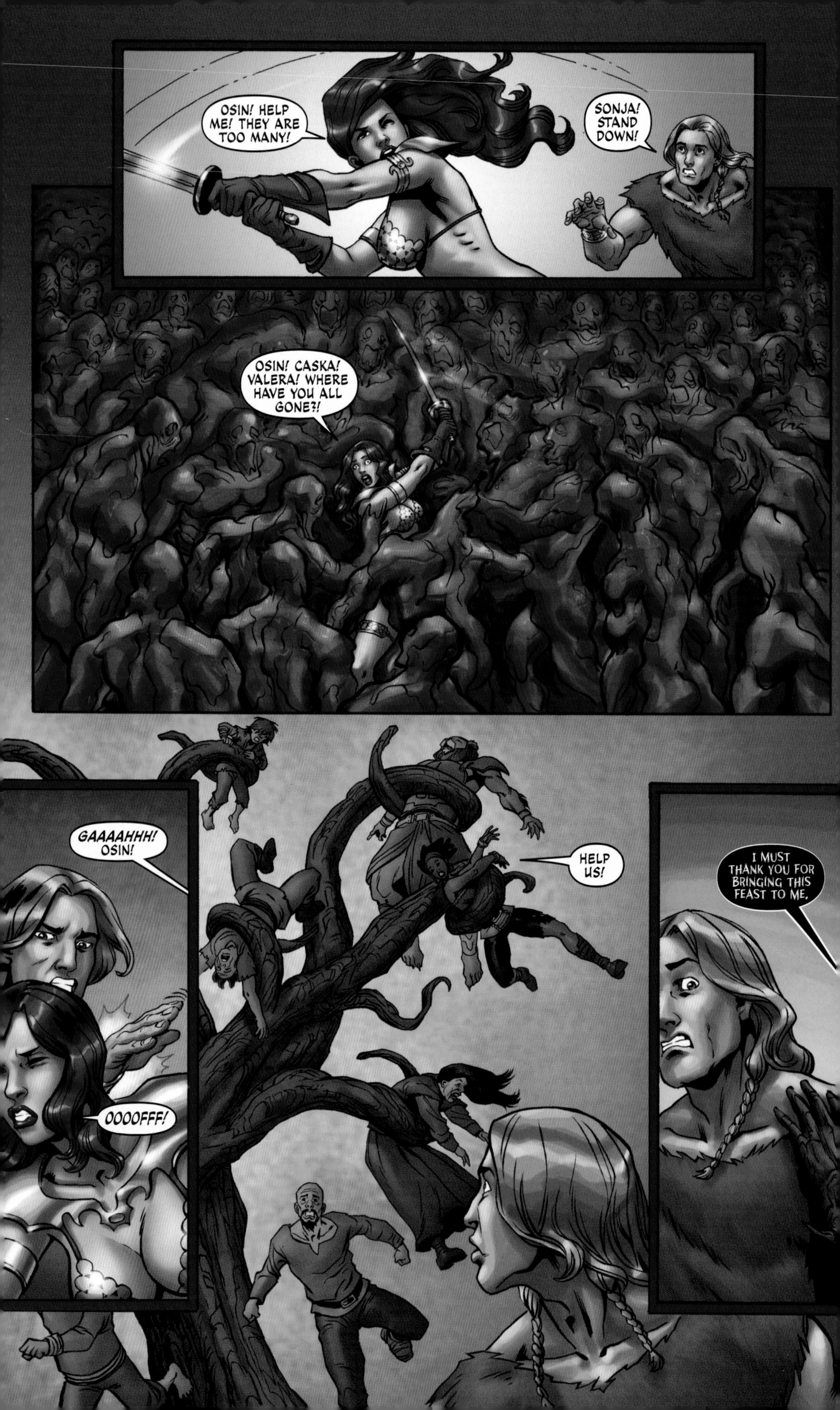
OSIN! HELP ME! THEY ARE TOO MANY!
SONJA! STAND DOWN!
OSIN! CASKA! VALERA! WHERE HAVE YOU ALL GONE?!
GAAAAHHH! OSIN!
OOOOFFF!
HELP US!
I MUST THANK YOU FOR BRINGING THIS FEAST TO ME.

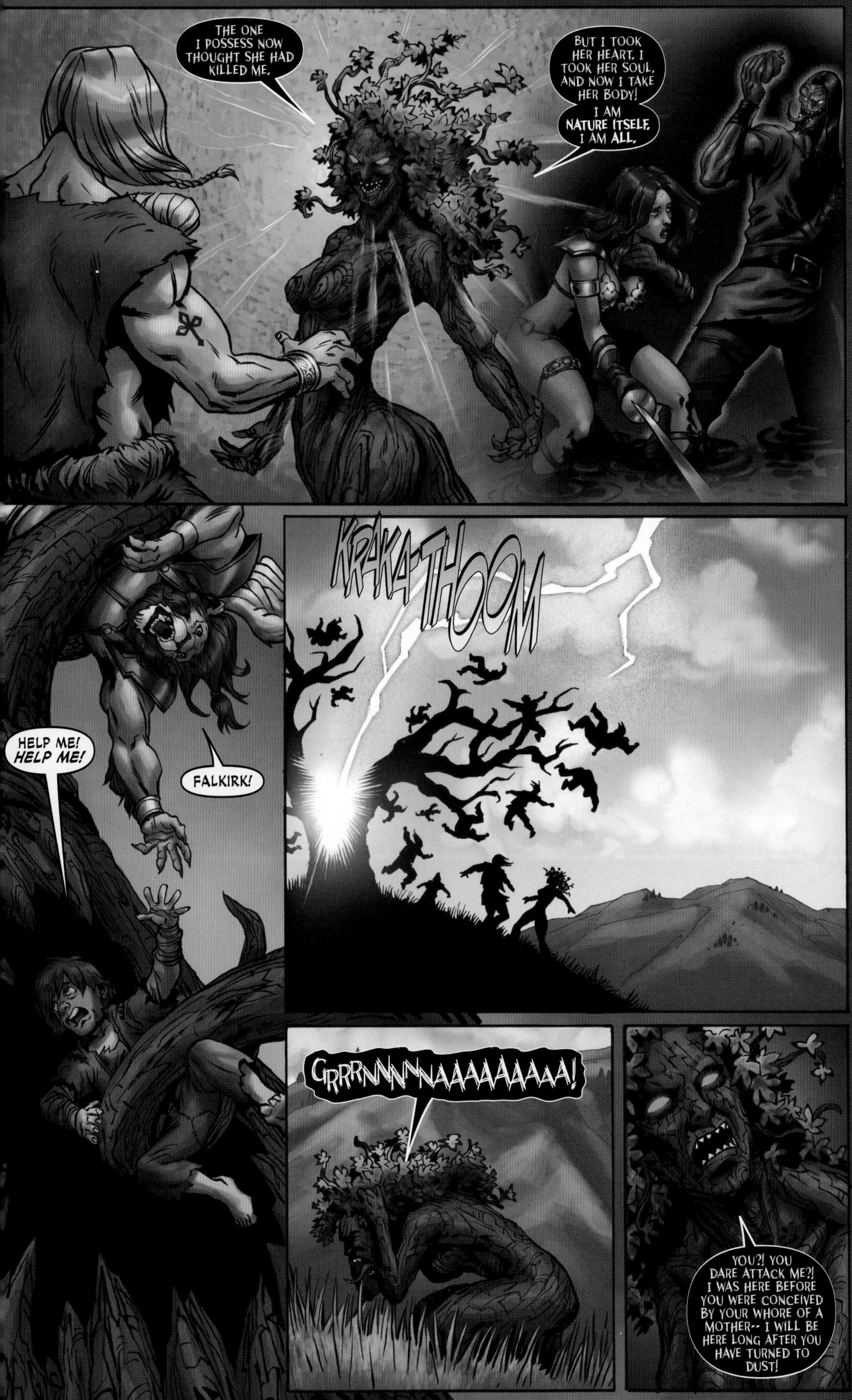

THE ONE I POSSESS NOW THOUGHT SHE HAD KILLED ME.
BUT I TOOK HER HEART. I TOOK HER SOUL, AND NOW I TAKE HER BODY! I AM NATURE ITSELF. I AM ALL.
HELP ME! HELP ME!
FALKIRK!
KRAKA-THOOM
GRRRNNNNAAAAAAAAA!
YOU?! YOU DARE ATTACK ME?! I WAS HERE BEFORE YOU WERE CONCEIVED BY YOUR WHORE OF A MOTHER-- I WILL BE HERE LONG AFTER YOU HAVE TURNED TO DUST!

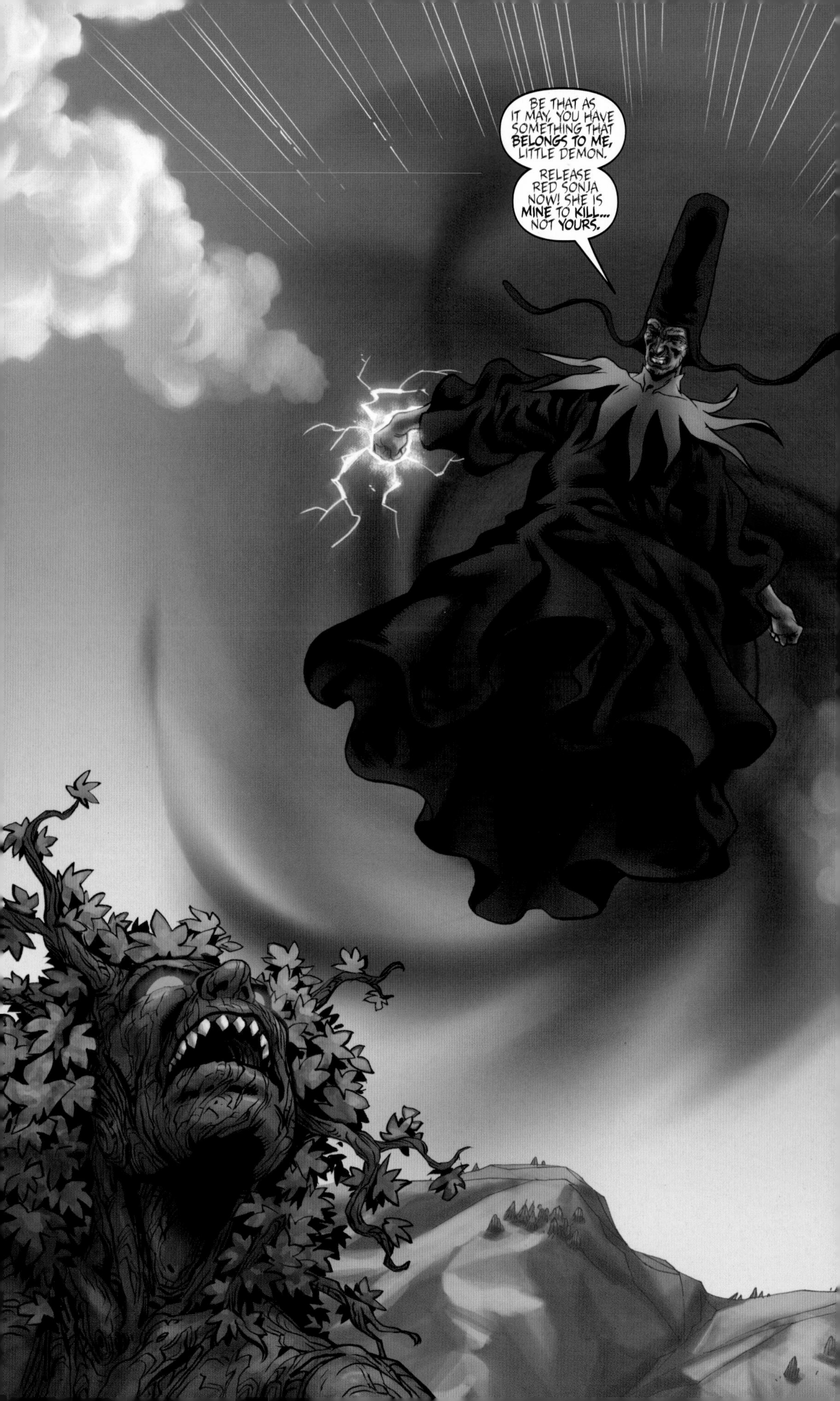
BE THAT AS IT MAY, YOU HAVE SOMETHING THAT BELONGS TO ME, LITTLE DEMON.
RELEASE RED SONJA NOW! SHE IS MINE TO KILL... NOT YOURS.

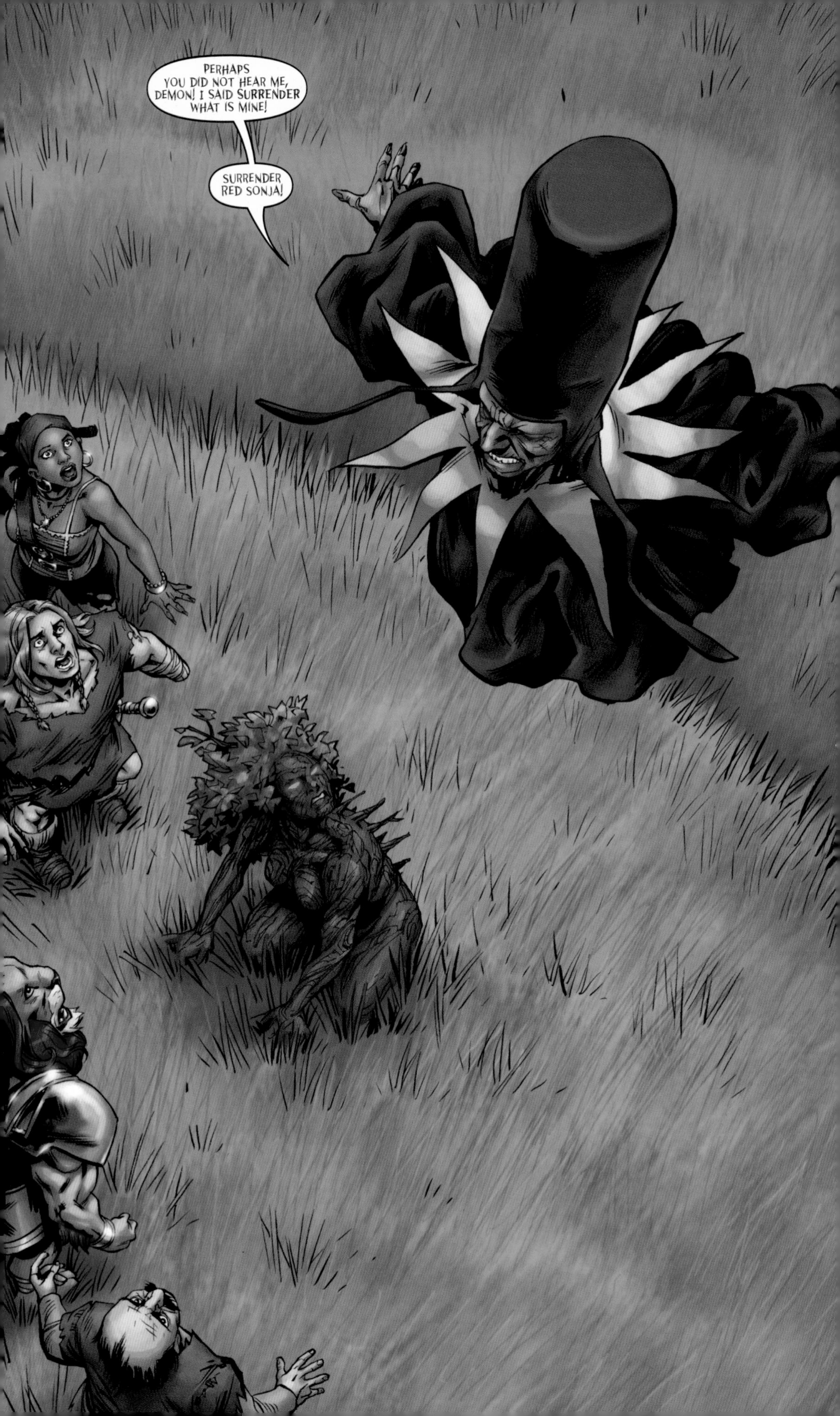
PERHAPS YOU DID NOT HEAR ME, DEMON! I SAID SURRENDER WHAT IS MINE!
SURRENDER RED SONJA!

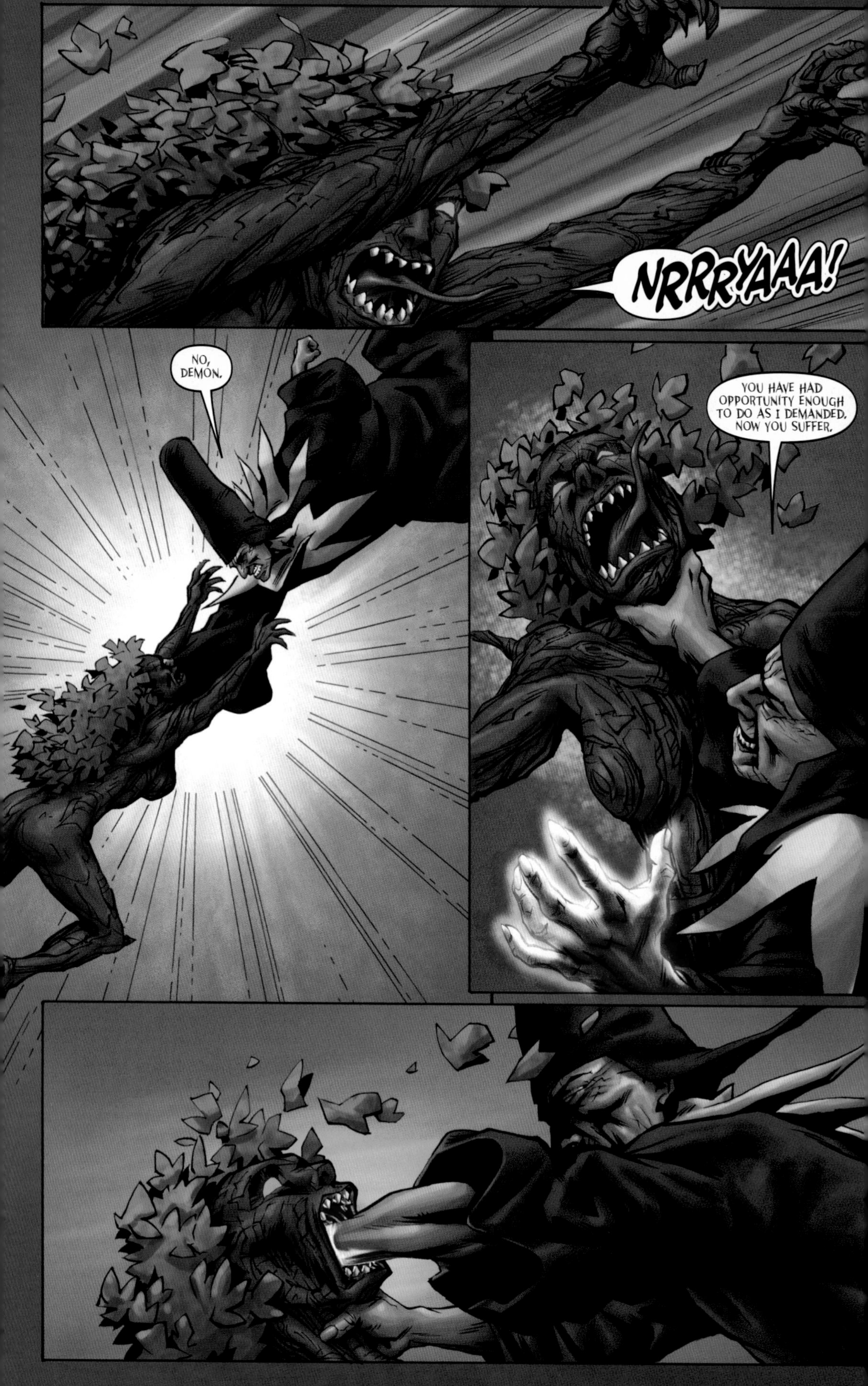
NRRRYAAA!
NO, DEMON.
YOU HAVE HAD OPPORTUNITY ENOUGH TO DO AS I DEMANDED. NOW YOU SUFFER.

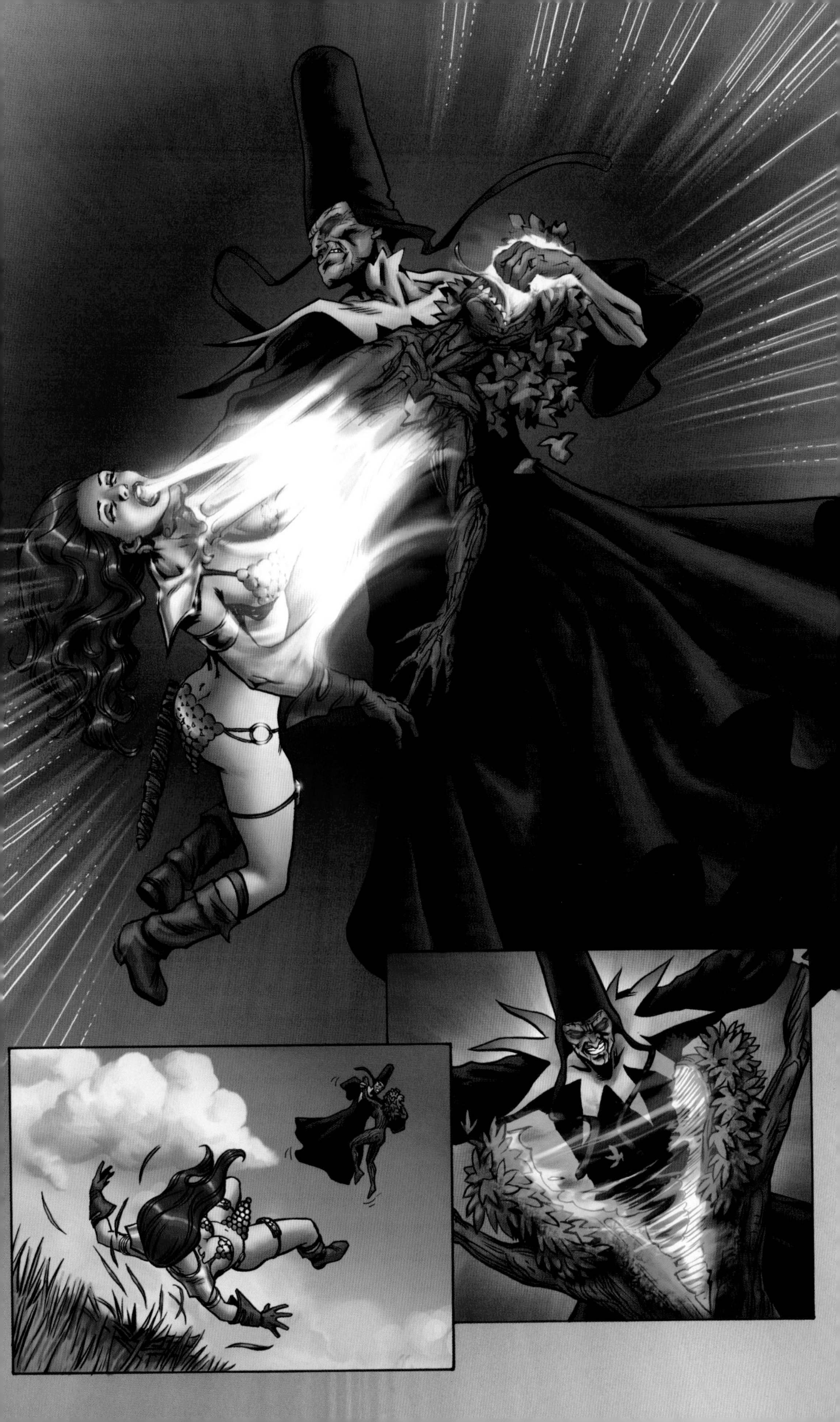

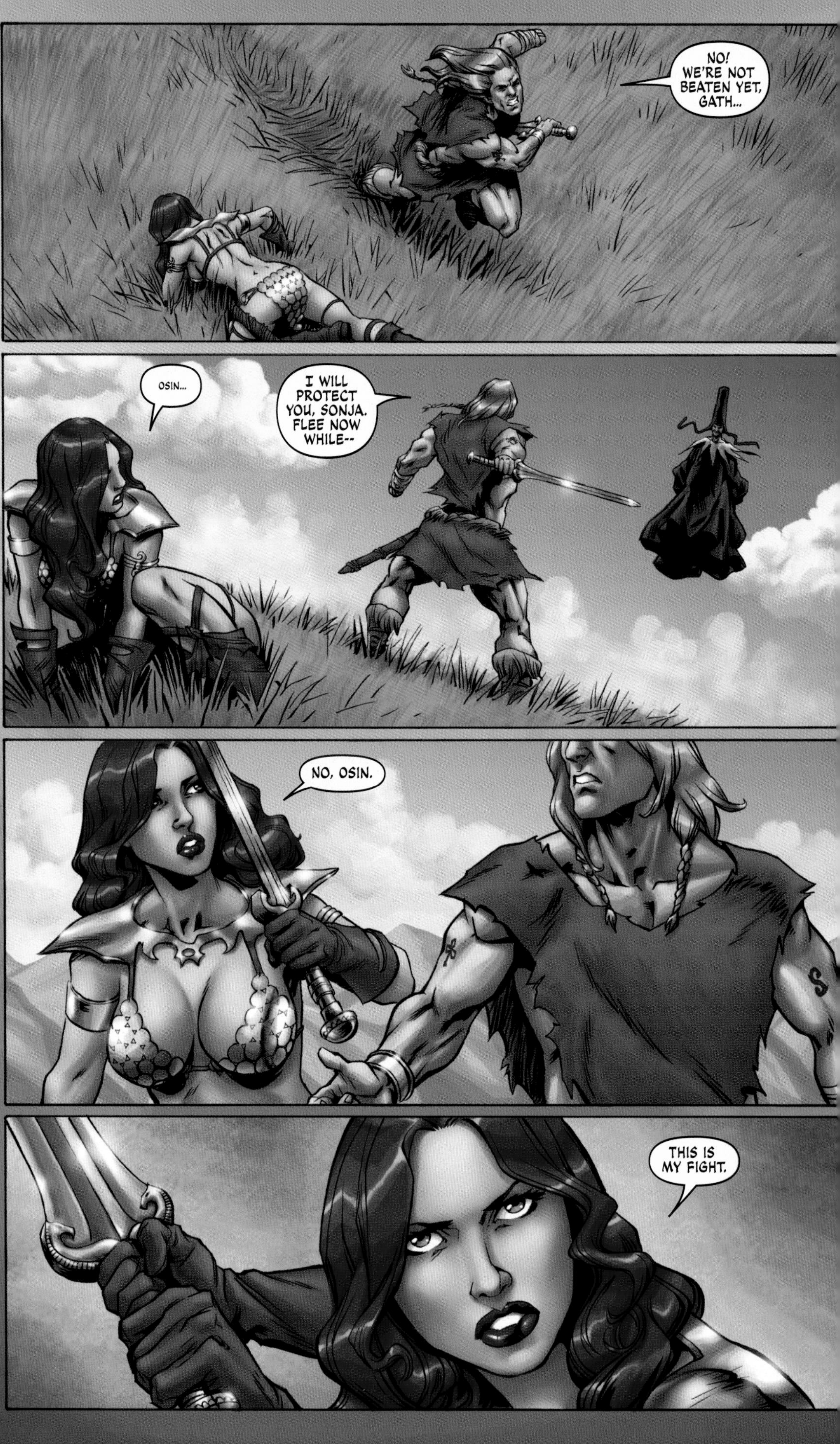

NO! WE'RE NOT BEATEN YET, GATH...
OSIN...
I WILL PROTECT YOU, SONJA. FLEE NOW WHILE--
NO, OSIN.
THIS IS MY FIGHT.

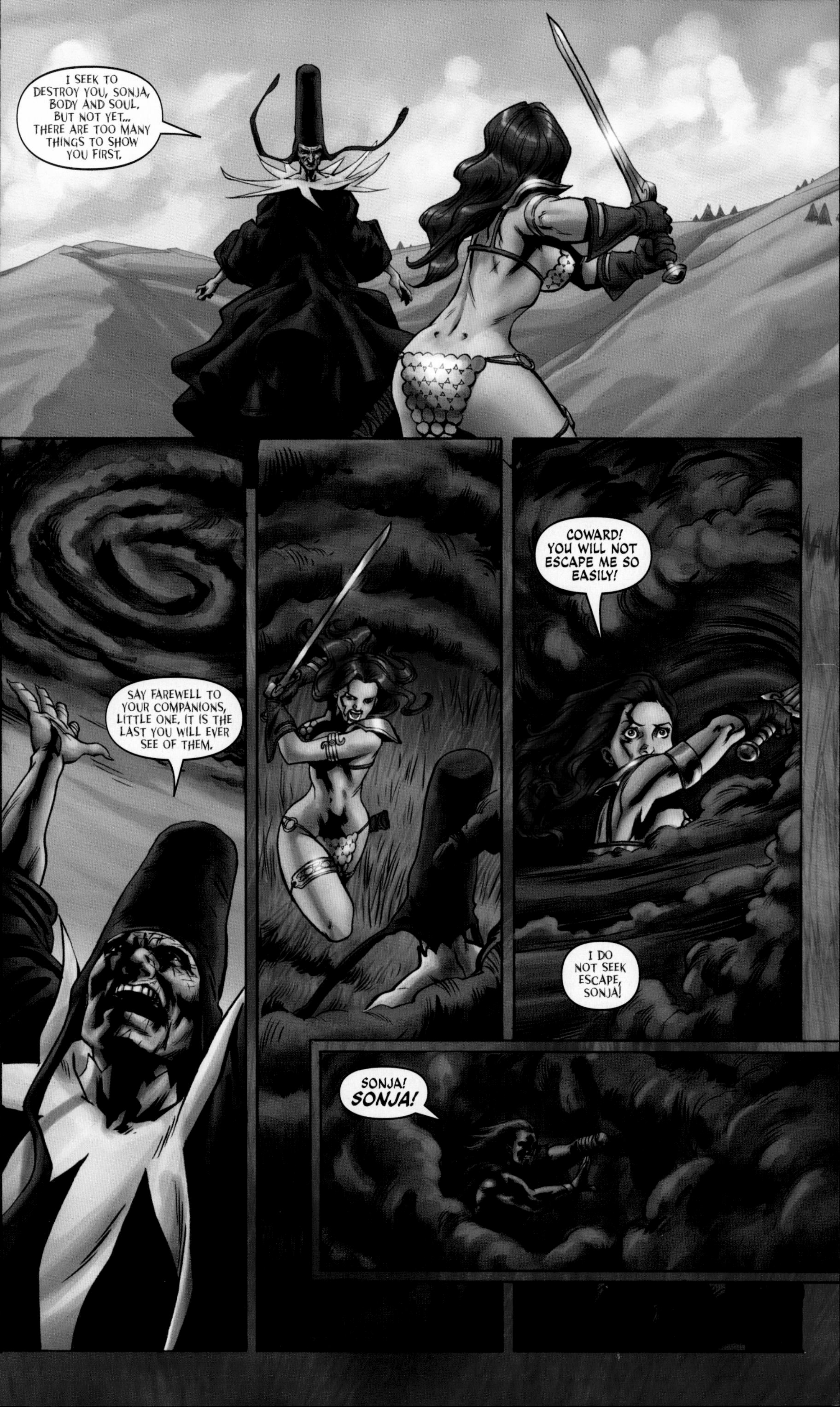
I SEEK TO DESTROY YOU, SONJA, BODY AND SOUL, BUT NOT YET... THERE ARE TOO MANY THINGS TO SHOW YOU FIRST.
SAY FAREWELL TO YOUR COMPANIONS, LITTLE ONE, IT IS THE LAST YOU WILL EVER SEE OF THEM.
COWARD! YOU WILL NOT ESCAPE ME SO EASILY!
I DO NOT SEEK ESCAPE, SONJA!
SONJA! SONJA!

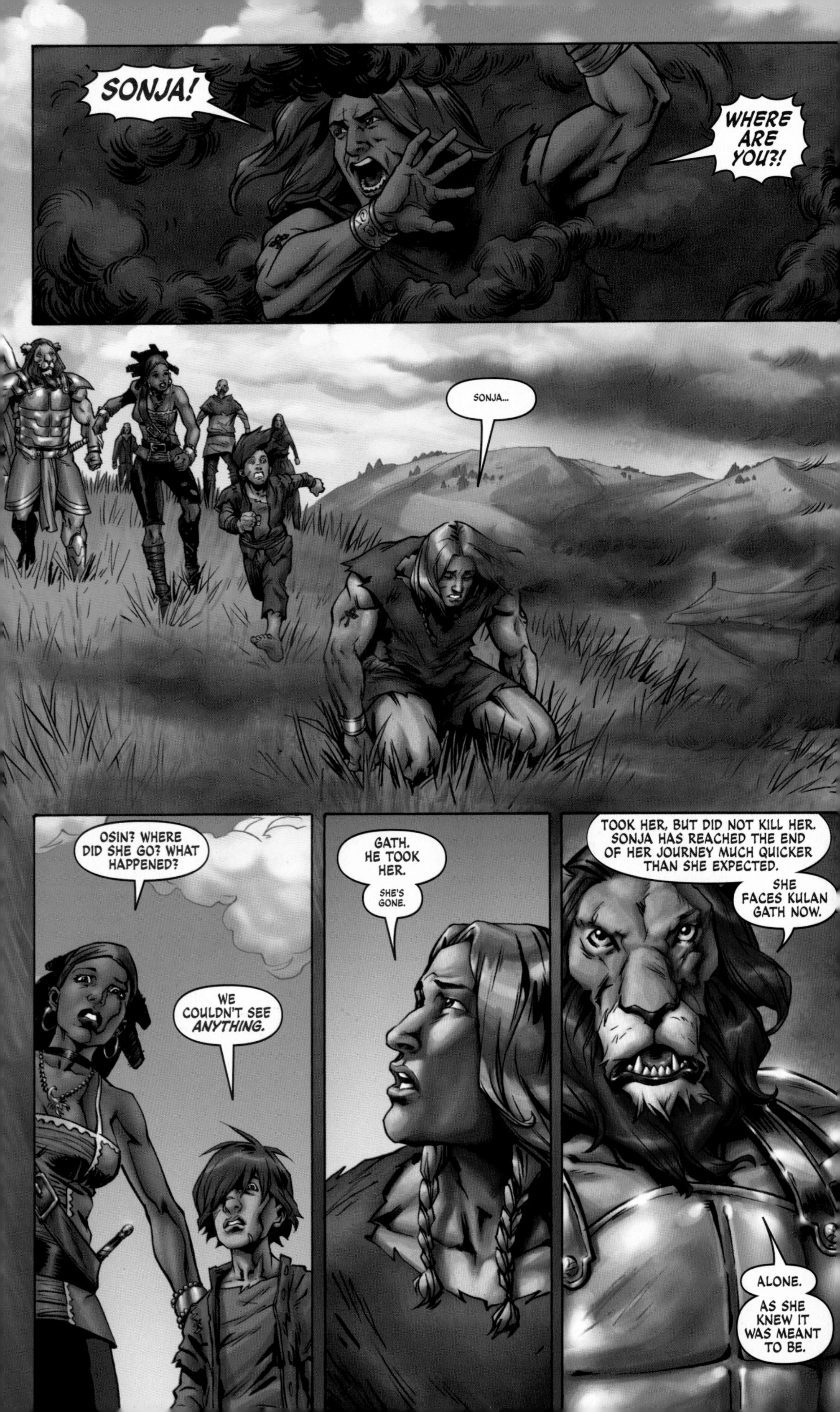
SONJA!
WHERE ARE YOU?!
SONJA...
OSIN? WHERE DID SHE GO? WHAT HAPPENED?
WE COULDN'T SEE *ANYTHING.*
GATH. HE TOOK HER.
SHE'S GONE.
TOOK HER, BUT DID NOT KILL HER. SONJA HAS REACHED THE END OF HER JOURNEY MUCH QUICKER THAN SHE EXPECTED.
SHE FACES KULAN GATH NOW.
ALONE.
AS SHE KNEW IT WAS MEANT TO BE.

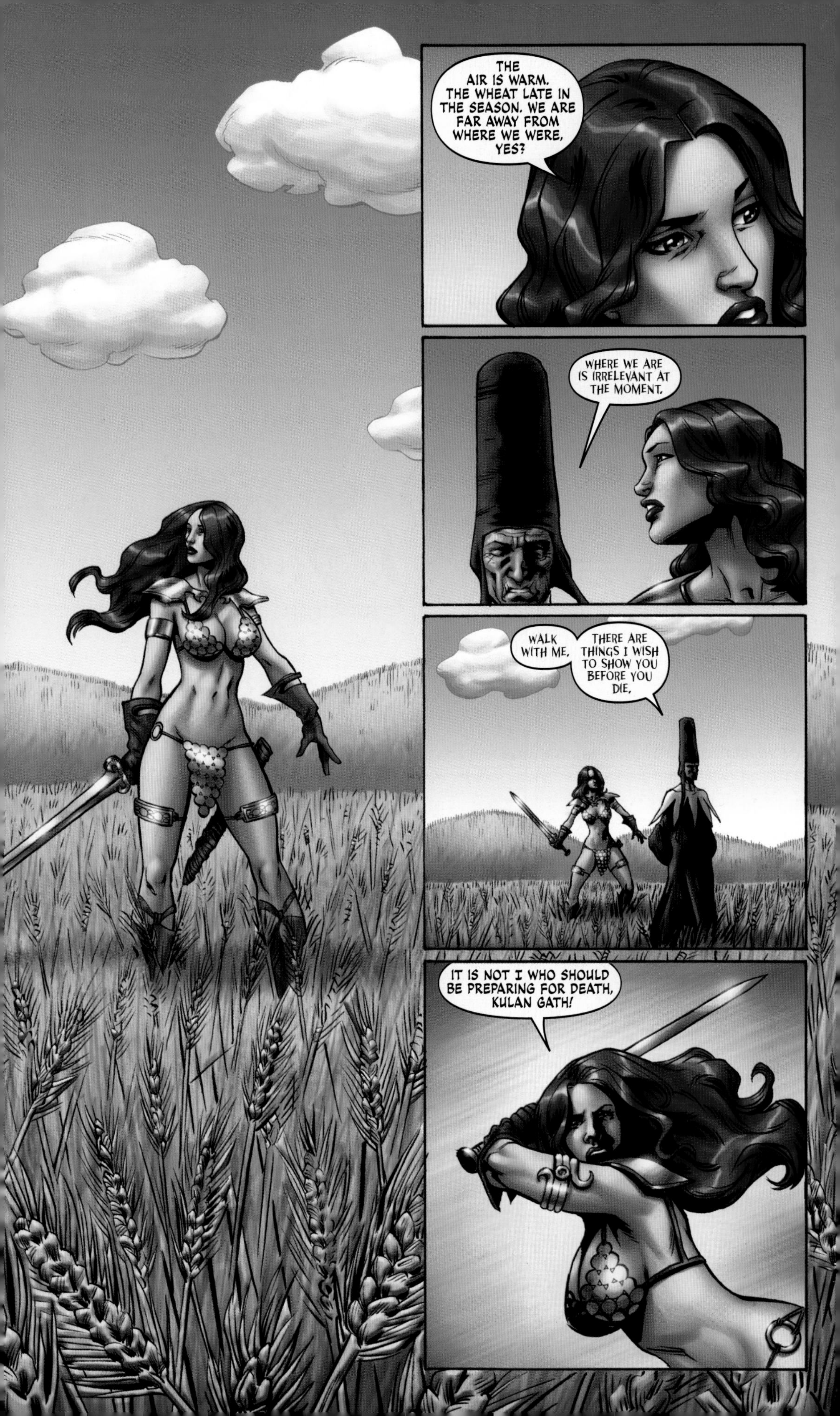
THE AIR IS WARM. THE WHEAT LATE IN THE SEASON. WE ARE FAR AWAY FROM WHERE WE WERE, YES?
WHERE WE ARE IS IRRELEVANT AT THE MOMENT.
WALK WITH ME.
THERE ARE THINGS I WISH TO SHOW YOU BEFORE YOU DIE.
IT IS NOT I WHO SHOULD BE PREPARING FOR DEATH, KULAN GATH!

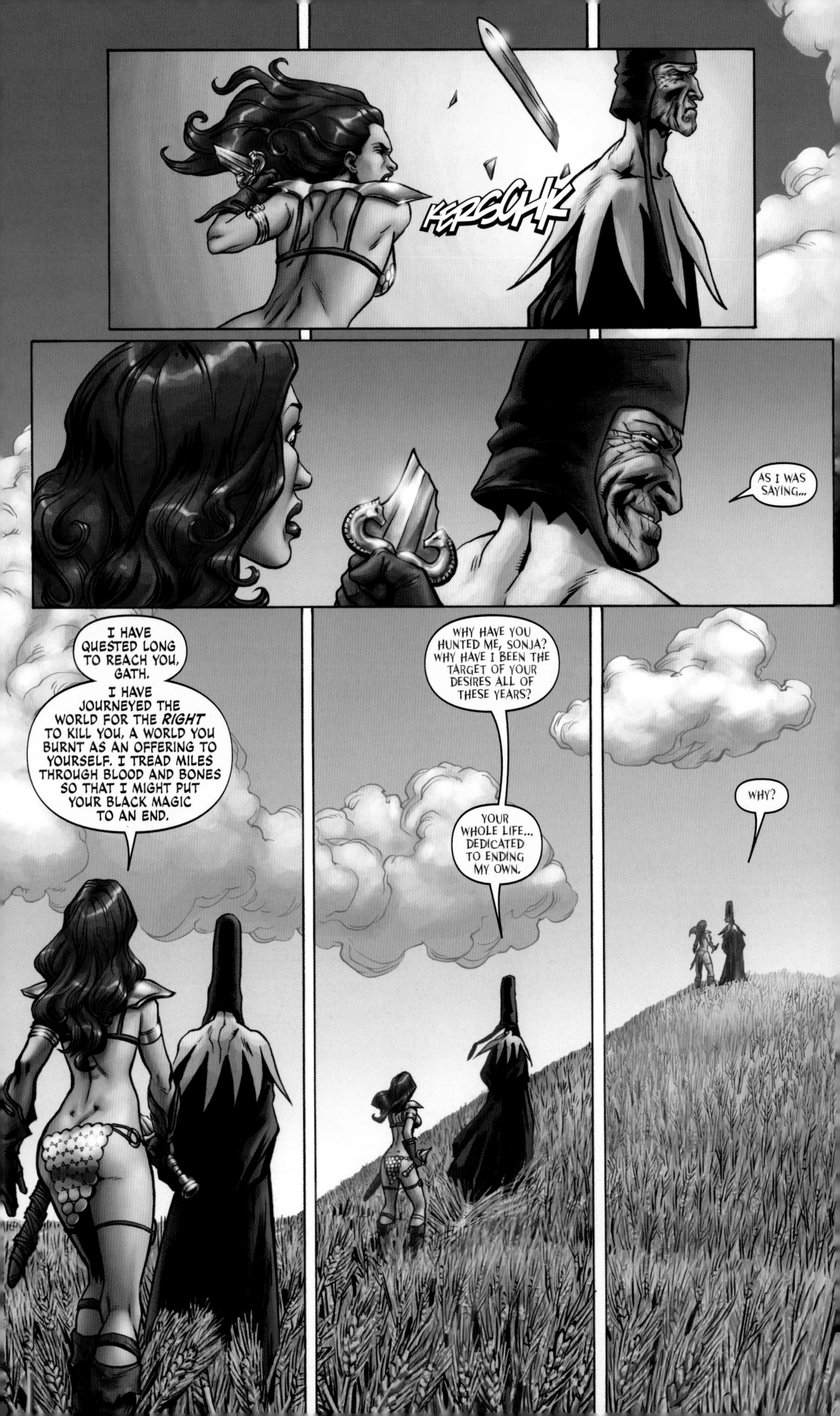
KERSCHK
AS I WAS SAYING...
I HAVE QUESTED LONG TO REACH YOU, GATH.
I HAVE JOURNEYED THE WORLD FOR THE *RIGHT* TO KILL YOU, A WORLD YOU BURNT AS AN OFFERING TO YOURSELF. I TREAD MILES THROUGH BLOOD AND BONES SO THAT I MIGHT PUT YOUR BLACK MAGIC TO AN END.
WHY HAVE YOU HUNTED ME, SONJA? WHY HAVE I BEEN THE TARGET OF YOUR DESIRES ALL OF THESE YEARS?
YOUR WHOLE LIFE... DEDICATED TO ENDING MY OWN.
WHY?

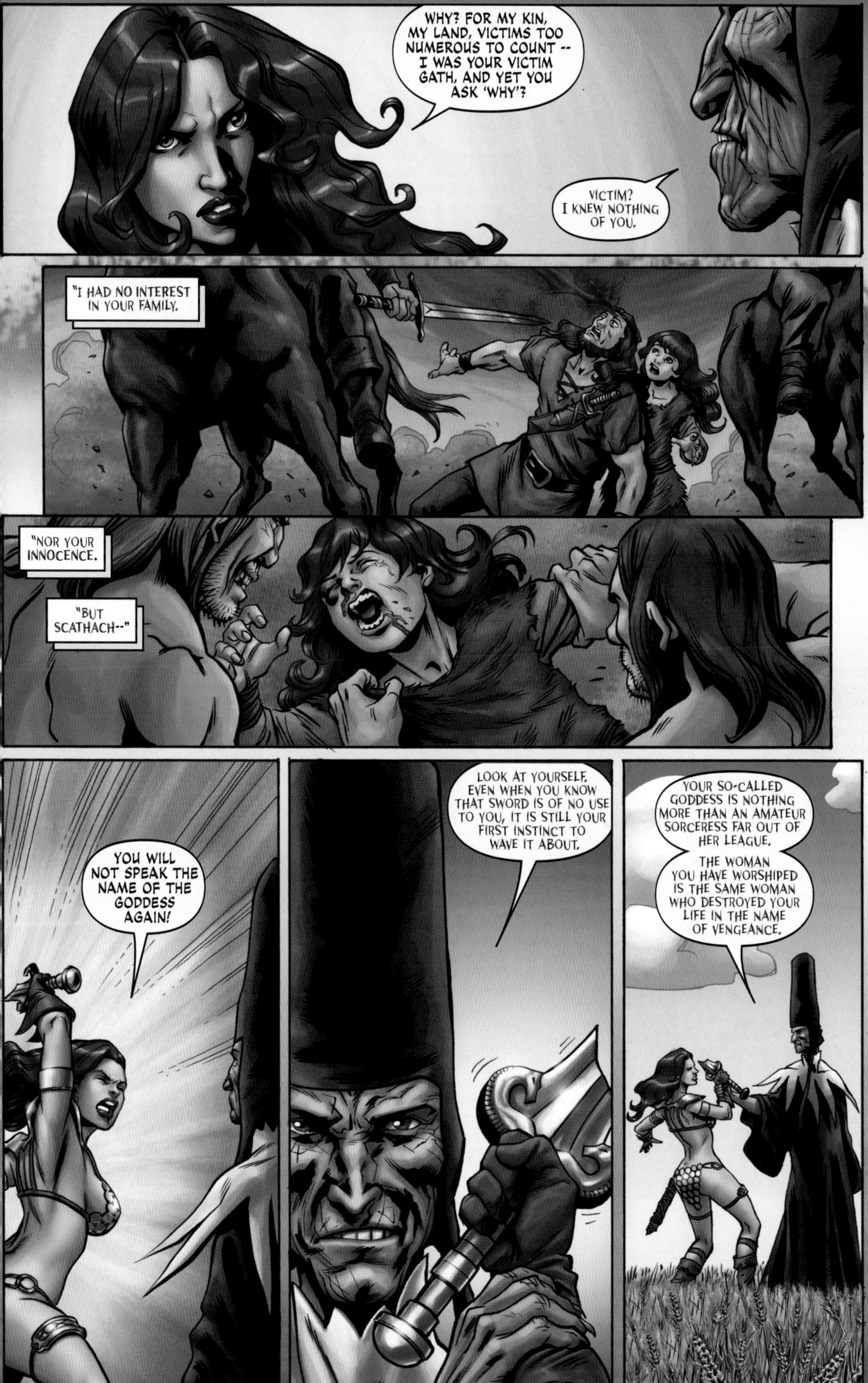
WHY? FOR MY KIN, MY LAND, VICTIMS TOO NUMEROUS TO COUNT -- I WAS YOUR VICTIM GATH, AND YET YOU ASK 'WHY'?
VICTIM? I KNEW NOTHING OF YOU.
"I HAD NO INTEREST IN YOUR FAMILY.
"NOR YOUR INNOCENCE.
"BUT SCATHACH--"
YOU WILL NOT SPEAK THE NAME OF THE GODDESS AGAIN!
LOOK AT YOURSELF. EVEN WHEN YOU KNOW THAT SWORD IS OF NO USE TO YOU, IT IS STILL YOUR FIRST INSTINCT TO WAVE IT ABOUT.
YOUR SO-CALLED GODDESS IS NOTHING MORE THAN AN AMATEUR SORCERESS FAR OUT OF HER LEAGUE.
THE WOMAN YOU HAVE WORSHIPED IS THE SAME WOMAN WHO DESTROYED YOUR LIFE IN THE NAME OF VENGEANCE.

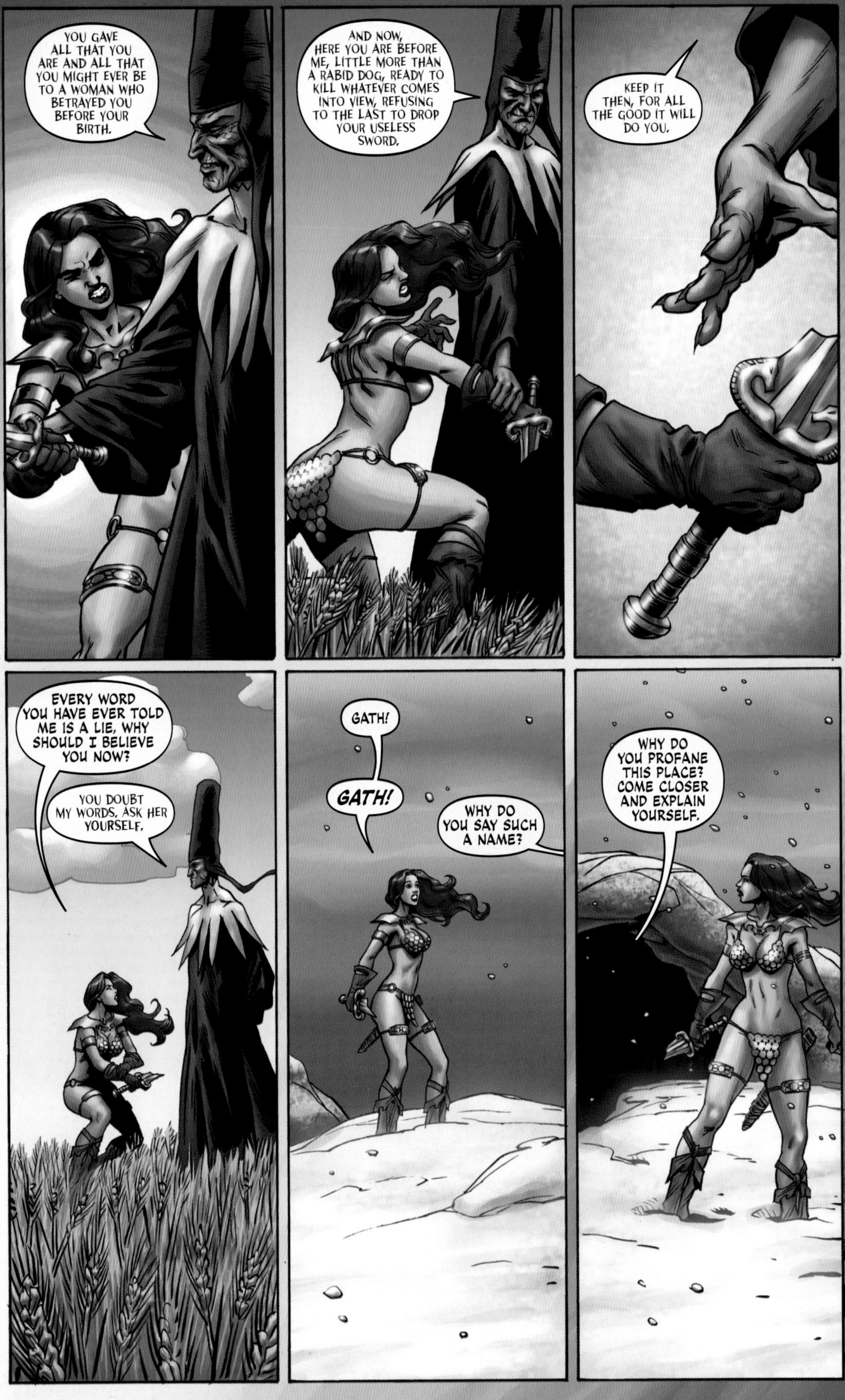
YOU GAVE ALL THAT YOU ARE AND ALL THAT YOU MIGHT EVER BE TO A WOMAN WHO BETRAYED YOU BEFORE YOUR BIRTH.
AND NOW, HERE YOU ARE BEFORE ME, LITTLE MORE THAN A RABID DOG, READY TO KILL WHATEVER COMES INTO VIEW, REFUSING TO THE LAST TO DROP YOUR USELESS SWORD.
KEEP IT THEN, FOR ALL THE GOOD IT WILL DO YOU.
EVERY WORD YOU HAVE EVER TOLD ME IS A LIE, WHY SHOULD I BELIEVE YOU NOW?
YOU DOUBT MY WORDS, ASK HER YOURSELF.
GATH!
GATH!
WHY DO YOU SAY SUCH A NAME?
WHY DO YOU PROFANE THIS PLACE? COME CLOSER AND EXPLAIN YOURSELF.

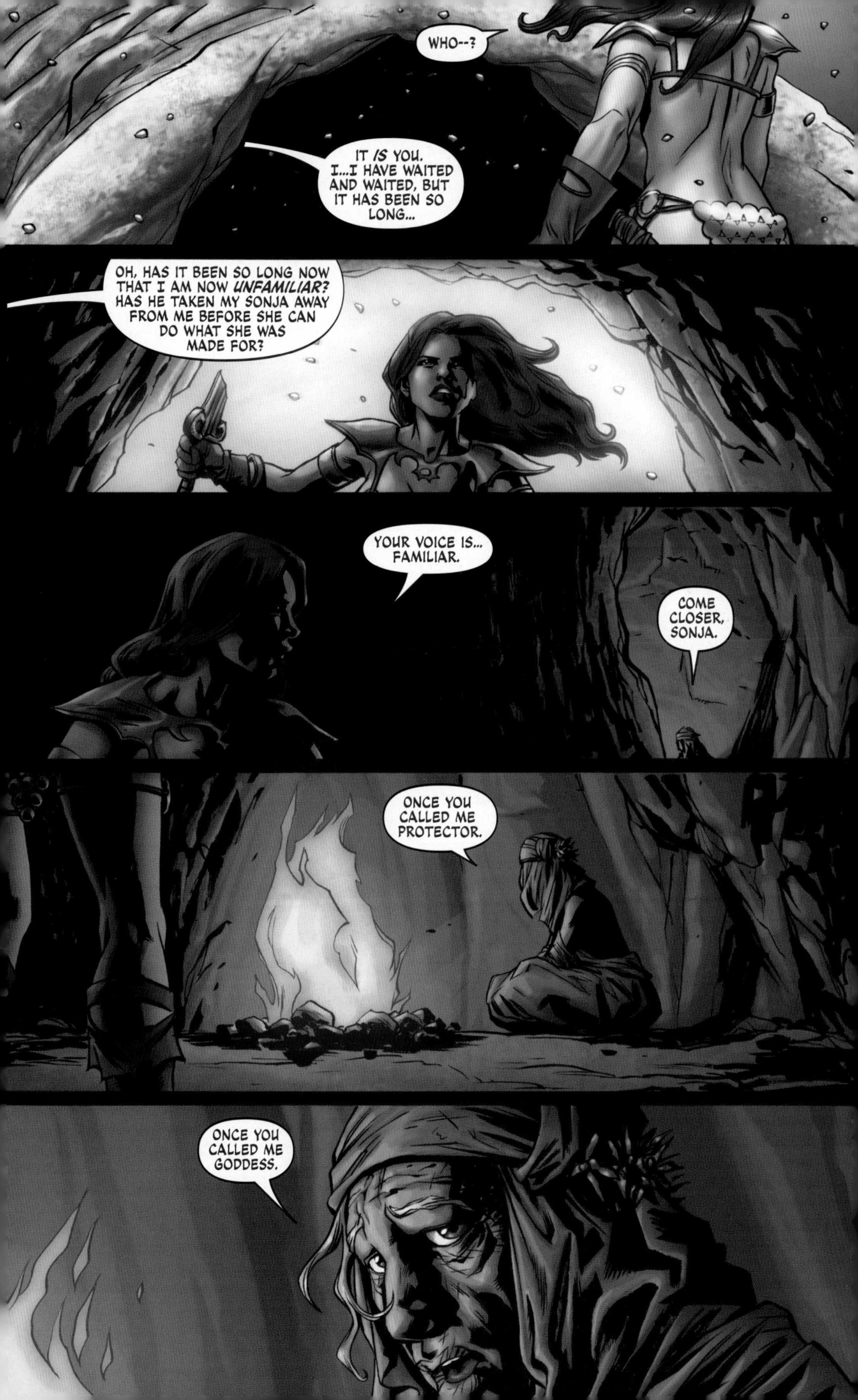
WHO--?
IT *IS* YOU. I...I HAVE WAITED AND WAITED, BUT IT HAS BEEN SO LONG...
OH, HAS IT BEEN SO LONG NOW THAT I AM NOW *UNFAMILIAR?* HAS HE TAKEN MY SONJA AWAY FROM ME BEFORE SHE CAN DO WHAT SHE WAS MADE FOR?
YOUR VOICE IS... FAMILIAR.
COME CLOSER, SONJA.
ONCE YOU CALLED ME PROTECTOR.
ONCE YOU CALLED ME GODDESS.

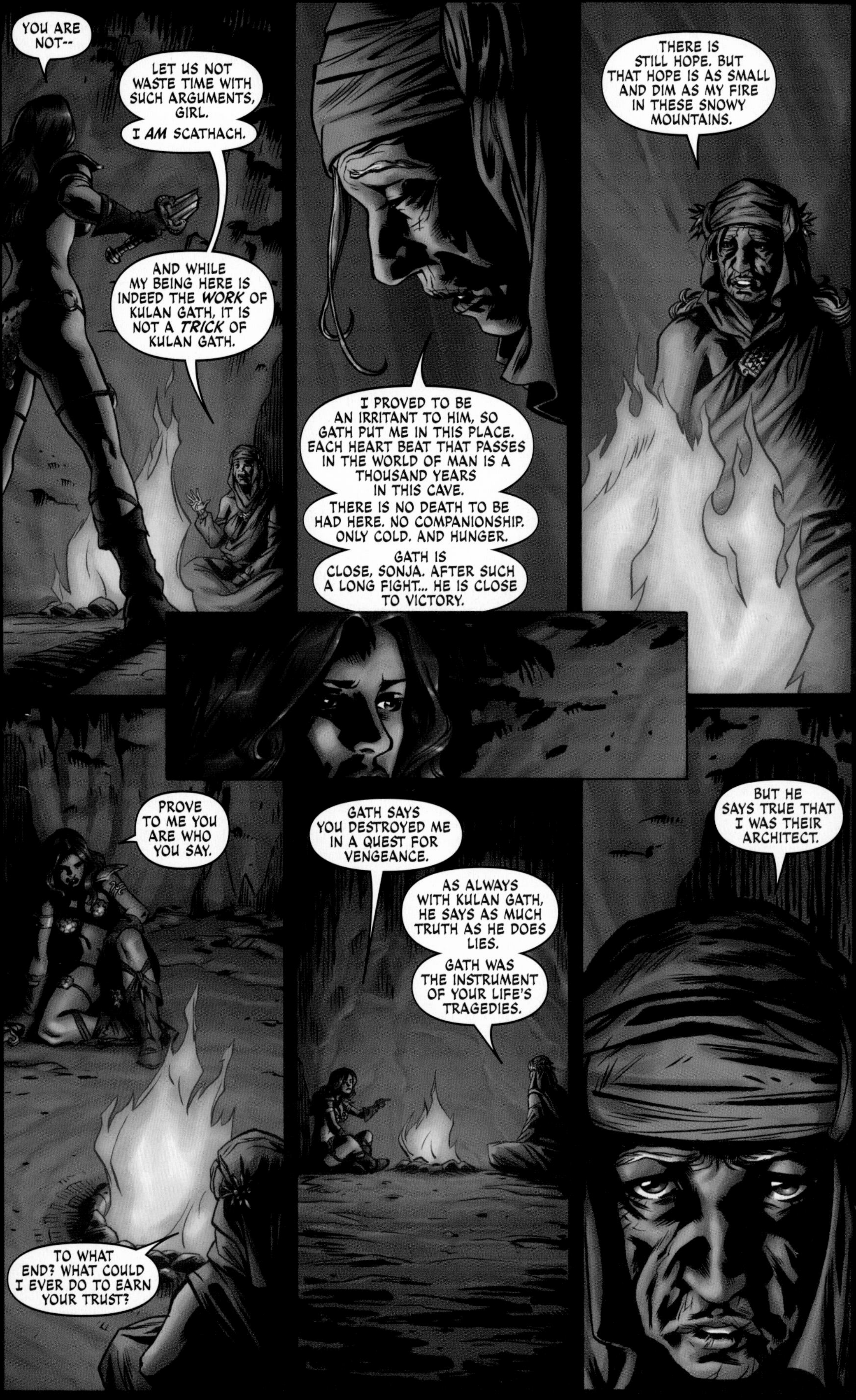
YOU ARE NOT--
LET US NOT WASTE TIME WITH SUCH ARGUMENTS, GIRL.
I AM SCATHACH.
AND WHILE MY BEING HERE IS INDEED THE WORK OF KULAN GATH, IT IS NOT A TRICK OF KULAN GATH.
I PROVED TO BE AN IRRITANT TO HIM, SO GATH PUT ME IN THIS PLACE. EACH HEART BEAT THAT PASSES IN THE WORLD OF MAN IS A THOUSAND YEARS IN THIS CAVE.
THERE IS NO DEATH TO BE HAD HERE. NO COMPANIONSHIP. ONLY COLD. AND HUNGER.
GATH IS CLOSE, SONJA. AFTER SUCH A LONG FIGHT... HE IS CLOSE TO VICTORY.
THERE IS STILL HOPE. BUT THAT HOPE IS AS SMALL AND DIM AS MY FIRE IN THESE SNOWY MOUNTAINS.
PROVE TO ME YOU ARE WHO YOU SAY.
TO WHAT END? WHAT COULD I EVER DO TO EARN YOUR TRUST?
GATH SAYS YOU DESTROYED ME IN A QUEST FOR VENGEANCE.
AS ALWAYS WITH KULAN GATH, HE SAYS AS MUCH TRUTH AS HE DOES LIES.
GATH WAS THE INSTRUMENT OF YOUR LIFE'S TRAGEDIES.
BUT HE SAYS TRUE THAT I WAS THEIR ARCHITECT.

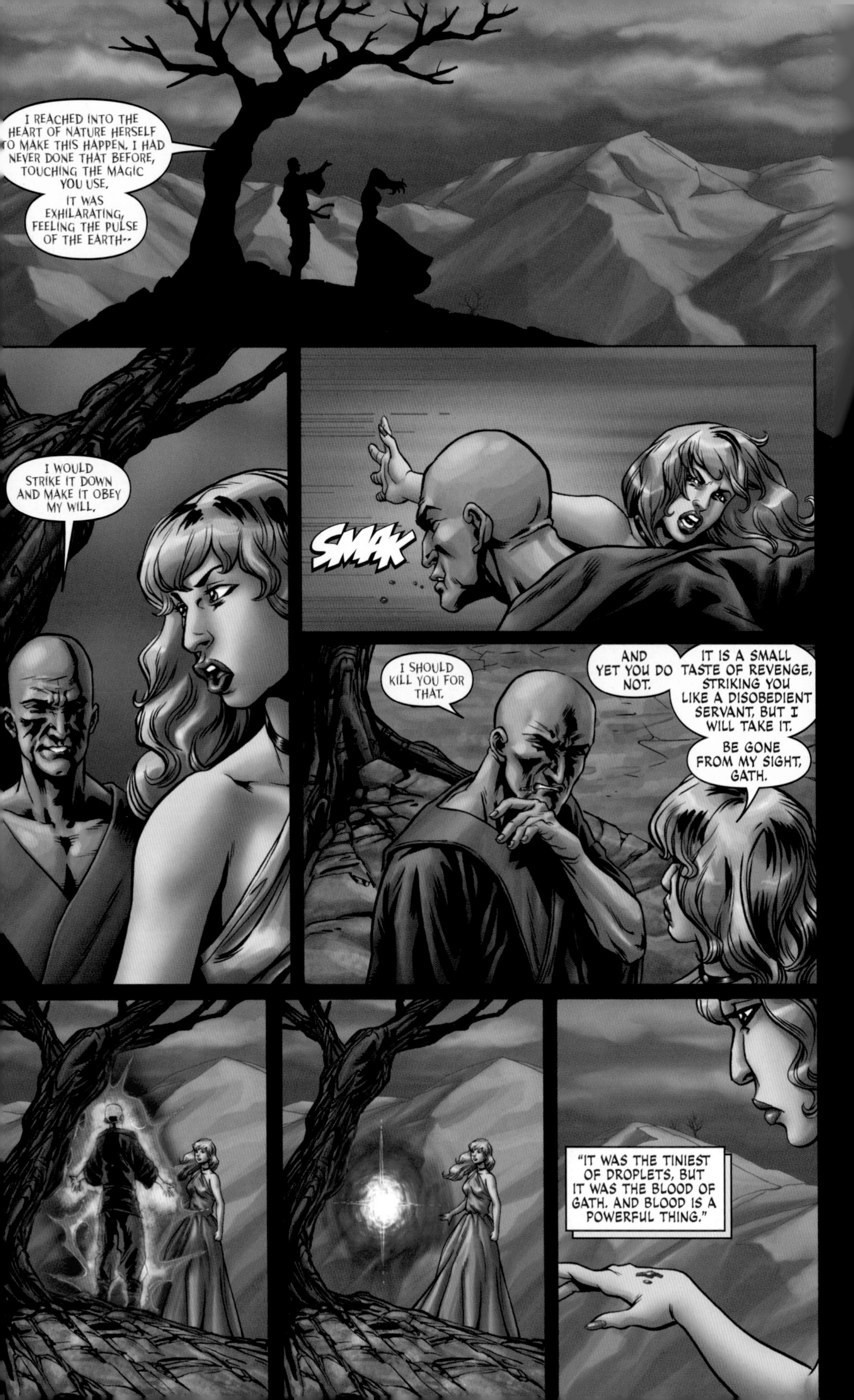
I REACHED INTO THE HEART OF NATURE HERSELF TO MAKE THIS HAPPEN. I HAD NEVER DONE THAT BEFORE, TOUCHING THE MAGIC YOU USE.
IT WAS EXHILARATING, FEELING THE PULSE OF THE EARTH--
I WOULD STRIKE IT DOWN AND MAKE IT OBEY MY WILL.
SMAK
I SHOULD KILL YOU FOR THAT.
AND YET YOU DO NOT.
IT IS A SMALL TASTE OF REVENGE, STRIKING YOU LIKE A DISOBEDIENT SERVANT, BUT I WILL TAKE IT.
BE GONE FROM MY SIGHT, GATH.
"IT WAS THE TINIEST OF DROPLETS, BUT IT WAS THE BLOOD OF GATH. AND BLOOD IS A POWERFUL THING."

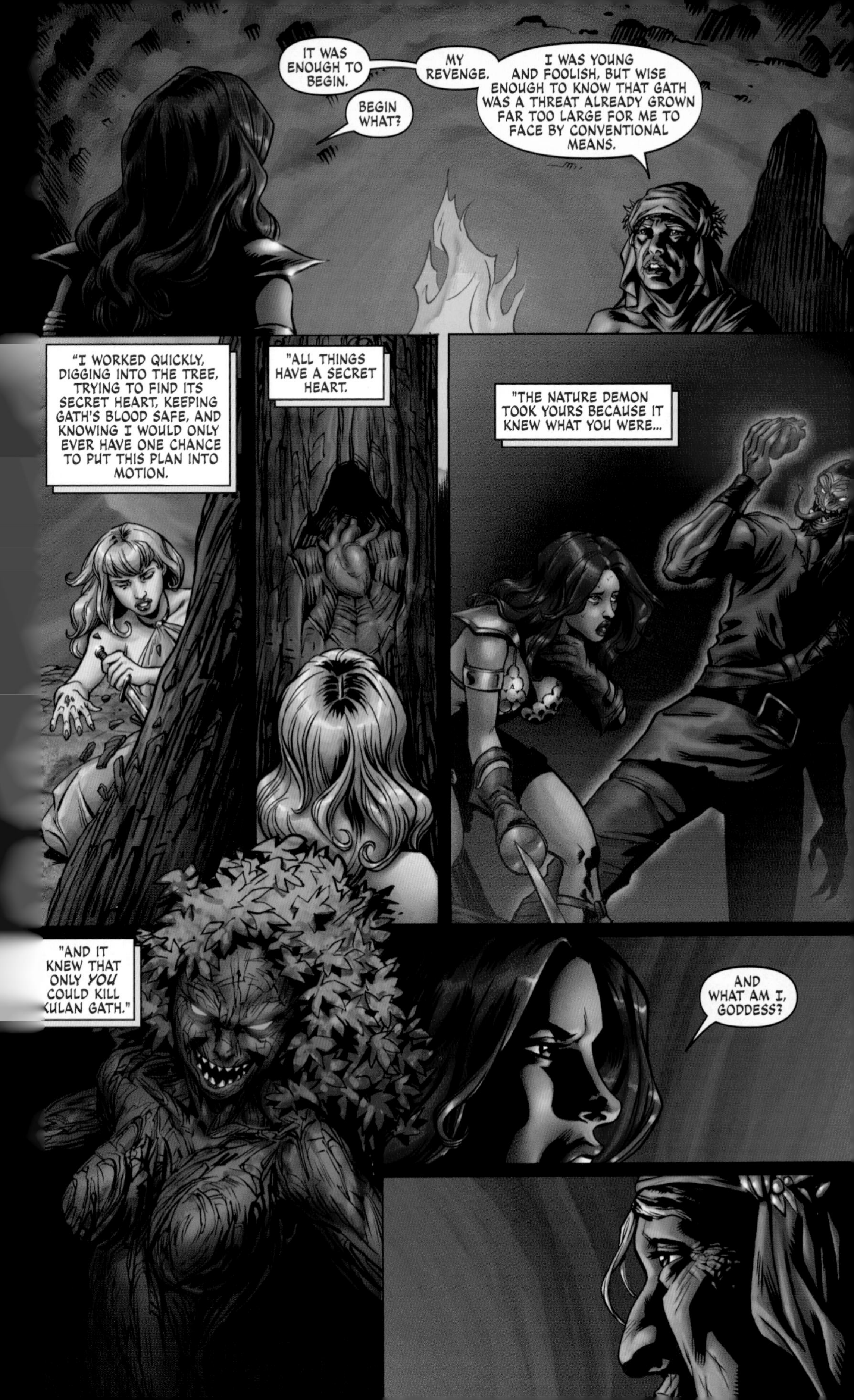
IT WAS ENOUGH TO BEGIN.
BEGIN WHAT?
MY REVENGE.
I WAS YOUNG AND FOOLISH, BUT WISE ENOUGH TO KNOW THAT GATH WAS A THREAT ALREADY GROWN FAR TOO LARGE FOR ME TO FACE BY CONVENTIONAL MEANS.
"I WORKED QUICKLY, DIGGING INTO THE TREE, TRYING TO FIND ITS SECRET HEART, KEEPING GATH'S BLOOD SAFE, AND KNOWING I WOULD ONLY EVER HAVE ONE CHANCE TO PUT THIS PLAN INTO MOTION.
"ALL THINGS HAVE A SECRET HEART.
"THE NATURE DEMON TOOK YOURS BECAUSE IT KNEW WHAT YOU WERE...
"AND IT KNEW THAT ONLY *YOU* COULD KILL KULAN GATH."
AND WHAT AM I, GODDESS?

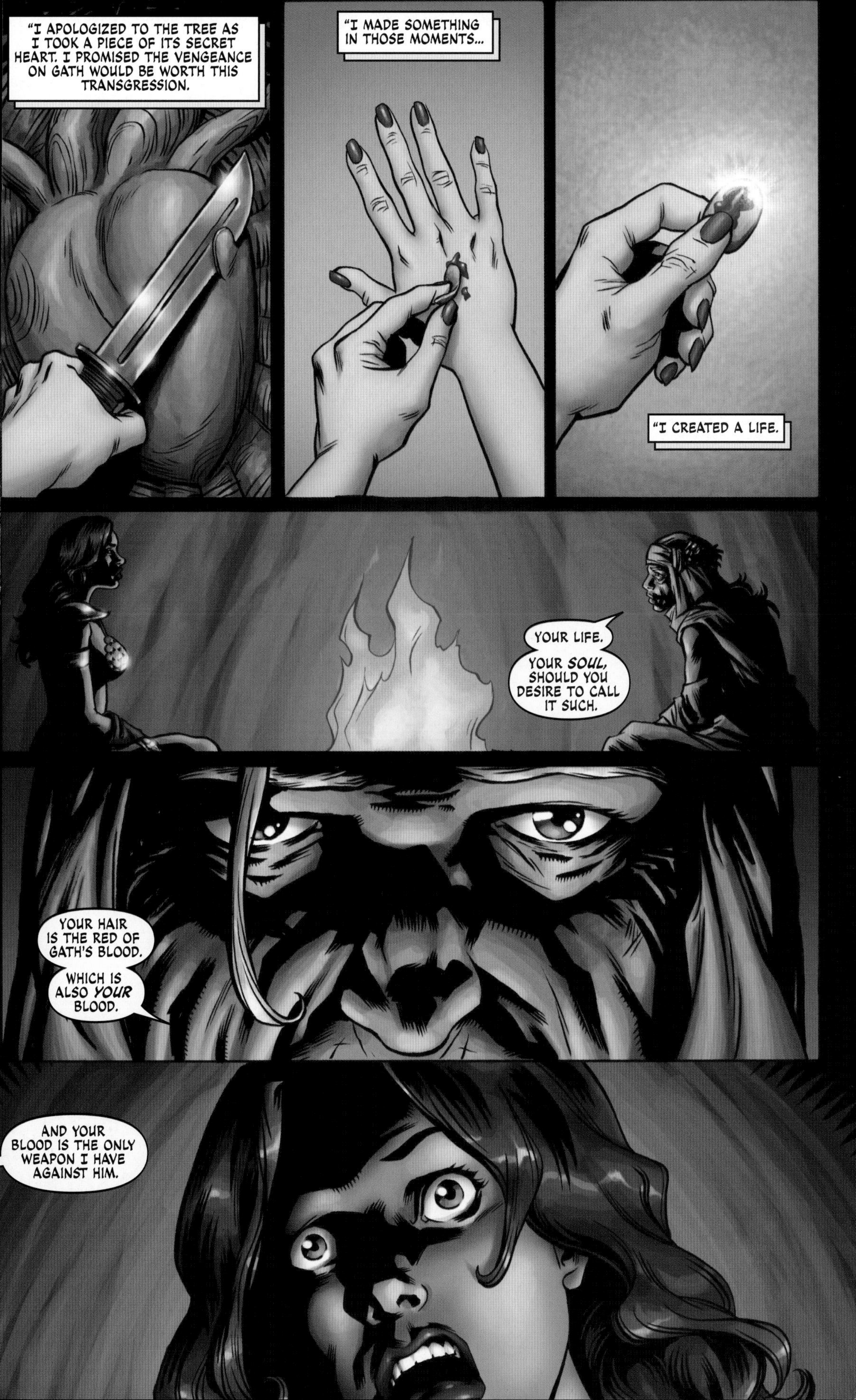
"I APOLOGIZED TO THE TREE AS I TOOK A PIECE OF ITS SECRET HEART. I PROMISED THE VENGEANCE ON GATH WOULD BE WORTH THIS TRANSGRESSION.
"I MADE SOMETHING IN THOSE MOMENTS...
"I CREATED A LIFE.
YOUR LIFE.
YOUR *SOUL*, SHOULD YOU DESIRE TO CALL IT SUCH.
YOUR HAIR IS THE RED OF GATH'S BLOOD.
WHICH IS ALSO *YOUR* BLOOD.
AND YOUR BLOOD IS THE ONLY WEAPON I HAVE AGAINST HIM.

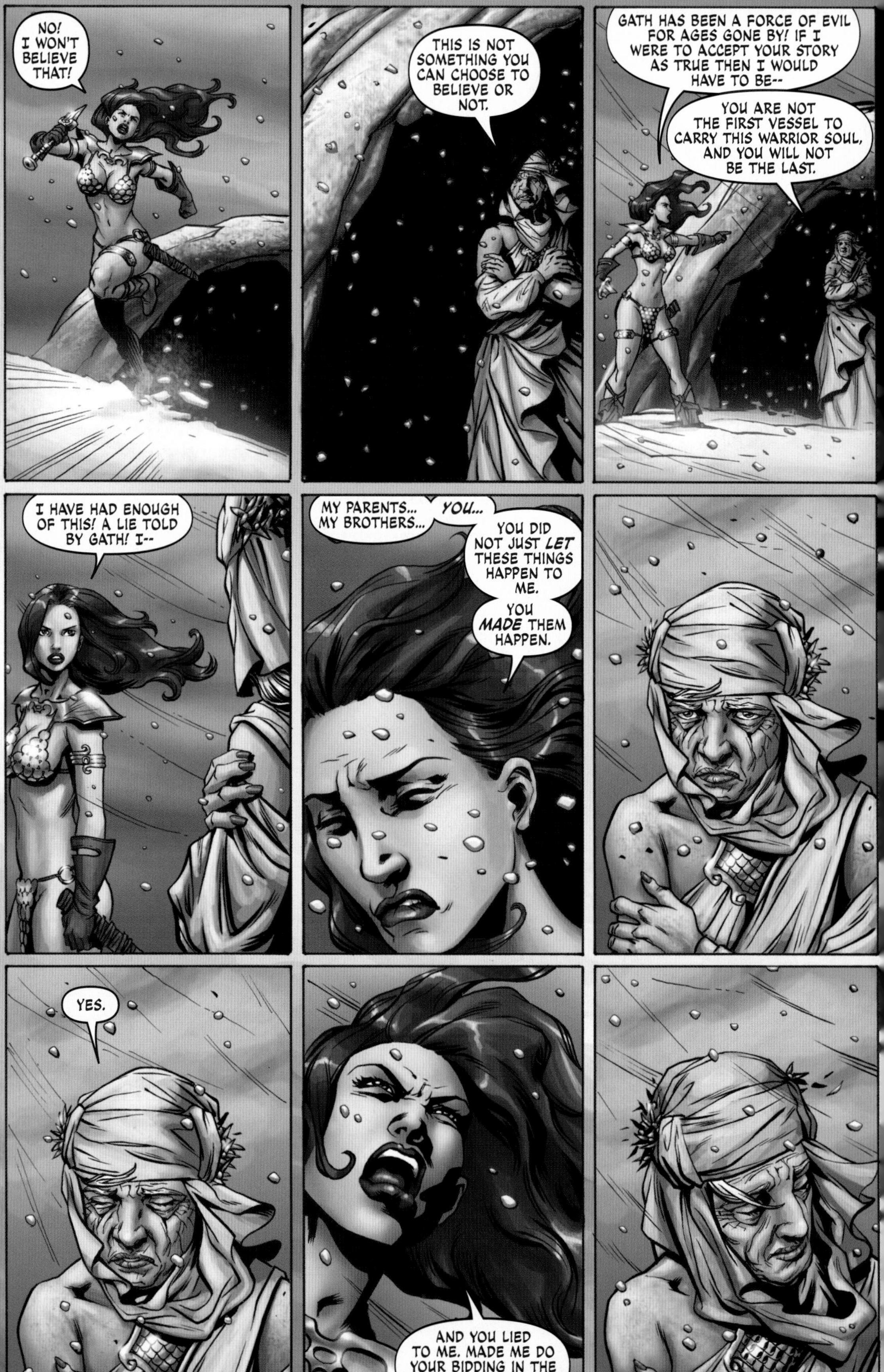
NO! I WON'T BELIEVE THAT!
THIS IS NOT SOMETHING YOU CAN CHOOSE TO BELIEVE OR NOT.
GATH HAS BEEN A FORCE OF EVIL FOR AGES GONE BY! IF I WERE TO ACCEPT YOUR STORY AS TRUE THEN I WOULD HAVE TO BE--
YOU ARE NOT THE FIRST VESSEL TO CARRY THIS WARRIOR SOUL, AND YOU WILL NOT BE THE LAST.
I HAVE HAD ENOUGH OF THIS! A LIE TOLD BY GATH! I--
MY PARENTS... MY BROTHERS...
YOU...
YOU DID NOT JUST LET THESE THINGS HAPPEN TO ME.
YOU MADE THEM HAPPEN.
YES.
AND YOU LIED TO ME. MADE ME DO YOUR BIDDING IN THE NAME OF DEFEATING... HIM.

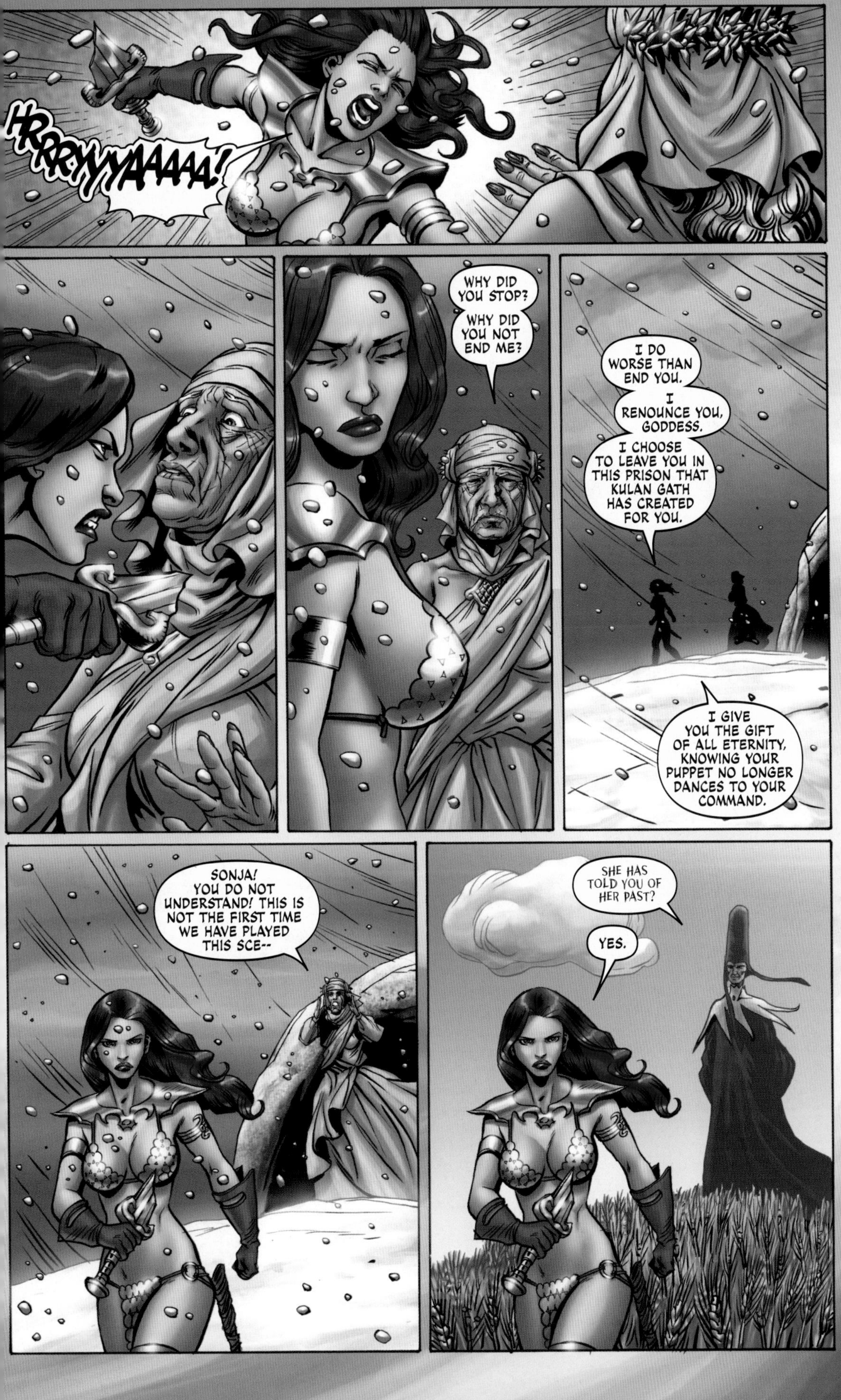
HRRRYYYAAAAA!
WHY DID YOU STOP?
WHY DID YOU NOT END ME?
I DO WORSE THAN END YOU.
I RENOUNCE YOU, GODDESS.
I CHOOSE TO LEAVE YOU IN THIS PRISON THAT KULAN GATH HAS CREATED FOR YOU.
I GIVE YOU THE GIFT OF ALL ETERNITY, KNOWING YOUR PUPPET NO LONGER DANCES TO YOUR COMMAND.
SONJA! YOU DO NOT UNDERSTAND! THIS IS NOT THE FIRST TIME WE HAVE PLAYED THIS SCE--
SHE HAS TOLD YOU OF HER PAST?
YES.

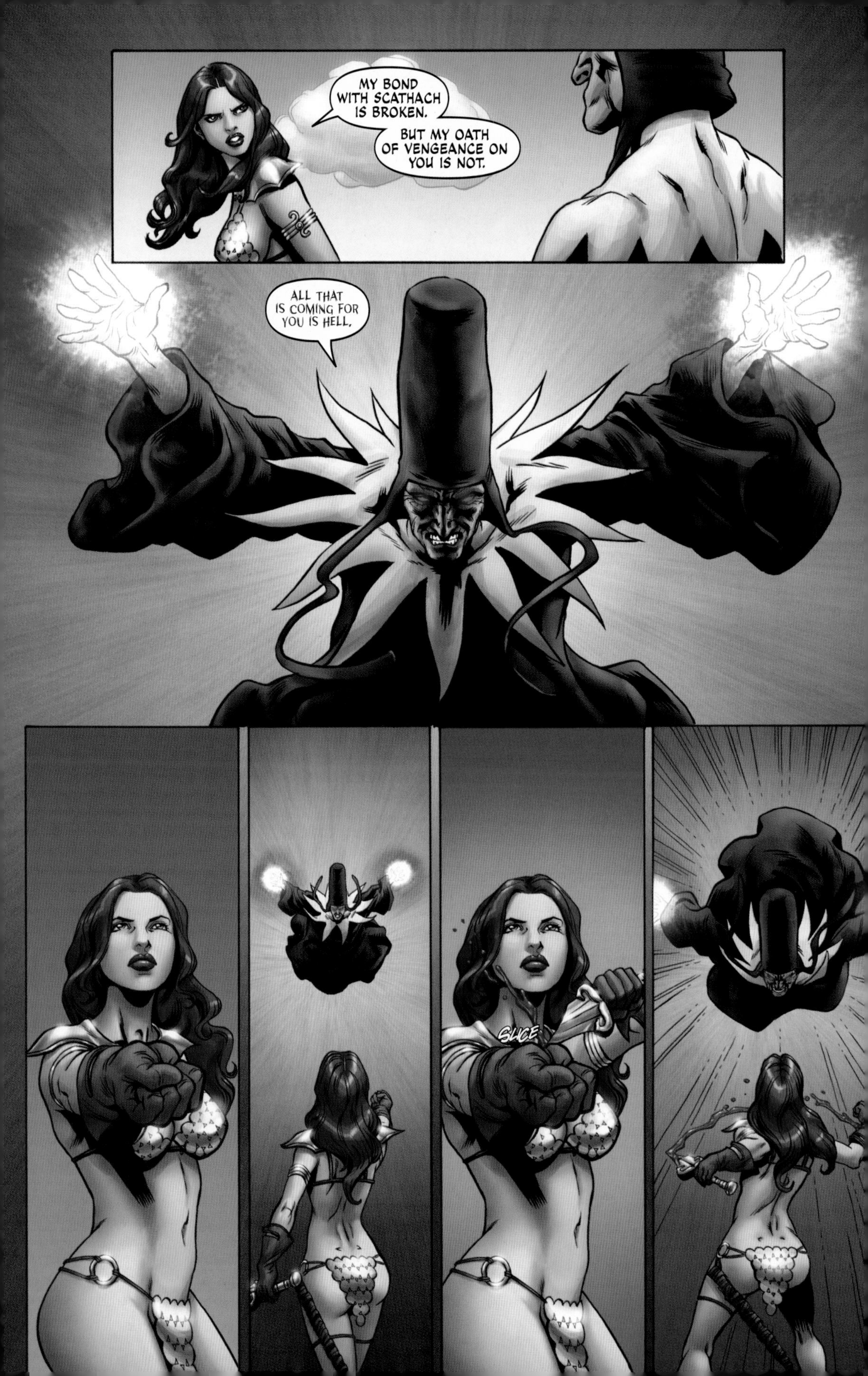
MY BOND WITH SCATHACH IS BROKEN.
BUT MY OATH OF VENGEANCE ON YOU IS NOT.
ALL THAT IS COMING FOR YOU IS HELL,
SLICE

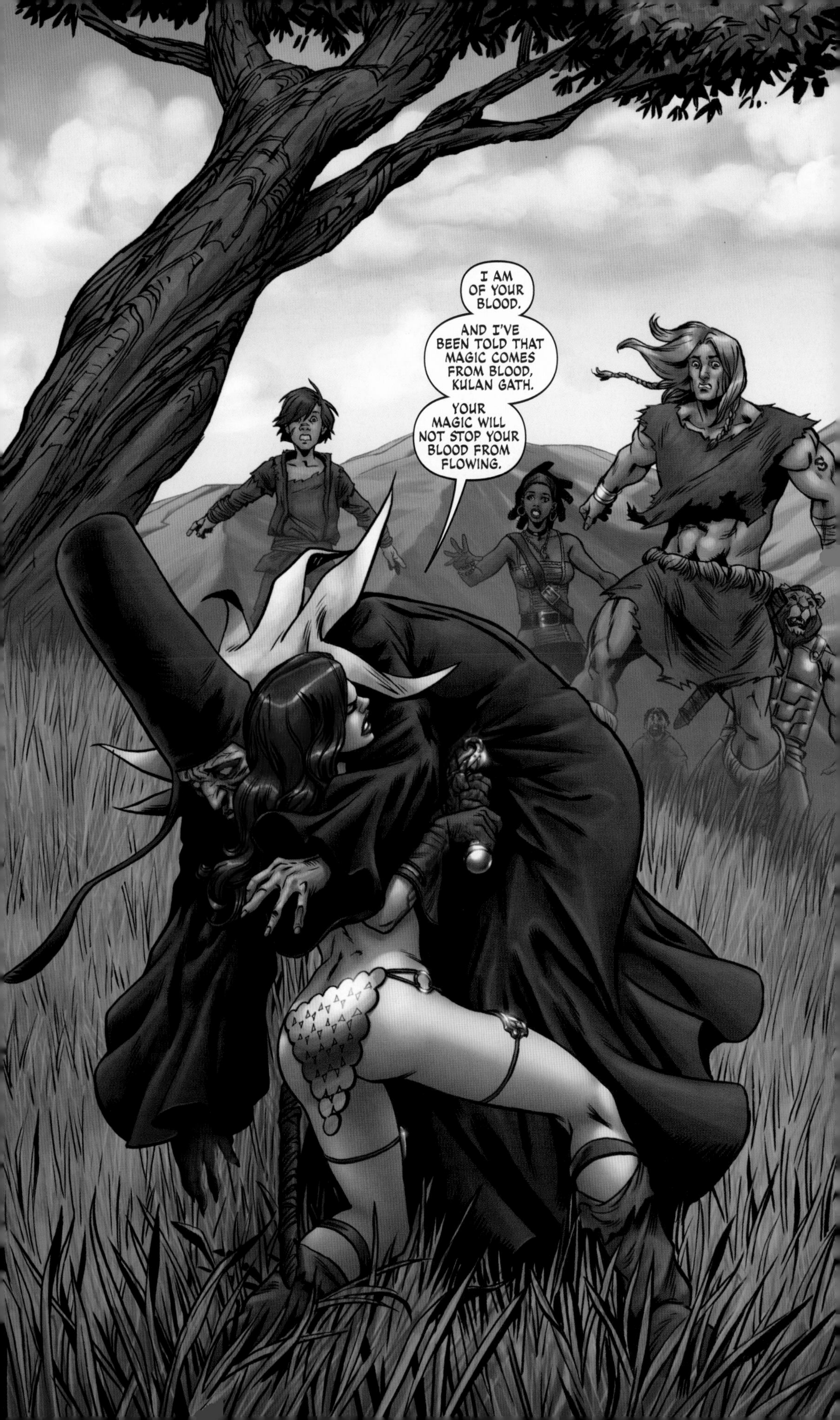
I AM OF YOUR BLOOD.
AND I'VE BEEN TOLD THAT MAGIC COMES FROM BLOOD, KULAN GATH.
YOUR MAGIC WILL NOT STOP YOUR BLOOD FROM FLOWING.

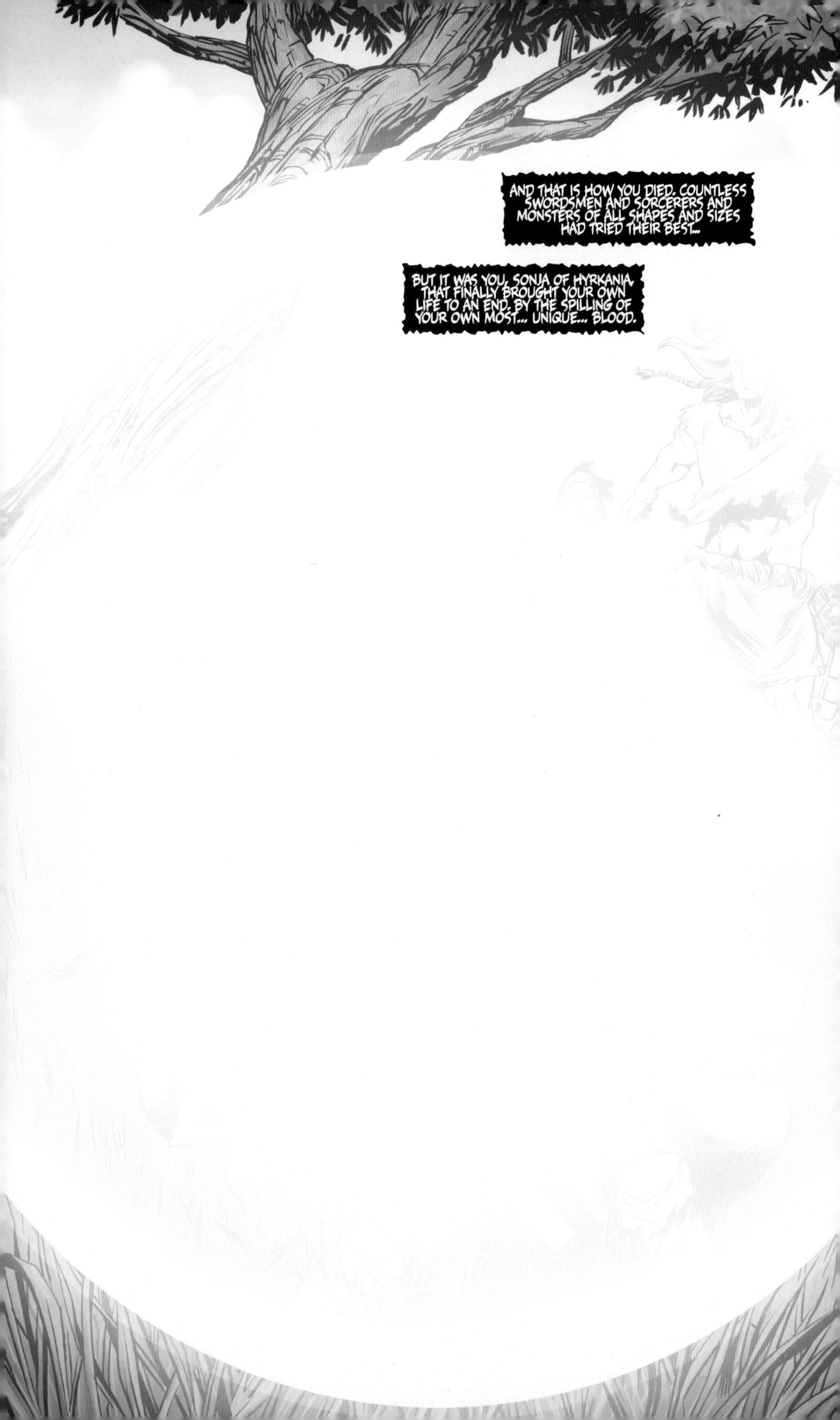
AND THAT IS HOW YOU DIED. COUNTLESS SWORDSMEN AND SORCERERS AND MONSTERS OF ALL SHAPES AND SIZES HAD TRIED THEIR BEST...
BUT IT WAS YOU, SONJA OF HYRKANIA, THAT FINALLY BROUGHT YOUR OWN LIFE TO AN END. BY THE SPILLING OF YOUR OWN MOST... UNIQUE... BLOOD.

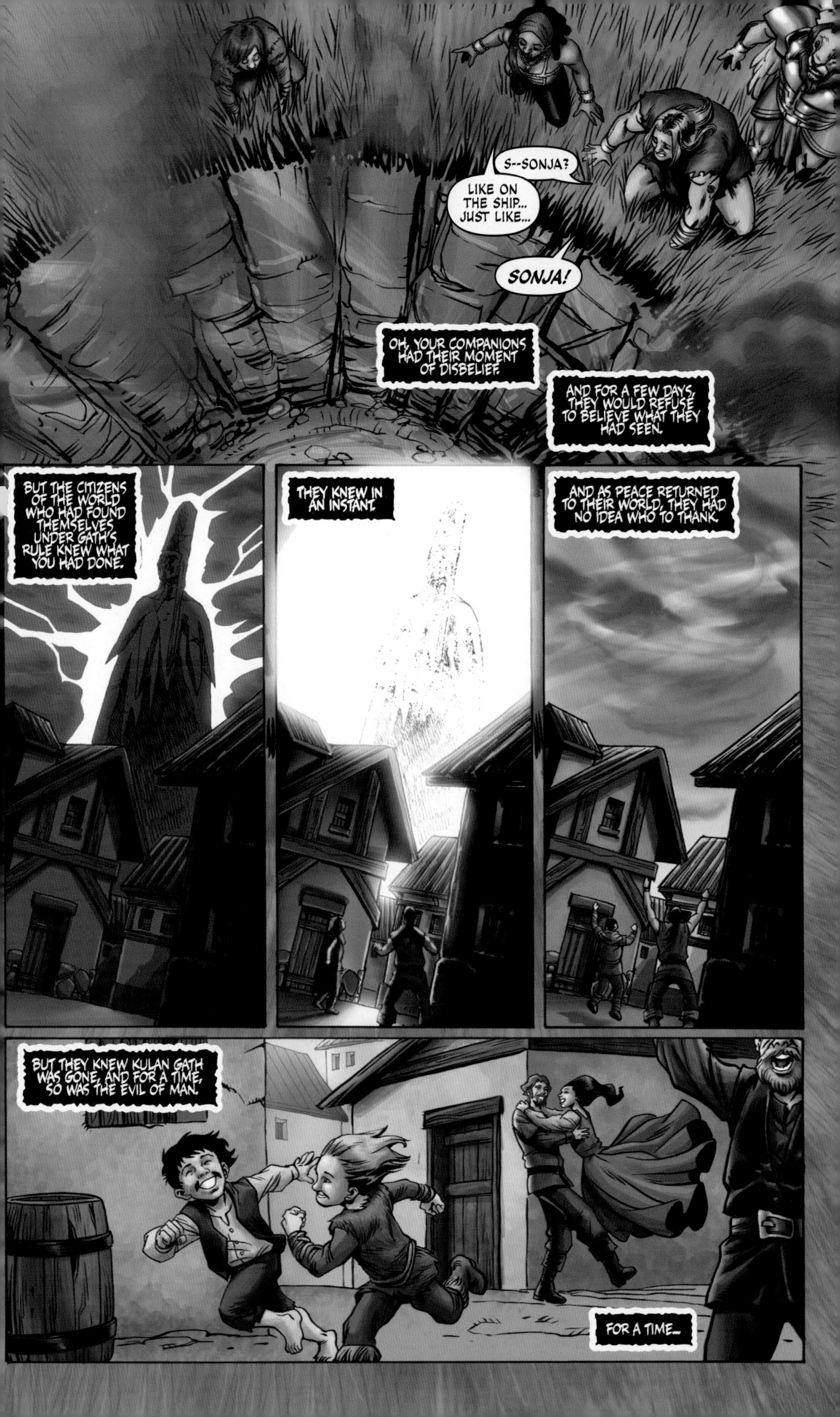
S--SONJA?
LIKE ON THE SHIP... JUST LIKE...
SONJA!
OH, YOUR COMPANIONS HAD THEIR MOMENT OF DISBELIEF.
AND FOR A FEW DAYS, THEY WOULD REFUSE TO BELIEVE WHAT THEY HAD SEEN.
BUT THE CITIZENS OF THE WORLD WHO HAD FOUND THEMSELVES UNDER GATH'S RULE KNEW WHAT YOU HAD DONE.
THEY KNEW IN AN INSTANT.
AND AS PEACE RETURNED TO THEIR WORLD, THEY HAD NO IDEA WHO TO THANK.
BUT THEY KNEW KULAN GATH WAS GONE, AND FOR A TIME, SO WAS THE EVIL OF MAN.
FOR A TIME...

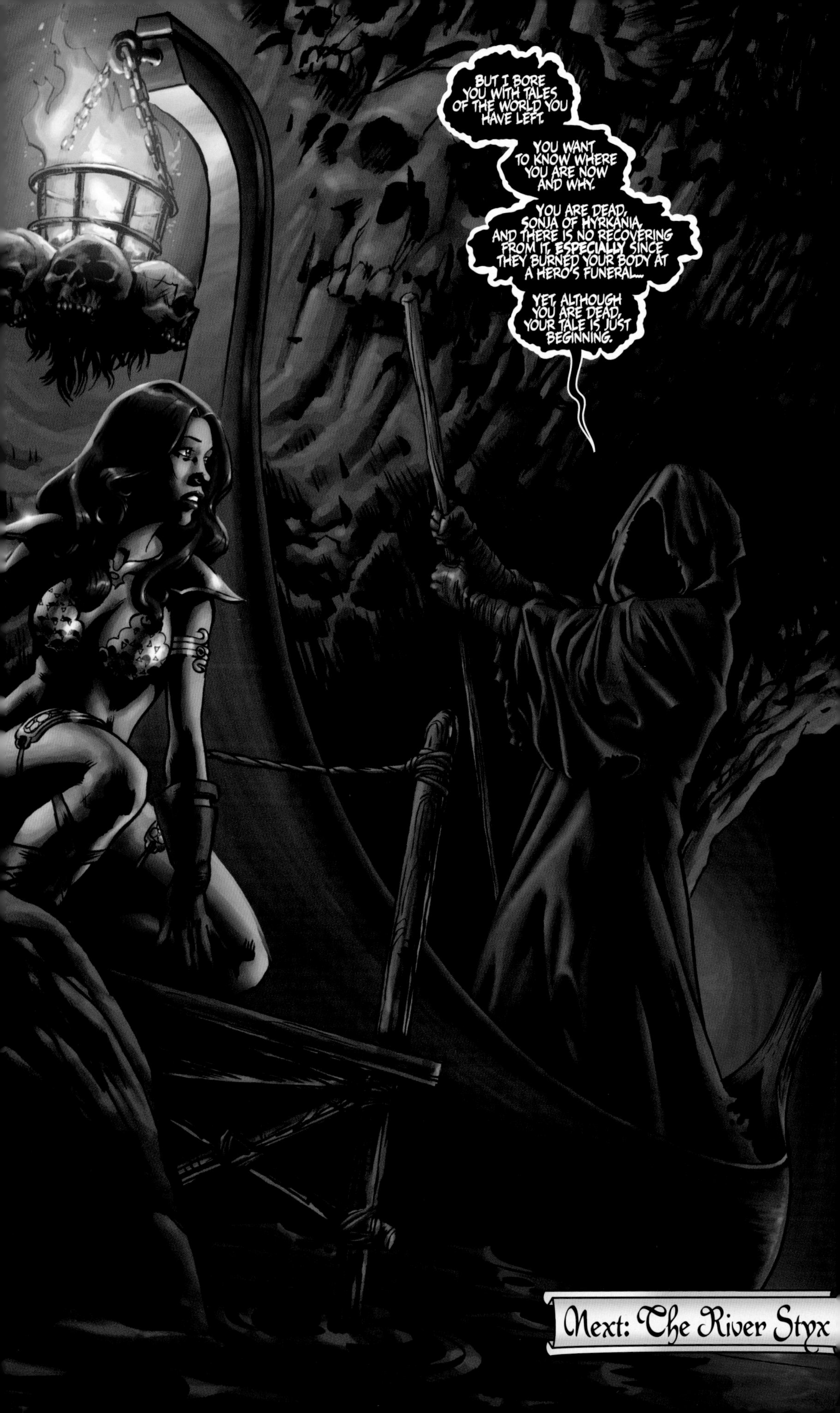
BUT I BORE YOU WITH TALES OF THE WORLD YOU HAVE LEFT.
YOU WANT TO KNOW WHERE YOU ARE NOW AND WHY.
YOU ARE DEAD, SONJA OF HYRKANIA, AND THERE IS NO RECOVERING FROM IT, ESPECIALLY SINCE THEY BURNED YOUR BODY AT A HERO'S FUNERAL...
YET, ALTHOUGH YOU ARE DEAD, YOUR TALE IS JUST BEGINNING.
Next: The River Styx

COVER GALLERY

ISSUE 25

116-117	•	Esteban Maroto
118	•	Art Adams
119	•	Mel Rubi
120	•	Ariel Olivetti
121	•	Paul Renaud
122	•	Mel Rubi (foil)

ISSUE 26

123	•	David Mack
124	•	Homs
125	•	Mel Rubi
126	•	Joe Prado
127	•	Ron Adrian (foil)

ISSUE 27

128	•	Dan Panosian
129	•	Homs
130	•	Mel Rubi
131	•	Joe Prado
132	•	Ron Adrian (foil)

ISSUE 28

133	•	Liam Sharp
134	•	Homs
135	•	Mel Rubi
136	•	Joe Prado
137	•	Ron Adrian (foil)

ISSUE 29

138	•	Greg Tocchini
139	•	Homs
140	•	Mel Rubi
141	•	Joe Prado
142	•	Ron Adrian (foil)

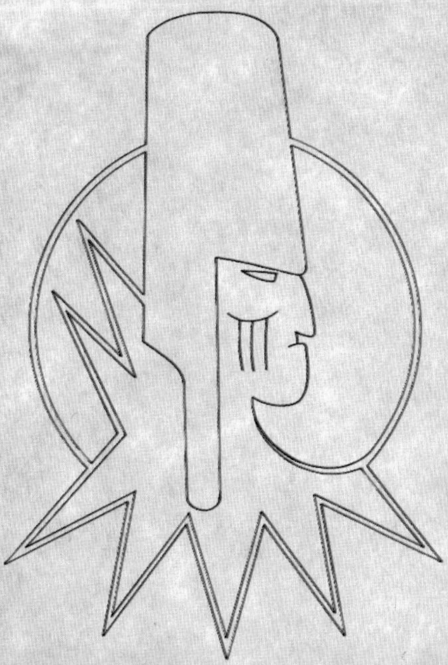

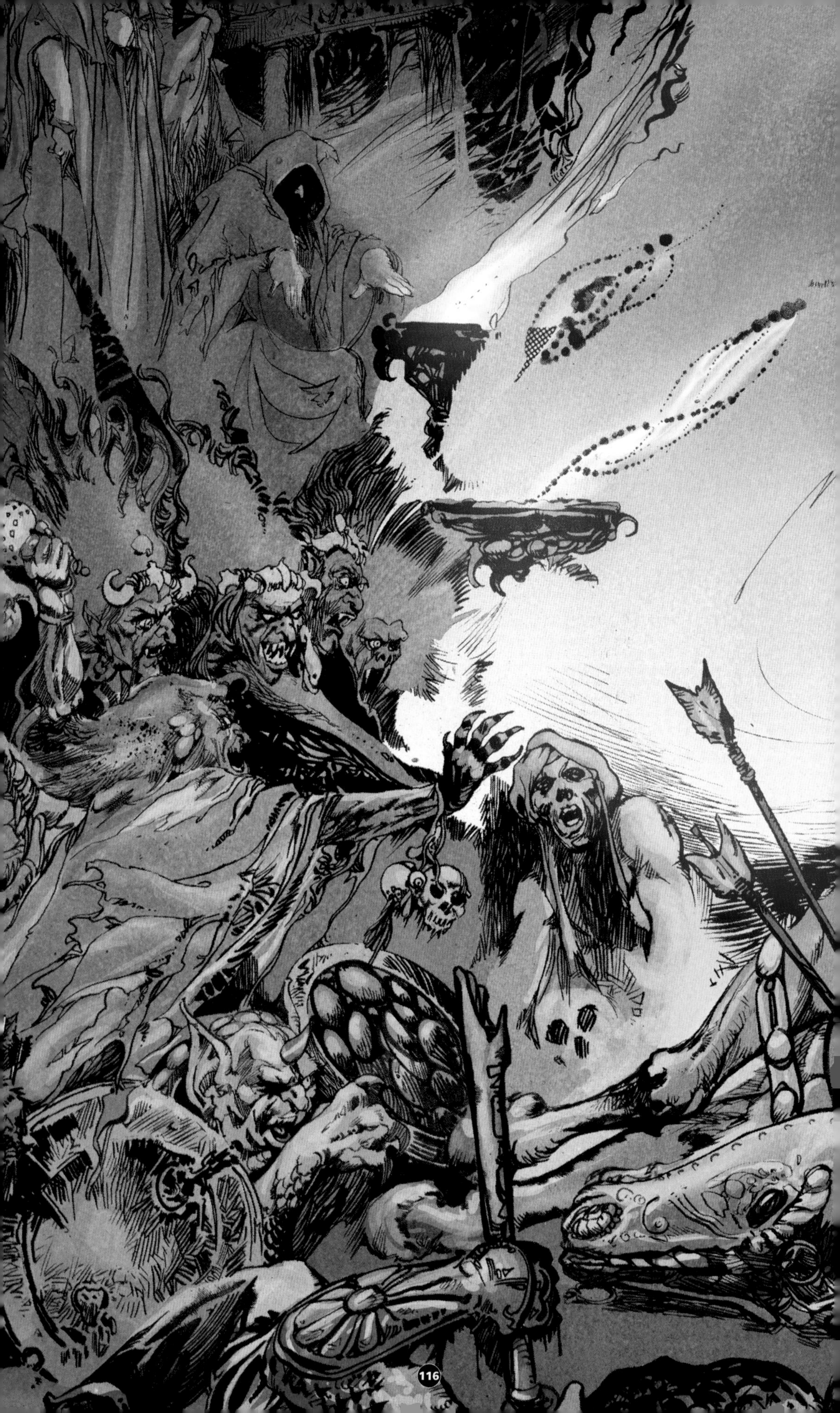

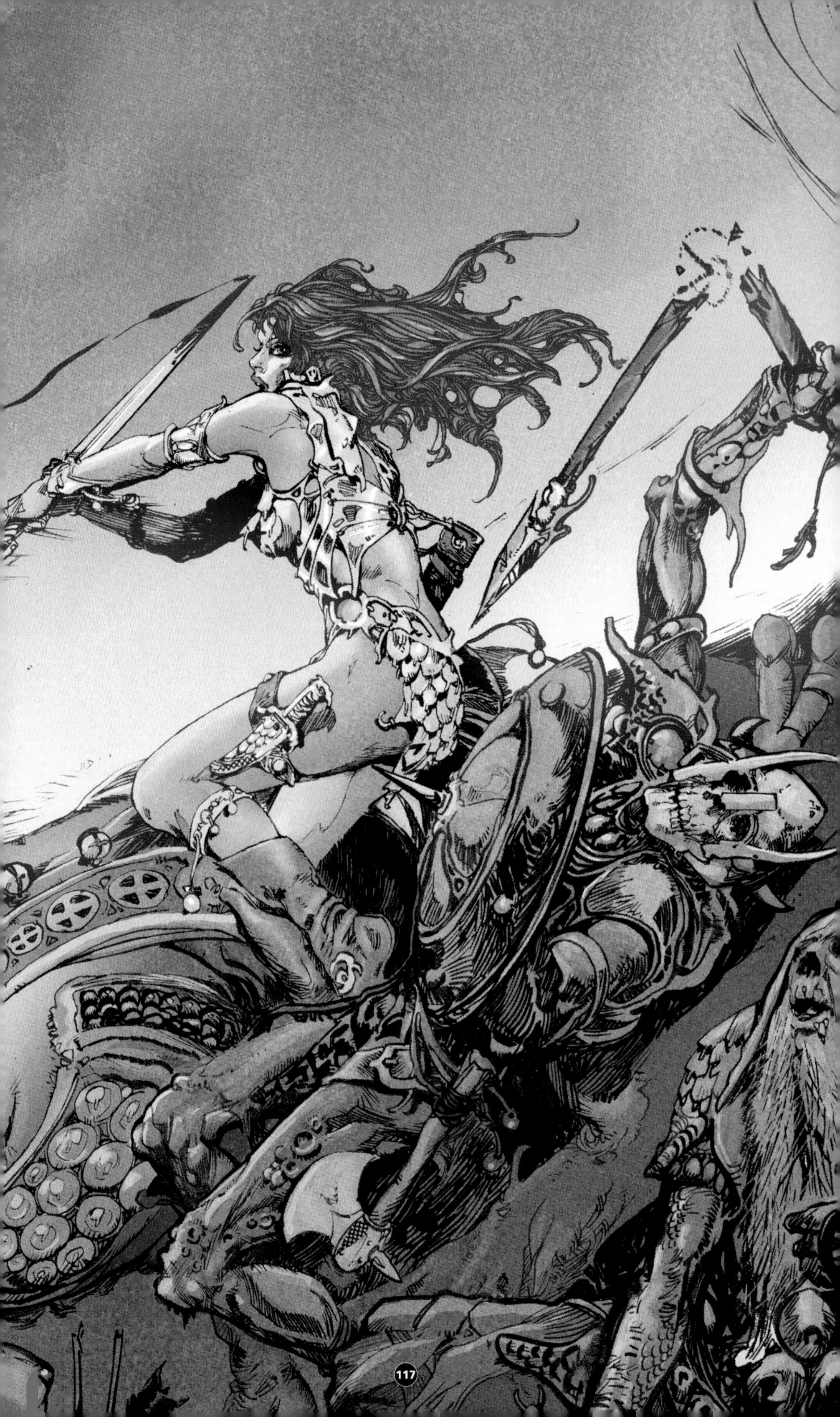

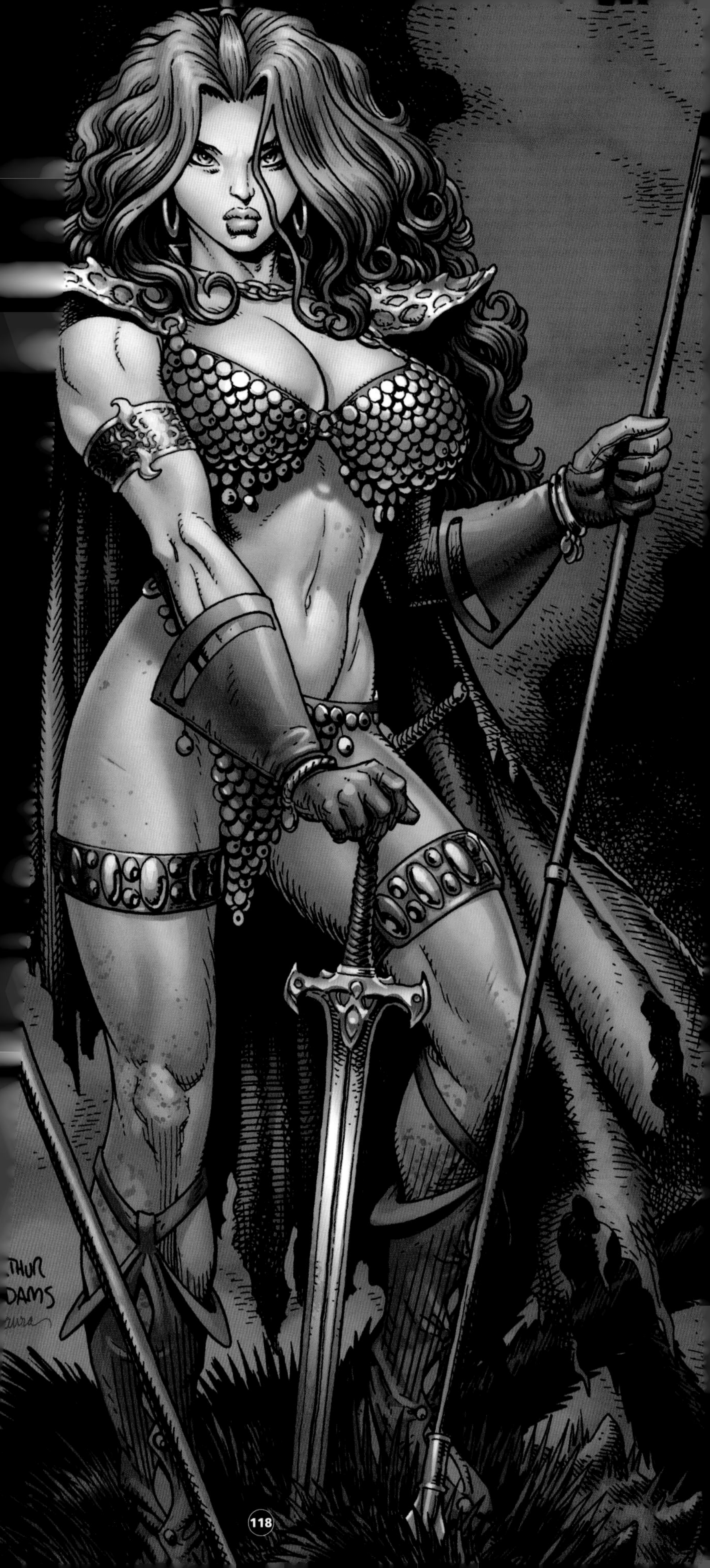

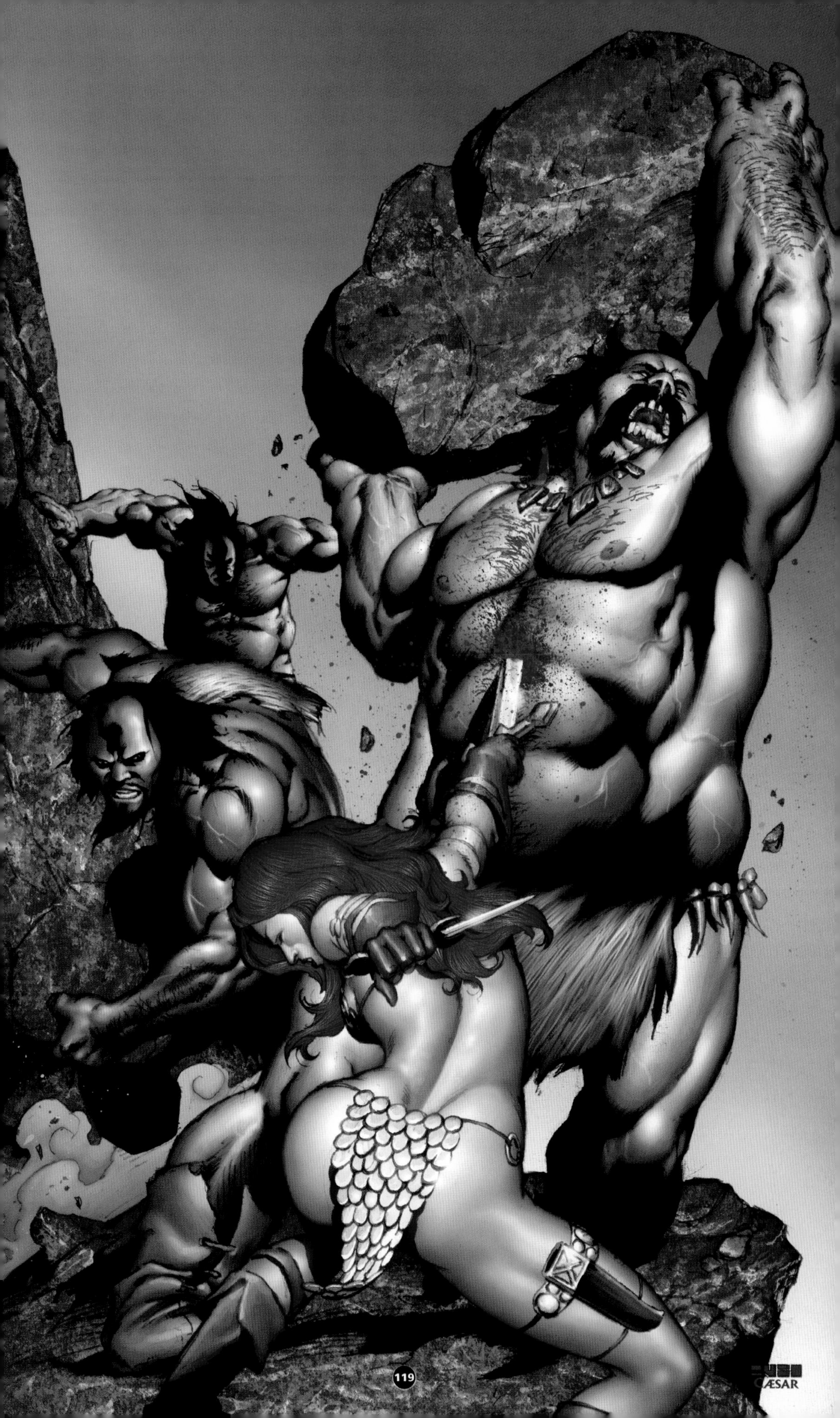
CÆSAR

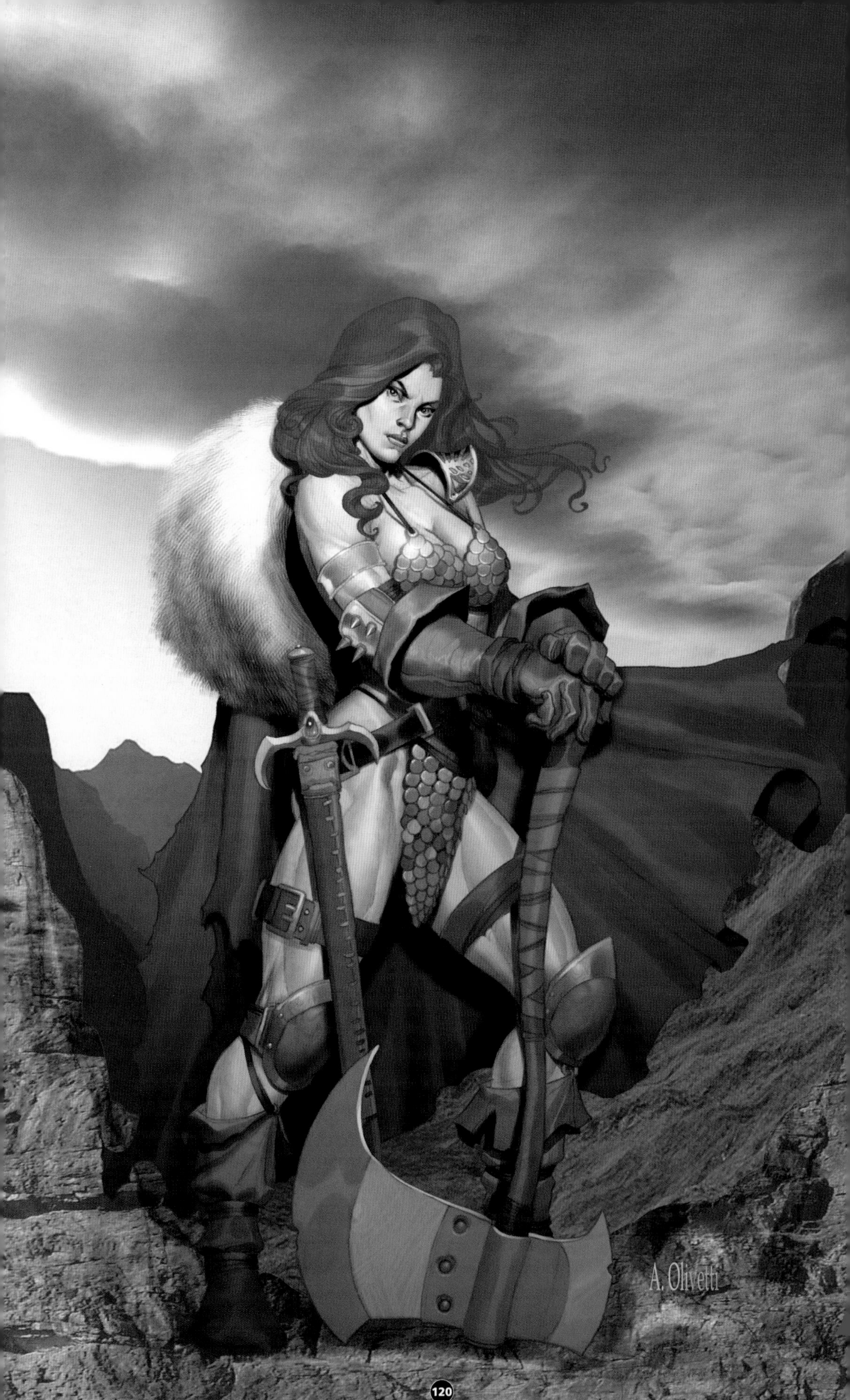
A. Olivetti

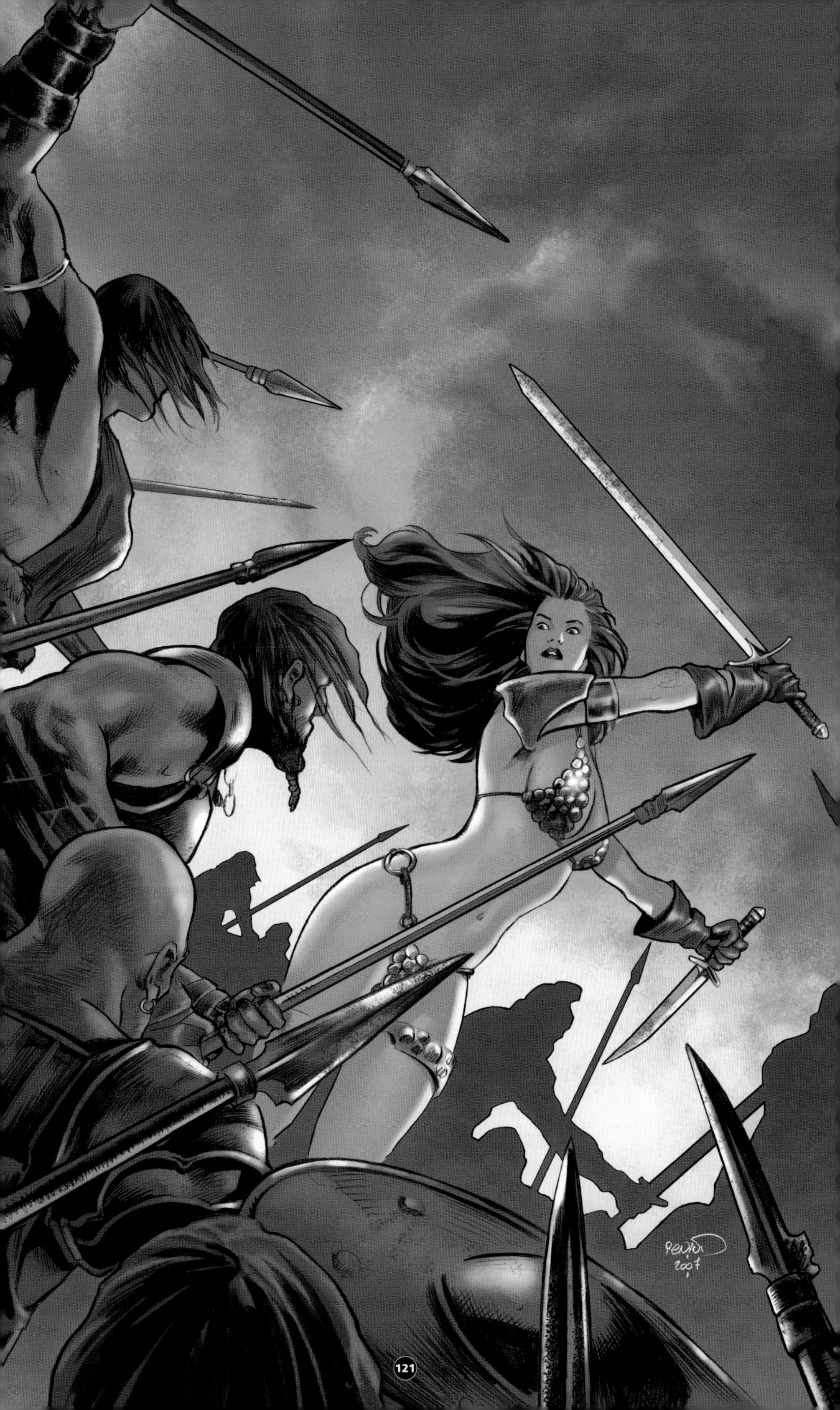

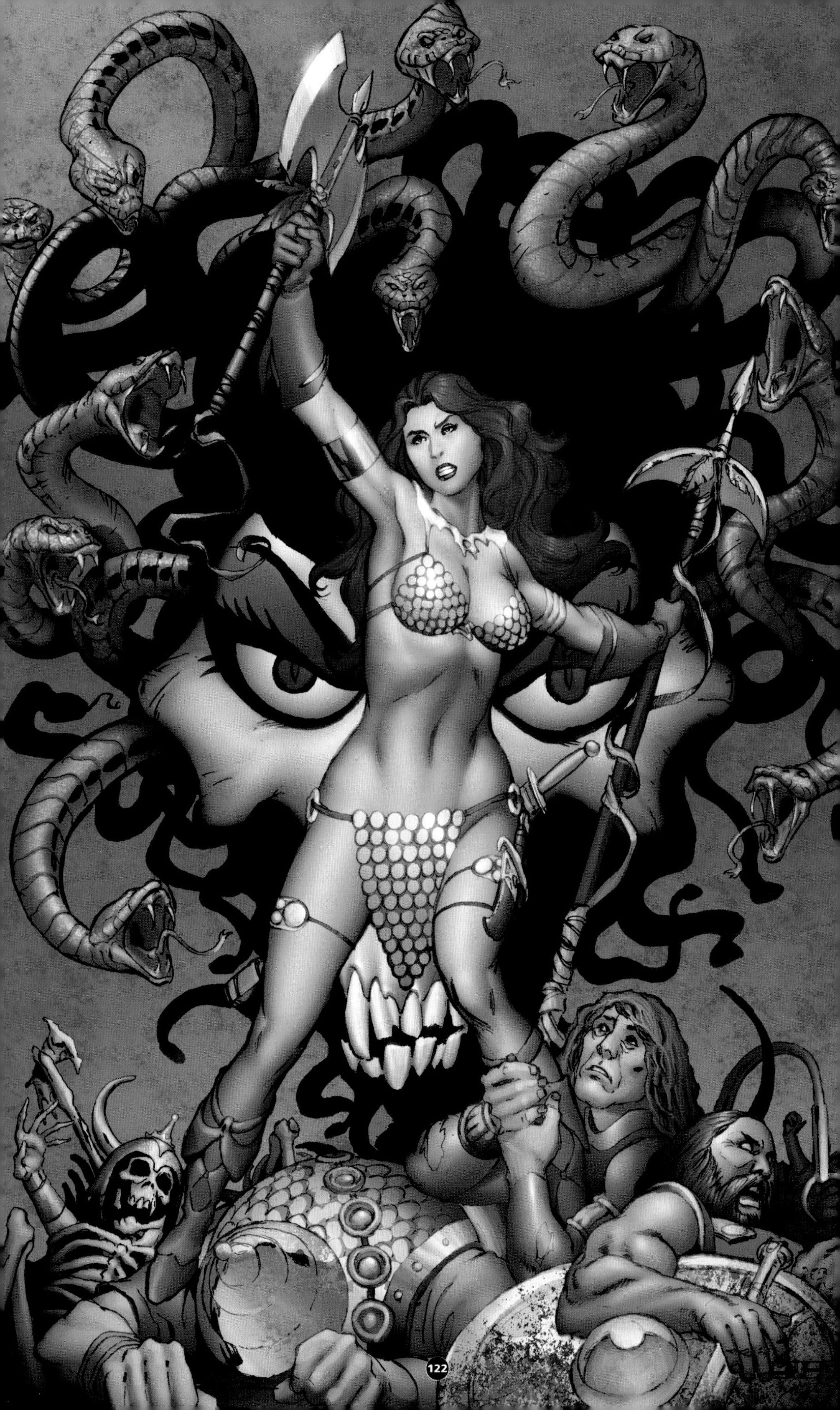

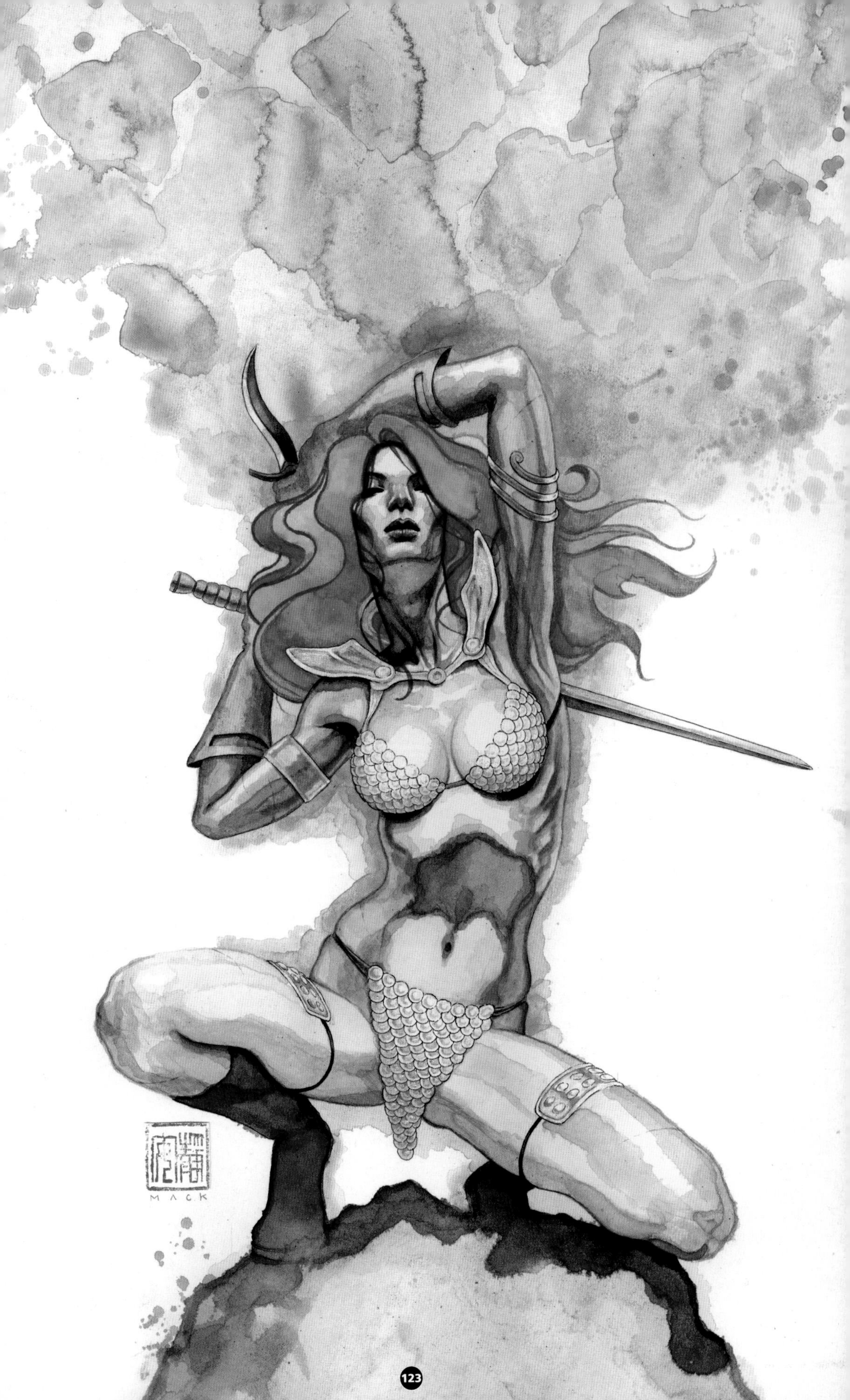
MACK

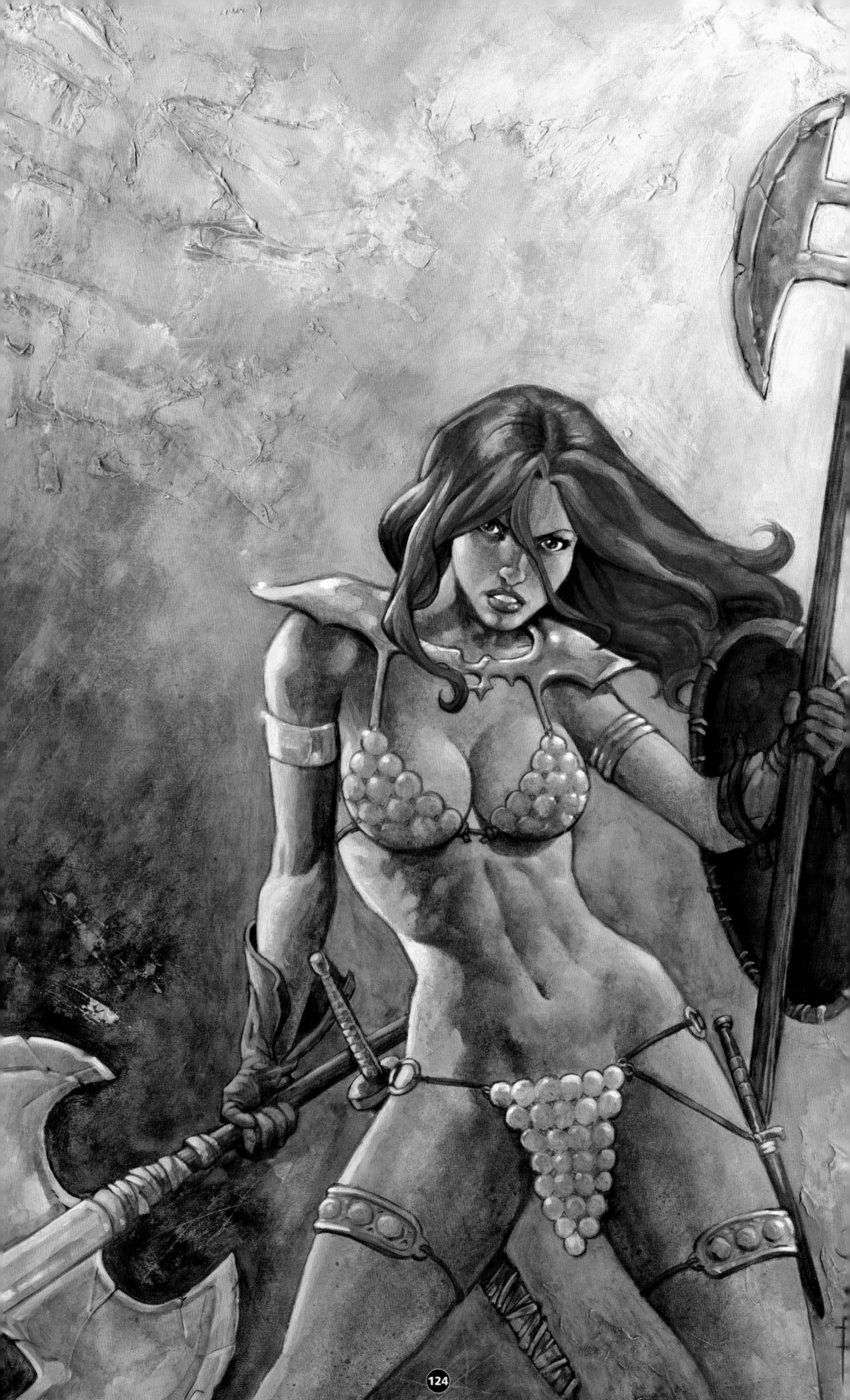

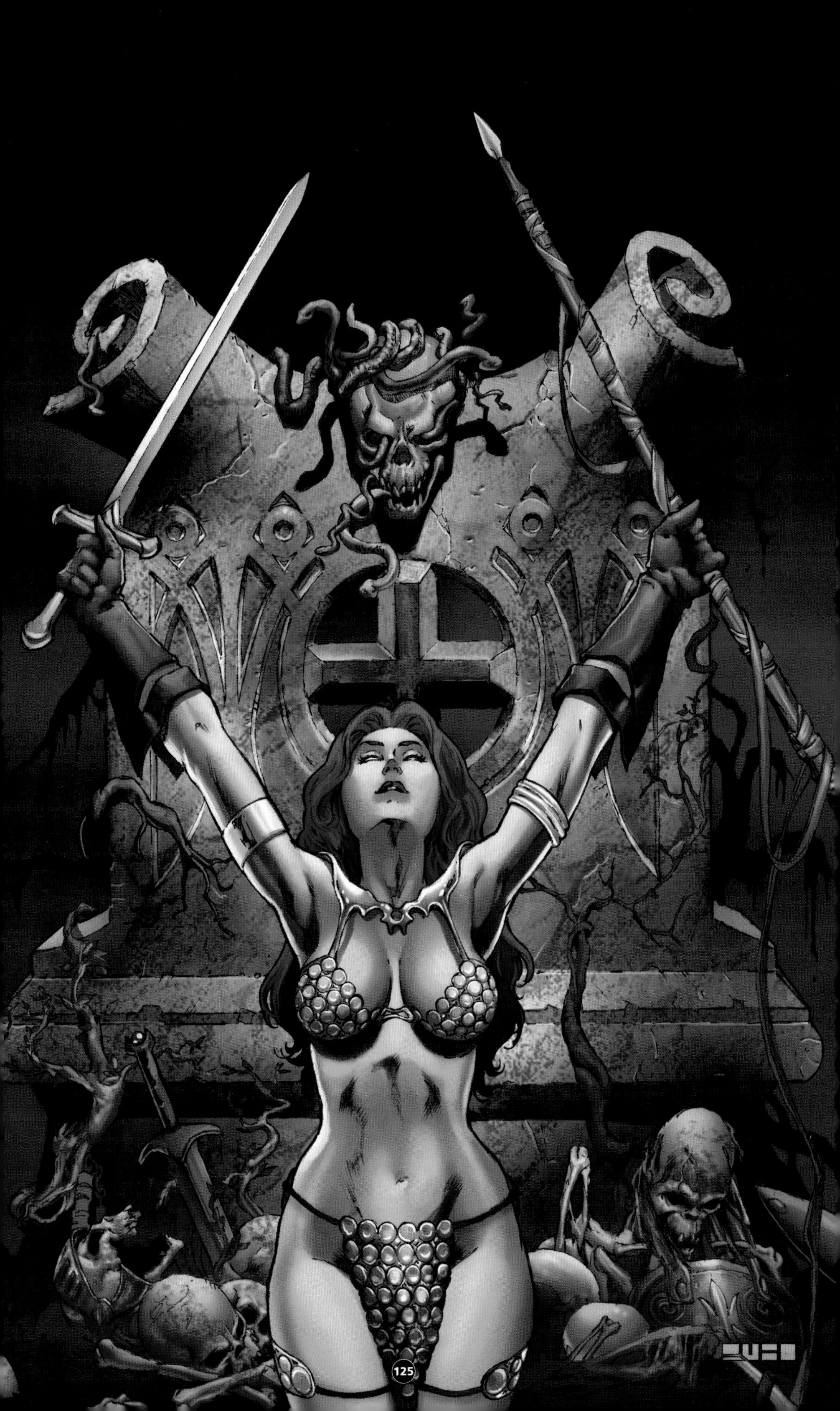

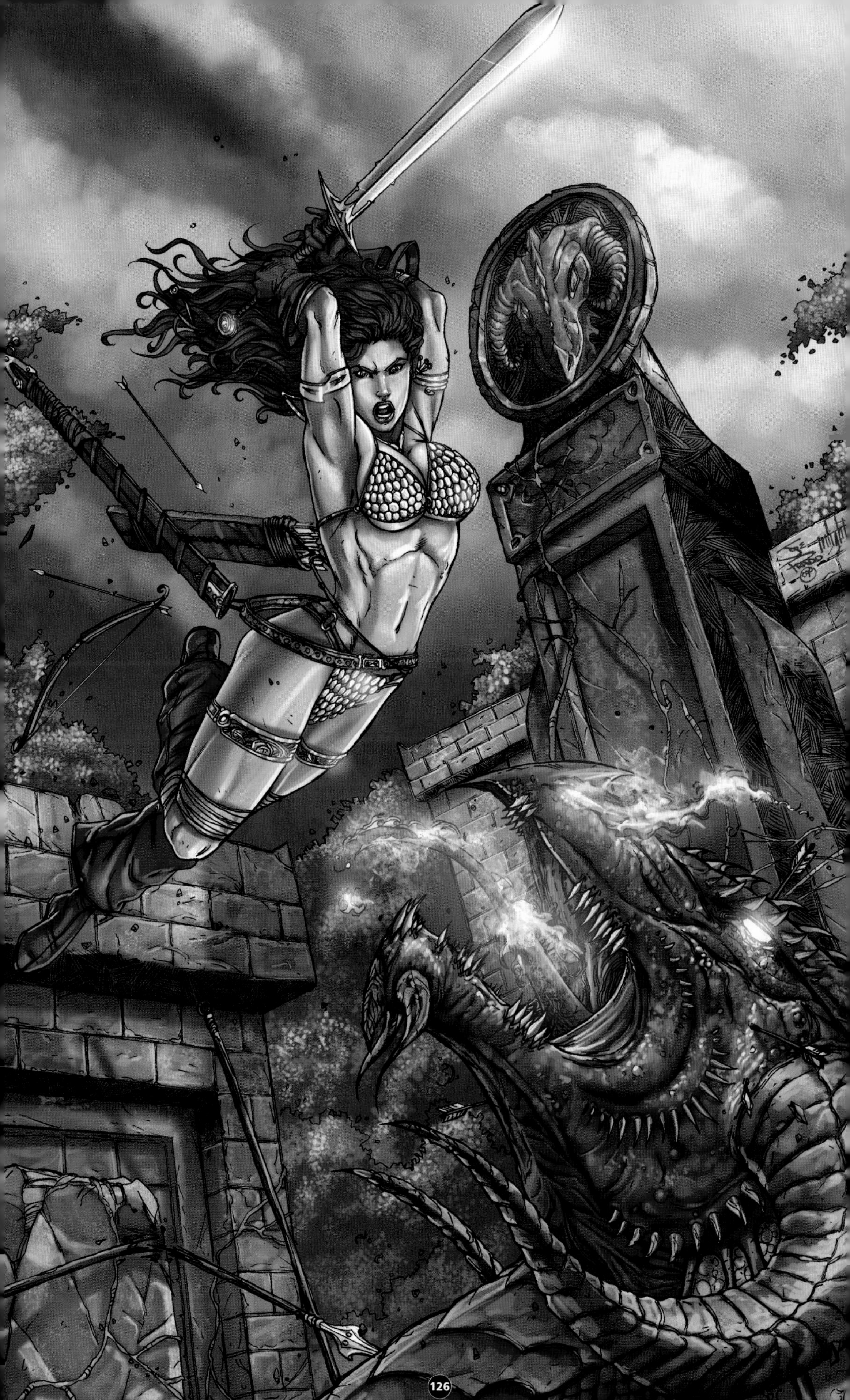

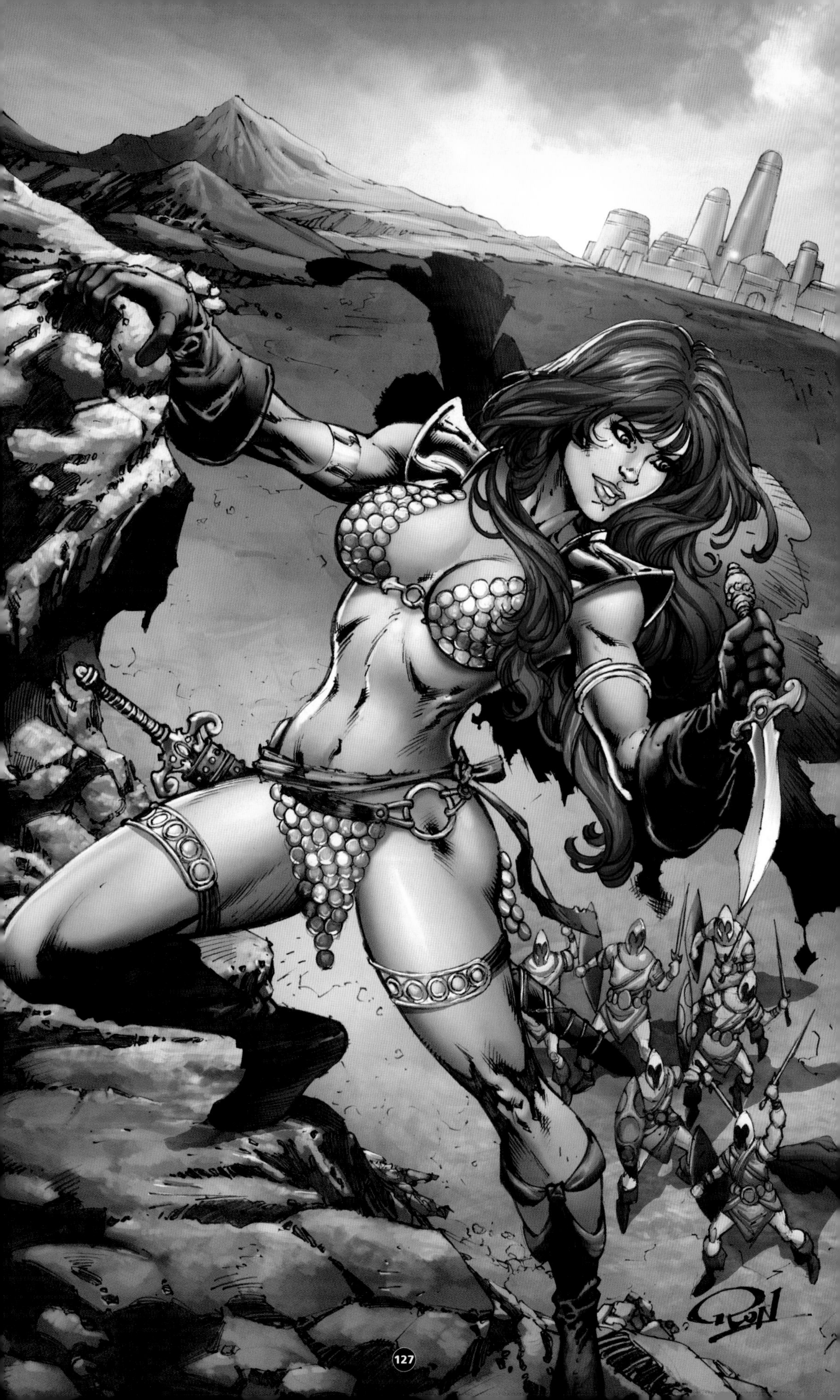

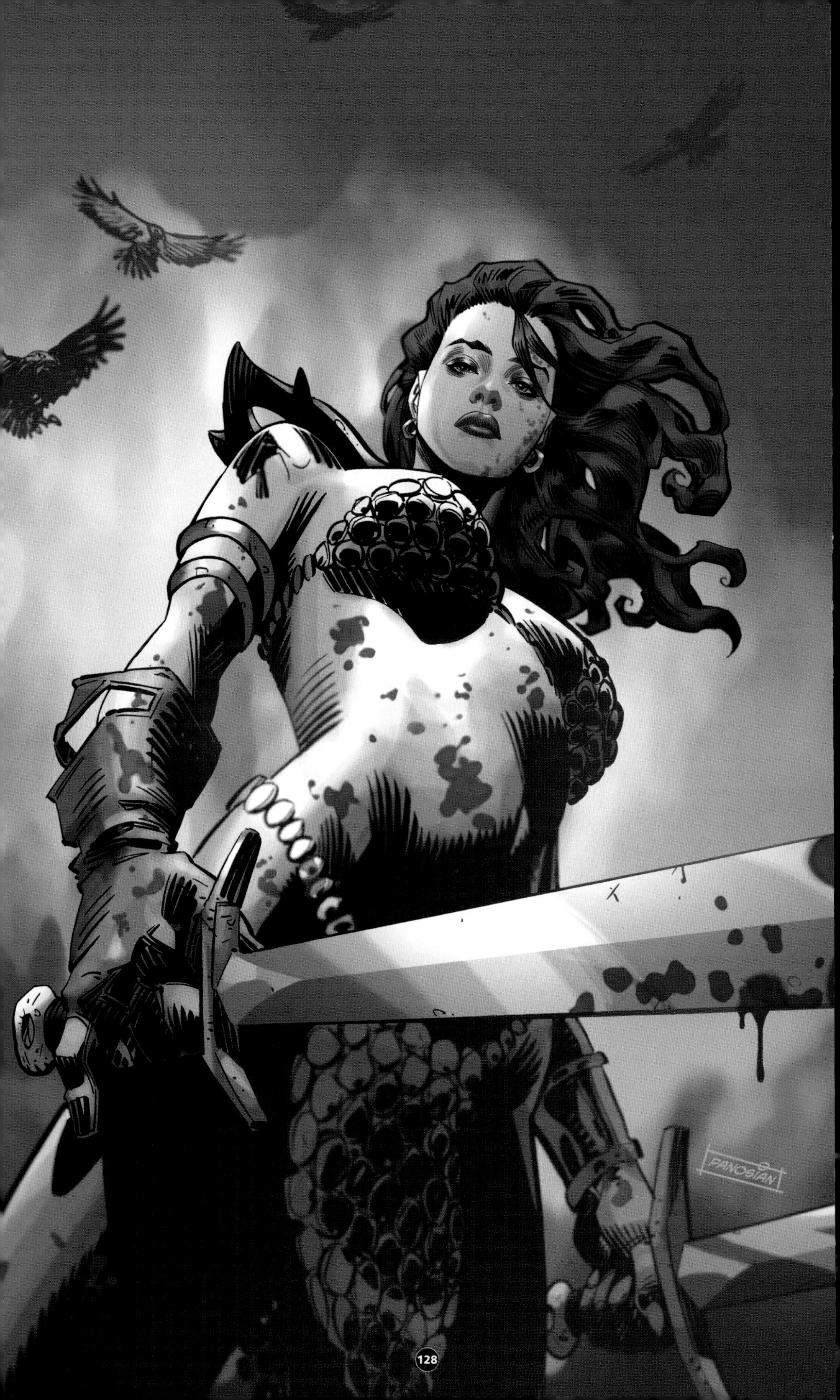
PANOSIAN

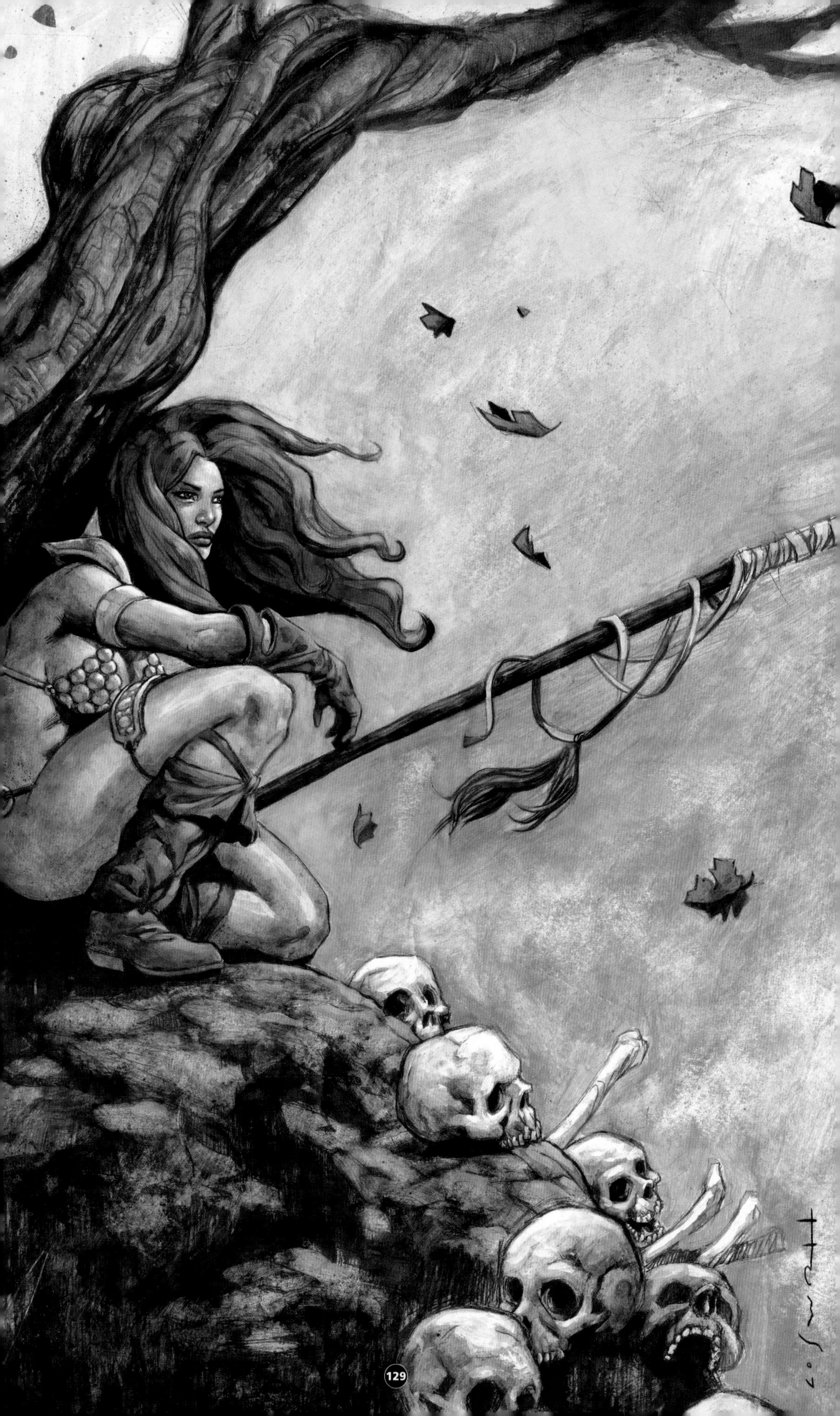

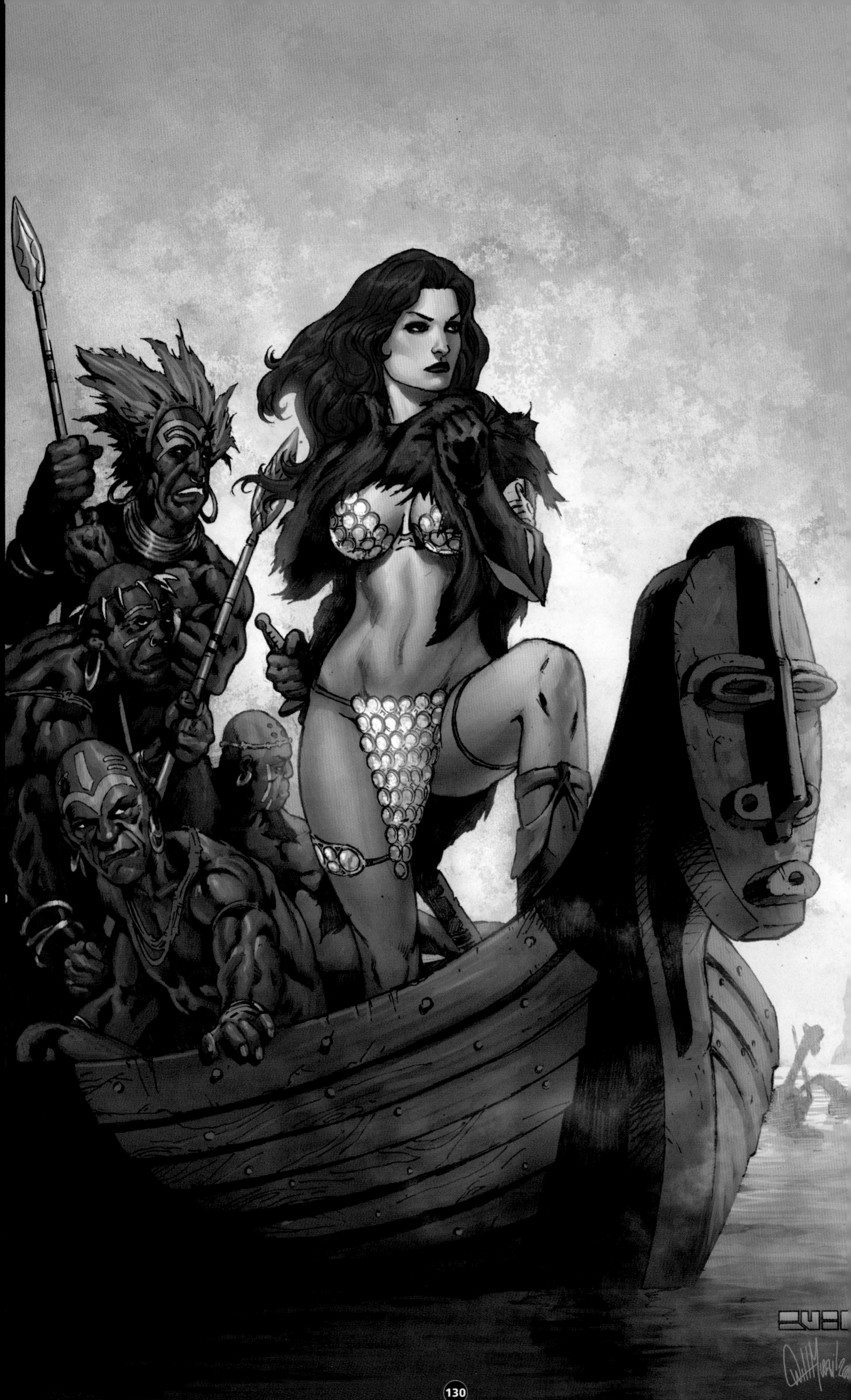

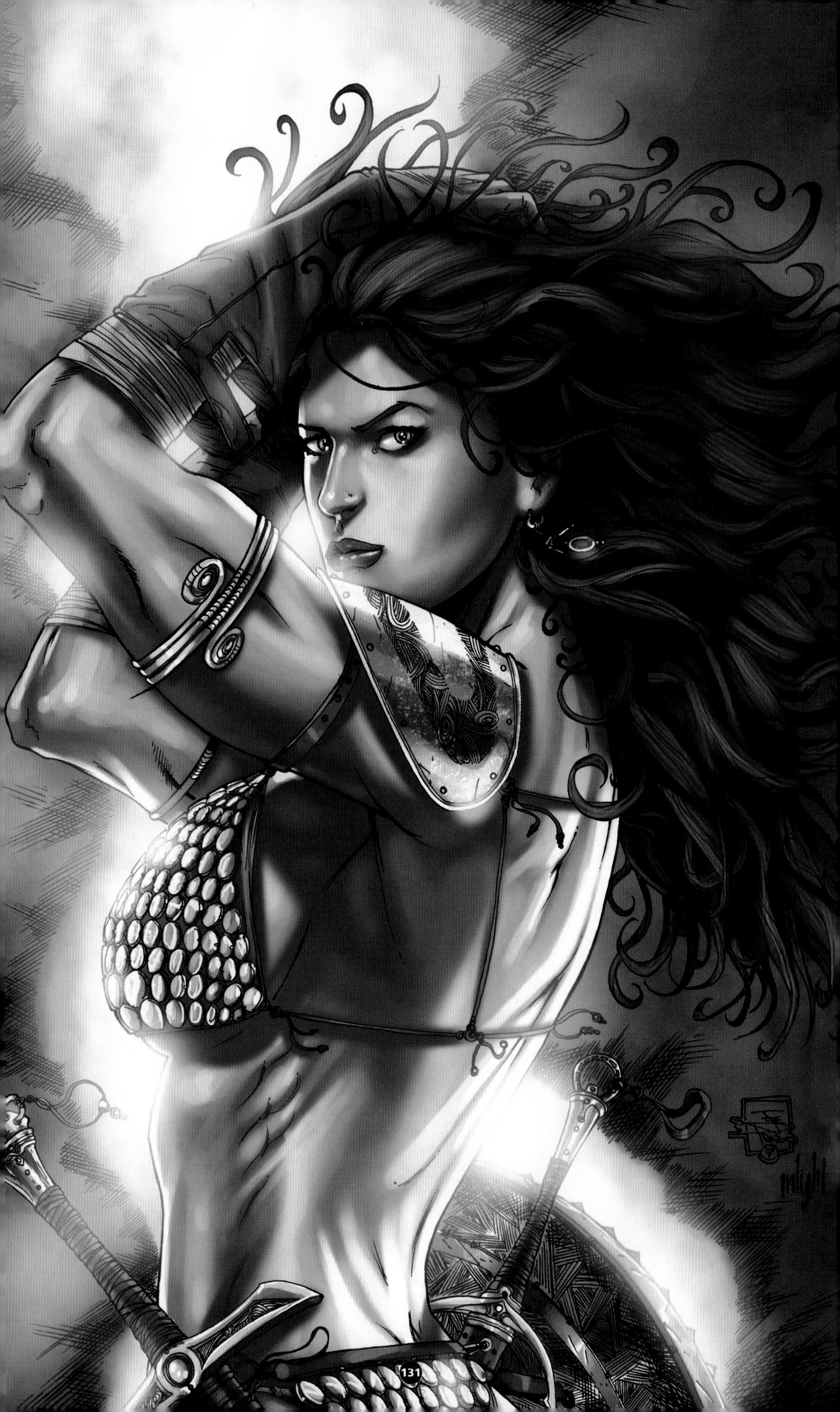

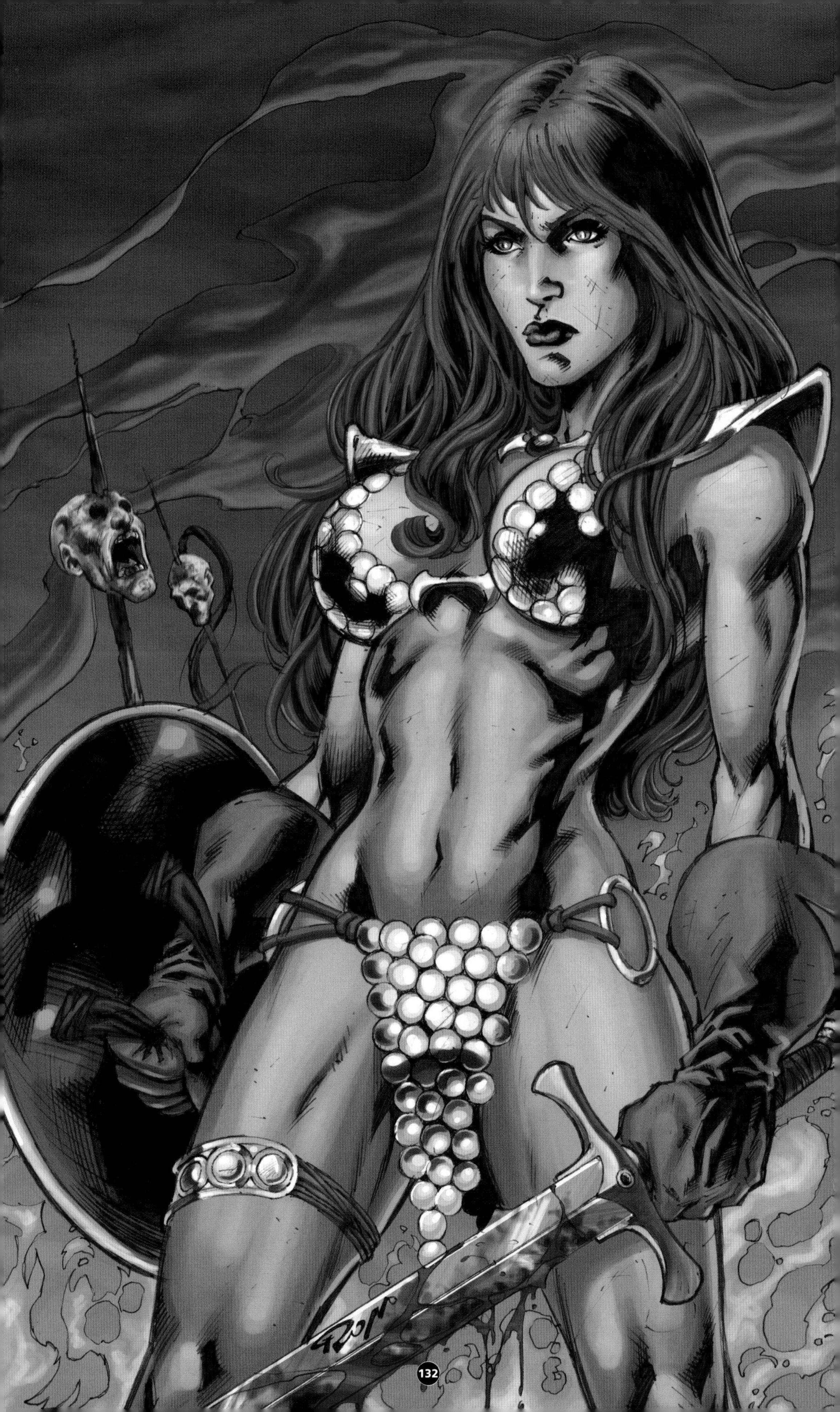

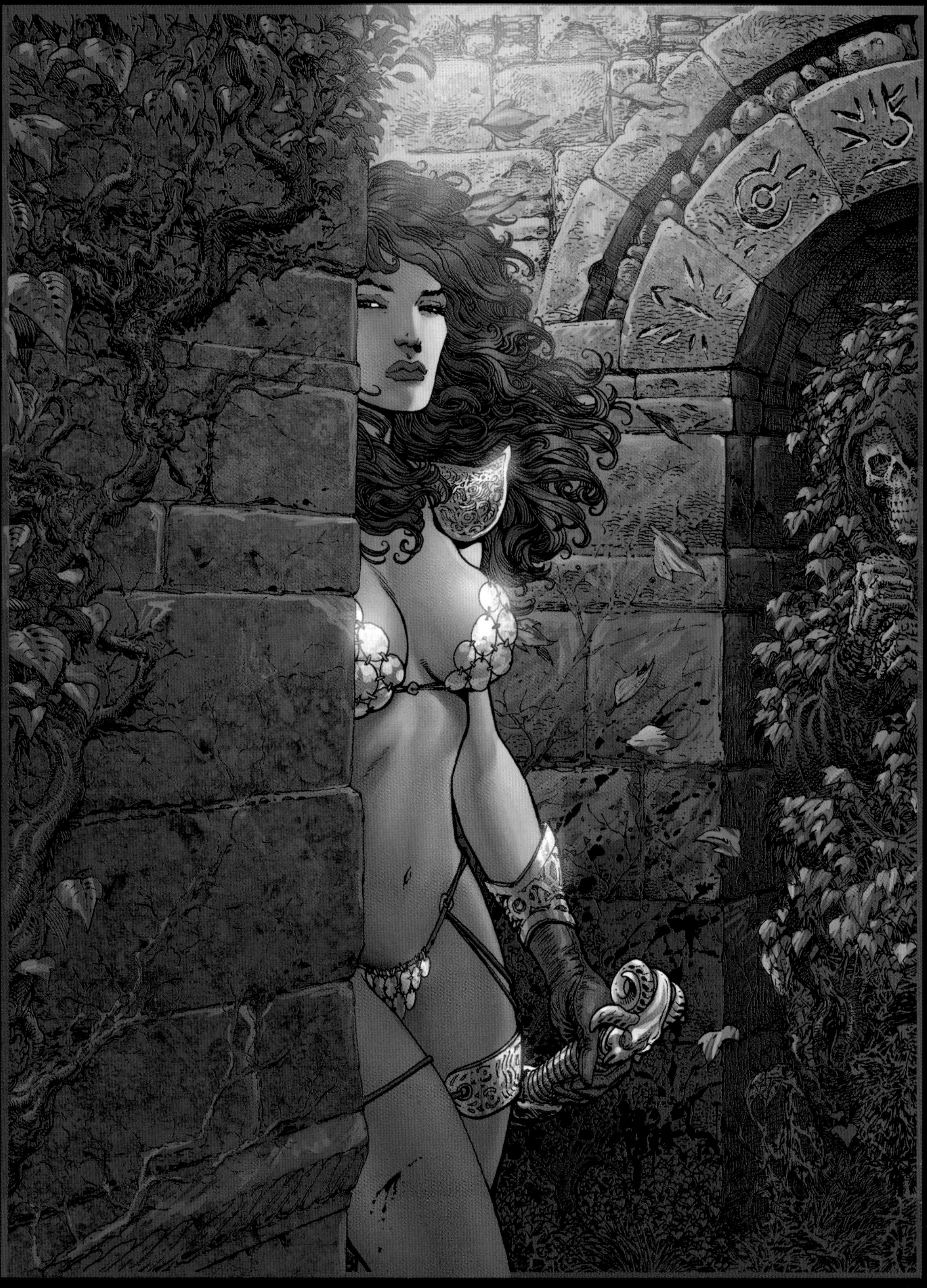

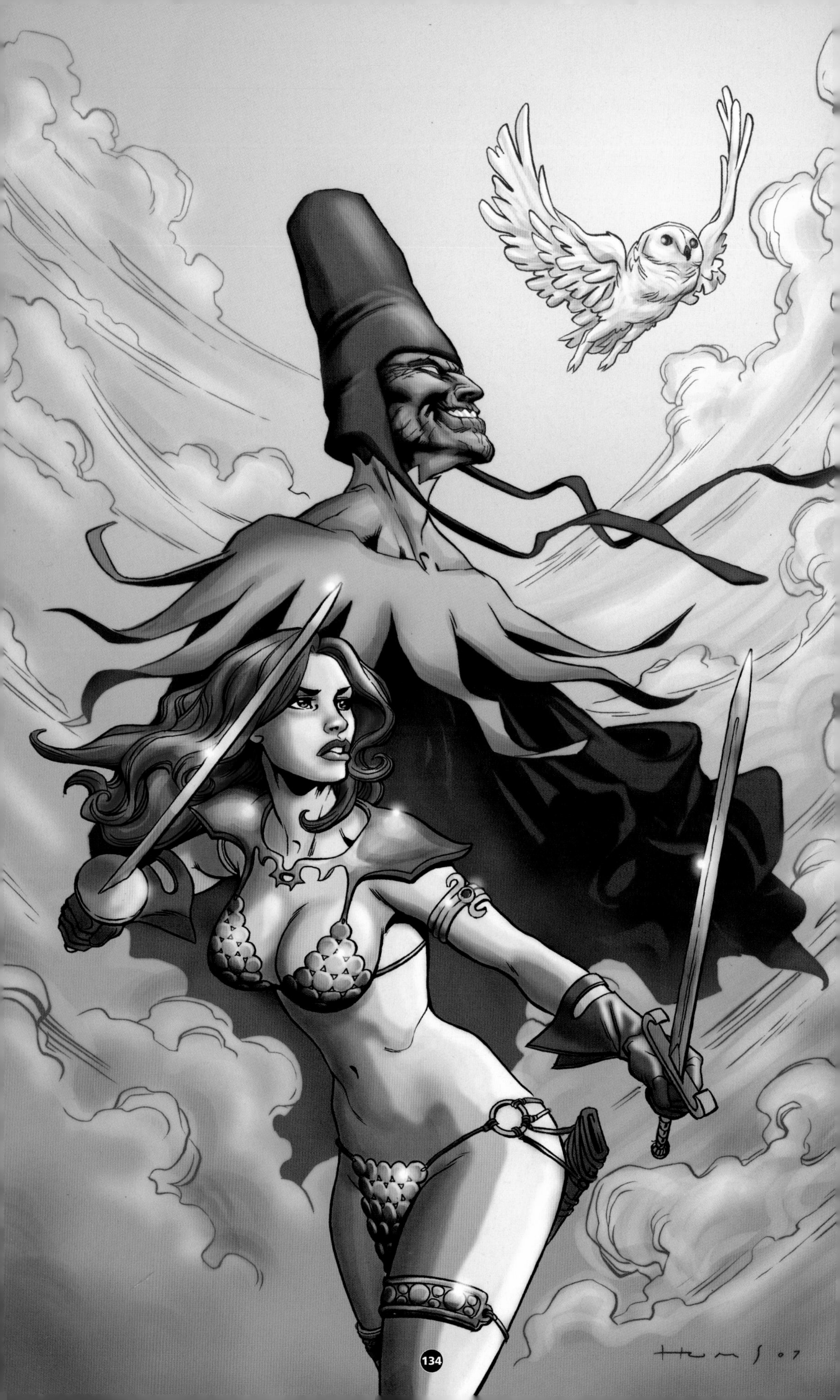

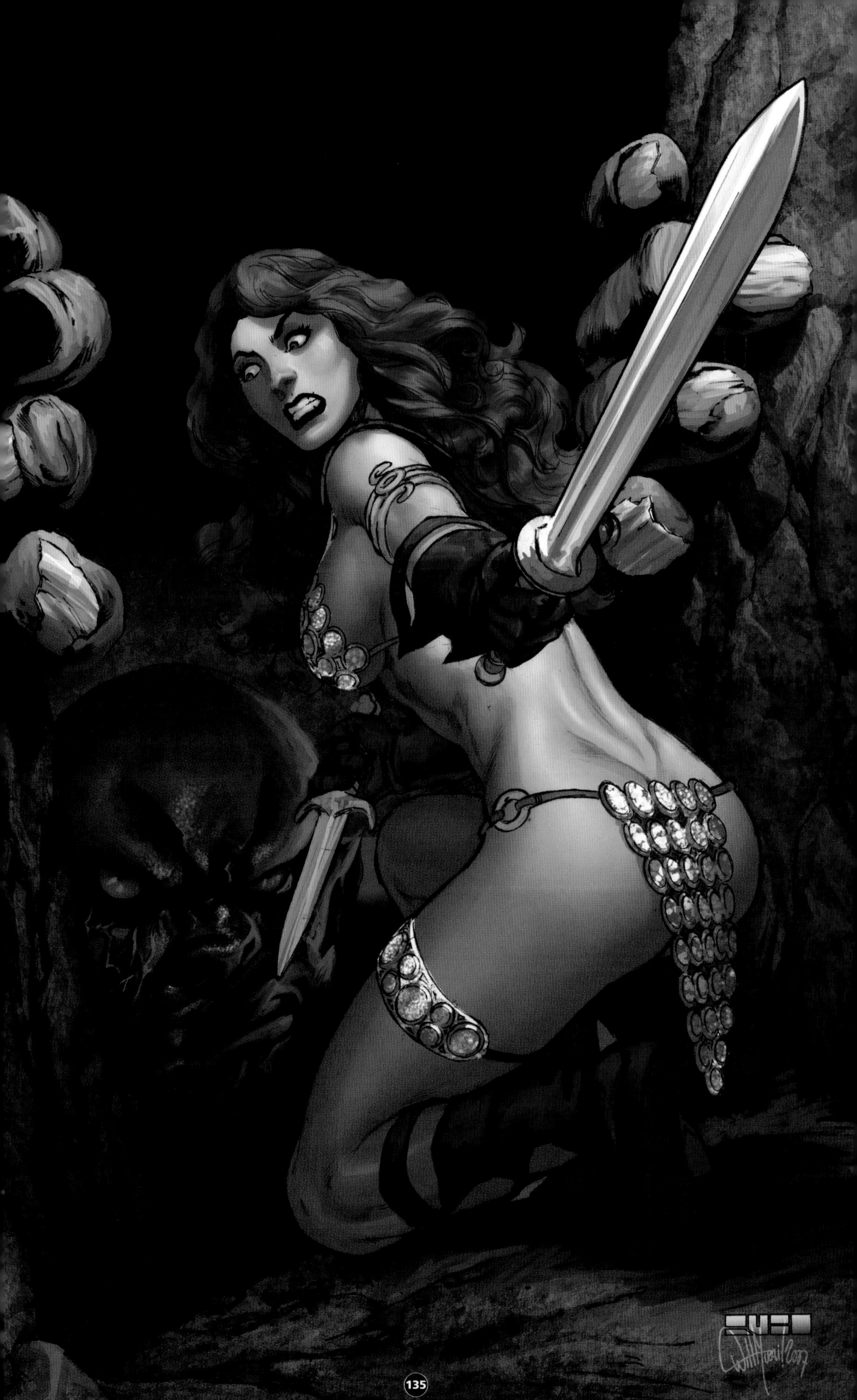

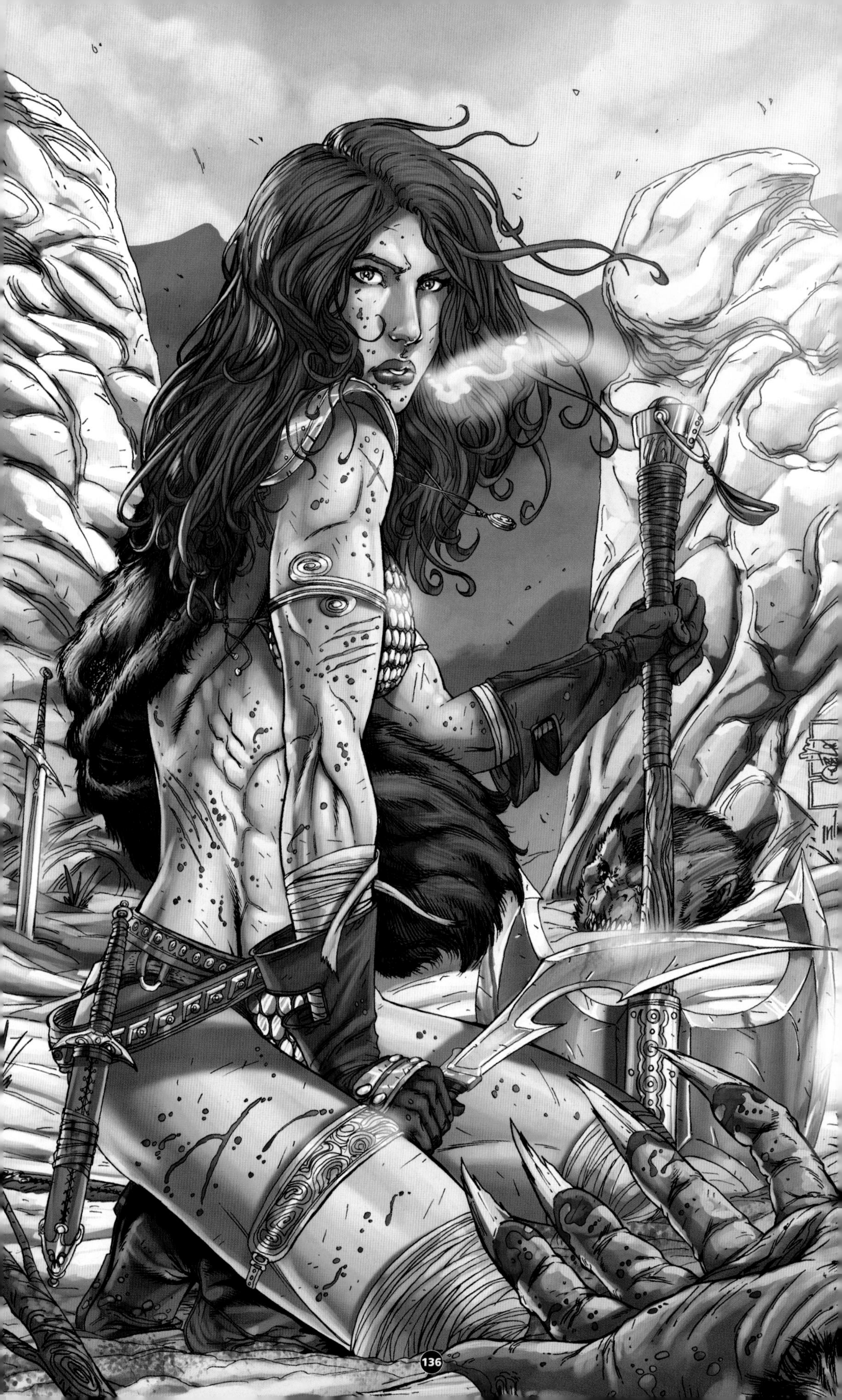

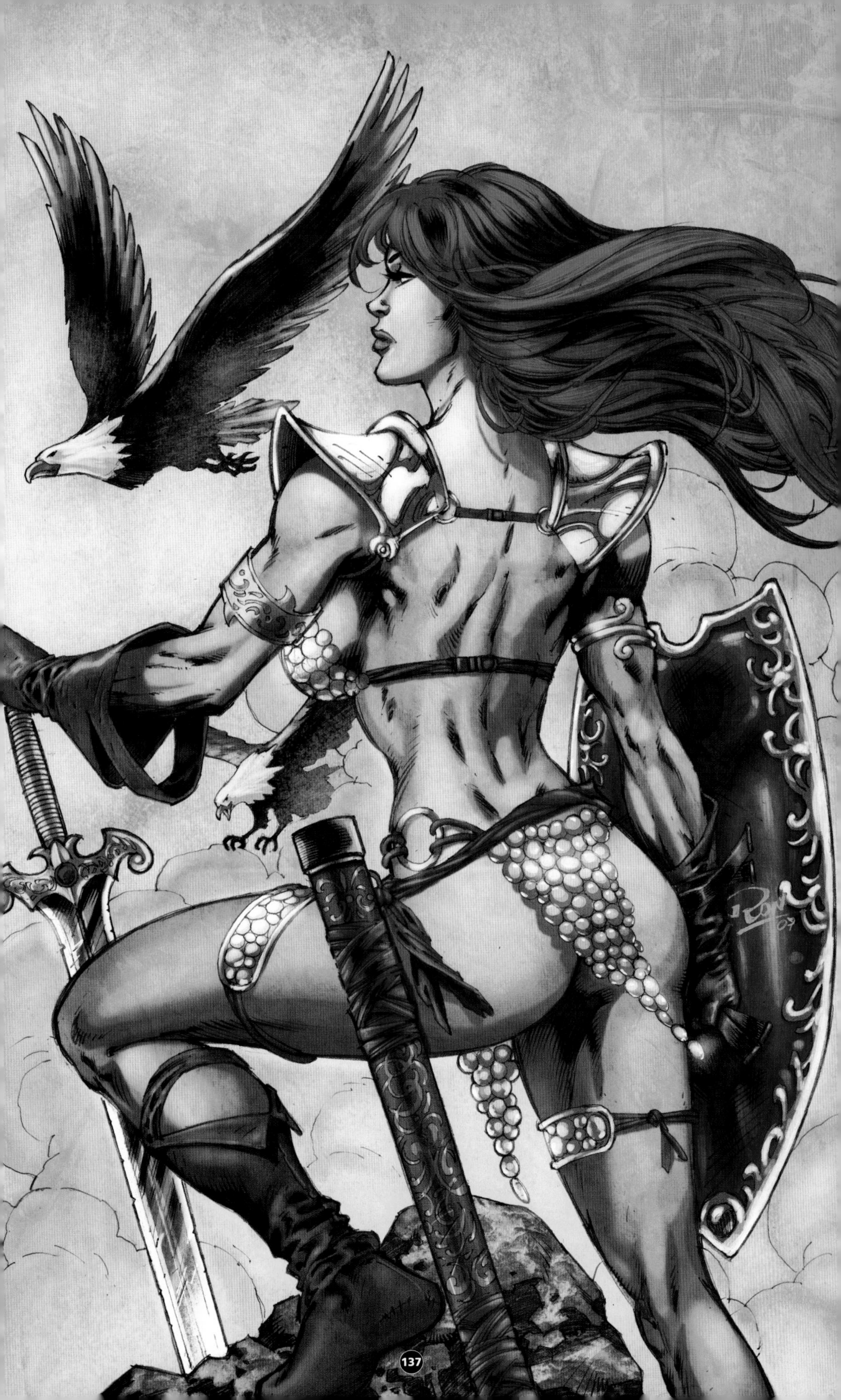

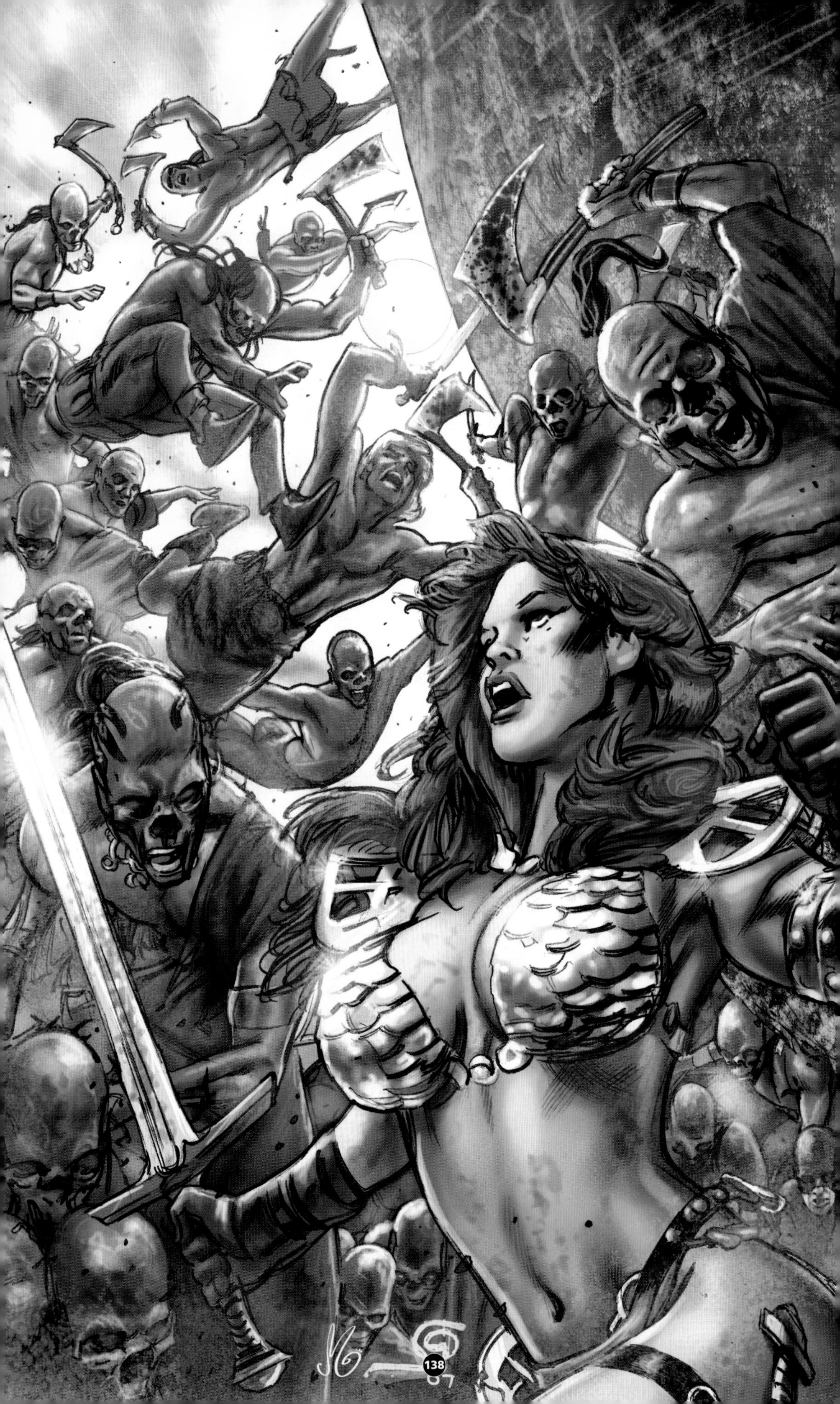

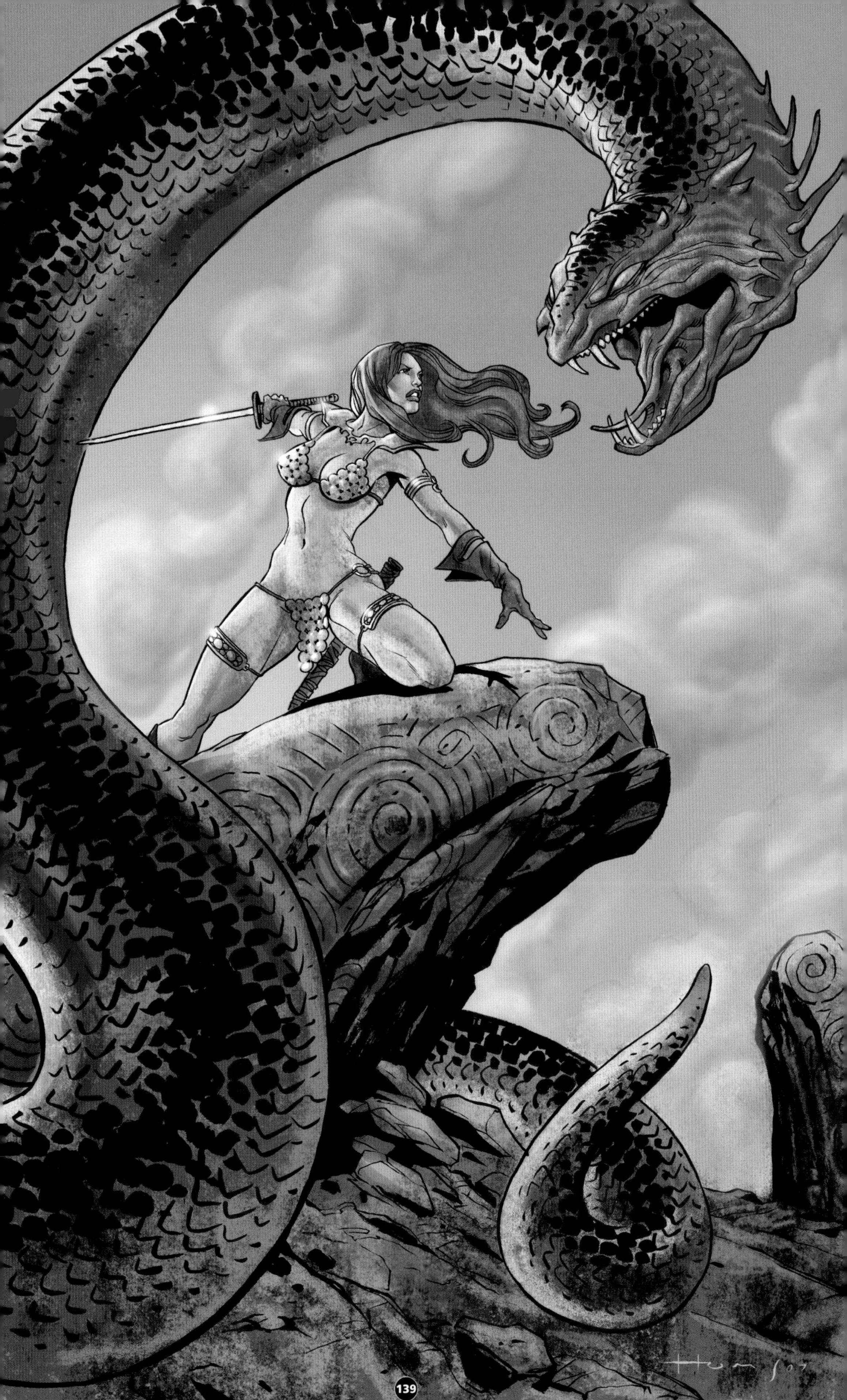

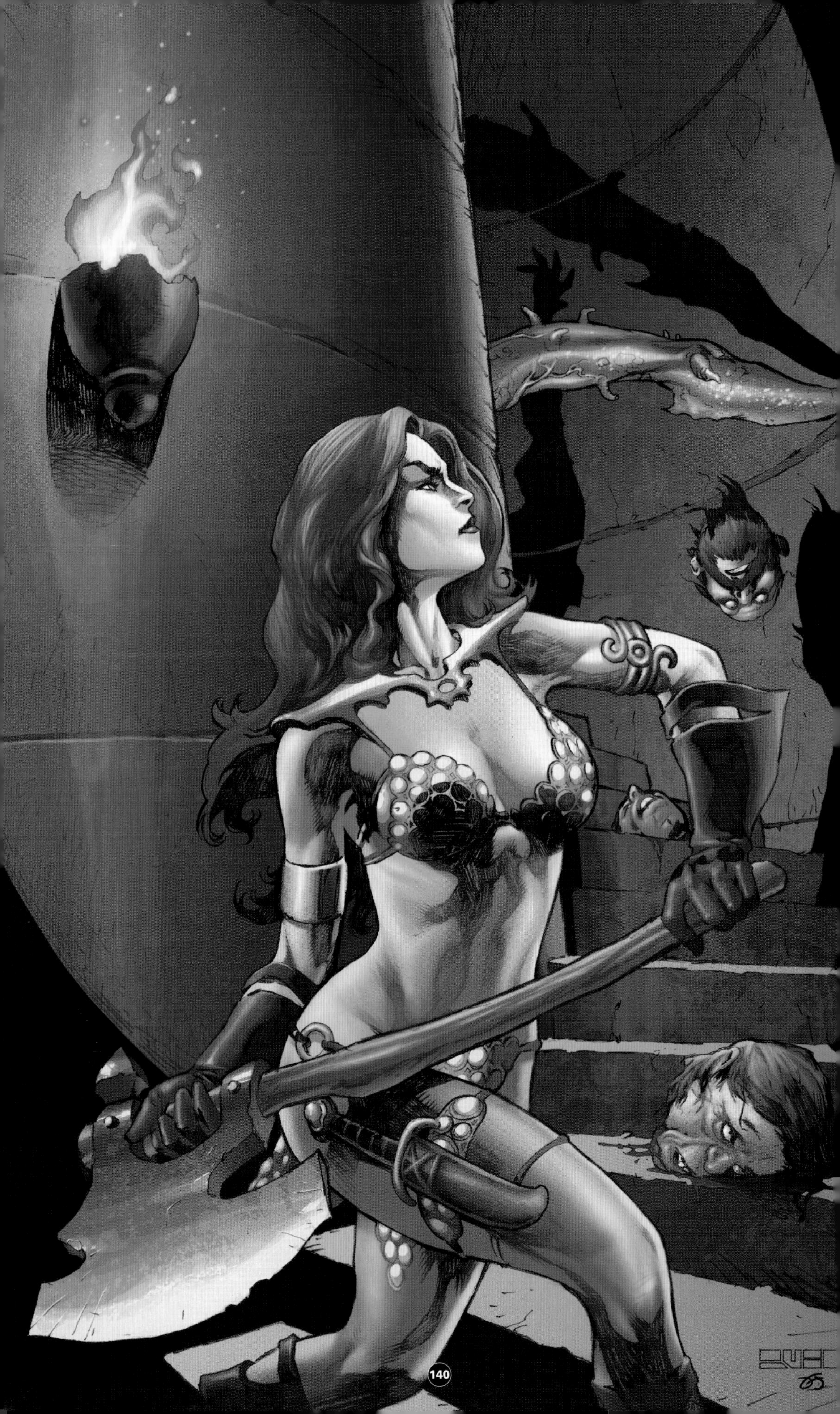

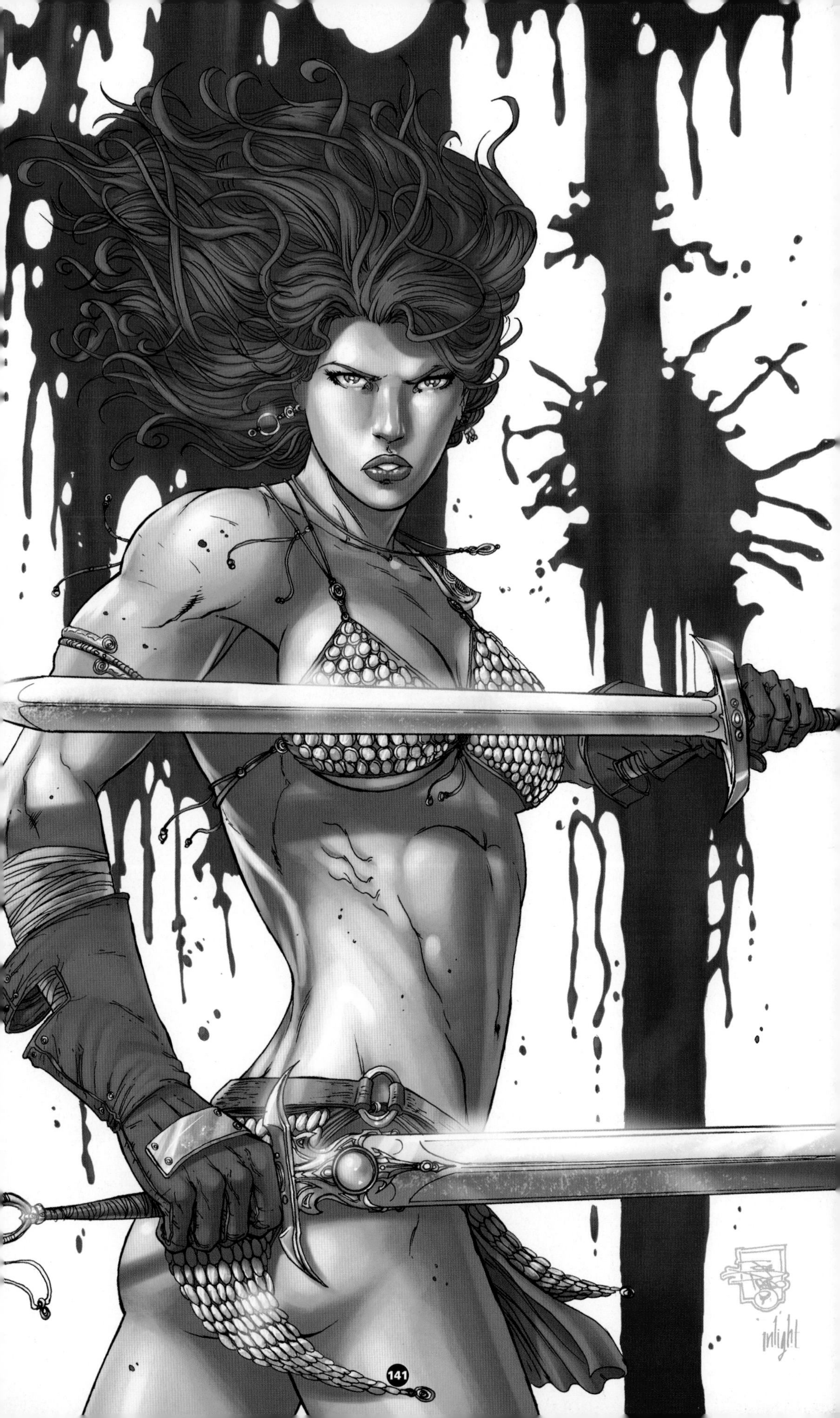

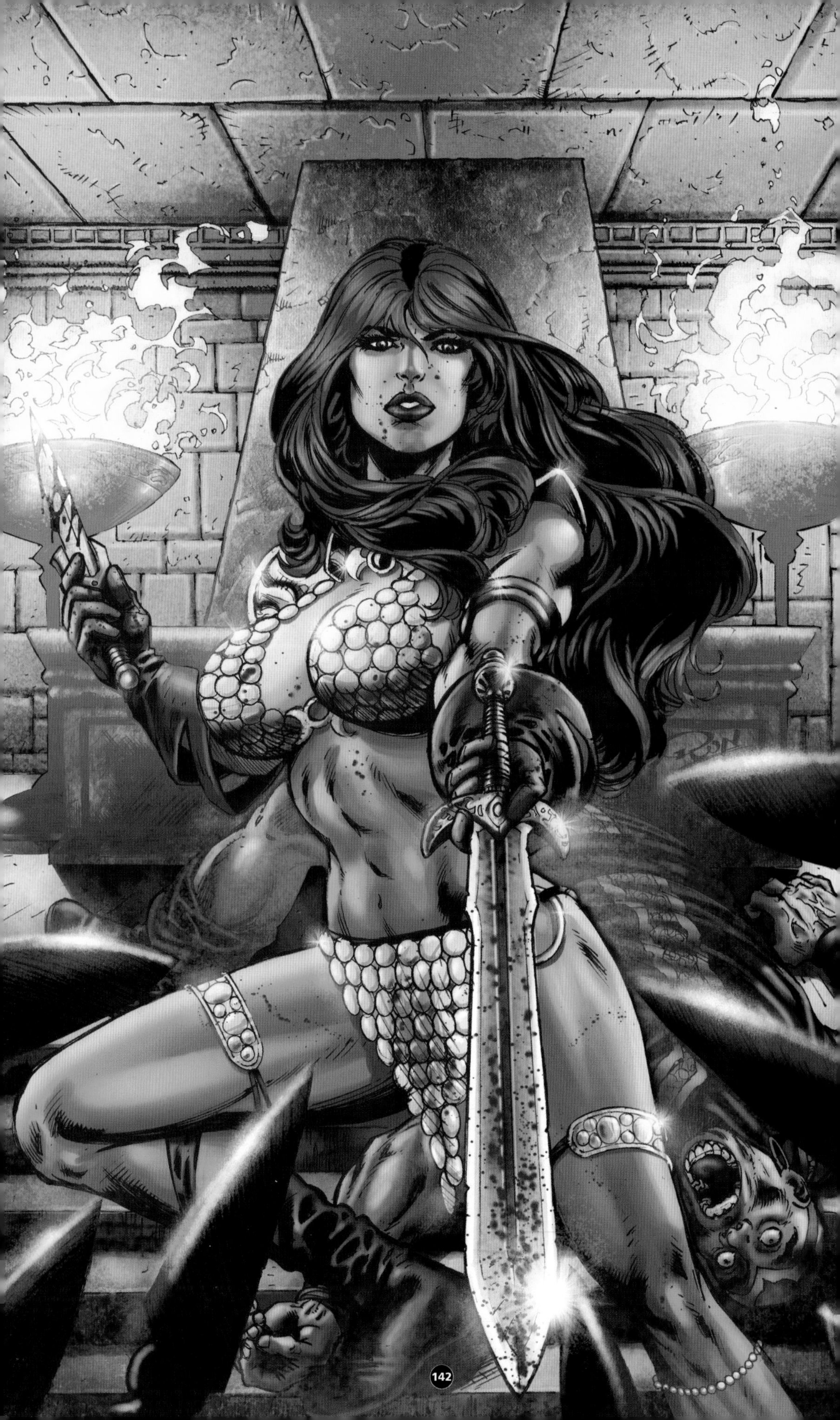

THE DYNAMITE ENTERTAINMENT COLLECTION

CURRENTLY AVAILABLE AND UPCOMING COLLECTIONS FROM DYNAMITE ENTERTAINMENT

Adventures of Red Sonja Vol. 1
Roy Thomas, Frank Thorne, More
SC ISBN: 1-933305-07-X

Adventures of Red Sonja Vol. 2
Roy Thomas, Frank Thorne, More
SC ISBN: 1-933305-12-6

Adventures of Red Sonja Vol. 3
Roy Thomas, Frank Thorne, More
SC ISBN: 1-933305-98-3

Army of Darkness: Movie Adaptation
Sam Raimi, Ivan Raimi, John Bolton
SC ISBN: 1-933305-17-7

Army of Darkness: Ashes to Ashes
Andy Hartnell, Nick Bradshaw
SC ISBN: 0-9749638-9-5

Army of Darkness: Shop 'Till You Drop Dead
James Kuhoric, Nick Bradshaw, Sanford Greene
SC ISBN: 1-933305-26-6

Army of Darkness vs. Re-Animator
James Kuhoric, Nick Bradshaw, Sanford Greene
SC ISBN: 1-933305-13-4

Army of Darkness: Old School & More
James Kuhoric, Kevin Sharpe
SC ISBN: 1-933305-18-5

Army of Darkness: Ash vs. The Classic Monsters
James Kuhoric, Kevin Sharpe, Fernando Blanco
SC ISBN: 1-933305-41-X

Bad Boy 10th Anniversary Edition
Frank Miller, Simon Bisley
HC ISBN: 1-933305-54-1

Borderline Vol. 1
Eduardo Risso, Carlos Trillo
SC ISBN: 1-933305-05-3

Borderline Vol. 2
Eduardo Risso, Carlos Trillo
SC ISBN: 1-933305-99-1

The Boys Vol. 1: The Name of the Game
Garth Ennis, Darick Robertson
SC ISBN: 1-933305-73-8

The Boys Vol. 2: Get Some
Garth Ennis, Darick Robertson, Peter Snejbjerg
SC ISBN: 1-933305-68-1

Classic Battlestar Galactica Vol. 1
Rick Remender, Carlos Rafael
SC ISBN: 1-933305-45-2

Classic Battlestar Galactica Vol. 2: Cylon Apocalypse
Javier Grillo-Marxuach, Carlos Rafael
SC ISBN: 1-933305-55-X

Darkman vs. Army of Darkness
Kurt Busiek, Roger Stern, James Fry
SC ISBN: 1-933305-48-7

Dreadstar The Definitive Collection
Jim Starlin
HC ISBN: 0-9749638-0-1
SC part 1 ISBN: 0-9749638-1-X
SC part 2 ISBN: 0-9749638-2-8

Dreadstar: The Beginning
Jim Starlin
HC ISBN: 1-933305-10-X

Eduardo Risso's Tales of Terror
Eduardo Risso, Carlos Trillo
SC ISBN: 1-933305-23-1

Highlander Vol. 1: The Coldest War
Michael Avon Oeming, Brandon Jerwa, Lee Moder, Kevin Sharpe
HC ISBN: 1-933305-31-2
SC ISBN: 1-933305-34-7

Highlander Vol. 2: Dark Quickening
Brandon Jerwa, Fabio Laguna
SC ISBN: 1-933305-59-2

Kid Kosmos: Cosmic Guard
Jim Starlin
SC ISBN: 1-933305-02-9

Kid Kosmos: Kidnapped
Jim Starlin
SC ISBN: 1-933305-29-0

The Lone Ranger Vol. 1: Now & Forever
Brett Matthews, Sergio Cariello, John Cassaday
HC ISBN: 1-933305-39-8
SC ISBN: 1-933305-40-1

The Lone Ranger Vol. 2: Lines Not Crossed
Brett Matthews, Sergio Cariello, John Cassaday, Paul Pope
HC ISBN: 1-933305-66-5
SC ISBN: 1-933305-70-3

Mercenaries Vol. 1
Brian Reed, Edgar Salazar
SC ISBN: 1-933305-71-1

Monster War
Christopher Golden, Joyce Chin, more
SC ISBN: 1-933305-30-4

New Battlestar Galactica Vol. 1
Greg Pak, Nigel Raynor
HC ISBN: 1-933305-33-9
SC ISBN: 1-933305-34-7

New Battlestar Galactica Vol. 2
Greg Pak, Nigel Raynor
HC ISBN: 1-933305-53-3
SC ISBN: 1-933305-49-5

New Battlestar Galactica Vol. 3
Greg Pak, Nigel Raynor, Jonathan Lau
HC ISBN: 1-933305-58-4
SC ISBN: 1-933305-57-6

New Battlestar Galactica: Zarek
Brandon Jerwa, Adriano Batista
SC ISBN: 1-933305-50-9

Essential Painkiller Jane Vol. 1
Joe Quesada, Jimmy Palmiotti, Rick Leonardi, Amanda Conner
SC ISBN: 1-933305-97-5

Painkiller Jane Vol. 1: The Return
Joe Quesada, Jimmy Palmiotti, Lee Moder
SC ISBN: 1-933305-42-8

Painkiller Jane Vol. 2: Everything Explodes
Joe Quesada, Jimmy Palmiotti, Lee Moder
SC ISBN: 1-933305-65-7

Raise The Dead
Leah Moore, John Reppion, Hugo Petrus
HC ISBN: 1-933305-56-8

Red Sonja She-Devil With a Sword Vol. 1
Michael Avon Oeming, Mike Carey, Mel Rub
HC ISBN: 1-933305-36-3
SC ISBN: 1-933305-11-8

Red Sonja She-Devil With a Sword Vol. 2: Arrowsmiths
Michael Avon Oeming, Mel Rubi, more
HC ISBN: 1-933305-44-4
SC ISBN: 1-933305-43-6

Red Sonja She-Devil With a Sword Vol. 3: The Rise of Kulan Gath
Michael Avon Oeming, Mel Rubi, more
HC ISBN: 1-933305-51-7
SC ISBN: 1-933305-52-5

Red Sonja She-Devil With a Sword Vol. 4: Animals & More
Michael Avon Oeming, Homs, more
HC ISBN: 1-933305-64-9
SC ISBN: 1-933305-63-0

Red Sonja vs. Thulsa Doom Vol. 1
Peter David, Luke Lieberman, Will Conrad
SC ISBN: 1-933305-96-7

Savage Red Sonja: Queen of the Frozen Wastes
Frank Cho, Doug Murray, Homs
HC ISBN: 1-933305-37-1
SC ISBN: 1-933305-38-X

Red Sonja: Travels
Ron Marz, Josh Ortega, Roy Thomas, more
SC ISBN: 1-933305-20-7

Scout Vol. 1
Timothy Truman
SC ISBN: 1-933305-95-9

Scout Vol. 2
Timothy Truman
SC ISBN: 1-933305-60-6

Six From Sirius
Doug Moench, Paul Gulacy
SC ISBN: 1-933305-03-7

Street Magik
Luke Lieberman, Kevin McCarthy, Rodney Buchemi
SC ISBN: 1-933305-47-9

Terminator: Infinity
Simon Furman, Nigel Raynor
SC ISBN: 1-933305-74-6

Xena Vol. 1: Contest of Pantheons
John Layman, Fabiano Neves
SC ISBN: 1-933305-35-5

Xena Vol. 2: Dark Xena
John Layman, Keith Champagne, Noah Salonga
SC ISBN: 1-933305-61-4

To find more collected editions and monthly comic books from Dynamite Entertainment, visit your local comic book store or call 1-888-COMIC-BOOK to locate the nearest comic store to you.

For more information visit
WWW.DYNAMITEENTERTAINMENT.COM